# Shakespeare's Younger Sister

Other books by Geoffrey Craig:

*Scudder's Gorge*

*The Brave Maiden*

*One-Eyed Man and Other Stories*

# Shakespeare's Younger Sister

by

Geoffrey Craig

*Golden Antelope Press*
715 E. McPherson
Kirksville, Missouri 63501
2019

Cover Design by Russell Nelson and Victor Freed



ISBN: 978-1-936135-84-4

Library of Congress Control Number:

Published by:
Golden Antelope Press
715 E. McPherson
Kirksville, Missouri 63501

Available at:
Golden Antelope Press
715 E. McPherson
Kirksville, Missouri 63501
Phone: (660) 665-0273
Website: www.goldenantelope.com
Email: ndelmoni@gmail.com

To Barbara and Danielle, with great love.

# Acknowledgments:

I would like to thank the following friends for their wise counsel and excellent critiques of *Shakespeare's Younger Sister*. Without their efforts, the book would be far less.

Barbara Teiger, Fran Chirch, Laurie Kritzer, Bill Sullivan, Ruben and Peg Shapiro, Lynn Nyquist, Kevin McCullough, Stacey Pramer, Tony Hyams and Bill Conrad.

I would like to thank Betsy and Neal Delmonico of Golden Antelope for their excellent editing and publishing work. This is my second Golden Antelope publication and, on both occasions, it's been a pleasure to work with Betsy and Neal. I would also like to thank Victor Freed for his notable assistance and suggestions.

# Author's Note:

Despite the use of some historical characters, this is a work of fiction, not history or historical fiction. With the exception of individuals such as William Shakespeare, Philip Henslowe, Richard and Winifred Burbage, Queen Elizabeth, Lord Burghley (referenced), Walsingham (Sir Francis—referenced) and members of the Shakespeare family (other than Constance, who is fictional), all the characters are fictional. With the exception of basic facts about their lives, I have also fictionalized the historical characters; and any resemblance, therefore, to their actual characteristics is purely coincidental.

While he had siblings, Shakespeare had no sister named Constance. While there is a Constance in *King John*, this is purely a coincidence.

While I have mentioned and utilized actual historical events and places to add context, background, color and authenticity, this does not alter the basic fictional nature of the story. As needed, I have made up places such as Fish Lane.

I have also not tried to replicate the language of Shakespeare's time, except to avoid where possible the use in direct speech of major words that did not exist in that era. To that end, I have used an etymological dictionary. Where only a modern word seems to fit the work, I have, occasionally, used in speech a word that almost certainly did not exist in Elizabethan England. I have occasionally adjusted a word in use in the 16th Century to a more contemporary meaning.

The issues surrounding a woman's place in society were debated in Elizabethan times.

Useful information was gleaned from a great variety of Internet sources (e.g. Internet Shakespeare Editions https://internetshakespeare.uvic.ca/ and the Shakespeare Birthplace Trust https://www.shakespeare.org.uk/explore-shakespeare/ ) as well as from the following books:

*The Time Traveler's Guide to Elizabethan England* by Ian Mortimer

*Understanding Shakespeare's England* by Jo McMurtry

*Elizabeth's London* by Liza Picard

*The Norton Shakespeare (Complete Works)*

# Table of Contents

# A Letter: Spring 1592

One morning in the marketplace, Constance Shakespeare was given a letter by a man she had never before seen. She was most anxious to read the letter but first had to complete the purchases for which her mother had sent her to the market. She was hesitant to open it amidst the press of people going from stall to stall. What if someone jostled her and she dropped the letter in the mud? Or a strong breeze tore it from her hand and whisked it away? Or that rascal, George Clopton, happened by and peered over her shoulder—out of deviltry or to see if she had another beau—and snatched it? No chances could be taken so she tucked the letter up her sleeve and continued her shopping.

Stratford-upon-Avon was a bustling town even if Constance feared it lacked the opportunities she so longed for. Not that she knew what those opportunities might entail. What she did know was that, as a woman (even one living in Elizabethan England), she would encounter obstacles in her quest. Her inner voice could not have spoken more clearly: "Constance Shakespeare, you are a woman; and your role in society is somewhat—no, quite—restricted. Which means you will have to struggle."

"To accomplish what?"

"Wait and you will find out."

Notwithstanding such apprehensions, in the thirty-fourth year of the glorious reign of Queen Elizabeth, Constance was certain that never had there been a time of such promise for women regardless of the limitations convention imposed on them. Constance listened closely to the dinner table conversations at home. Her father, John Shakespeare, was an astute man, if stern in the treatment of his children and often inflexible in his views, which he freely expressed. On religion, however, a topic fraught with danger even in Elizabeth's reasonably tolerant reign, he held his peace. His guests included the most knowledgeable and important men in Stratford. She, therefore, had a grasp of recent English history and was grateful that it was Elizabeth and no longer her older sister Mary who occupied the throne. It was best to forget Mary's brief but abhorrent reign when good Protestants were burnt at the stake. Constance shuddered just thinking about it.

But the morning was too full of sunshine for such thoughts. It was considerably warmer than during the past few days, and Constance felt the sap of life running fast in her veins. She felt like doing a somersault or leaping up and clicking her heels together or, at the very least, breaking into song. She concluded, sadly, that the marketplace in her hometown would not be the best site for the daughter of a well-to-do citizen to do any of those things. It might not be properly understood. Stratford's more sober inhabitants would think she had gone quite mad; and if such behavior were reported to her father, God alone knew what the consequences might be.

Constance was basically a happy person. She loved her family and friends, especially her best friend, Emma Loveney. Her ambition, furthermore, to be something more than a wife and mother did not preclude her thinking about marriage as any eighteen-year-old English woman surely would—especially one from the upper ranks of society in a small but growing provincial town.

"I might be awfully naive," she thought, "but why should marriage, especially to the right person, necessarily stand in the way of other accomplishments."

She wasn't sure if George, her first, and so far only, beau was that right person. His mind, for one thing, seemed too occupied with physical matters; and where his mind ranged, his hand was sure to follow. Not that she didn't enjoy a bit of kissing and so forth; but it really couldn't compare to reading, which she did with alacrity and wide-ranging tastes. Although Constance's formal education consisted solely of a spell of tutoring that concentrated on reading, the basics of French, music (playing the virginal), dance and, most importantly from her Father's perspective, table manners and the virtue of obedience to him and other male members of the household (like her older brother Will, who had attended grammar school but not university), Constance nevertheless had a keen mind with a natural talent for learning and absorbing information. She closely observed the world around her and retained everything. She was careful, however, not to display too much of this talent for it might not have accorded well with the expectations for a young woman of her station. The shelves in her father's parlor contained numerous books that appealed to her inquisitive mind and, at least temporarily, satisfied her hunger for knowledge. Like her friends, almost all of whom were literate, Constance loved exhilarating tales, known as romances; but she had also delved into deeper works such as Sir Thomas More's *Utopia* and the newly-issued first three books of Edmund Spenser's *The Faerie Queene*, both of which could be found in her father's collection and which she had perused more than once.

She was lying on her bed one afternoon re-reading More's fascinating work when her older sister, Joan, dashed into the room they shared, paused to see what Constance was doing and then grabbed the book out of her hands.

"Cannot you read," said Joan, "some thrilling tale of chivalry instead of this dreary nonsense."

"Have you read it?"

"No, and I have no intention of doing so... ever."

"Then you are a fool. Please give it back."

Joan did and smiled.

"It's a beautiful day. Why don't you take a walk along the river with George and kiss him—just as I saw you doing the other day."

"You saw nothing of the kind."

Constance was quite competent at playing the

virginal. She particularly liked the compositions of William Byrd and Giles Farnaby. Yet she knew that playing music, while a proper interest for a well-born lady, would in no way satisfy her longing for something more important.

When she arrived home and finally was able to read the letter, she could not have been more excited. She read it over and over before putting it away in the sleeve of her dress. She had considered hiding it between her ample breasts; but George would likely pay a call in the evening and, if left alone with her for even a couple of minutes, would caress her, which she briefly allowed him to do between kisses. He would then seek to persuade her to find a time and a place to go further; but she, so far, had demurred. While Emma, who had lost her own virtue a few months ago, teased her for being foolish, Constance saw no good reason to lose hers. She hoped she would recognize a good reason when, and if, one came along.

Opportunities to lose one's virtue were not lacking in Stratford. One misty morning, for example, she happened to be walking past Holy Trinity Church—where the Shakespeare family worshipped—just as the vicar was coming out the front door. He said that he needed to speak to her on a matter of some urgency and would she please come inside the church. Curious as to what this matter could be—as the vicar rarely spoke to her after services but rather fawned over her father—she followed him into the church. The vicar asked how she was faring to which she replied:

"Fine" and then without further preamble asked whether she retained her virtue. Astonished, Constance could only nod in the affirmative and murmur: "Yes".

"Excellent," said the vicar, "since losing your virtue would lead you straight to perdition unless, of course, you gave yourself to a Man of God, such as myself, and in the service of God."

She was about to ask him if he mistook her for the town idiot or a simple country girl when he pulled her to him and gave her a wet kiss on the lips.

"To the vestry, my beauty," he said, pulling her by the hand. "Quickly now. We haven't all day."

Constance not only resented the vicar's assumption that she was stupid, she also found him exceedingly ugly with a large wart on the end of his nose, sunken cheeks, a slight hunch to his back and claw-like hands. His breath, furthermore, reeked of scallions and garlic; and while she was not unaccustomed to strong, earthy smells (George's breath was hardly that of a rose), that which emanated from the vicar's snaggle-toothed mouth was disgusting. She jerked her hand free, hurried down the main aisle and out the front door with the vicar's admonition to hold her tongue ringing in her ears.

Constance and Emma lived four houses apart on the same muddy lane. Constance's father made an excellent living as a glover and leather worker as well as a dealer in hides and wool. Master Loveney, Emma's father, was proprietor of a successful fulling mill that employed a dozen young women. Both families lived in large, half-timbered houses of two stories, which was not common in Stratford at that time.

When Emma allowed Harrye Shawe to pluck her flower, she not only immediately told Constance about the happy event but also asked when she would allow George to do the same for her. The letter she had received that morning made her wonder if a good reason had made its appearance and if she should, therefore, let George resolve the matter as he so ardently desired.

Emma was not that happy with Harrye. She called him "Blockhead" because he seemed unable to accomplish the most important task she had set for him.

"What fools men be," Emma said. "They seem to think following a woman's instructions is a slight on their honnor. You'd think he'd do whatever I ask considering what I do for him."

"What is it that you do?"

"Touch him. Kiss him. In just the right place and just the right way."

"You what?" shrieked Constance, in a voice ringing with shock.

"Hush, you fool. Do you want to wake the dead, or Father, who'll whip us both?" Emma grinned. "I once did it with that old whore, Sidney Cooke. Met her by chance when I was taking a promenade in the woods near the river. Some promenade. She taught me a thing or two and didn't even charge me."

"Emma Loveney, you're going straight to Hell."

"I haven't noticed any horned men with forked tails following me around town so I'm not worried."

"But with another woman?"

"It was just the once; and if the Devil catches me by the hair, I will have had my share of fun and shan't care a whit about the consequences."

"I certainly would if I were you."

Constance feared that Emma was being foolhardy. She wondered if Emma were one of those women who preferred women to men. She knew they existed and wondered how they went about it but decided that was one subject, close as they were, that she would refrain from discussing with her friend.

Having read the letter for the sixth time—and thus having committed it to memory—and with it safely in her sleeve, Constance did a little jig but stopped when she realized that, even though she had gone to the attic to read the letter away from prying eyes, someone in the house might hear her heels clicking on the floor and inquire as to what made her so happy on such a miserable, drizzly afternoon (the morning sunshine having completely disappeared—a not uncommon event given England's volatile weather). She hurried down to her room to fetch her cloak—trying to be dead quiet, an impossible task given the creaking nature of the old, attic staircase. She had to see Emma and didn't want her mother saddling her with any further chores.

That morning, she had swept out the main floor and replaced the rush mats although why the servant girl couldn't do it was beyond her. Mother had said she had other tasks for the girl who was, to Constance's way of thinking, a lazy twit. Her mother had then sent Constance to the market to buy a cut of beef, some vegetables and several of that novelty, the potato, which had only recently been introduced into England. Constance had the devil of a time pronouncing the word but did like how the thing tasted. Her mother planned on using all those ingredients in the stew that she was making for dinner. Although John Shakespeare could afford a cook, his wife was used to and actually enjoyed cooking.

Instead of doing chores, Constance had planned on spending the morning and afternoon with her nose in a romance. But the letter—which had been delivered to her near a meat stall by a tall, lean fellow, who walked with a distinct limp and a cane and whose face was partly hidden by a broad-brimmed hat pulled low over his forehead—took precedence over the romance no matter how captivating the story. The book relates how a homely young woman, on finding her new husband in bed with another man, goes to the vicar of the village church with her sad tale. The vicar reports the young men; and the soon-to-be widow, tears streaming down her cheeks, stands at the foot of the gallows as both men have nooses placed around their necks. For the remainder of her days, she curses both her husband's lover and all vicars, leaving room in her heavy heart only for the husband, whom she comes to believe was the victim of strong ale.

The man with the limp handed her the letter and whispered: "Let no one else see this." Then he limped away, as inconspicuously as possible considering the loud tapping of his cane on the cobblestones. What she had seen of his face revealed a man roughly in his late twenties, with a trim, dark beard, a straight nose and full lips. His eyes, near as she could tell, were blue. From the rich cloth of his cloak and stylish hat, she assumed that he was a man of substance. Had she, at that moment, thought any further about him, she would have assumed they would never again meet, little suspecting how important a role he would play in her life.

Taking her heavy woolen cloak from the chair where she had draped it after returning from the market, Constance slipped unnoticed out of the house and hurried down the lane as the drizzle turned into serious rain. She pulled her hood as tightly as possible around her face and prayed not to fall on the slick, muddy roadway. Wet or not, she had to see Emma. Two subjects needed immediate consideration. Should she comply with her brother, Will's, request as laid out in the letter? And if so, should she first let George have what he so desperately wanted? Her poor brain was reeling. She hoped that Emma would help sort out these possibly life-changing decisions.

Constance ducked under the cover overhanging the front door at the Loveney house. The rain and dripping water had caused a large puddle, which she stepped around, to form in the roadway near the heavy oak door. She shivered and knocked as loudly as possible. Bets, the servant girl, opened the door a crack, peeked out and anxiously asked: "Who is it?"

"It's me."

Constance pulled back her hood a smidgeon.

"Oh, Miss Shakespeare, I didn't expect you, or

anyone, to call in this fearsome weather."

"Expect me or not, let me in this instance or I'll have Master Loveney ship you back to Scotland where you shan't find a situation as easy as this one."

"Easy, you say, when my poor arms ache all the time from scrubbing and washing clothes and my back feels like it will break in two from lifting chairs and chests to sweep under them. I swear the Mistress can spot a mote of dust or a morsel of food from across a room; and if she finds the least one, she'll take the rod to me and her arm is strong as..."

"Are you going to stand there blathering or are you going to let me in out of the cold? Or would you rather wait until I catch the death of me?"

"Of course, Miss Shakespeare. I mean of course not."

Bets opened the door just wide enough for Constance to edge through. She took off her cloak, shook it and handed it to Bets.

"See that you hang it near the fire to dry out."

"You're not going to cause me trouble with the Master, are you?"

Constance rubbed her chin, deep in thought.

"Please."

Constance laughed.

"For what: not letting in any stranger who knocks on the door? Of course, I won't unless it's for being the silliest goose in all of Stratford. I was just having a touch of fun, which I need with all the heavy questions weighing on my mind."

"Thank you, Miss Shakespeare. You are an angel."

"That's to be seen. Now, I presume Miss Emma is at home, probably up in her room, lazing about."

"Shall I tell her you're here?"

"No need. I'd like to surprise her."

Constance tiptoed up the stairs, pausing briefly on the landing to be sure no one was around, and then continued up the curving staircase to the second floor. She moved quietly along the corridor with its wide planks covered with rush mats and heavy rugs. She pushed open the door to Emma's room, stuck her head in and called out: "Guess who?" Eyes closed, Emma was resting against thick pillows; a book lay open by her side. She opened her eyes and looked at Constance in surprise. Her lips parted in a broad smile.

"The Devil's Assistant," laughed Emma, "here to carry me off straight to Hades or some other such delightful place."

"Someday you may regret all your joking."

"Don't be such a doomsayer." Emma sat up. "Come in and shut the door." Constance did as requested. Emma picked up the book and showed it to her. "I had planned to practice on the virginal, but I thought to read a little first. This so-called romance, however, is hardly worth the name: exceedingly dull." Emma dropped the book on the bed. "So I've been dozing and dreaming about Harrye. He is improving in certain important respects."

"Emma Loveney," said Constance, not without an

ill-concealed grin, "you are far and away the most wicked girl in town, if not the whole shire. Now listen carefully. We have serious matters to discuss."

Emma made room on the bed for Constance to sit.

"What is so serious that it brings you out on an afternoon such as this?"

Constance drew the letter from her sleeve. It had gone slightly damp, and the ink had run in a few places.

"It's from my dear brother, Will, whom I haven't set eyes on since his last visit to Stratford to see Anne and the children and the rest of the family. That was, as I recall, two years ago. I've often wondered why Anne, like a proper wife, doesn't go to London with the children to live with him; but that's his affair, not mine."

"You need to pay attention to the town gossips."

"Who say?"

"That, first of all, since she's a good eight years older than your brother, he got tired of sharing her bed."

"I can hardly credit that."

"Credit whatever you will. When Anne was twenty-six, and most attractive by all accounts, and he as green a lad as ever was, he delighted in her bed. But after a few years, with Anne no longer so sprightly caring for three little ones and a house, he sought lusher pastures and, I wager, found them in London."

"Will wouldn't do that."

"My dear, dear Constance, you have so much to learn about men."

"And women too, it would seem."

"Of that I have but scant knowledge."

"But some knowledge."

"Changing the topic, the town gossips also say that Anne kept after Will to earn enough money to support them in comfort when all he cared about was filling pages with nonsense. According to Charity Gage, he replied to Anne that the money will come when it will come."

"Charity my buttocks. I wouldn't believe a word that homely old woman says. She is bilious beyond telling."

"He ran off and left her and the children, didn't he?"

"To make his fortune in London and thus to provide for them as she wishes and far better than he ever could in this town. Now he's a famous actor and theater owner and will soon be rich as Croesus."

"We shall see what we shall see. I wager he's still scribbling nonsense."

"Now that's nonsense."

"Enough idle chatter. Let me read the letter. That is, after all, why you came."

Constance handed Emma the letter.

"If some of the words are indecipherable, tell me. I know the letter by heart."

"I am not surprised." Emma smiled and started reading. "Some letter." She pointed to a word that looked like raindrops on a window pane. "Pray tell, this would be?"

"Domestic."

"That makes sense. And this mess, here, towards the end?"

"Two days, more or less."

"I see. Well, there's no mistaking: 'With brotherly affection, William.'"

Constance retrieved the letter.

"Tell me, right away, Emma. Should I do what he asks?"

"Are you an even greater fool than I had imagined?" She gave Constance a playful tap on the arm. "If you don't do it, by God's grace, I shall."

"I knew you would say that. Oh, Emma, you are such a good friend."

She hugged Emma who touched Constance's hair.

"I so envy your mass of curly hair. If I had curls like that, I'd consider whether there might be a better beau in this town than Harrye Shawe although I doubt it."

"Harrye has some admirable qualities."

"Yes, he does."

"Your father seems to like him."

"That's so important," said Emma with a touch of sarcasm.

"Perhaps he'll give him a place at the mill."

"Then I can read romances all day, if I can find any good ones, have children and grow fat."

"You will do nothing of the kind, except for the children. Now, tell me," said Constance, taking back the letter, "is it time to let George ... you know?"

"If you like, but I wouldn't think much on that subject. If I'm not mistaken, you'll have far more interesting opportunities where you're going."

"Poor George."

For Will's letter had requested that Constance come as quickly as possible to London to assist in his domestic arrangements.

# Passage: Spring 1592

Clouds so covered the moon that not a sliver of light escaped. She had never experienced such darkness, and to say she was afraid would be an understatement of the gravest sort. Back in Stratford, she was rarely out at ten in the evening and, later than that, only for revelries such as May Day or the feasts and caroling on Christmas Eve. But the town was well-lit on those occasions by a plenitude of lanterns and torches. Now she could not even see where she was stepping and had once stubbed her toe against a rock in the center of what you might call a road and another time had inadvertently strayed from the road and tripped over a limb, falling to the damp, cold ground. She got up, her leg bruised and sore and, fearful that she had lost something from her leather satchel, had diligently examined the bag and searched the ground around the limb as best she could. Fortunately, she seemed to have lost nothing.

She had left Stratford just after midnight. From supper until that hour, she had lain on top of her bed trembling with excitement. She had hidden the satchel under the bed. Joan had been sound asleep in her bed for several hours and didn't stir when Constance left. She had told no one, except Emma, about the letter. Her father—a solemn, if caring, and exceedingly strict man who would not hesitate to give an errant child or apprentice a sound drubbing—would never have permitted a willowy chit of eighteen with a turned up nose, high, rosy cheeks and a sometimes unruly head of auburn curls to prance off to London on her own. Will would have known this; else why the secrecy involved in delivering the letter? She wondered if the man with the limp were a friend of his or a highly paid messenger. She suspected the former. Why would a man who appeared well-off travel that distance, at some risk to body and soul, for even a large sum?

She had thought of taking a lantern but feared aggravating the sin of running away. Her father will be furious in any case and even more so were he to find a piece of property missing. Not that he thought of her, and his other children, as property; but he did think of them as fully subservient to his will. In this regard, love did not enter the equation. She was, nevertheless, certain that he loved her but equally certain that he suspected nothing of her independent spirit and her ardent desire for a life that included accomplishments beyond marriage and raising children. She could not bear the picture of a tedious future as the wife and bearer of sons, and lesser-valued daughters, for a stout tradesman or member of the lower gentry - should her father manage to reach that high. The very idea filled her with a palpable dread that penetrated to her very core. She had no objection to marriage but knew that the only way to achieve her goals would be a husband of her own choosing who would respect her mind as much as her fertile body. That she had a good mind she knew not only from the ease with which she devoured books but also from her ready ability to follow the serious, thought-provoking and intensely fascinating conversations at the table when her father had important guests to dinner or supper.

That her father knew none of this was apparent from the fact that he spoke to her of little besides her knitting and playing the virginal. For a man so careful of his property, she was surprised that he didn't notice that books were frequently missing from their accustomed place. She read in the privacy of her room; and even though Joan taunted her for her choice of books, she also respected Constance's request to keep the matter between the two of them. She feared her father would question why a woman should read such works.

She had also not taken a lantern as she dreaded drawing attention to herself from anyone else who, although highly unlikely, might be abroad at such an hour. But now Constance wished she had brought the lantern—sin or not. She could see nothing of the road and could barely make out the shapes of trees and the dim outlines of the nearby ranks of hills. She didn't know how long she had been walking; but she had not reached Ettington, some five plus miles from Stratford and where she hoped, in the morning, to find a coach bound for London. How she would pay her fare was a matter to which she had given little consideration other than thinking to inform any coachman that her brother—the successful, well-known actor and theater impresario—would amply reward him when he left her at the door of his palatial residence. It would not have mattered had she given the subject any thought as she had no money to take. Her father had occasionally given her a few shillings for a purchase and had wanted the change so she had no savings. She was not, however, about to let her penury interfere with seizing this possibly once in a lifetime opportunity.

Her feet were sore from her stiff shoes; her arm ached from carrying the satchel; her calves, unused to the prolonged exercise, felt as if they would scarcely go another foot, and her body shivered in the night air. Yet she persevered, driven forward by the pot of gold at the end of the rainbow: her new life as mistress of Will's household. She wondered how many servants he had and how they would like taking orders from a snippet of a girl. She realized there would be much to learn. Will might even want her to keep his accounts, a matter about which she knew nothing. During his last visit to Stratford, while short on details, Will had left the impression that he was a prominent, if not the most prominent, London actor, well-known also for his skill in the running of theaters and the object of much bitter envy due to his resounding success despite his not having attended a university, the graduates of which, he stated, were young fops, better suited to mincing around the stage in outlandish, tight-fitting clothing than getting down to the business of serious acting. She had drunk in every word.

When she could make out the roofs and white walls of the cottages of Ettington, her spirits lifted; and she hurried forward, eager to find an inn that might shelter her until a coach departed, hopefully no later than dawn. But the high spirits lasted no longer than a few moments as an icy wind sprang up, seemingly out of nowhere, and cut through her cloak with no greater difficulty than a honed knife slices butter. She pulled the cloak as tight as possible and kept going, her shivering increasing as the wind gained strength. March, indeed, could be a cruel month. She found an inn in Ettington; but hard as she pounded on the door, no one answered.

"Sound asleep, one and all," she muttered to herself.

She could not sit on the frigid ground, and no bench was in sight so she had no choice but to forge onwards to Pillerton Priors which, although she had never been there, was she believed but a few miles further on. At least, she was going in the right direction; and the further she went, the less likely she was to meet someone who would recognize her. As she left the village, she glanced over her shoulder for a final look at the place where she had hoped to rest. She had not gone much more than half a mile from Ettington when the roadway began to narrow. She paid little attention as her mind was occupied with the warm fire she prayed awaited her in Pillerton Priors. The road narrowed further and became rutted and cluttered with sharp stones. To cross a gurgling stream, she lifted her skirt; but her shoes got soaked and became very uncomfortable. A wedge in the clouds allowed a little moonlight to seep through. She stopped; all around were fields, trees and hedgerows. She started again, cursing silently at the ill maintenance of the roads in these parts.

"Lazy folk," she said aloud, startling herself, and then stumbled, taking a few quick steps to keep from falling. What she had thought was a road had abruptly ended. She was in a field. About twenty yards away, she saw white forms. One lifted its head, and she heard the familiar, "Baa." She wanted to cry but simply turned around and struggled back. When she reached the road, she realized that it took a wide curve to the right. Cursing herself, she decided, would be a waste of the time and energy she needed to reach Pillerton Priors and that blazing fire. As she neared the village, a fine rain began that dampened her cloak.

A sleepy-eyed boy dressed in ill-fitting shirt and trousers finally answered her persistent knocking at the inn's door.

"What the devil is a girl like you doing out at this time of night?"

"Is there a fire going?"

"Not bloody likely at this hour."

"I'm chilled to the bone," she said. "Can't stop shivering."

"I'll put you in the stable. You can bed down with the horses. They and the straw will warm you up good and proper."

"Is there a coach to London tomorrow?"

"Early in the morning. Want me to wake you? You'll need to be up early to get a place."

He led her across the cobbled courtyard. She felt as if she would collapse at any moment. She couldn't remember ever being so tired. The rain having stopped, the sky had cleared; and moonlight glistened on the wet paving stones. Light seeped under the stable door. The boy opened it for her. A half dozen horses stood or were lying down. Fresh manure steamed, and the stable was redolent with its odor. She recoiled at first but, as the boy left, sliding the door closed, she realized that it was far warmer in the stable than outside. She searched for a pile of clean straw and, finding one in a corner, burrowed into it. She looked around. A pitch fork and two shovels hung on a grimy wall. Sheaves of hay were stacked against the opposite wall. Warming up, she lay her head back and was immediately asleep.

The boy was as good as his word. She sat up and rubbed her eyes. Her cloak and shoes had dried during the night; and even after only a few hours' sleep, she felt rested and reasonably warm. The boy handed her a chunk of hard rye bread and a steaming mug of cider, which warmed her further. She could have kissed him then and there for, not having a penny on her, she had not entertained the slightest idea when or how she would obtain food. She knew where her mother kept the market coins; but her inner voice had told her that if leaving without permission was a serious matter, taking money from her mother to abet her plan would have constituted an even more grievous sin than taking a lantern. She must surely arrive at Will's sometime the next day and could, if necessary, go with nothing further to eat until then. It would be a small price to pay for the life that lay ahead.

The bread wasn't what she was used to; but then, she didn't suppose London would be either. She refrained from kissing the lad, fearing it might stir undesirable emotions in his skinny chest. Had she any money, she would have given him a ha'penny. Thinking further on it, she decided a quick kiss would do no harm. After all, he had saved her from a frigid night and grave hunger. Moreover, he was not bad looking. She bestowed a kiss on his lips. He blushed.

"Oh, milady, I've not been kissed by such as you before."

"Meaning you've kissed your fair share of scullery maids and serving girls? And have you rolled with them in the straw in this very stable?"

"God's blood, milady, I'm an honest man."

"You're not quite a man although your lips had a manly flavor. As for being honest, you can roll with a maid in the straw and be an honest lad so long as you give as good as you get."

"Milady seems familiar with..."

"That'll be enough. Had I a ha'penny about my person, I'd gladly give it to you. You must, instead, treasure the kiss you received from such as me."

"Treasure it I will although it be hard to eat."

Constance laughed heartily, gave him another brush of the lips and hurried out the door.

In the courtyard, the coach was standing at the ready. She had not even heard the horses being led out of the stable. The coachman, a burly fellow wearing a padded doublet, heavy wool trousers, a cloak and a woolen cap, held a steaming mug in both hands. He had a prominent wen on the tip of his heavily-veined nose. When speaking, he made a slight whistling sound due to two missing front teeth, the rest of which were yellowed from constant pipe smoking. She approached him warily.

"Yes, miss?' he asked in a curt tone.

"Have you a place in your coach for a young woman of character?"

"And what sort of character would that be?"

"Of the best," Constance said, allowing a touch of pique into her tone.

"Which is why you've adorned your cloak with straw."

Constance took off her cloak, quickly brushed off the straw and put it back on. The coachman watched with an evil grin.

"I need to go to London," she said, softening her tone.

"As do the rest of my passengers." He removed his cap and scratched at the rough tufts of hair that blossomed from his scalp. "I have one last place inside the coach, but it will be three shillings."

"I'm afraid, my good man, that I quite forgot my purse and don't have the three shillings; but I'm staying in London with my brother, William Shakespeare. He's a rich actor and..."

"No actor, in London or anyplace else, is rich," said the coachman with a smirk. "I know as I see the plays with great regularity."

"You mustn't see them with such great regularity or you'd know of my brother."

"Never heard of him. Nor do I expect I ever will. So it's three shillings unless..." The coachman smiled broadly. "...you care to pay in kind."

"Sirrah," came a voice behind Constance. "I recommend you hold your filthy tongue unless you wish it cut clean out."

Constance turned around and beheld a vision. Not over ten yards away stood the most handsome man she had ever laid eyes on. He was tall, smooth-shaven, mid-twenties in age, she guessed, and wore a doublet of fine wool. Over the doublet was an elegant jerkin, embellished with pearls and needlework in gold and silver, whose pleated lower section ballooned to his mid-thighs. His hose, skin-tight, showed to advantage his muscled calves; and he sported a modest codpiece. A low-cut ruff encased his neck and on his head, at a jaunty angle, sat a wide-brimmed hat with a feather angled backwards. His hand rested lightly on the hilt of a sword in a scabbard attached to a wide, studded leather belt. Affixed to the shoulder above the scabbard was a waist-length cloak. Constance felt that she might swoon at a moment's notice.

"But, my lord, this... this... why I never... I mean it's an honest fare... yes..."

"Are you, perhaps, deaf, Sirrah? Or lacking in the

understanding of the Queen's English?" The young man slid the sword an inch out of the scabbard. "Did I not say to hold your filthy tongue?"

"Yes, my lord."

"Then hold it."

"Yes, my lord."

"Here are two shillings, more than enough for you to take this charming young woman to London so that she can find her immensely successful brother." The young man took a purse from his jerkin, removed two coins and threw one at the coachman who caught it mid-air. The second coin was thrown low and landed between two cobblestones. "Surely," said the young man, "it is no trouble to bend over." Which the coachman did with alacrity. Smiling at Constance, the young man politely asked: "What did you say your brother's name was?"

"Shakespeare... William Shakespeare."

"Alas, I do not know of this fine actor...."

"And theater owner," interjected Constance, bowing her head.

"Yes, of course. I will endeavor to remember his name. It should not be difficult as it does sound trippingly on the tongue." He took Constance's satchel from her and, lightly guiding her by the elbow, steered her towards the coach. "You shall sit next to me."

"How can I ever thank you?"

"No need."

"My brother will insist on repaying the two shillings."

"I would never dream of such a thing." He stopped at the door to the coach. "Allow me to introduce myself. I am Edmund Gavell, eldest son of the Earl of Pennyford. At your service." He opened the door and helped Constance into the coach. She sat in the middle seat, facing backwards and next to a plump man with thick jowls. Lord Edmund handed up her satchel and, stepping gracefully into the coach, sat on her other side. Across from her, sitting stiff as a musket rod, was a scarecrow of a woman, middle-aged and with sunken cheeks, heavily rouged. Her cloak was pulled tightly around her. On either side of her sat two young girls, whom Constance judged to be several years younger than herself.

"Good morning, ladies," said Lord Edmund.

The woman nodded, murmuring, "Good morning, my lord," while the two girls twittered like birds and partially hid their faces with the backs of their hands.

"Mistress Sedley," explained Lord Edmund to Constance, "is taking her delightful nieces..." The girls twittered even more excitedly. "...up to London where they will stay for a time with her brother, a well-to-do tradesman or, perhaps more accurately, a wealthy merchant. The gentleman on your other side, who delights in his suckling pig and puddings, is none other than Squire Chichester who owns a pleasant manor hereabouts." With a slight wave of his gloved hand, Lord Edmund continued: "Let me introduce to you ladies and gentleman our new traveling companion: Miss... oh, dear, I haven't learned your first name." At this, he twirled his hand as if to indicate the insignificance of the oversight. "...Miss Shakespeare."

Constance leaned towards him and said softly: "Constance."

"Indeed... Miss Constance Shakespeare who is traveling to London to visit her exceedingly famous brother."

At that, the coach jerked forward and Constance was thrown against Lord Edmund.

"I'm so sorry."

"Not at all," he said and patted her arm, smiling graciously.

Leaning slightly forward, Constance stared out the window as fields and rolling hills swept by. Never having been in a coach before, she felt they were going at break-neck speed although Lord Edmund explained that, were they on their own horses, they would be traveling much faster.

"I'm taking the coach as I had to retrieve a trunk from our country estate and deliver it to Father in London. It contains some important papers related to a matter of law in which Father is interested. I am so delighted now at the inconvenience to which the trunk put me."

Lord Edmund glanced quickly at Constance, admiring her youthful beauty.

"Where is the trunk?" asked one of the nieces.

"Well-secured on top of the coach and watched over carefully by my man-servant."

"I didn't know anyone was on top of the coach besides the coachman," said Constance.

The nieces giggled. Mistress Sedley snapped at them to hush this instant and turned a condescending smile on Constance. "Of course, there are riders on top. In addition to the coachman and Lord Edmund's servant, the coachman has an assistant; and there is one other passenger."

"Thank you, Mistress Sedley, for the kind explanation. This is all quite new to me and very exciting."

"So it would seem although I would have thought that a fine, young lady like yourself would've known something about riding in a coach. They are not so rare, nowadays, even in the country towns." Mistress Sedley leaned back in the seat, well satisfied with herself.

Constance blushed. Before she could think of anything to say, Lord Edmund broke in: "I should imagine that Miss Shakespeare has wisely spent her time on her father's estate, learning the virginal and other feminine arts rather than gadding about in a coach and four."

Constance decided to leave it at that.

"I see," said Mistress Sedley.

"What will you do at your brother's?" asked one of the nieces.

"My brother wrote me that he needs assistance with his rather large household. I shall manage his domestic affairs."

"So the baggage can read," said Mistress Sedley in a whisper that she did not believe the others could hear.

"What did you say?"

"Talking to myself, Lord Edmund."

The coach was cold; and Constance, still suffering from the effects of the previous night's ordeal, began to shiver violently. Lord Edmund noticed and pulled a blanket from under the seat. He spread it over her skirt and above her waist. Saying that he also was cold, he covered his own legs and stomach.

"Is your father's manor near Pillerton Priors?" asked Mistress Sedley.

"Not far," said Constance.

"You are from Warwick, Squire Chichester," said Mistress Sedley, "which is not so very far from here. Are you familiar with a Squire Shakespeare or perhaps, a knight of that name?"

"No knight, but I have heard of a John Shake..."

"Stop this instant," commanded Lord Edmund, and the coach fell quiet. "I suggest the lot of you refrain from further pestering Miss Shakespeare, who is obviously cold and fatigued." He looked hard at Mistress Sedley. "Am I understood?"

"Yes, my lord. I am simply curious as to why her father, seeing as she is so young, did not accompany her to the coach."

"Mistress Sedley," cautioned Lord Edmund.

"He did accompany me but had to leave on the instant, having urgent business in Stratford."

"Business so early?"

"Mistress Sedley, pray accommodate my request or suffer the consequences."

"Sorry, my lord."

Absolute silence enveloped the coach. Nothing was heard save the hooves of the horses striking the hard-packed dirt road and an occasional "move along there" from the coachman as he encouraged the horses to keep up their pace. Constance again leaned forward to look out the window. The weather had cleared, and the trees along the road glistened in the morning sun. The coach swayed, and Constance felt nauseous. She prayed she would not be sick. Could she ask that the coach be stopped? How mortifying! But what choice had she if the nausea worsened? She was so preoccupied with not getting sick that, at first, she didn't notice the hand on her skirt. Starting at her knee, the hand moved slowly, as if of its own accord, up the outside of her left thigh. She looked at Squire Chichester who sat placidly looking out the window, hands folded on his lap and, apparently, noticing nothing.

"The road surface is not bad right now," said Lord Edmund.

"Yes," she agreed.

"It will surely get worse. Some of the holes near London would swallow this coach in its entirety."

"Oh dear, how frightening."

She gazed straight ahead although she could see, slightly to her left, that Lord Edmund's hands were underneath the blanket. All symptoms of nausea vanished. The hand moved to the inside of her thigh and began a stroking movement. She stiffened. What could she do? "Nothing," came the immediate answer. Without Lord Edmund's protection, which he would certainly withdraw if she made even the slightest attempt to remove his hand, she was at the mercy of the persistently nasty Mistress Sedley. A tiny sigh escaped her lips. The hand increased its pressure, pushing down on her thigh as it stroked and reaching further up. She wanted to look at Lord Edmund but dared not for fear Mistress Sedley or the nieces would think something amiss. Dear God, what would happen then? Realizing that staring straight ahead could be as bad as staring at Lord Edmund, she looked in the opposite direction: past the Squire's head and out the window. A pasture full of cows rolled past and then a copse thick with oak and sycamore. Then something odd occurred. She didn't want the hand to stop; and when it moved from her thigh to between her legs, she became still as a mouse at the edge of its hole. The hand rubbed back and forth and in a circular motion without stopping. The insides of her thighs were wet and a sensation was building—a sensation she had never before experienced. She knew something was about to happen. She forced herself to continue looking out the window. Another field with cows came into view. At the same moment, it happened. A powerful spasm coursed through her body.

"Oh my," she said quite loudly, startling everyone except Lord Edmund, "look how many cows are in that pasture."

"Indeed," said Lord Edmund and laughed, causing Mistress Sedley to wonder what was funny about a field dotted with cows. He removed his hand from Constance's leg.

Just then, the coach hit a rough patch; and the passengers were bounced around in their seats. The nieces thought it was great fun and a diversion from the boredom of traveling with Auntie Sedley; but the impact on Constance's bladder, while a diversion, was hardly fun. She squeezed her legs together and hoped she could contain the urge until they reached a rest stop. Unfortunately, she had no idea when that might be. She grimaced, fearful of the awful consequences should she wet herself. For starters, in her satchel, she had only a sleeping gown, a bodice and a spare set of undergarments—nothing approaching a full set of clothing, not even a skirt. In Stratford, shops abounded where she could remedy the problem; but she doubted they would come across any such on the high road to London. Every bump jostled her and worsened the situation. The urge to pee was well-nigh overwhelming, but she held on with grim determination. She had occasionally experienced this potent sensation when walking about town with Emma, but at those times, relief was not far away. Once, she remembered, while they were walking on a country lane, the urge hit them both simultaneously; and they were forced to retreat, laughing gleefully, into the bushes on the side of the lane. If only, she thought, that surly coachman would experience the same need and stop the coach. Then an idea for her salvation occurred to her. After all, she and Lord Edmund were now on somewhat different terms.

"Excuse me, my lord," she said with feigned diffidence, "but I am in some need of... refreshing myself."

"Oh, my dear Constance, I do apologize. I should have offered. My servant, at all times, packs a flagon of excellent wine. I shall..."

"No, my lord, it is not wine that I require but a brief pause in our journey."

"Ah."

Making a fist, Lord Edmund struck the top of the coach several times. When that proved of no avail, he opened the door and called for the coachman to halt. This achieved the desired result. The men found satisfactory bushes on the near side of the road while the ladies retreated to the far side. Clambering down a modest embankment, they entered a copse ten yards distant. The three young women raised their skirts and squatted; but Mistress Sedley, equally austere in all her habits, moved further into the woods. The nieces, flanking Constance, thought this as much fun as bouncing in the coach—as well as quite daring.

"Suppose," said Ester, the younger niece, "a peasant or yeoman should happen by and see us. Wouldn't that be dreadful?"

Both nieces burst into laughter. Constance remained silent: grateful for the relief.

Wynefreed, the older niece by a year, leaned towards Constance and, in a low voice she hoped her Aunt could not hear, said: "What did Lord Edmund do to you in the coach? Did he pluck your flower?"

"I should think not."

"Oh, don't be coy. I saw his hand move under the blanket."

"He was simply adjusting my skirt, which had fallen out of line."

"Oh fiddlesticks! Do you think we're innocent children? We may live in the country, but we know a deflowering when we see one."

"Then you know less than you think. My flower is quite intact."

"Will you tell him to do it to us?" asked Ester.

"Don't be absurd," snapped Wynefreed. "He's not likely to do that."

"Do what?" asked Mistress Sedley, who had just come up behind them. "And who might he be?"

Constance stood up quickly while the nieces almost fell over.

"Help them improve their French," said Constance. "I imagine Lord Edmund is quite adept at the language."

"What a splendid idea. Thank you, Constance, if I may call you Constance, for suggesting it. I will speak to Lord Edmund directly."

When, back in the coach, Mistress Sedley broached the subject and said that it was at Constance's suggestion, Lord Edmund replied: "Avec plaisir" and, under the blanket, gave Constance's thigh a modest squeeze.

By the time the coachman stopped, near midday, for a light repast at a stone and stucco inn, The Reindeer, in the market town of Banbury, Constance was beyond famished. When Lord Edmund asked what she would like, Constance said: "Anything, really." At his direction, the serving girl brought her a mug of cider and a hot soup. To her delight, the soup had cubes of turnips, carrots and mutton floating in the broth. Sitting at a dark oak table with Lord Edmund and Squire Chichester, she drank the cider and devoured the soup with as much grace as any person could command who had walked miles through heavy weather, slept in a bed of straw and eaten nothing but a chunk of bread for nigh on to twenty-four hours. When she asked for a second bowl of soup, Lord Edmund laughed and signalled the serving girl. He paid the bill and handsomely tipped the girl to whom he gave an endearing smile that caused her to prominently sway her buttocks as she crossed the ill-lit room with its small, glazed windows and wide-planked flooring.

After eating, Lord Edmund took Constance on a short walk around the town, showing her, in particular, one of Banbury's crosses, the Bread Cross. They returned to the coach; and Constance whiled away the afternoon dozing off from time to time or listening to the French lesson Lord Edmund was giving the nieces. Late in the afternoon, as the sky began to darken, they arrived in Aylesbury. Now, Lord Edmund told Constance, they were only about forty or so miles from London and would arrive there the next day sometime in the afternoon.

"You must be anxious to see your brother."

"I am, thank you, my lord."

He told the innkeeper to provide Constance with her own room. When Squire Chichester suggested that he and Lord Edmund share a room to reduce expenses, Lord Edmund replied that, while he appreciated the kind gesture, he was not a good sleeper and did not wish to disturb the excellent Squire throughout the night.

Lord Edmund invited Mistress Sedley, the nieces, Squire Chichester and Constance to join him for supper. As an inn, The Speckled Trout dated back over a hundred years, having previously been a manor house for a further hundred years. The dining room had a low, beamed ceiling and wide floor planks fastened by wooden nails. Light came from candles on the tables and in wall sconces. Painted cloths, with pastoral and Biblical scenes, hung on the walls. A low fire burned in a hearth and, in one corner, a young man at a virginal played variations on a popular melody. The music brightened up an otherwise somber room.

"I've heard that piece," said the Squire, "but for the life of me, I cannot place it."

"I believe," said Constance, "that William Byrd wrote it. Quite popular among courting couples back home."

"You don't say," said the Squire.

"Is it now," commented Lord Edmund.

"It is delightful," said Wynefreed.

"I should so love to dance," said Ester, "with a handsome fellow."

"Ester!" said Mistress Sedley, sharply, thus ending the conversation about music.

Since dinner, a good number of hours earlier—a good number, indeed, it seemed to Constance who was again famished—had been quite modest compared to what was typical for a nobleman's midday meal, Lord Edmund ordered an array of delicacies instead of the usual, small number of dishes generally served at supper. The two serving girls carried in platter after platter. First came roasted meats well-seasoned with spices such as salt, pepper, rosemary, mace and cloves: mutton, veal, goose, coney and, the inn's piece de la resistance, swan. Additionally, a capon had been baked in a hard pastry (used only for cooking, not eating) with oranges, prunes, dates, honey and cinnamon added for flavoring. Fried turbot and eel followed, accompanied by boiled cabbage, artichokes and a recently introduced vegetable that was all the rage: cauliflower. To accompany these superb dishes, Lord Edmund had chosen, from the inn's excellent cellar, a dry, white Burgundy from France and an aromatic red wine from Spain.

No sooner had the fish course been taken away, then a bowl stuffed with plums, peppins and cherries was brought in as well as an apricot and gooseberry pie straight from the oven.

"it is quite fortunate that today is not a fish day," said the Squire, "or we would not have had nearly as sumptuous meal. I thank you, my Lord."

"You are most welcome," said Lord Edmund, "but no thanks required."

Mistress Sedley pushed back from the table, her eyes glazed over and her stomach ready to burst. "I too wish to thank you," she said to Lord Edmund. "I feel so stuffed you could roast me on a spit. We must to bed."

She nodded at the nieces. "Thank Lord Edmund, Wynefreed and Ester, and let's move along."

Constance also could barely stay awake, but she fervently wished to hear the gentlemen's conversation so she forced herself to sit upright and remain at the table. The Squire began by praising the quality and variety of the meat dishes and then held forth on the enchanting bouquet of both wine selections. Lord Edmund demurred, exclaiming: "You are too kind. A modest repast."

After a few more pleasantries, the conversation turned to the subject of the various perfidious plots against the life and rule of their beloved monarch.

"It is most fortunate," said the Squire, "that in the last half dozen years, we have not seen another of these damnable conspiracies."

"Not since the execution six years ago of that fool Babington and his cohorts."

"Don't forget," said the Squire, "the involvement of that French—might as well have been French seeing where she was raised—whore, Mary, Queen—hah!—of Scots."

"I haven't forgotten," said Lord Edmund.

"Lost her fool head and good riddance if you ask me. Were it up to me there'd be a goodly supply of Catholic heads garnishing poles on castle gates."

Lord Edmund put a hand on the Squire's shoulder and spoke in a calm, yet firm, voice: "There be many loyal Catholics in the country who want nothing to do with plots and assassinations." Lord Edmund relaxed his grip on the Squire's shoulder and continued: "Things do seem to be quieter."

"As the son of an important earl and also a London resident, you would be in a better position to know than myself, a rude country fellow. I dare say, however, that the manner of Babington's departing is giving pause to those Catholics pining for a return to the old religion. Hanging by the neck for a brief time and then, still alive and kicking, castrated, drawn and quartered is a suitable end for such vile elements. I'd have loved to hear the traitor screaming with his innards spilled into the mud."

Constance gasped. She feared she would faint and collapse in a heap on the floor. She fought back the powerful urge to vomit. Neither she nor her friends had ever witnessed an execution with the exception, of course, of Emma who had snuck off to see one despite her father's strictures on the subject. When he learned of her disobedience from a customer who had seen Emma standing within a few yards of the gallows, he had, with gusto, taken a paddle to her behind. For the next couple of days, she had found sitting at table a problematical business.

"Squire Chichester," snapped Lord Edmund, "please remember: we have a woman of tender years and good character with us."

Looking abashed, the Squire apologized to Constance who assured him that, as she was going to live in London, she needed to become more worldly-wise.

"In which case," said the Squire, "you may find it of interest that when the executioner, having just separated Mary's head from her body, held up the head by its hair, the bleeding thing dropped from his hand and fell to the floor. It seems the vain strumpet had worn a wig to her execution and had, in truth, short, grey hair."

Despite her shock, Constance could not help laughing and was quickly joined by the Squire and Lord Edmund.

"Since Walsingham's death," asked the Squire, "who has replaced him as the Queen's master of spies?"

"I wouldn't know," said Lord Edmund.

"Whomever it is, he needs to pay close attention. There may be loyal Catholics, but secret ones abound. Sly fellows who pass themselves off as Church of England but, behind the mask, long for a restoration of the old ways. They hide in their dens throughout the country. I've heard of a few in Stratford, Miss Shakespeare; but I'm certain you are innocent of any such knowledge."

"I am astounded," said Constance. "I've heard of none. My father is a hard man and would not permit such goings on anywhere in our neighborhood."

"Just the type that bears watching. I venture to say that..."

"Now," interrupted Edmund, it's time we all took to our beds. We depart early on the morrow."

As he left Constance at the door of her room, he bid her a good sleep and then ambled down the hall to his own room. Constance's room was small and furnished with a table by the bed, a straight-backed chair, a chest and a few pegs in the wall. A basin and an ewer of water stood on a second table while a chamber pot was under the bed. She undressed quickly, put on her sleeping gown, slipped into bed and blew out the candle on the bedside table. As she drifted off, she heard, in the sleep-filling recesses of her mind, the door open and close and soft footsteps cross the room. Frightened, she opened her eyes and saw Lord Edmund, dressed only in his hose and a shirt, standing by the bed and sweetly smiling.

"May I join you?"

"I am confused, my lord."

"I thought you might like to repeat the sensations from earlier in the day."

The memory caused a quickening of her nerves.

"They were rather nice, but..."

"But?"

"I've never done this before."

"I am an excellent tutor."

Her inner voice whispered that here indeed was a good reason. She had never met anyone like Lord Edmund.

"It might be a good idea."

"I'll take that as a yes." He lay down next to her. "I won't harm you in any way. You may tell me to stop if you wish."

"Thank you, my lord."

He kissed her on the lips, gently and without pushing his tongue into her mouth. She gave him a slight kiss back. He put an arm around her shoulders, drew her against his chest and kissed her again, this time letting his tongue caress her lips. He put his hand beneath her gown and ran it up her thigh, gently stroking as he went. She felt herself get wet as she had in the coach. She kissed him more fervently. He took her hand and placed it on the bulge in his hose. She had never before touched a man's organ, always pulling her hand away whenever George had moved it in that direction. The feel of Lord Edmund's hardness sent a thrill up her spine. She shivered.

"What should I do, my lord?"

"Stroke it, very gently."

She did as bidden, and he kept moving his hand as he had in the coach. When she felt that potent sensation building, she let out a soft moan; and he stopped.

"Have I done something wrong, my lord?"

"Not at all. We just need to progress further."

He stripped off his hose and undergarment, leaving on only his shirt, and pushed up her sleeping gown until it revealed her hardened nipples. He spread her legs and swiftly, but gracefully, lowered himself onto her almost bare body. He gripped her by the upper arms and pushed. Realizing that she was a virgin, he entered her very slowly so as to cause the least amount of pain. She gave a small, sharp cry.

"The pain will subside quickly."

It did. He moved back and forth, still slowly, but at the end of each thrust, he pushed firmly against her pelvis. She began to feel the wonderful, quickening sensation. She moaned as the feeling spread throughout her body. Saying, "Hush, now," he covered her mouth with his; but increasingly intense moans still escaped her lips. As the feeling subsided and her body began to relax, he thrust once quite vigorously and could not prevent his sharp cry from echoing around the narrow room. He stayed on top of her for a couple of minutes and then slid to her side. He took her in his arms, blew into her ear and kissed her creamy throat. Then they both fell into a deep sleep.

He rose well before dawn and was dressing when she awoke. She held out a hand and drew him to the bed.

"Was that pleasing?" he asked.

"Yes," she answered. Her eyes grew thoughtful. "When shall we do it again?"

"We shall, but I cannot for sure say when. In London, I hope."

"I understand, my lord."

"My dear, Constance, given what we did last night, you may call me Edmund, but not in public."

He left, closing the door behind him without a sound.

"Now I have been truly deflowered," she thought. "Won't Emma be proud of me."

# Arrival: Spring 1592

Breakfast was laid out on a long table and consisted of bread, butter, pickled herring and a choice of ale or cider. Constance chose the cider and washed down a second helping of herring with copious draughts. Not generally very hungry at breakfast, she assumed the activities of the preceding night had much to do with her keen appetite.

"Hungry, are we?" asked Lord Edmund with a chuckle.

"Surprising as I am not generally hungry in the morning." She hesitated. "Maybe not surprising..." She hesitated again. "...my lord."

"I am especially hungry this morning," he said.

She made a slight curtsy and felt satisfied that she had told the truth. Lying was a trait she heartily condemned and believed permissible only in the most extreme circumstances or to avoid wounding another's feelings.

As they walked to the coach, she asked Lord Edmund if she could sit next to the window so as to see more of the countryside than she had the day before. He readily assented although the Squire put on a glum face.

"Why Miss Shakespeare, I thought you liked sitting next to me."

"Indeed, I do; but then, I so want to see the country as it is my first time traveling anywhere outside of Stratford.

"So be it." A smile lit up the Squire's jowly face. "I can see the advantage of that seat. The countryside is, indeed, worth observing."

As the coach rolled along, the road seemed smoother than yesterday; and she was more comfortable. She gazed at the wide fields in some of which grazed cattle and the ubiquitous sheep while others were divided into sections bordered by narrow paths. Each section was divided into strips. She asked Lord Edmund what was the meaning of this pattern.

"Tenants of each manor are assigned one or more strips for growing crops. In this region, the principal crops are wheat, corn and barley. The paths allow the tenants to access their strips of land. Some of the land, on the other hand, may be leased to yeomen who pay rent and farm it. The open fields where you see animals grazing may be manorial or village land with the animal's owners having grazing rights. Does that satisfy your curiosity?"

"It does, my lord."

"Do you have a thirst for knowledge?"

"I do have a thirst for knowledge ... and much else, my lord."

At that, Wynefreed laughed and said: "What else, Miss Shakespeare"?

"Life's varied experiences."

"Which would include?"

Mistress Sedley pinched Wynefreed's arm. The girl cried: "Ouch" to which Mistress Sedley said: "Hold your impudent tongue or a little pinch will be the least of it." Wynefreed lowered her head but looked up under a mass of light brown hair and winked at Constance. Fortunately, Lord Edmund had, at that moment, looked out the window.

While the landscape consisted mostly of fields dedicated to crops and animals, the road also passed through stretches of thick, dark forest. In one such forest, Ester, in a quivering voice, asked: "Will we meet robbers in the forest?"

"Do not concern yourself," replied Lord Edmund in a soothing tone. "My servant and the coachman are well armed and prepared to deal with any robbers. I also would join the fray should it be necessary."

"It would, furthermore, be a most daring band of cutthroats," said the Squire, "who would disturb a coach once they discovered it carried the son of a powerful earl. There is far less dangerous prey about."

They traversed frequent villages and occasional towns. In one village, a child waved as the coach sped by. In the towns, Constance observed the number of houses that were made of brick rather than wattle and daub (a frame filled in with a mixture of plaster and reeds or small branches). One village seemed deserted. No people were in sight, and the houses were in bad repair, as if abandoned. Furniture and household goods lay in the street. In the middle of the village, the coachman had to stop while his assistant and Lord Edmund's servant cleared two tables and several chairs that blocked the road. That accomplished, the coach moved on.

"Where is everybody?" asked Constance.

"Enclosure," replied Lord Edmund through gritted teeth.

"What is that?"

"The lord of the manor hereabouts has forced the villagers from their homes and fields so he can create open space for sheep farming or preserves where he can hunt deer or boar at his leisure. It is as cruel a practice as one can imagine, and my father will have none of it on his lands. Have you not seen vagrants and wandering families in Stratford?"

"Yes, but I thought they were good-for-nothings too lazy to work."

"They'll work hard enough if given a chance."

"I beg to differ with your lordship," said the Squire. "Sheep farming is more extensive when land is enclosed and, thus, improves our trade with overseas markets. And why should not a lord of the manor use his land for hunting or in whatever fashion he so chooses? It is, after all, his land."

"It has furthered unrest in the towns and countryside and poses a risk to the stability of the regime. Have you no pity, furthermore, for the poor wretches who can barely, if at all, provide for their wives and infants?"

Edmund glared at the Squire.

"You are the son of an earl and a lord in your own right so I will defer to your superior judgment."

"Nonsense. You may hold whatever opinion you wish."

"So long as I care naught for keeping my head attached to the rest of my body."

"You are playing the devil's advocate which I find noxious in the extreme." Edmund playfully tapped the Squire's arm. "That alone could deprive you of your head."

"Just what I said, my lord."

Edmund threw back his head and laughed heartily.

"I was only..."

The coach stopped suddenly, and Edmund was thrown against Constance while the Squire practically landed in Wynefreed's lap, causing her to squeal. Edmund touched Constance's hand as he straightened up.

"So sorry, Miss Shakespeare."

"Quite all right, my lord."

The coachman's assistant—a young fellow relatively new to long journeys carrying aristocrats, among whom he included the Squire and Mistress Sedley—warily approached the door and, trembling with anxiety, knocked. Edmund opened the door and asked: "What has happened?"

"A... a... a... bridge, my lord."

"What about a bridge?"

"We... we... cannot cross it," the young man said hurriedly.

"And why is that, young man?"

"Because... because...."

"Rest easy, my lad; no one intends you any harm."

This reassurance seemed to calm the young fellow and restore his command of the language.

"Thank you, my lord."

"I am delighted that you have found your tongue even if we still are ignorant of the source of our problem. Let me assist you," continued Edmund, with a chuckle. "Are we confronted by a stubborn ox who prefers this bridge to any other part of the shire? Or, perhaps, a pair of sheep are mating in the middle of the bridge and expect us to wait until the marriage is consummated? In either case, you have my permission to drive them off."

Edmund smiled at the lad in a kindly fashion, and the lad ventured a modest smile in return. A low rumble of laughter escaped from Constance and the Squire. Mistress Sedley glared in turn at each of the nieces, daring them to laugh.

"It is neither an ox nor mating sheep, my lord."

"Well then, if it's a pig's carcass, just heave it into the stream. Since It may take two of you to perform such a Herculean task, my servant will be of assistance; but whatever the obstacle, show a lively spirit, my lad. We are all anxious to see the tower of St. Paul's, truncated as it still is from that lightning strike of some thirty years ago."

"An excellent warning that was to the damnable Catholics," interjected the Squire.

"Would you please lay aside your religious bigotry," said Lord Edmund, irritably, "at least until we resolve our dilemma." He turned back to the young man. "Well, my lad?"

"Yes... I mean, no."

"This is becoming difficult again."

"I mean there are no obstacles such as you mention, my lord. The bridge is out of sorts."

"As in someone down with a fever?"

"No, my lord, the bridge is in need of repair; and we must go through the stream."

"Clarity at last. Many thanks. Let us then tarry here no longer and move briskly into the stream."

"We cannot do that."

"God preserve us," said Edmund, shaking his head and unable to stifle a laugh. "Pray tell, why not?"

"Coachman says it is not safe for the passengers to stay in, or on, the coach while he traverses the stream. He begs my lord, and the other passengers, to cross on foot."

"And get my feet wet," cried Mistress Sedley. "Not on your life."

"I'm afraid you must," said Edmund. "The coachman makes good sense. Suppose the coach should topple over in the stream? You might get more than your feet wet. You might drown."

"Heaven forbid," said Mistress Sedley, her eyes stark with fear.

"The men shall carry the ladies," said Edmund. "Your feet shall stay dry as if they had never left the coach."

"I should think not," said Mistress Sedley. "No man has ever carried me, and none shall carry my nieces. Far better to get our feet wet." She tossed her head peremptorily and pushed Ester. "Out... out... and be quick about it."

They all clambered out of the coach. Edmund's servant and the male passenger had already climbed down, leaving only the coachman. Edmund walked to the bridge. The sides were crumbling and the flooring was deeply rutted and looked on the verge of falling into the stream.

"A disgrace," muttered Edmund angrily. "I shall see to it that the authorities deal with the manor owner responsible for maintaining this bridge." He returned to the knot of people waiting for him to organize the crossing. "This is one of our serious problems," he said to the Squire. "So many people fail in their duties." He turned to Constance. "Shall I carry you across, Miss Shakespeare?"

"Thank you, my lord, but I shall be fine. I don't mind getting a little wet. I'm certain I'll be drier than I was... never mind."

With that, Constance felt her way cautiously down the bank. At the bottom, she took off her shoes, rolled her skirt up to her calves and made it fast with a pin. With her shoes in one hand and her satchel in the other, she stepped into the stream. The water, colder and moving faster than she had anticipated, swirled around her ankles and calves. She briefly regretted not accepting Edmund's offer but, thinking too late now, started gingerly across. The stream bed was slippery in places, especially when running over smooth rocks; and she almost fell once or twice but, nevertheless, made good progress.

"I'd be delighted for someone to carry me," said Wynefreed, looking directly at Lord Edmund.

"I'd be happy to accommodate you," said the Squire, with a leering grin.

"Did your ears fail you?" snapped Mistress Sedley at Wynefreed. "Under no circumstances. Now move smartly."

Wynefreed, gravely disappointed, moved towards the bank, followed by Ester and Mistress Sedley.

"Squire Chichester," said Lord Edmund, "the least we can do is assist the ladies down the bank. You stand at the bottom." He nodded to the male passenger. "You halfway down, and I shall stay at the top."

The three women made it down the bank without incident and, rolling up their skirts a couple of inches—far less than Constance—started across. The men followed. "Careful, it's slippery in places," Constance called from the opposite bank. No problems occurred until, halfway across, Mistress Sedley stepped on a large, slimy rock and, crying out, fell sideways into the stream. Edmund rushed forward and, crying over his shoulder for Nicholas, his servant, to fetch a blanket, scooped up the struggling and drenched Mistress Sedley and carried her to the stream's edge. Even wrapped in a blanket, she shivered uncontrollably. The nieces rubbed her furiously until, gradually, the shivering subsided. She thanked Lord Edmund for rescuing her—"I could well have drowned"—and acknowledged that she should have taken his advice in the first place.

Once all the passengers were safely on the opposite bank, the coachman slapped the reins and headed the horses towards the bank. Taking but a tentative step down the slope, the lead horse balked and backed up, throwing the whole team into confusion. The coachman swore and cracked his whip over the back of the lead horse and his mate; but neither would budge.

"Let me try," said the assistant, who had returned to his place next to the coachman. The coachman nodded, and the young lad climbed down and approached the lead horse. He spoke quietly, knowing just the right tone to calm the animal. After speaking a minute, he grasped the bridle and edged the horse towards the lip of the bank. Trustingly, the horse moved forwards but still hesitated at the edge.

"It's fine, Robbie," murmured the young lad to the horse and stepped over the edge. Robbie followed, slowly picking his way for the first couple of steps and then moving with greater assurance. The team, united again, went down the bank and into the stream. The assistant walked beside them. Lord Edmund, watching from the opposite bank, let out a deep-throated shout: "Well done, my lad, well done." The rest of the passengers took up the chorus and bellowed: "Well done, indeed." The lad grinned with pleasure.

When the coach reached the bank, Lord Edmund

slipped a crown into the lad's hand and clapped him on the back. The coachman called for the lad to climb back on the coach. The other passengers found their places, and the journey resumed. As they approached within a few miles of London, Constance observed that, in each village, there were considerably more houses lining the road than in the country villages or towns. Packed closely together, the houses seemed, to her, to be one continuous town punctuated here and there by a few open fields.

Suddenly, Constance screamed; and all conversation ceased.

"What is it?" asked Edmund.

Constance could only point dumbly out the window. Edmund leaned over and looked. Five bodies, two of which were women, hung from gallows and swayed in the breeze. Crows picked at their faces. Edmund placed a hand on her arm.

"It's Tyburn," he said, "the execution grounds. Those are dastardly criminals, and you should feel no pity for they have committed unspeakable deeds. Innocent folk have suffered at their hands."

Constance nodded but still could not speak. She denied neither the criminals' malignancy nor the horror of their crimes; they surely deserved their punishment. It mattered little, however, what the criminals had done. Her reaction at seeing the drooping bodies was not one of pity but rather of revulsion. The sensation was visceral and terrifying. She turned away. She never wanted to see such a sight again. She knew that some went to executions as a form of entertainment, of sport; but that was not her. Wynefreed and Ester also looked out but did not appear to be horrified. The three of them, nevertheless, remained silent until after the coach had passed Newgate and entered the city of London.

The coach stopped at an inn near St. Paul's, and the journey was over—or just begun in the case of Constance. Expressing a hope to see them again, Constance bid farewell to Mistress Sedley and the nieces, who started along Newgate Street towards Cheapside. Constance looked around. She had never seen so many people in one place. Newgate Street was jammed with riders on horses, carts, the occasional carriage or litter (carried by four men) and a multitude of pedestrians hurrying along, entering and leaving the myriad of shops and stepping carefully around the rotting carcass of a dog that lay in the street. Seeming to her oddly out of proportion to the rest of the building, she gazed up at the stump of St. Paul's spire, a squared-off tower left after the lightning strike and resulting fire that sent the upper part of the spire crashing through the cathedral's roof. The cathedral was, nonetheless, far larger than any church in Stratford; and she was awed by its power and beauty.

"May I take you to your brother's house?" Lord Edmund interrupted her reverie. "My father's carriage is here. The driver has been waiting for some time."

"Will it not be a bother, my lord?"

"It will be my pleasure."

"Would you mind my accompanying you?" asked

Squire Chichester. "My lodgings are not far from Pennyford House."

If looks could kill, Edmund's glance of disdain and fury directed towards the Squire surely would have done so. "Not at all," Edmund said in a tone that, to anyone with even a modicum of perception, would have indicated that the Squire's place in London society was, henceforth, far from secure. Constance handed Edmund her brother's missive, which contained the name of the parish and the street.

"I see," said Edmund.

Constance gawked at the sights, enchanted, as the carriage moved slowly along crowded Cheapside. She was amazed to see buildings of five stories with elaborate carvings and was no less impressed with the numerous goldsmiths' shops, grocers' establishments and apothecaries. Passing through Stocks Market, she saw stalls where fish and meat, laid out in great slabs, were sold. They were now on Lombard Street and, after passing Grace Church Street, turned off the main thoroughfare into a neighborhood of lanes and private houses. The carriage worked its way slowly through a warren of ever narrower lanes. The road surfaces were no longer paved but were heavy with mud. Although it was only mid-afternoon, the overhanging eaves of the houses and the smoke belching from fireplaces and (in the better homes) chimneys made the scene they passed through seem almost as dark and thick as her mental image of the underworld.

Finally, the carriage could go no further; the

driver, climbing down from his seat while holding the reins tightly since the horses, in such unfamiliar territory, were growing restless, informed Lord Edmund that he would have the devil of a time turning around.

Helping Constance from the carriage, Edmund told her that they must proceed on foot. The stench hit Constance as soon as she left the carriage. Clearly, the neighborhood lacked much in the way of sanitation—visible proof of which soon became apparent. Meanwhile, Edmund stopped a middle-aged woman, attired in a coarse dress and apron, and asked her where Fish Lane, for that was the street mentioned in Will's letter, could be found. Staring in amazement at the elegantly-dressed nobleman, the woman pointed in the direction towards which the carriage had been headed. "Two lanes further down, my lord," and, grinning lecherously, the woman continued, "and if I can be of further assistance to your lordship, do not hesitate to ask. I live just along here."

"Careful of your tongue," said Edmund, in a tone quiet enough to be threatening.

Performing a rough curtsy, the woman hurried down the lane. Edmund took Constance by the arm and walked with her towards Fish Lane where they encountered a man standing at the corner, smoking a pipe. When asked for the home of William Shakespeare, the man took the pipe from his mouth, blew a puff of smoke that engulfed Constance and pointed with the pipe down the lane. "Third building on the right. Second floor," he said as if annoyed at the interruption in his smoking. Edmund glared at the man but left his sword sheathed.

"I best leave you here," he said to Constance. "I'll watch to see you safely reach your brother's home." He touched her hand. "Come see me at Pennyford House. You'll be most welcome. It is on the river. You'll have no trouble finding it. We have a garden facing the river, which I believe you will find most pleasant."

Her mind reeling, Constance walked down Fish Lane. It was so dark that she barely missed stepping in a pile of offal in the middle of the lane. She found the smell practically overpowering and unlike anything she had experienced in Stratford which, notwithstanding her occasional complaints, she now realized was pristine in comparison. The door to the house was unlocked. She entered and climbed a set of dark stairs, the air fetid from the odor of urine. She knocked on the second-floor door, waited, and then knocked again, more loudly.

"Go away, damn you," someone inside shouted.

She knocked again, as hard as she could, and shouted, "Will, it's me."

"Cannot you let a man work in peace?" the same voice cried out, but now she heard footsteps. The door was flung open, and Will bellowed: "Did you not hear me, you shameless strumpet? I have half a..." He stared, astonished, at Constance. "It's you," he cried, laughing. "You've arrived at last." He pulled her into his arms and hugged her tightly. "Thank God for his tender mercy and that I'm back from the theater. We ended rehearsals early today. Otherwise, who knows what you'd have done—except that I generally forget to lock the door."

Constance freed herself and, stepping past Will into the room, looked around in horror and dismay.

# A Man's Home Is His Castle: Spring 1592

Recoiling in disgust at the sight that greeted her in Will's front room (she had as yet no idea if there were other rooms of a similar condition, but she feared the worst), she felt her stomach churn and had to exert every ounce of her considerable willpower not to push past Will, rush or tumble down the stairs, burst into the street and search for the first coach to return her, posthaste, to Stratford into the loving arms of her mother and the acceptance of whatever punishment her father would deem suitable to the circumstances.

It was not so much the stained clothes that lay scattered in heaps around the room—mostly on the floor but also on a trestle table (upon which also rested several plates with the decaying remains of one or more meals) beside an interior wall, and on a sizeable ladder-back chair—that caused her gorge to rise and vomit to threaten to spew forth. It was also not the chaotic stacks of books, papers and writing instruments that cluttered a second table under a window and across the room from the first. Nor was it even the distinct odor of urine that, apparently, crept into the room from an open door between the trestle table and the ladder-back chair. Unaccustomed though Constance was to the sight of such disorder—her father's house, the only home she had so far known, representing the epitome of cleanliness and orderliness (even the rush floor mats were changed thrice weekly)—none of what she had so far taken in would have caused immediate and headlong flight. No, what did it for her was the head of a sheep, the eyes gazing emptily and, she thought, forlornly, from a shelf next to the fireplace amid a jumble of spoons and glasses.

Will flung an arm around her shoulders.

"It's not as tidy as one might like, but you can put it right in no time."

"What about the servants?" gasped Constance.

"A novice actor and scribbler of plays and verse can hardly afford servants."

"Not even one?"

"Why, my beloved sister, do you think I was so anxious for you to come to London? Do you think I like living in this fashion?"

"What about that strumpet you were not so anxious to see?"

"She would consider cleaning, washing and cooking beneath her dignity."

"But it's not beneath mine?"

She removed his hand and took a step towards the door. He grasped her upper arm and, in a not unkindly way, spun her around.

"Patience, my dear Constance," he said, letting go her arm, "is a virtue much to be admired and wished for. It is only a question of time until I bring forth plays that the theater-going world recognizes to be as superior to the works of Thomas Kyd or that reprobate, Christopher Marlowe—or any of the other triflers and braggarts who gull an audience into thinking the dross they put on the stage is worthy of their pennies—as our beloved Queen Elizabeth is to a peasant tilling his field. Then, but only then, my beloved sister, shall you have at your command more servants than you can possibly find tasks for them to perform. Does that enchanting prospect satisfy you, at least for the moment?"

"But Will, I thought you had already achieved such eminence. I recall your saying, last time you were in Stratford, that you were one of London's most prominent actors as well as a theater owner or manager or something like that."

"Did I say all of that? Well, my dear, that is the world of the theater. We are such stuff as dreams are made on and so on and so forth. You shall quickly learn to trust no one in the theater to tell the whole truth or, for that matter, any part thereof."

"Not even my brother, it would seem, whom I believed to the fullest."

"And shall again, trust me. Meanwhile, I greatly admire your courage and daring in making the journey. I assume you were obliged to leave without Father's permission as it would almost certainly not have been granted."

"I snuck out in the middle of the night."

"Brave indeed. I shall write Father and advise him that you are safe in London with important work that will greatly benefit the family. That should mollify him."

"Will he believe you?"

"He may or may not, but he will pretend to do so. Father, as you know all too well, is a difficult man. He and I had, shall we say, intense disagreements. It was one cause for my marrying so young and to the first woman who would have me."

"Do you not love Anne?"

"Our marriage produced heat but little warmth."

"And heat doesn't last?"

"A keen insight—for a..."

"For a woman," Constance interrupted. "Why, thank you." To minimize her sarcasm, she glanced at the sheep's head and again fought the urge to vomit. "So that is why you left her and your children?"

"That and the lure of London and the theater." Will grew silent and thoughtful. "And other reasons."

"Which are?"

"Enough of your questions."

"Just one more."

*"C'est quoi?"*

*"Ça traite de la religion."*

"You know some French?"

"The basics only."

*"Ton question."*

"A squire traveling with us railed against secret Catholics. Are there such in Stratford?"

"I cannot say for sure, but I have my suspicions. It is four short years since the glorious defeat of the evil Spanish Armada, and there may be some who prayed for its success. I care little for formal religion but even less for such traitors. They should be found out and quickly dispatched. Now a question of my own."

"Yes."

"Have you brought any gold crowns? Wisely secluded in your purse?"

Constance looked abashed. She smiled weakly and, taking a small purse from her satchel, shook it to demonstrate the lack of any coins whatsoever.

"Not a one, I'm afraid, dear brother, nor any of the silver kind either."

"Bother," said Will. "We shall, however, endure. I've enough for the next few days. I've half-finished a play about Richard that will bring in a pocketful of gold sovereigns."

"The Lion-Hearted? What a noble subject!"

"Not that imbecile who imagined himself a conqueror but who won battles and not the war as he never reconquered Jerusalem. The fool then gets himself captured on the way back from the Holy Land and has to be ransomed. No, no, Richard the Third, a towering figure of a man with a veritable tragic flaw. I know not whether it be true, but I'm making him a hunchback with a withered arm. Jolly good, wouldn't you say?"

"It will be a marvel of the stage; of that I am sure."

Will patted Constance's cheek. His face took on

an expression of intense excitement. He grasped her hand.

"You have not seen the remainder of our dwelling. Come, I will show you."

Constance pointed at the sheep's head.

"First, do you think you could dispose of that?"

*"Sans doute."*

Will picked up the offending object, pushed open the window by his work table, peered down at the lane below and tossed out the gory item. He slapped his hands together and grinned at Constance. "Gone," he said. "Would have done nicely in a soup but gone and not to be missed." A dank, odoriferous gust slipped through the window. Constance trembled. Will closed the window. "Come along," Will said, and grasped her hand again. Constance shuddered, considering what the hand had previously touched.

They passed through the open door into a narrow, rectangular-shaped room. The only furniture in the room were a bed, with three leather-covered books lying next to the two pillows, a chair and an indented table with a basin. A cloak hung over the back of the chair, and an ewer rested on a shelf under the basin. Trousers, doublets and jerkins hung on pegs in the wall. The acrid odor of urine emanated from a chamber pot which stood on the floor at the foot of the bed. A single window was over the bed.

"Will, you must empty the chamber pot more frequently."

"I know, but I forget as I am so busy with my

work. I am often so involved with working out a scene that I have to run like the devil to rehearsals. I have a role in a miserable play: "The Moor's Wife, A Tragedy". 'Tis a tragedy, all right; and a more odious piece of horse dung I've not yet encountered in the theater."

"Of what does it treat?"

"Some horse's ass of a blackamoor marries a French nobleman's daughter and then kills her because he falls in love with her maid."

"Whom he wishes to marry in her stead?"

"Marry? Not in the least. He simply wants to play the beast with two backs with the more-than-willing maid. Oh, excuse me, Constance."

"Quite all right, Will. I am not naive."

"I see. Well... well." Will rubbed his chin. "In any case, why the dolt feels he needs to murder his poor wife just to consummate his lust is never explained and is, in any case, beyond me."

"Hardly sounds suitable for your acting genius."

"You hit the mark there. As for the dialogue, I could do better while fast asleep. The low-born playwright wouldn't know an iamb if he met one in the street."

"Perhaps you should improve upon it with your own play."

"Someday, I will do just that. In the meantime, I will spare your delicate nostrils." Will picked up the chamber pot, climbed onto the bed, opened the window and threw out the contents of the vessel without a single look. "That resolves it. No more noxious odors." He replaced the chamber pot and picked up a book from the bed. He showed it to Constance but held it some distance away so that she could not touch it. Intricate designs filled every inch of the leather cover except the date and title section. Constance leaned towards the book and read: *Fifth Volume of the Chronicles of England* and could make out nothing further.

"*Holinshed's Chronicles,*" said Will. "An invaluable resource for history plays, which are all the rage in the theaters these days. My three plays on Henry the Sixth have made quite a favorable impression although not as lucrative a one as I would have liked." He made a twirling gesture with his index finger. "I'll show the popinjays who dare ridicule my brilliant endeavors." He twirled his finger again. "But come, let me show you where you'll sleep."

He led her through a second door into a cramped space containing a bed, a chair and a small table. A chamber pot, fortunately empty, was under the table. The chair stood next to a window. She looked out and saw a small garden plot which, she assumed, was in the rear of the building.

"There's no basin," Constance said, nodding at the table. "Where do I wash?"

"Are you cognizant of how extraordinarily beautiful you've become, my dear sister?"

"Where do I wash, Will?"

"You can use my basin when I'm not in the room. I spend a great amount of time at my writing table or at the theater. You didn't answer my question."

"I was aware of no such transformation."

"I truly doubt that unless there are no longer mirrors in Stratford."

Constance laughed softly.

"Well, thank you, brother."

"How old are you now?"

"Eighteen."

"And no marriage proposals?"

"I know of none."

"Strange... very strange, at your age. Father must be holding out for gentry or maybe even a 'Sir.' Would you like to be Lady Somebody or Other?"

"I hadn't thought about it."

"I also doubt that. You are quite the mystery woman." Will sighed. "And it's almost too late. Father better hurry if he wants a knight for a son-in-law." He sighed again. "Oh well, my good fortune. At least, it's someone's." He left her room, passed through his and entered the front room. She followed. He sat at the writing table and motioned for her to sit in one of several other chairs, from which she first had to shove aside dirty clothes. "Your duties," he said without preamble, "will not be onerous. You shall shop for food and prepare the meals, of which I partake no more than two a day. I cannot abide breakfast—no time—have to write all morning—other than some bread and ale; but you may have whatever you fancy. Dinner and supper are the meals for me although we must move smartly through dinner as I often have to rush to the theater."

"Who has cooked your meals up to now?"

"I sometimes dine in the taverns with my fellow actors and playwrights and for the rest, I throw something together although cooking would hardly be the right term. Cheese and a salad make for a quick and adequate supper."

"I thought you didn't care for your fellow playwrights."

"Oh, I like them well enough. I just wish they recognized how far above them I shall climb. Although, I must say, they occasionally turn a reasonable phrase or two."

Will laughed and said, with a twinkle in his eye: "Don't take too seriously what we writers say. We are Herculean in our capacity for exaggeration and the spinning of tales. Truth lies not in the facts of the matter but somewhere deep down in the matter itself—in the essence of the thing. But then, you needn't worry about such literary pettifoggery. You are, after all, a woman."

Constance bristled but decided not to comment. After all, it was her first day on the job.

"We shall dine together, which will be pleasant for us both. As to other duties, you shall wash the clothes and sheets which, as you've noted, are in some need of attention. And finally, you shall keep our lodgings clean—clean as an infant's bottom—perhaps not the most apt analogy but you understand the point. There are those who've said my writing would improve with better metaphors and similes. These, of course, are idiots; and one should keep an ample distance from idiots. Would you not agree, sister?"

"In no uncertain terms, brother."

"Well then, have I made your duties clear?"

"As crystal."

"Once finished with your work, you are free as the breeze—now there's a simile worth noting—provided you comport yourself in the manner appropriate to an up and coming family. You might consider starting an herb and vegetable garden in the back."

"Of course," said Constance, her mind drifting back to an inn in Aylesbury and wondering how far Pennyford House was from Fish Lane. "An infinity," she thought, "in spiritual, if not in temporal distance."

Will extracted some coins from a pocket in his doublet and handed them to her: six shillings and three groats.

"Try to make this last for tonight's supper and to-morrow's dinner. I'll give you whatever I can. With you here to prepare the meals, I will have less recourse to the taverns with no loss to either my purse or my work. We shall enjoy a quiet existence as I write my way into fame and fortune. Now off with you. The thought of a meat stew has my mouth watering."

"We passed the Stocks Market on our way here. There was plentiful meat, but is there one closer that is equally good?"

"We?"

"One of my fellow passengers was kind enough to bring me almost to Fish Lane in his father's carriage."

"So you have already made a friend in London."

"I would hardly go so far as to call him a friend,"

said Constance, convincing herself that this was one of those circumstances that permitted a small lie.

"I see."

"No, you don't," thought Constance, "or maybe you do, which would be far worse."

"In any case, Leadenhall Market, where you can buy meat, is completely satisfactory and not more than a fifteen-minute walk. If you then proceed up Corn Hill, you will find vegetables and fruit. You can also find shops there to buy soap, which you'll need to wash the clothes as well as our faces and hands. Buy the pure Castile soap, which is white. Avoid like the plague the black and grey soaps that will ruin our faces and hands along with the clothes. To get there, ask anyone on the street for directions." Will went to the trestle table and pulled from underneath it a basket and a bucket, handing both to Constance. "There is a water conduit on Grace Church Street. Fill the bucket on your way home."

Constance had one foot out the door but turned back.

"Will," she said, pertly, "do you truly think, because I have to do the housework, that I'm lower than a strumpet?"

"Don't be daft. It was merely a figure of speech. Shall I explain what that means?"

"I know what it means."

Leadenhall Market was comparatively easy to find. She only had to ask directions twice, and only once did she have to retrace her steps. The larger streets were paved with cobblestones; but the smaller ones consisted of either beaten earth or plain mud no better than the country roads she had experienced on her way to London. As she entered the market, she had to stop as a herdsman drove a herd of sheep across the square. She watched the tranquil animals ambling along and wondered if they had any idea what awaited them. Probably not or they might not have gone so peacefully to their fate. She thought about the sheep's head in Will's lodgings and why it had so sickened her. After all, many used them as food. Possibly it was the Squire's remark about Catholic heads garnishing poles, a sight she hoped never to see even if the idea was to deter others from committing the most ghastly of crimes. When the sheep had passed, she edged her way through the crowded market and began looking in the stalls that sold meat. Mutton would be nice, she thought, so she examined the offerings at a few stalls. She saw a joint that looked fresh and asked the butcher for a price.

"Three shillings the pound, my pretty one."

"Three shillings!"

"And a bargain, if I say so myself."

At that price, it might be nigh on impossible to squeeze two meals out of the coins Will had given her. She stared at the mutton while she tried to calculate in her head what she would need for other provisions, a virtually hopeless task as she had no idea what other high prices lay ahead of her. London clearly was not Stratford.

"You can get it a good bit cheaper," a voice whispered in her ear.

Startled, Constance turned around and found herself face-to-face with a smartly dressed woman, whom she judged to be about thirty. The woman had a broad and pleasant, if not beautiful, face; her forehead was high and her nose aquiline. Her cheeks were smooth, unblemished and with only a hint of rouge. She wore a simple chain of pearls around her neck; her only other jewels were a border of emeralds and sapphires affixed to the narrow brim of her round-topped hat, which also had a gay feather ruffled by the breeze. Knowing an aristocrat when she saw one, Constance dropped a short curtsy and said: "Thank you, your ladyship."

The woman smiled and gave a brief nod. "That is quite all right. You are obviously new to London. You will adapt." She turned to the servant who was accompanying her. "Come along, Iris. We have much shopping to do." The two moved off, the servant carrying two large baskets already weighed down with crusty loaves of bread and piles of vegetables and fruit.

The butcher put on an expression of agreeableness and remarked with somewhat forced courtesy: "Since the Duchess has deigned to take an interest in a country lass, I'll do you a grand favor and offer the cut at two shillings six the pound. Try what you will, you won't find this quality mutton at even close to the price elsewhere in the market."

"One shilling ten," said Constance, "I'll take a

pound and wrap it securely, please. I have other purchases to make."

"The devil take you but seeing as you're so comely..."

"Thank you," said Constance and, looking around, noticed that the woman was in front of another stall but gazing in her direction.

"Duchess?"

"Yes, my pretty: Susanna Marsham, Duchess of Bastrow, who," said the florid-faced butcher, glancing quickly in the Duchess's direction, "must think you deserving, or hopeless. You did give her a right proper curtsy for a simple country girl." He cut the meat, weighed the thick piece and wrapped it in a heavy, greasy paper. He handed it to her, and his lips parted in a slight, but engaging, smile.

Constance put the package in her basket and smiled at the butcher in return.

"Shall I give you all my trade then?"

"You are a saucy one. As Lady Marsham said, you'll adapt."

Constance continued into Corn Hill where she bought garlic, carrots, cabbage and turnips for the stew that she thought would be the safest dish for an inexperienced cook. She found a small flagon of olive oil, a loaf of heavy bread, cheese, apples and pears. To flavor the stew, she picked up salt, pepper, dried rosemary and ground cloves. She also purchased a packet of coarse flour. She had two shillings and a groat left. She walked back up Corn Hill, looking around at the stalls and shops. Suddenly, she heard a cry of: "Watch yourself, you silly girl" and looked up to see a gentleman astride a cantering horse headed straight at her and not more than thirty yards away. Next to him rode a woman sitting side-saddle. Constance jumped back, the loaf of bread flying from her basket. The man pulled up. His horse's flared nostrils were inches from Constance's chest, her bodice frothy from the animal's harsh and spumy breathing. Drops of sweat cascaded down the horse's sides. Constance shook with fear. A hoarse cry sprang unbidden from her open mouth. The woman didn't slow her horse and gave Constance a disdainful look as she rode past, twisting in the saddle and calling out: "Hurry up, Roberte."

Constance struggled to calm her fluttering heart. Roberte leaned over, tweaked Constance's chin and said: "Pay attention, young miss, if you want to survive in London." He laughed, pulled his horse aside and rode on, trampling the loaf in the mud and hollering: "Coming, darling." Constance glanced despairingly at the flattened, mud-encrusted loaf; and, anger now welling up, she returned back up Corn Hill to replace the devastated loaf with a smaller, far less crusty one. She found the Castile soap at a shop near Leadenhall; and now with four pence left instead of the shilling she had planned on saving for herself and getting angrier with each step, she marched towards Will's lodgings, stopping first at Grace Church Street for water. She had to wait in a line of five women. The young woman in front of her looked in Constance's basket and said: "Nice provisions, you have there."

"I had a sight better until some high and mighty gentleman and his haughty lady on their fine horses almost knocked me off my feet. I lost a beautiful loaf of bread and had to buy a much worse one."

"These nobles care little for us common folk. Get out of the way whenever you see one is what I say."

"I know a rather nice one," said Constance, her anger cooling a bit, "and a Duchess helped me in the market today so maybe they're not all so terrible."

"A Duchess? Aren't you the fine one, all friendly with a well-born lady."

"It's nothing of the sort. She just taught me to haggle with a butcher. I won't ever see her again; of that you can be sure."

"I've never spoken to a Duchess in my life so you have me there." The young woman grinned. "I'm Madge."

"I'm Constance."

"Pleased I'm sure."

"Do you live near here, Madge?"

"Just over by the Pewterers' Hall."

"I've no idea where that is."

"Why everyone knows Pewterers' Hall. Are you certain you're not daft?" Madge laughed uproariously and pinched Constance's arm. "I'm just having fun with you; but in truth, you don't know?"

"I'm new to London."

"When did you arrive?"

"This afternoon."

"That solves the mystery. Where are you living?"

"At my brother's lodgings. On Fish Lane."

"Now that's something of a nasty area. Does your brother have a trade? A tanner, perhaps, or a carpenter or joiner?"

"He's an actor and playwright: Will, I mean William, Shakespeare." Constance, knowing now the truth of the matter, continued with care. "Might you have heard of him?"

"Can't say that I have but then I've only been to the theater once. My husband took me to a tragedy. Very bloody affair. The stage was full of bodies at the end. What did you say your brother's name was?"

"Shakespeare... William Shakespeare."

"Shouldn't be hard to remember his name as it's an odd one." Madge's turn had come. She held her bucket under the flowing pipe. When it was almost full, she started to walk away but stopped. "Since you're new," Madge said, "would you like me to show you around?"

"That would be very kind of you."

"My father and husband are watermen and are gone all day and into the evening. Once my work is finished, I am my own person. Shall we meet here tomorrow at two o'clock?"

Concerned about the amount of work she faced the next day, Constance said: "The day after would be better. I imagine tomorrow will be filled up with chores."

"That's understandable as you've just arrived."

"What is a waterman?" asked Constance.

"They each own a wherry—a small boat—and row passengers across the river or up and down. Hard labor it is."

"Would you be able to show me where Pennyford House is?"

"What business would you have at Pennyford House?"

"None at all."

"And being new to London, how would you even know about Pennyford House?"

"A friend from Stratford came to London to visit family and told me it was quite beautiful and should be seen to be believed."

"I see," said Madge, with a look of suspicion. "It is an imposing house and belongs to one of England's most powerful earls. I will show it to you, but the Earl of Pennyford is a man to avoid."

Fearing that she would spill water on her dress, Constance pulled the bucket away from the pipe when it was three-quarters full. She made it back to Fish Lane without losing a drop. Looking in the basket, Will asked, in a harsh tone, where the ale was. Shamefaced, she replied that she hadn't thought of it.

"I can see that you spent most of your time in Stratford learning about figures of speech. Mother has neglected her responsibilities."

"I will go back out if you tell me where I can find it."

"I will go. I've finished a scene, and you need to start cooking."

She took the clothes off the trestle table and added them to one of the heaps on the floor. She would deal with the clothes tomorrow. She found a basin in a cupboard next to the fireplace and washed the dishes and utensils that were on the table. Then she hung an iron pot over the fire, poured in oil and, giving it time to heat up, added the herbs, garlic, salt and pepper. She chopped the meat, set it in the pot and then proceeded to rinse a couple of carrots, the cabbage and a turnip. She diced the vegetables, stirred the sizzling meat and breathed in its delicious aroma and, when it had nicely browned, added the vegetables. She pulled a chair up to the fire and poured in water and flour, stirring constantly until the stew was thick. She tasted the juice and found it nicely hot. She cranked the lever and pulled the pot far enough above the fire to prevent the stew from burning but, at the same time, keeping it hot. She rested her head against the back of the chair and, exhausted from such a strenuous day, soon drifted off to sleep.

"Doesn't that smell good," said Will as he came into the room and then laughed heartily as, startled, Constance practically leapt from the chair. "You've had a long day of it," he continued in a now kindly tone. "We'll eat and then you can go to bed."

# "She Is No Strumpet": Spring 1592

It took her the whole of the next day and the better part of the following morning to clean the lodgings and wash the clothes. Despite the hard work in the malodorous lodgings and her fleeting thoughts the day before of retreating to Stratford, she felt no temptation to quit. She knew that, once she had thoroughly cleaned and aired out the rooms, keeping them clean would not be such a difficult task. She also knew that, were she to return to Stratford, she would never have another chance to leave. Her father would see to that. She would probably, post-haste, be married off to a fat merchant. Despite the stench, the offal and carcasses in the streets, the mad horsemen—and horsewomen—, the jostling crowds and the sky-high prices, London was where she wanted to be. In just one day, she felt the excitement of the city coursing through her body.

"Compared to London," she thought, "Stratford is stale beer."

She would make mistakes, like forgetting the ale;

but she would learn, and she would make Will's lodgings comfortable—whether he could ever afford a servant or not. With her free time, she would see London and find something suitable to her ambitions.

"What will it be? Who can tell?"

Will had neither a broom nor a mop so when, on the morning after her arrival, he gave her money for food, she insisted that he add a few shillings so that she could buy basic cleaning equipment.

"I cannot clean this rotten sinkhole without those items as well as a tub for washing your smelly clothes and a basket for carrying them to the yard to dry. No, don't look at the grocery basket. I need a bigger one."

Reluctantly, he gave her a half pound and told her it had better be enough for the equipment as well as a few days' food or they would soon run out of money.

"They don't mint coins at the theater," he said petulantly.

After shopping, she began by sweeping out all three rooms. So much dirt had accumulated that she was forced to sweep it into the tub she had bought for washing clothes and then carry the tub down the stairs and into the garden where she dumped the contents into an unused corner. She then mopped the floors, laid down rush mats and sprinkled them with sweet-smelling rose petals, cowslips and chamomile. She wiped down the small, but glazed, windows after which she cleaned the furniture and turned her attention to the grimiest parts of the walls, which required several trips to the conduit for water. She stopped after three hours and shook her arms, which were aching so badly she thought they might fall off. All this time, Will had sat at his table scribbling away.

"Brother Will," she said, sweetly. "I could wish for some help with these walls, especially the places I have trouble reaching."

Will brusquely turned his chair around and stared at her as if he had seen a ghost or a witch or worse. "Certainly, you jest," he said and turned back to his papers.

"Not at all. This is hard work, and I am becoming sore and tired."

Will swung around again.

"Constance, do not trifle with me."

"I am far from trifling."

"I can only hazard a guess at what Father would say if he heard you, but allow me to supplement your obviously incomplete education."

"Please do."

"First lesson: curb your mockery and your tongue."

"It would seem I am lower than a strumpet, at least the fancy ones you must be accustomed to."

"I shall ignore that choice bit of impertinence. Second lesson: I am a man and men, at least in the England of tradition and manners, do not, I repeat, do not clean homes nor do washing nor prepare meals—and they should not, thinking of my own feeble attempts at that endeavor—nor...nor...perform any number of other domestic activities whatever they might be.

Third lesson: I am working diligently at winning my fame and fortune. While fame alone will not put on our table a tasty stew like the incomparable one you made last evening for supper for which, by the way, did I not highly compliment you?"

Constance nodded and said: "Yes."

"So then, as I was saying, before I interrupted myself..."

Constance smiled but did not laugh at which Will looked disappointed.

"...while fame alone will not purchase our necessities, although it will be a valued first step, the fortune that is sure to follow will not only allow me to continue my work in some comfort but will also alleviate the harshest aspects of your burden. Both of our labors are, and will always be, important; and please remember that, when you are finished with yours, you may take your rest and entertain yourself as you will while mine are never done."

With that, Will picked up his pen again and bent, deep in concentration, over the script of *Richard III*. Constance glared at him, picked up the broom and made as if to hit Will over the head but thought better of it and put the broom in a corner. She finished the wall in two more hours and then prepared dinner. She roasted a haunch of pork over the fire and made a salad of leafy greens, cucumbers, onions, leeks, parsley and rosemary, tossed with a dressing of olive oil, vinegar, salt and pepper.

"Another excellent meal," said Will, smacking his

lips. "You will make a very satisfactory housekeeper. I am sorry for the earlier harsh words, but there is much you need to learn about the world—things Mother should've taught you. Once I have become preeminent in the London theater, I shall endeavor to find you a suitable husband. The experience you are acquiring in taking care of what I admit are my less than lavish surroundings will serve you well as mistress of a home full of servants."

Constance wondered if she could stay seated while she profusely thanked Will or if she needed to genuflect to his august presence. She voted for staying seated.

"Thank you, Will. That will be most kind of you."

"Not at all."

Right after dinner, Will left for the theater.

Since it was a relatively warm afternoon, she decided to wash at least some of the clothes, giving them time to dry in the garden. Again, she needed to make several trips to the conduit. During none of them did she see Madge. Arriving home from the theater, Will expressed great satisfaction as he held a clean, sweet-smelling shirt to his nose. Rising at dawn the next morning, she finished the clothes and cleaned the walls in the back rooms. By then, it was time to turn her attention to dinner for which she fried sole, halibut and eels in a pan and roasted vegetables in a pot on the small brazier. As they were eating, Constance worried about meeting Madge on time and asked Will for the hour. He opened the cumbersome object dangling from his neck and said:

"Getting towards two although this mechanism is rarely accurate. Why do you wish to know?"

Taking up and rinsing the now-empty plates, Constance explained that she had made a friend at the water conduit who had offered to show her around London.

"A young woman of substance, may I presume?"

"Yes, indeed. She manages a large household for her husband and father, who lives with them. I believe they are well-to-do tradesmen."

Constance smiled inwardly, well-pleased with another fabrication that circumstances required.

"Off with you then. You've worked hard these past two days and deserve a little promenading. Be sure to return in time to fix supper. I will be home from The Rose, where the play that fiend Henslowe is putting on is not worth a fig, and raging with hunger much like a bear in the bear-baiting arena near to The Rose."

She hurried as fast as she deemed lady-like, afraid that Madge would have thought she wasn't coming and left swearing at the rudeness of country girls. But Madge was waiting by the conduit and smiled at her. Constance apologized for being late.

"I'll wager that brother of yours kept you working. I'm my own master during the day as my men-folk take their midday meal at a tavern where they serve cheap food and cheaper ale. It's a miracle they don't turn over their boats and give themselves and their passengers a good soaking and a hard swimming. The currents in the Thames can be fearful."

Madge took Constance by the arm, and they started towards the river. They passed through Grace Church Market with its imposing columns that indicated stalls from various counties. Two horses pulled a cart filled with barrels across the square while two oxen pulled another cart loaded with baskets of fruit and vegetables.

"From the suburbs," explained Madge, "just outside the city gates. Still good farmland out there although more houses are going up every year. I wonder, before long, where our provisions will come from as they build on all the land. I grew up in a squalid village down in Kent. My father was a farmer; but after my mother died, he brought us children—the three remaining ones—up to London, looking to make his fortune. Being a waterman is better than farming a few strips of land but not much, I'll warrant you." Madge pointed to her left. "Our house, which makes it sound grander than it is, is a few lanes in that direction."

They continued down Grace Church and soon crossed Lombard Street passing The Bell Inn on the right.

"Perhaps we'll stop here," said Madge, "for a tankard of ale when we've finished our promenade."

"I have three groats with me."

"That'll do nicely."

They turned left on Little East Cheap; and Madge pointed out Butchers Hall, a large building in the Tudor style. Not much further on, they approached the immense stone walls of The Tower. They stopped near the outer wall, and Constance stared up in amazement at the imposing structure with its towers at each of four corners.

"That," said Madge, with not a little pride, "is the most famous sight in all of England, if not the world: The Tower of London. Traitors have lost their heads in The Tower, and monarchs have resided there. The Crown Jewels are kept there as well as wild animals and all sorts of armor. We won't be able to see any of that."

"They must be afraid we'd steal the lot and make ourselves rich," said Constance, giving Madge a nudge.

"We'd lose our heads if we tried," said Madge with a laugh.

"Not if we succeeded and ran off to France."

"Stop your foolishness."

"I was only jesting, but I'll stop. Who knows if there might not be spies in the neighborhood."

"You are such a piece of work," said Madge, taking Constance again by the arm, "as would make a dead man laugh."

They passed through a gate and strolled around the forecourt until Constance stopped abruptly, recoiling at the sight of a scaffold upon which stood several gallows. Her mind fled back to Tyburn and the bodies swinging from their nooses. Her stomach churned, and she made an involuntary gagging sound.

"Whatever's the matter?" asked Madge.

Constance pointed at the scaffold.

"Oh that," said Madge. "Nothing to be alarmed at. No one you know will ever swing from one of those."

Madge laughed and gently pulled Constance, still speechless, along the fortress wall and through another gate. Now in the main enclosure, they wandered past the fortress and into a garden where Madge guided Constance to a bench.

"Feeling any better?"

"Yes, thank you."

"Why did a simple gallows upset you so?"

"I read a book once about a man who gets hung for committing a wicked deed, and I have occasional dreams about it."

"Lucky then that I can barely read."

"Also, on my way into London, I saw bodies dangling from nooses at Tyburn." Constance was briefly silent. "It sickened me. Both things together, I suppose. I had a friend in Stratford who snuck off against her father's wishes to see an execution. She was adventurous in more ways than one."

"I go to Tyburn from time to time. It's quite the sight. I was planning on inviting you but now I won't." Madge stood up. "Let's walk along the river."

"Splendid. I've not seen it."

They walked along Thames Street, catching glimpses of the river. They approached London Bridge, and Madge told her it might be better not to look at the far side. Constance glanced anyway in that direction and saw the numerous heads stuck on poles affixed to the top of a building.

"Oh," cried out Constance.

"I warned you."

"You did."

"Are you to be sick?"

"No," said Constance in a weak voice. "They are sufficiently far away. At least, I cannot look into their eyes."

"Nor can they look into yours."

At that, both young women laughed and continued along Thames Street until Madge led them down a side street that ended at the river. There she hailed an oarsman in a wherry to take them across the river to Southwark. "Two pence," said the oarsman; and Madge agreed. As they crossed, Constance marveled at the river's width and all the boats plying up and down and across in each direction. Madge pointed out the fourteen-sided Rose, and Constance said that's where Will was performing.

"The theaters abound with strumpets, mingling in order to seek custom among the throngs of young—and not-so-young—men. You should never go alone."

"I am sure that Will would not allow it."

Madge also showed Constance the bear-baiting and bull-baiting arenas and said that, given her own willingness to attend executions, it was strange how little she liked the baiting of animals.

"It's mostly the dogs that get killed. The bears squeeze them or batter them to death. The sport is excessively cruel." She pointed to the bridge. " I don't suppose you'd like to walk across?"

"I am not ready for that."

Madge sighed and led the way to the river where

she signalled for a boat smaller than a wherry—known as a sculler and rowed by one man—who took them across for a ha'penny each. Madge instructed him to row upstream a ways before crossing. As they approached the north bank, Madge drew Constance's attention to a very large, brick mansion with multiple chimneys and a garden bordering the river.

"There be your Pennyford House. Mark where it is in relation to the bridge in case you've a mind someday to take a closer look."

"Why should I?" asked Constance, carefully noting how far it was from the bridge. "I can see it perfectly well from here. Thank you for showing it to me."

Madge had the waterman row along the shore towards the bridge so that the heads would be as far away as possible. As the tide was coming in, the current grew swift and turbulent. Shouting: "The arches ho," the waterman aimed his boat towards one of the bridge's middle arches and shot through at tremendous speed. Constance screamed with delight; Madge simply laughed. Pleased with his skill, the waterman smiled and directed the boat to a landing just below the bridge. Agreeing that they much deserved a glass of good ale, the two women linked arms and walked up Fish Street (not to be confused with Fish Lane where Will lived) to the crossing with Candlewick Street, where Fish Street became Grace Church Street. Just beyond stood the proud Bell Inn. They found seats at a table in the wood-paneled hall and, savoring their ale, talked amiably about the day.

"Excuse my curiosity," said Constance after a few minutes, "but have you any children, Madge?"

Madge looked away. Constance waited patiently. Madge turned back, brushing the tears from her eyes.

"Three, but they all went to God at a tender age." Constance put a hand on Madge's. "I am so terribly sorry." Madge allowed herself a thin smile. "Peter and I keep our hopes up. The vicar in our parish tells us that we must pray hard and that, if we do, someday God will hear us and bless us with a healthy child. Unlike my sister, who was always on her knees begging for sons and who was rewarded with five of them and four still alive, I care not whether it's a son or a daughter so long as the child lives past the two years that the oldest of our three reached and grows to be a fine man or woman and provides Peter and me with grandchildren. I would like more but will settle for one if that be God's wish, but I don't want to go to my grave without having raised at least one child to adulthood."

"I will pray every day that God grant your wish."

The two women finished their ales in silence. They left the inn and, before parting company, Madge said: "Perhaps the sister of an important theatrical gentleman will come visit my home one day."

"Will is not so important, at least not yet, and I'd be happy to visit. I think we shall be excellent friends."

Over supper, Will asked her what she had seen and how she now liked London. Constance described her promenade, leaving out only the scaffold and gallows, and mentioned that she and Madge had passed

The Rose.

"When," she asked, "will I be able to see you act, especially in one of your own plays?"

"Perhaps when I finish *Richard the Third*, which will be my best so far, and perhaps ever. I have a few more ideas but not that many. One thing is certain: do not go alone to The Rose. I shall take you when I deem it appropriate and not before. You can invite your new friend whose name is?

"Madge"

"Madge what?"

Constance looked shocked and embarrassed.

"I don't know."

"You had best find out."

A week later, Will left right after dinner without even taking the time, as he often did, to smoke his pipe. Constance hurriedly washed the dishes and then put on the best of the two new outfits that Will had bought for her. She walked impatiently down Grace Church and, just past the Bell Inn, turned right on Candlewick, which she followed to Dowgate. Turning left, she passed the Tallow Chandlers Hall and the Skinners Hall—both imposing buildings. She had seen Madge twice in the last week: once at the conduit and once when they had walked, meeting at an agreed time, to Moorgate and, passing through the city wall, had strolled past the adjacent fields and along the pleasant lanes. They saw women laying out wash to dry and men practicing with longbows and muskets. Today, however, Constance hoped not to meet Madge by accident as she had another objective in mind. Turning onto Thames Street, she continued parallel to the river until she reached the brick mansion that she had seen from the boat a week ago.

She walked up a path to a huge wooden door and rang a bell suspended on a rope. She waited a minute and then rang again. The door slowly opened, and a liveried servant stood in the doorway, looking her over with undisguised contempt.

"Is Lord Edmund at home?" she asked, her voice wavering despite the many times she had practiced the line.

"Lord Edmund does not receive...."

"Who is there, Seyton?" sounded a familiar voice that made Constance shiver.

"No one, your lordship."

"Move aside, please," said the voice and, seconds later, Edmund was in the doorway. "Oh, my word... Constance." He smiled broadly. "Do come in." He turned towards Seyton who was standing in the shadows behind the door. "That will be all, Seyton. You may go." Seyton glided out of sight.

"What a surprise! I should say: 'What a delightful surprise!'" Edmund turned her slowly around in a full circle. "My dear, you look as ravishing as ever and, apparently, flourishing in those less than wholesome surroundings. How are you faring?"

"Well, my lord...."

"We are not in public."

"Of course." She rendered him a smile that sent a quiver up and down his spine. "I'm doing passably well, Edmund, considering my brother's lodgings." She paused. "I've made a friend: an excellent young woman who, sadly, lost all three of her children; not one reached even two years."

"All too common, I fear. It might help if we cleaned up the city. Dumping offal in the street and... well, waste... in the river is doubtless not the wisest course of action. But enough complaints. I didn't know if I would see you again."

"Nor I you but I had hopes."

"Isn't hope grand?"

She laughed and nodded in agreement. He took her hand.

"But come: I must show you the garden of which I'm certain I bragged enormously. It really is quite modest."

"You did not brag in the least."

She was amazed at the hall, having never seen anything like it. Her father's hall was puny in comparison. Three stories in height, the top two stories were veiled by wooden screens, occasionally punctuated by stained glass windows showing Biblical images as well as scenes from contemporary country and city life. Elaborately carved wooden columns topped by figures of men and women in various poses—some lewd, others devout, many satirical—circled the room. Such a plethora of decorations made Constance giddy. She would've liked to study each column, but Edmund led her towards the far end of the hall.

"This is quite astounding," she managed to say.

"Father's pride and joy, but I find it overly elaborate. My tastes in art..." He paused. "...and other matters tend to be simpler."

"Well, I've never seen anything like it so, please, let me look at one or two columns."

"Of course. I was being inconsiderate. Look at as many as you like."

Constance admired three columns and then walked on. Edmund again took her hand. They left the hall and entered the dining room, equally large but with far less decoration. In the center stood a table that, Constance guessed, could seat upwards of twenty. They passed through a doorway in the far-left corner and walked down a hallway lit, even in daytime, by candles in wall sconces. They passed a door and Edmund explained that it opened into a room where all the dining utensils and linens were kept. Edmund opened the next door and motioned for Constance to look in. She saw a huge kitchen with a large stove, several long tables and two fireplaces, only one of which now had a fire in it. Two women were at work. One was preparing pies while the other was trimming meat. Edmund greeted the women who gave a quick bow of their heads, said: "Good day, your lordship" and returned to their work. Edmund closed the door.

"They pay scant attention to us. They are such excellent cooks that they can afford to virtually ignore us. They are irreplaceable. We have another kitchen below ground, but it is only used for important occasions when we have many guests. Father and Mother are in the country today and are not expected home until tomorrow or the day after so supper will just be me unless my sister decides to dine at home instead of with friends. You'd be welcome to stay."

"And who would fix Will's supper?"

"Ah, yes, Will."

A door at the end of the hallway opened onto the garden, a large area bordering the river and laid out in squares and rectangles separated one from the other by thick waist-high hedges. Edmund showed her where they grew herbs, flowers and vegetables. He took her to a stone bench overlooking the river. When they sat down, they were out of sight of the house.

"My friend, Madge, took me around part of London a week ago; and I saw this garden from the boat. I had asked her to point out Pennyford."

"This friend: is she a merchant's wife or daughter? How did you meet?"

"They are in trade and quite wealthy." She squeezed his hand. "No, Edmund, I won't fool you as I did Will. Her father and brother are watermen; and while I have not yet seen her dwelling, I imagine it is as humble as our lodgings or more so. We met filling our buckets at the conduit on Grace Church."

"Filling your bucket? What a different life from mine. Yet, perhaps, I adore you all the more because of it."

"If I may ask, Edmund, because I've thought a good deal about you, are you by chance married?"

"You were honest with me so I shall be with you. Yes, I am married—a political marriage as are most at my rank. My wife and two sons spend most of their time at our country home. I visit from time to time. My wife and I do not get along—in many ways."

He leaned towards her; and they kissed, at first tentatively and then with the passion she remembered from the inn, which seemed an eon ago. He put a hand on her bodice and then ran it along her thigh, albeit on the outside of her skirt. She caressed the back of his neck and then put a hand in his crotch, which gave him a frisson that flowed through his entire body. He stood up and guided her to her feet.

"The large bed in my room," he said, caressing her cheek, "has a feather mattress which will be ever so much more comfortable than either this bench or the ground."

"is it safe?"

"There is no one in the house but servants, and I tip them generously—more so than Father."

She was barely aware of her surroundings as Edmund led her back through the house via a different door from the garden and down a back passage and up a circular flight of wooden steps. They entered a long hallway. Edmund led her past an immense curved stairway that arched up from the ground floor. They continued along the hall until they turned into a smaller hall and stopped at the first door. Opening it, he showed her into a large, well-furnished room with a bed that was larger even than she had imagined. She hardly had time, however, to look around before Edmund was undressing her and taking off his own clothes. He lay her gently on the bed; and she sank into the feather mattress, which was every bit as comfortable as Edmund had indicated and so different from the thin pad on her bed at Will's. She would have liked to luxuriate, if only for a minute, but had not the chance as Edmund was on top of her, kissing her mouth, her breasts, her navel and, to her great surprise, her sex. He stayed there long enough for the feeling to rise and her moans begin. Then he slid back up her body, somewhat to her disappointment and blew gently in her ear.

"Ready?"

"Oh, yes."

It did not take long for their mingled cries to fill the room. They fell into a deep sleep in each other's arms.

The roar, "Edmund," accompanied by the sound of heavy boots stomping along the hall, caused them both to bolt upright. Terror in her eyes, Constance looked questioningly at Edmund who, grimacing, said only: "Father." The roar was heard again; it echoed throughout the hall. "Damn it. Home early," said Edmund as he leapt from the bed and began hurriedly dressing. Now there was pounding on the door.

"Edmund, you contemptible whoreson, get out here immediately."

Dressed in an unseemly fashion, Edmund gave

Constance, who was frozen in place, the briefest of kisses and hurried out the door. Recovering her senses, Constance got out of the bed and, as fast as she could, threw on her clothes, leaving many of the buttons undone as she silently cursed women's complicated outfits. Desperate, however, as she was and even through the closed door, she could clearly make out what Edmund and his father were saying.

"How dare you, sir?" the Earl spoke in a fury and only slightly lower in volume than his roars.

"Father, please, lower your voice."

"Do not, sirrah, tell me what to do."

"Father, this must remain between us."

"I shall determine with whom it remains," the Earl growled. "I demand an explanation."

"I was entertaining a lady and wished to show her..."

"A lady?" interrupted the Earl, angrily. "A whore, you mean." Stunned, Constance stopped dressing for an instant, a horrified expression darkening her face. She heard the sound of a slap and gathered the remainder of her clothes into a bundle.

"Father," Edmund exclaimed, bewildered.

"How dare you bring a strumpet into my home?"

"She is no strumpet."

Constance pulled back the door and saw Edmund facing a large, florid-cheeked man with a cropped beard that ran along the line of his chin and jaw. She burst through the partly open door, brushed past the Earl and, shouting over her shoulder: "I am no strumpet", ran down the hall. Turning into the main hall, she quickly came upon the broad staircase and, clutching her bundle, charged down the stairs. Smiling evilly, Seyton waited by the door, which he opened with a contemptuous bow.

"Farewell, Constance," he said with pleasure. "I don't expect we'll be seeing you here again. Unless, of course, the Earl invites you to a family supper."

Constance fled through the open door, which Seyton hurriedly closed behind her. As fast as possible, she put on the rest of her outfit before venturing onto Thames Street. Trying to attract as little attention as possible, she practically ran towards home, sobbing all the way. Where Grace Church crosses Lombard, she almost ran into Madge, into whose arms she fell, crying like a hurt child.

Seyton was right in one respect: she would not see the interior of Pennyford House again, but Edmund was a horse of an entirely different color.

"You need ale," said Madge and led her to the Bell, not twenty paces away. After taking a few substantial swallows, Constance related the whole story, leaving out only what Edmund did to her and she to him to cause them to make so much noise. Madge smiled and touched her hand.

"Did you climax?"

"Is that when your body is quivering so hard you feel the earth is going to break in two?"

"You certainly climaxed or came, which is another word for it."

"I couldn't help moaning. I was embarrassed."

"As I said, you came." Madge's expression became hard as stone, and she looked at Constance with cold, penetrating eyes. "And I warned you, did I not, to stay away from the Pennyford clan."

# A Horse, a Duchess and a Sonnet: 1592-1593

As spring turned into summer, the weather grew warm and the lodging stifling. If Constance kept a window open for long, the rooms would begin to smell of urine and worse—just like the stairs. She was now more used to London's varied, powerful and—more often than not—wretched aromas; but she still didn't like them in the lodging. So beads of sweat rolled down her back, sides and between her breasts as she cleaned or cooked. When Will was not there, she wore only one layer of clothes in order to stay cooler. One day in July, the heat was unbearable so that, after Will had gone to the theater and she had finished throwing out the dinner remains and washing the dishes, she lay down hoping to sleep. But the spirit of sleep must not have liked the heat either because he, or she, wouldn't visit however much Constance twisted and turned. She thought of going to Madge's house but could not summon up the energy to walk even that relatively short distance. Finally, she gave up counting sheep, slipped out of bed, wiped her face with a damp cloth and wandered around the three rooms, totally bored. She stopped at Will's writing table and noticed a manuscript with *Richard III* written on the cover. Ignoring a tremor of anxiety, she sat down at Will's table. She ran her hand over the manuscript, opened it and started reading, which was challenging as Will's handwriting was careless at best and, at worst, almost incomprehensible.

She read on, however, as the story was compelling even if the versification and dialogue were, to her way of thinking, awkward in a number of places and, for some reason she did not fully comprehend, left in those places a good deal to be desired. She had no experience in writing—other than the odd letter—and certainly none with plays so maybe she was wrong. But the more she read, the more she felt the work could be improved upon. In any case, reading was better than doing anything else in the awful heat. Nearing the end of the play, in Act V, Scene IV, she came upon a line that seemed particularly egregious. In fact, the same clumsy line was repeated further on. Brow knitted, she stared thoughtfully at the line and read it over several times.

"What," the line read, "would I not give at this moment for a damn horse."

Something was clearly not right, but she could not figure out what. Then she did something that, years later, still astonished her. She picked up a pen lying on the table, dipped it in ink and wrote on a spare bit of paper lying on the table:

"The lack of a horse thereof will cost me dear right now."

No. She crossed it out.

"Dear God in heaven, furnish me a horse for my need is great."

No. She somewhat liked the first part but not the second.

"Dear God in heaven, without a horse, consider me doomed."

No, yet again. She sighed in exasperation. She had no idea it could be this hard. Try again, she told herself.

"Pray, God, a horse or I am the most forlorn of men."

No... no... no. One last time and, if no luck, she would go to Madge's.

"A horse...."

Yes. She had to start with a horse and not God.

"A horse, a horse...."

Closer.

"A horse, a horse!" She paused and studied the paper. "My kingdom..." Even closer. "...for a horse." She laughed out loud, crossed out Will's line and wrote in the manuscript: "A horse, a horse! My kingdom for a horse!"

"Since I have that one right," she said, half out loud, "let's see what else I can do."

She started at the beginning and made several changes, each one taking time and numerous attempts but becoming easier, faster and smoother as she moved through the manuscript. It became much easier after she intuited Will's rhythmic structure. As she worked, she lost track of time; but she reached—after four hours—her line about the horse and felt a surge of satisfaction at her work. Studying that last line with great pleasure, she neither heard the footsteps on the stairs nor the door opening.

"What in hell are you doing?"

Constance dropped the pen, leaving a blotch on the paper, and turned to see her brother, red with anger, standing in the doorway.

"Just.... just...."

"I see 'just.... just'...." He strode, his expression fierce, to the table and looked at what she had done. "Why you impudent... uh... wench." He read the line again and slammed the manuscript on the table. "This is our master script. God only knows what you might have done had I not forgotten this..." He stabbed the manuscript with his forefinger. "...and had to come home. We are rehearsing several plays, and this was the final one on the schedule. I didn't realize I had forgotten it until we were ready to start the rehearsal. I should beat you soundly." Stepping towards her, he raised his hand. Constance screamed and, rising from her chair, backed away. "Don't be a ninny. I won't hit you; but do this again, and I'll see you to a nunnery. Now get back to work or go visit Madge." As she hurried to her room, Will picked up the manuscript, studied the line briefly, tucked the manuscript under his arm and left. Constance followed shortly thereafter.

She went to Madge's house and said she needed ale—strong ale. Despite the heat, therefore, they hurried to the Bell. Constance and Madge kept no secrets from each other so as soon as the tankards were served and Constance had taken a deep draught, she related what she had done in a voice trembling with a mixture of fear and excitement. Madge burst out laughing.

"Oh, if I could have only seen his face," Madge said. "Men think they know everything."

A week later, Will took Constance and Madge to the opening performance of *Richard III*, in which he played Henry Tudor, Earl of Richmond and the future King Henry VII. As a special treat, instead of having them stand in the pit, he bought them seats—the cheapest, to be sure, but seats. The two women were hypnotized by the performance; and Constance beamed as she realized—as well as memory could serve—that Will had reversed almost none of her changes. In the middle of the battle scene in Act V, Scene IV, she thrilled to hear Richard shout: "A horse, a horse! My kingdom for a horse!".

And that, then, was that.

One day in early August, it rained heavily all morning but cleared up in the afternoon. Constance went to market, marveling at the dazzling light reflected off the cobblestones. Not a cloud in the sky, the sun was as brilliant as she had ever seen it. The morning rain had also cleared out the dreadful heat and clamminess of the previous two days which, as she worked or walked to Madge's, had caused sweat to coat her body and permeate her dress. Today, however, it was warm enough for her to wear nothing but a simple dress, bodice and apron but not so warm, with a pleasant breeze off the river, as to make her uncomfortable. In sum, she felt on top of the world: light-hearted, confident and, as men turned to look at her, sure of her beauty although the subject of a husband had not come up—either in the two letters she had received from her father or with Will since the conversation when she had first arrived. Will had apparently accomplished what he had promised that first day in the matter of her departure as her father's letters only said that he hoped she was working hard and serving well her brother's needs. Will might have told her father that he, Will, would deal with the marriage question although, if so, he had done precious little—to her knowledge—about it. On the other hand, he might have persuaded her father that her services were so vital to his continued success in the theater that she was more valuable as a housekeeper than as a wife—even to a member of the gentry. It was not an implausible deduction as Will had not only a skilled pen but also, apparently, some sway with her father. Will was, apparently, content with her management of the household.

Constance missed her family and had written them several letters: to her mother, to Joan and one to her father. She described London, mentioned Madge and spoke of her duties in taking care of Will's household without either lying or revealing the true nature of their lodgings. She was pleased at her subtlety. In none of the letters did she express any desire to return to Stratford for, in truth, she had none.

She had not corrected any more of Will's work. She noticed that his manuscripts were now kept in a box on the floor. At least, it made dusting his table far easier.

Arriving at Leadenhall, she carefully avoided a pile of horse dung and what looked like cow's intestines that a butcher had tossed from his stall. She went immediately to Master Thursby, whom she had patronized ever since her first day's shopping. While they still bargained, primarily because they both enjoyed it, she knew that he gave her the best prices—knew as she occasionally checked at other stalls and made sure that he saw her.

"Well, Mistress Shakespeare, what will we serve brother Will this evening? Perhaps a leg of mutton or a nice cut of beef? Or a roasted swan? I have a lovely one."

"I think beef if you please, Master Thursby."

"I have just the right cut for you." The butcher picked up a loin of beef from his table and showed it to her. "That will be fine," she said.

"I must tell you that I saw *Richard the Third* the other day. A fine performance. Your brother wrote an excellent work and did a credible job as Henry Tudor. One line in particular caught my attention for its insight and dramatic import."

"And which line might that be," said Constance holding her breath.

"A horse! A horse! My kingdom for a horse!"

Constance let out her breath and smiled.

"I see you have the line by heart."

"And why not? It was perfect for the situation. Have you seen this masterpiece?"

"Will took Madge and myself. We had seats."

"What an excellent brother."

"Now, Master Thursby, how much is the loin?"

"Two shillings six, the pound, Mistress Shakespeare."

Constance looked at him askance.

"Master Thursby," she said slowly, and working to conceal a grin, "I have much to do today and, therefore, have little time. You wouldn't want me to take my trade to Master Quibble across the square, now would you?"

"You wouldn't think of such a thing."

"Wouldn't I?" She smiled. "One shilling eight."

"It is an exceptional loin." He didn't smile but looked straight at her. "Two shillings, as you're in such a hurry."

"Done."

"I see you've gotten much better at this," said a soft voice behind her.

Constance turned around and, seeing the Duchess of Bastrow, dropped a short curtsy.

"Your ladyship," she said.

"No need to curtsy every time we meet, even if

it's only on occasion and by chance."

"Thank you, your ladyship."

The butcher handed Constance the wrapped meat, which she placed in her basket.

"Master Thursby," said the Duchess, "that did appear an excellent cut of beef. Pray give a similar piece to Iris..." The Duchess paused briefly. "...at the same price or better."

"Certainly, your ladyship."

"Iris, you may then go home. We have shopped enough for one day."

"Yes, your ladyship."

Iris did a short curtsy and turned her attention to the butcher, who was cutting a loin for the Duchess.

The Duchess looped her arm through Constance's, who had no idea how to react, and started off through the square at a leisurely pace. Constance walked closely at her side.

"Have you completed your purchases?"

"Not quite, your ladyship."

"You know, my dear, that your ladyship this and your ladyship that can be almost as tiring as constantly being curtsied to by... by friends. I have a name: Susanna. You may call me that... when appropriate."

"Thank you, your... Susanna."

"Much better. And what is your name?"

"Constance... Constance Shakespeare."

"Are you married, Constance?"

"No."

"Do you then live with your parents?"

"My brother."

They had left the market and were strolling along Corn Hill. Constance wanted to stop at a shop she frequented for vegetables; but the Duchess seemed engrossed in their conversation, and Constance did not know how to divert the flow of conversation to her shopping.

"Is your brother a merchant?'

"He is a writer of plays and an actor."

"Ah, the theater. I sometimes have plays performed at my home. I should do so more often. Perhaps I shall ask your brother to put on a play for me." The Duchess was thoughtful. "I don't know the name, Shakespeare. What has he written?"

"Most recently, *Richard the Third*."

"Yes," said the Duchess, cheerily. "I have a gentleman friend who saw it. Interesting historical interpretation, he opined. Perhaps I shall ask your brother to put on that one." The Duchess suddenly stopped and looked around. "Here I am talking when you have purchases left to make."

"This is where I do most of my shopping."

"I have an idea. Have you been to the tower roof at St. Paul's?"

"I've not had the chance."

"If you would defer your shopping for a little while, I'll take you there. The climb up the stairs is daunting, but the view of London from the top is astounding. Shall we?"

"That would be nice."

They crossed the Stocks Market and entered Poultry, which they followed to Cheapside. Passing numerous elegant homes, they continued on Cheapside until they reached St. Paul's. The climb up the narrow steps of the tower was, indeed, exhausting; but the view, as promised, was magnificent. Constance gazed, admiringly, at the river, the mansions on Cheapside, the Moor Fields, where she had walked with Madge, the Leadenhall Market and even the Tower. She greatly enjoyed looking at all the roofs of London and the different types of houses: from brick mansions to half-timbered taverns to the sparse wattle and daub houses of the common folks.

"Is it not true, Constance, that this is worth the agony of the climb?"

"It certainly is... Susanna." Constance's expression showed agitation and worry. "I am sorry, but calling a Duchess by... I mean, all my life, I've been taught...."

"I do understand. You should call me what you wish." The Duchess waved her hand to encompass the tower roof. "We are lucky. On a Sunday, the roof is crowded; and it is much harder to enjoy the view." The Duchess pointed to the east, towards Cheapside. "Do you see that brick house on Cheapside? With three chimneys?" Constance looked in the direction the Duchess was pointing.

"Yes."

"That is my house. Well, the Duke's to be exact; but it is where I live when in the city. We passed it walking here. In back... you cannot see it from here... we have a charming garden with a small, intricate labyrinth. Have you ever tried one?"

"Never. I don't really know what one is."

"You soon shall. Come along." As they started down the stairs, the Duchess stopped and turned around. "A labyrinth can be quite difficult and frightening because it is easy to lose your way; but don't worry: I know my way around it backwards and forwards."

The house, with its wood panelling intricately carved, reminded her of Pennyford; but the garden was completely different. Instead of neat squares and rectangles with benches scattered around, the Duchess's garden was more sylvan in nature with small trees and a profusion of flowers in seeming chaos. Small rabbits dashed for cover in the shrubbery as the two women approached, and a doe nibbled on a shrub—unafraid and accustomed to humans. In the center of the garden stood a box-like structure of hedges with an opening in one corner.

"We tried to make the garden as close to nature as was possible in a huge, grimy city. I think we partly succeeded. The Duke is very fond of the garden. It brings him peace of mind. He is a close advisor to the Queen and sits on the Privy Council. He is expert in criminal, trade and diplomatic questions. He also has a country estate, which requires frequent visits and attention. I go there occasionally but find London so much more interesting, exciting and, frankly, enticing. His myriad duties result in long days and many absences from home. When here, he refreshes himself by sitting in the garden contemplating, I suppose, the state of the realm. He is much concerned with the increase in vagabonds wandering the highways and byways. He feels for, but also fears, them. Robberies in the country are on the increase. But enough of tiresome matters. Once more unto the breach although for you, dear Constance, it is presumably the first time. The idea is to find the center, beyond which you cannot go, and then your way back. You lead. Give it your best try."

With the Duchess following, Constance entered the labyrinth. She walked down short passages, turned many corners, came to dead ends—forcing her to back track—and went down one passage from which, at the end, she could see the entrance through the hedge but had not the remotest idea either how to get there or in which direction lay the center. She looked helplessly at the Duchess who stood behind her. Tears of frustration sprang to her eyes. The Duchess handed her a handkerchief.

"Do not berate yourself. No one, at least that I know of, works it out on the first try. Follow me."

With practiced assurance, the Duchess navigated passageways and numerous twists and turns until, without ever doubling back, she led Constance into the center where there was a double seat with a back. Wearied from their exertions, the two women sat on the seat.

"Was not that fun?"

"So long as I don't have to find my way back."

"You can try, and I'll give you clues along the

way. You will have little trouble."

Having provided that reassurance, the Duchess leaned towards Constance, put her arms around her and kissed her full on the lips. Surprised, Constance tried to pull away; but the Duchess held her firmly and kissed more intensely, her tongue pushing between Constance's lips and exploring her mouth. The words: "No, stop, please" formed in Constance's head, but she couldn't utter them whether from fear or some other cause she couldn't tell. Then an image of Emma appeared in her brain and, thinking of what Emma had once told her, Constance stopped trying to pull away and let her body relax. She kissed the Duchess back; and giving Constance a winsome smile, the Duchess stroked her cheek and neck, then let her hand play with her breast. Constance felt excitement rising.

Without warning, and perhaps deliberately not giving Constance the chance to object, the Duchess rose from the seat, dropped to her knees in front of Constance and lifted Constance's skirt. The Duchess put her head inside the skirt and adjusted Constance's legs so that her thighs rested on the Duchess's shoulders. Pushing on her belly so that Constance slid backwards and rested firmly against the seat's backrest, the Duchess pulled down Constance's undergarments.

"Oh dear God," muttered the Duchess, hoarsely.

Constance shivered when the Duchess licked and kissed her. Firmly gripping Constance's upper thighs, the Duchess nibbled, pulled at and, finally, more and more rapidly and forcefully, tongued Constance's clitoris. The climax started, slowly at first and then gathering energy and speed until Constance knew that it wouldn't stop, that she couldn't stop it even if she wanted to and that she couldn't help uttering a moan that grew in volume and intensity until her orgasm was complete. The Duchess withdrew from inside the skirt and looked questioningly at Constance.

"Susanna," Constance said. "That was... something."

"You came very powerfully."

"Without doubt."

"Would you please return the favor."

At first, Constance found the taste, and odor, strange and, perhaps, unpleasant but, out of respect for and in awe of the Duchess, she continued caressing and fondling Susanna with her tongue. Gradually, she got used to what she was doing and began to enjoy it. As Susanna uttered short and then longer moans, she found herself getting excited. Susanna's cries resounded with ecstasy; and she murmured with vehemence: "Don't stop. In God's name, don't stop." Constance responded with an inarticulate sound and increased the vigor of her tonguing. Susanna stiffened, her pelvis arched and she cried: "Yes." Her body relaxed; and, slowly, Constance withdrew from beneath her skirt.

Susanna pulled Constance onto the seat and, putting an arm around her shoulders, drew her close. They sat in silence for a couple of minutes. Constance was sleepy but dared not go to sleep. She had little idea as to how she felt about what had just happened. Confused at the very least. Frightened out of her wits a distinct possibility.

"You have not done this before, have you?"

"No."

"You were superb. My climax was, to say the least, intense. Did you like doing it to me?"

Constance hesitated, trying to think of what to say.

"Tell me the truth. We women must be honest with each other if only because the men so seldom are... with us and, perhaps, with themselves."

"Not at first but then yes."

"A good answer. Am I your first lover?"

"I've had one other: a man... very brief."

"Would you like to come here again? Remember: honesty."

Struggling with her feelings, Constance said: "I'm not sure, but I think so."

Susanna stroked her cheek and then kissed her lightly on the lips.

"You are so beautiful and pure. Now don't tell me I'm beautiful because I'm not, at least not any longer; and flattery is a form of dishonesty. But I'm not bad-looking, am I?"

"No."

"If you decide to return, come here next Thursday at two in the afternoon. If you're not here then, I shall understand and not blame you in the least." Susanna's tone changed, turning serious and not a little fearful. "There is one thing of critical importance that I must tell you. And you must swear on your immortal soul to obey me."

"What is it?"

"Do you swear?"

"Yes."

"You must tell no one about this, not your brother nor that young woman with whom you go to the market occasionally."

"Madge?"

"I don't know her name, but I presume that's the one. I've seen no other. Do you have another friend?"

"No. But please, why are you so worried? Is it because we've committed a mortal sin?"

"It is because even duchesses can lose their heads."

Constance gasped and then whispered: "I swear."

"Now you must finish your shopping or your playwright brother will be hungry and cross."

Constance was almost at Stocks Market before she realized that she had not purchased the other items she had planned for supper. Her mind was in turmoil. Had she just condemned her soul to the perpetual flames of Hell? Even if not, her head was certainly at risk. If the authorities would cut off a duchess's head, they would waste little time wondering what to do with the head of a common, unimportant girl from Stratford, that is if they didn't find it more convenient to simply hang her. She, furthermore, had no understanding why she had responded so fervently to what Susanna had done. When she had previously thought of such things, which was rare in the extreme, she had recoiled in horror, so unnatural did it appear. She doubted not, however, that she had enjoyed it. She had also liked what Edmund had done to her, kissing her just where the Duchess had. With Edmund, however, while she had lost her virginity without being married, her head was not in jeopardy. Emma, unmarried, had lost her virginity almost a year ago; and perhaps some of her other friends had lost theirs as well. The notion of pregnancy did not enter her mind.

Forgetting, if only briefly, the matter of hellfire and the gallows, she asked herself which of the two partners in love-making did she find more appealing? To her dismay, she could not answer the question. Time, perhaps, would tell her. She would have loved to talk it over with Madge, who might be able to resolve the dilemma; but she had sworn not to, and she believed in keeping oaths. Yes, she would likely go back next Thursday; and if so, she would ask Susanna whether they were going to Hell. A duchess, particularly one who made love with other women, should know the answer. She turned back towards Cheapside and hurried to her favorite grocer.

Two days later, in the morning, she happened to come across Madge in Leadenhall Market; and they arranged to meet for a promenade in the afternoon when they had a respite from work until they needed to prepare supper. They walked, as they often did, to Moorgate and, thence, into Moor Fields. The weather had again changed, and it was blistering hot. Constance regretted her several layers of clothing.

"Perhaps," said Madge, "we should go to the Bell. It will be cooler, and we can have some refreshment."

"Let's rest, first," said Constance, pointing to a nearby tree that would provide some shade.

As soon as they were seated, Madge said: "I hear from Master Thursby that, the other day, you were strolling with the Duchess of Bastrow. You do keep fancy company."

"On my first day in London, as you know, she helped me in the market. We were both at the butcher's, and we walked through the market together. She does not act like a duchess—or how I would imagine a duchess to act."

"I see." Madge gave Constance a sly look. "Master Thursby didn't see where you went after leaving the market."

"Only up Cheapside to a grocer's shop. Nothing further. She went on her way. "

"Well, if you're not inclined to tell the full story, then we'll change the subject. I have news of my own. I am with child."

"Oh, Madge. That is wonderful." Constance gave her friend's hand a firm squeeze. "I am so happy for you, and I will fervently pray this child will live to a ripe old age."

On the following Thursday, Constance walked up Cheapside to the Duchess's house. She had given her decision some considerable thought, weighing the possibility of damnation against the powerful sensations she had experienced. The sensations won; and besides, there was something in the way the Duchess spoke to her that was most appealing. Looking around nervously, Constance approached the door and knocked. Almost immediately, Susanna opened the door and stood there smiling.

"Come in." The Duchess closed the door. "No one is here except a very old servant who is quite deaf and spends most of her day sitting by the kitchen fire. I've made sure we have a couple of hours to ourselves." The Duchess took Constance in her arms and kissed her fully on the mouth. She led Constance up a broad staircase and down a short hall, hung with family portraits, to her bedroom. A large wooden chest with intricate carvings of wood nymphs, satyrs and cupids stood against one wall. Opposite was a long table with carved human figures as legs; on it were neat piles of books and several rolled up maps. A tapestry with hunting scenes, a medieval castle and a river hung on the wall facing the immense four-poster bed with thick, velvet curtains on each side. Two chairs with lion's head armrests stood near the bed.

The Duchess turned Constance around and lovingly kissed the back of her neck, then gently inserted her tongue in one of Constance's ears. Slowly, she undressed Constance, kissing her eagerly where each piece of clothing fell away. Completely naked, Constance did the same for the Duchess. Now both naked, they got into bed and commenced their intense love making, with Constance more sure of herself this time. Afterwards, they lay encased in each other's arms and talked.

"Did you enjoy it today?" asked Susanna.

"Yes."

"As much as with the man ... or perhaps, more?"

"I don't know. I keep thinking about that."

"You are thoughtful. I like that."

"Do you not love the Duke?"

"I love him very much, and our intimacy is both vigorous and playful."

"Then why women?"

"I am drawn to both sexes and see no reason to deny either side of my nature. We shall see whether you are the same. At least, if I limit my infidelities to women, I won't confound the Duke's lineage."

"Meaning you won't become pregnant?"

"Precisely and neither will you." Susanna grew solemn. "I believe the Duke knows but chooses not to raise the subject. Occupied as he is with state business, he appreciates domestic tranquility. And, I believe, is content knowing that I love him and, I flatter myself in thinking, is enthralled with the ways I find to please him—even after years of marriage."

"Do you have children?"

"We have tried, very hard, but have not been blessed."

"I am so sorry."

"Not as sorry as I am. It is the greatest disappointment of my life. But, right now, let's not dwell on sad things."

Susanna kissed and then sucked at Constance's nipple, which swelled up and turned hard.

"Again?" Susanna asked.

Before Constance left, they worked out a method for signalling when it was safe for Constance to come to the house. Constance would go to the market at the same time in the morning unless she was unable or not desirous of seeing the Duchess that day. The same flexibility, naturally, held true for Susanna who, when she did come to the market, would be accompanied by Iris. Otherwise, it might seem odd. Acknowledging Constance, the Duchess would say: "Good morning, Mistress Shakespeare" if it were prudent for Constance to come to the house that afternoon. If it were not, the Duchess would say: "How nice to see you". Whatever else they might say would be irrelevant.

"If the Duke accepts your arrangements, then why the secrecy?" asked Constance.

"Servants, my darling, talk constantly and to God knows whom. Not for the first time have servants, deliberately or not, cost masters their heads."

At the front door, Susanna quickly kissed Constance.

"By the way," she said. "I have spoken to the Duke about a performance of your brother's play. He is favorably disposed, but it is not yet settled. I will keep you informed as matters progress."

Over the course of the next month and a half, Constance visited Susanna every week and, occasionally, twice in the same week. She began to have intimate feelings for the Duchess although she was not sure if the word love applied. While she found their love making pleasurable in the extreme and their conversations fascinating, she could still not answer the question, concern for her immortal soul notwithstanding, whether she preferred men or women or, like the Duchess, was drawn to both. At this point, she certainly had far more experience with a woman than her brief encounter with Edmund.

Susanna loved literature, especially poetry, and had given her a copy of Geoffrey Chaucer's *Canterbury Tales*, which she had been reading with great pleasure. "I would like to have inscribed it for you," said the Duchess, "but prudence won out over sentiment. Nevertheless, be sure no one else, especially your brother, sees it, as curiosity as to how you came by it would surely be aroused." She kissed Constance and stroked her breast, letting her hand stray over Constance's belly. "I do have strong feelings for you."

"And I you."

Constance thought occasionally about the subject of marriage. Will had said nothing about it nor had her father in his latest letter. While she still expected to marry at some point, she was not averse to postponing the event. After completing her chores, her days were her own; and she loved the freedom to read, to wander around London—with or without Madge—and to spend time with Susanna. She was uncertain how to ensure that marriage, especially after children were born, allowed her at least a modicum of her present freedom. Unless, of course, she found a husband on her own but how likely was that in the London that she knew. She particularly wondered if she would have to give up Susanna. Possibly not but that would mean deception, a practice that she thought likely to be destructive of a healthy marriage. She also wondered if Will would someday let her help with his work. Almost certainly not given the care he now took to keep his papers private. She would never dream of opening the box.

One afternoon in early October, she was entering Cheapside on her way to see the Duchess when, her mind focused on where she would soon be and what she would be doing, she bumped into a young woman. She murmured, "Excuse me" and kept going.

"Constance," the young woman cried out.

Constance turned around and saw that it was Wynefreed with Ester by her side.

"How nice to see you both," lied Constance.

"Where are you going with such grim determination?" asked Wynefreed.

"To the grocers. Purchases for supper."

"What are you going to carry them in?" asked Ester.

"Oh my word, I was in such a hurry that I've forgotten my basket."

Ester giggled, and Wynefreed said: "You always were a mysterious one."

"Since you've no basket," said Ester, "you'll

either have to buy one or go back home to fetch it."

"We'll go with you to make sure you get a good one," said Wynefreed.

Constance realized that, as she was going to Susanna's, she had no money with her.

"I best go home."

"We'll still go with you," said Wynefreed. "What fun it will be."

"I don't live in the most elegant surroundings."

"No matter," said Wynefreed.

"It will be an adventure," said Ester. "Just like Robin Hood."

With a sigh, Constance started back down Poultry.

"What have you been doing?" asked Wynefreed.

"Taking care of my brother's lodgings. Reading when I have the time."

"I thought," said Ester, "that he had many servants and that you were to see they did their work."

As they would soon discover the truth, Constance saw no point in lying and said that matters had not turned out quite as she expected. Ester laughed, and Wynefreed, pinching her arm, told Ester to mind her manners. At Leadenhall Market, Constance again tried to dissuade the girls; but they insisted on continuing.

"Aunt Blanche will be so surprised that we met you," said Wynefreed.

"And so angry that we walked so far in this neighborhood," giggled Ester.

"Ester, did I not warn you?"

"You haven't told me what the two of you have been doing?"

"I have momentous news," said Wynefreed. "I am to be married next year."

"But you cannot be more than fourteen."

"I'll be fifteen in a month, and he is very wealthy so I will be quite the lady."

Constance concealed her shock. While some girls were married at an early age, this seemed extreme. No such arrangement had been made for any of her acquaintance. She doubted Wynefreed was ready to be a wife; but expressing her opinion would hardly improve matters, and the girl seemed quite happy at the prospect.

As the neighborhood grew poorer and darker, Constance could see that the girls were becoming disturbed. By the time they reached Fish Lane, they were in something of a tizzy although Wynefreed slightly less so than Ester. Since it had rained heavily during the night, the narrow street was a quagmire. Davy, the impoverished, rough-clad, filthy, stinking and inveterate pipe smoker, stood pretty much where he had on the day she had first come to Fish Lane although he now greeted Constance warmly as they were on good terms if not exactly friends.

"Good afternoon, Constance," said Davy. "You departed from our stylish neighborhood not more than a half hour ago and here you are back again and with two new servants for your foppish brother's household."

Wynefreed and Ester gaped at Davy with horror

etched on their youthful faces.

"These are not servants, Davy, but acquaintances that I made on my journey to London from Stratford."

"Please to meet you ladies," said Davy with a deep bow, extending his pipe to a point where the smoke curled up Ester's nostrils, causing her to sneeze fitfully.

"We best be getting home," said Wynefreed.

"I cannot let you travel through this neighborhood alone," said Constance.

"We shall be fine."

"No, you will not. I am going with you at least as far as Cheapside."

"But your basket?"

"Let me worry about the basket," said Constance, taking each girl by the arm and starting off. Over her shoulder, she called out: "Good-bye, Davy, see you again sometime."

Davy gave her a puzzled look as he saw Constance almost every day.

Constance did not let go of the girls until they reached the beginning of Cheapside. "You must come visit," said Wynefreed as she started up Cheapside. "I shall." Constance watched until they were out of sight and then realized that she had no idea where the girls lived, not that she cared all that much and not that she couldn't find out if she wished. She rang the bell at Susanna's front door, fully an hour later than expected.

The Duchess opened the door and pulled Constance inside. Anger suffused her face. "Where have you been?" Constance started to answer, but the Duchess cut her off. "Most people do not keep a Duchess waiting."

"Did you consider I could've been attacked by a robber?"

"Were you?"

"No."

Constance explained in detail what had happened and ended by asking: "Would you have liked me to bring them here?" She then curtsied, the sarcasm of the gesture not lost on the Duchess.

Susanna took Constance in her arms and whispered: "I'm sorry. Will you forgive me?"

"Only if you take me right to bed."

Later, as they lay satiated, Susanna said: "Sometimes this nobility business is more than I can manage. I wasn't born to it. My family were only country gentry. I was elevated when the Duke married me." She sighed. "I might have been more at ease living on a country manor."

"Then we would not have met."

"You are wise beyond your years. And I have news for you. The Duke plans to request your brother to mount a production of *Richard the Third* in our house. He will shortly receive the invitation—although invitation is hardly the word for it."

"That is wonderful. I cannot thank you enough."

Constance went silent and thoughtful.

"I am good at reading you. Something is not

quite right."

"Who will the Duke invite to the performance?"

"Personal friends, high government officials. The Queen might attend but one can never be sure."

"The Queen?" Constance gasped.

"The Duke will mention it to her. She might be interested as the subject deals with her grandfather's conquest of the throne. Or then again, she might prefer to avoid the subject." Susanna played with Constance's hair. "But you didn't really answer my question."

"Will the Duke invite the Earl of Pennyford and..." Constance hesitated. "...and his son... Edmund?"

"Well, well, which one was it? I hope, Edmund. I'm not fond of his father whom I consider a brutish type."

"Edmund."

"You do travel in high circles." Susanna laughed and then grew serious. "We have to include them. The Earl may not come, and Edmund..." Susanna toyed with Constance's breast. "...is the soul of discretion. It will be fine." She continued her caresses. "Shall we?"

Will was astounded when the letter arrived by messenger. Constance, excitement racing through her body, watched as he read the letter, put it on his writing table and picked it up to read again. He did this three times before turning to Constance who, rather than stare at him, had begun the pretense of sweeping out the front room, ignoring the fact that she had completed that task not thirty minutes earlier.

"You can have no idea what I'm holding in my hand."

"Of course not, dear brother, as I haven't had the opportunity to read what appears to be a letter."

"It is without question a letter—and one which will change forever our fortunes and the history of the English stage."

"That is indeed quite something. May I read this incredible document or would you rather read it to me or, failing that, describe its contents?"

"I dare not let it out of my hands for fear it will dissolve into thin air and blow out the door like any common breeze."

Constance laughed.

"I doubt such a phenomenon is possible, dearest Will; but let's not tempt the Fates. At the same time, please do not keep me in this state of suspense."

Pacing up and down the room as if he were on a stage, Will read in a theatrical voice: "To Master William Shakespeare, Theatrical Impresario: His Grace, Leonarde Marsham, Duke of Bastrow, requests that said Master Shakespeare and His Company of Actors shall come to Bastrow House in Cheapside, London at three in the afternoon on Wednesday the Twenty-Eighth of October in the year of our Lord, One Thousand Five Hundred and Ninety-Two to perform his Historical Play, *Richard the Third* before a Select Audience of Peers and Gentlemen and Gentlewomen and which may include Her Majesty, Elizabeth the First, Queen of England and

Ireland." William stopped pacing and waved the letter in an almost royal fashion. "The Queen," he said, a tremor in his voice.

"Yes," said Constance, willing herself not to smile and careful not to say "Susanna,"—"The Duchess told me the Queen likes the theater and might wish to attend."

Will stared at her, unable to utter a word.

"I had better explain."

"I should think so."

"The first time I went to Leadenhall, a butcher—who now provides all our meat at excellent prices—tried to get the better of me; and the Duchess, who happened to be nearby with her servant, gave me sound advice. Since then, we have occasionally met, purely by chance, in Leadenhall or Stocks; and she has been gracious enough to exchange a few polite words with me. The butcher, on the first day, told me who she was. On one of those occasions, I told her about *Richard the Third*; and she remarked that the Duke, who values the respite from his many duties that theatrical performances provide, might want a performance in Bastrow House. It was only the other day that she mentioned that the Queen might attend as Henry Tudor, the character whom you portray, was her Grandfather."

"And why, pray tell, dear sister," his voice a mixture of sarcasm and disbelief, "is this the first time I've heard of this friendship?"

"Hardly rises to the level of friendship, dear brother, as..." She almost said: "Susanna" and wondered if the privilege were now worth the risk. "...the Duchess, after all, is a duchess. I've known of the letter for a mere couple of days and thought you would like to hear of this by the Duke's own hand and not my telling of it, which would not be nearly as exciting."

Will kissed Constance on the cheek and said: "You were right. It is quite thrilling to see it on paper." He paused thoughtfully. "What other secrets are you keeping from me?"

"None whatsoever, except that Madge and I chatter like silly girls and wonder whether she is to have a boy or a girl."

Will told her that the last part of the letter, which he had not read aloud, asked Will to furnish a list of appurtenances and furniture, if any, that would be needed for the performance.

That evening, as she prepared supper, Constance pondered whether, were she the Duke's lover rather than his wife's, she could be more open with her brother and whether a satisfactory marriage with a gentleman of standing might not have resulted from the affair. Whether a gentleman of standing would allow her the freedom she so cherished was altogether another matter. Better to stay unmarried until she was more sure of her course whatever that should prove to be. She was also uncertain as to the durability of Susanna's feelings for her. They seemed indeed strong at present, but one never knew. The precise nature of her own strong feelings continued to be somewhat of a puzzle to her. Did they constitute love or some other emotion?

She did not mention these concerns later in the week when she and Susanna were lounging in bed after a torrid love-making. She merely described Will's surprise and pleasure and said that the company was furiously rehearsing for the special occasion and that Will's stature within the company had increased immeasurably for which she, Constance, owed a debt of the utmost gratitude to Susanna.

"Not at all. I would like to give you other tokens of my feelings—all right, let me be honest—my love for you; but sadly, that is not possible. It would be far too dangerous."

At the mention of the word "love", Constance felt her heart beat more rapidly and a sense of excitement saturate her body. This was the first time that someone had used that word to describe feelings for her in such a context. She suddenly realized that she felt the same but was unsure what to say so she remained silent until Susanna changed the subject to what Constance should wear to the performance.

She found her voice when she visited the next time. She brought the Duchess a single pink rose. A duo of tears ran down Susanna's cheeks when Constance handed her the rose. "I understand," she said, taking Constance in her arms and kissing her fervently. Once in her bedroom, she laid the rose on a pillow; they were both careful of it as they made love.

"I will have to dispose of it after you leave," Susanna said, "but I will always treasure the memory."

"I know."

The hall at Bastrow House was brilliantly lit the afternoon of the performance. An open space had been created at one end with rows of chairs facing what would serve as the stage. Space was left behind the chairs so that the Duke's guests could gather and converse. Liveried servants moved among the guests carrying bottles of claret from Gascony, white wine from La Rochelle and Spanish sack, a dry, amber wine. A long table stood by the rear wall. On it were flagons of cider and ale for those who did not care for wine, wheels of French cheese, platters of sliced apples, pears and plums, bowls filled with dates, figs and grapes and plates piled high with fruit and cheese tarts. Glasses, pewter tankards and goblets were arranged at one end of the table. Looking at the sumptuous delicacies, Constance remembered that most or all of the guests would have eaten a large dinner not that long ago. She, herself, was far too nervous to eat a thing. She glanced around the room and guessed there to be fifty to sixty guests. She did not see the Duchess.

The guests strolled around the room, sipping decorously, parading their stylish outfits (a virtual obsession with the upper ranks of Elizabethan society and not a few of the lower ranks as well) and conversing with friends and acquaintances but generally speaking ignoring those they did not know. The nobles especially steered clear of the ostentatiously wealthy merchants that the Duke—attuned to the power of such individuals and how useful they could be in furthering the administration's objectives—had invited. A few guests sampled the delicacies but, as Susanna had explained to Constance, most of the eating would take place after the performance.

She was wearing a new outfit that Will had bought just for the performance. The bodice had an embroidered neckline. The pale burgundy overskirt with a pattern of flowers parted in the front to show her light yellow underskirt. She had refused to wear a ruff, saying they were uncomfortable in the extreme; she sported a high-crowned round hat with a feather slanted to the rear.

"Can we afford it?" she had asked about the outfit.

"We cannot not afford it," Will had replied.

Suddenly, the Duchess was by her side and saying in a low voice: "You are the most beautiful woman in the room." Before Constance could reply, the Duchess had glided away.

She wished Will could see all the elegantly-dressed, high-born guests; but long before the first guest had arrived, the actors had been shown to a room off the hall where they could dress and lay out their props. Given the small size of the hall relative to The Rose and the difficulty of moving furniture in the allotted space, the company had decided to perform on a bare stage. In the actors' humble opinions, they only needed their voices to bring the play to life.

The Duke approached and said that he was glad to meet the Duchess's young acquaintance who, as he understood it, was the moving force behind this afternoon's performance. Saying, "Thank you, Lord Bastrow", Constance made a curtsy. The Duke smiled and walked away.

Two young gentlemen in gaily-colored doublets and tight hose came up to Constance. They introduced themselves as Andrew and Valentyne. The first asked why they had never seen her in society or at court. Valentyne proposed that they all go to a dance after the boring history play was finished. Constance smiled demurely and replied that it would not be possible. Valentyne was about to attempt persuasion when a third man approached the group. Seeing him, Andrew and Valentyne made short bows and backed a few steps away. Constance looked at the newcomer and, having been prepared by Susanna, said simply: "Why, Lord Edmund, how nice to see you."

"And you, Miss Shakespeare. It has been some time since that rough coach ride to London. We had to cross a stream on foot if I recall correctly."

"Indeed, you do."

"It is so nice to see you in such agreable surroundings. I am looking forward to finally seeing one of your now famous brother's plays."

Hearing this, Andrew and Valentyne turned to leave; but Edmund said, in a tone that brooked no refusal: "No, stay, both of you. Miss Shakespeare and I would be most interested in your views on the theater."

At that moment, a murmur ran through the crowd; and everyone turned towards the door. Two liveried footmen entered the room and stood at each side of the door. Flanked by the Duke and Duchess, Elizabeth entered the room. The men bowed, and the women curtsied. The Queen wore an extraordinarily high ruff, a pearl-encrusted bodice that came to a point just below her waist and a wide, flowing skirt. The intricate pattern of small crosses was the same on her bodice as on her skirt. Her sleeves puffed out at the shoulders. She did not wear a crown nor did she carry the sceptre and orb. Greeting men and women that she knew, Elizabeth allowed the Duke and Duchess to guide her to where Constance and the three men stood. The men bowed. Her heart pounding, Constance made the deep curtsy that, first naked—with them both laughing uncontrollably—and then clothed, she had perfected under Susanna's tutelage. The Duke said something to Elizabeth in a low voice that she alone could hear. Andrew and Valentyne melted into the crowd. Elizabeth seemed not to notice although, in truth, she missed nothing.

"Lord Edmund," said the Queen.

"Your Majesty."

"I didn't know you had an interest in the theater."

"Newly acquired, Your Majesty."

"I see."

The Queen turned her attention to Constance.

"I understand, Miss Shakespeare, that it is your brother's play we are to see and that he performs the role of my grandfather."

"Yes, Your Majesty."

"I hope he is not as tight-fisted as Grandfather."

"He is most generous, Your Majesty."

"I have not heard of him as prominent in the theater, but I eagerly await the presentation."

With that, Elizabeth continued her progress through the crowd, stopping now and then for a word with someone, until she reached her seat in the front row. The Duke and Duchess sat on either side of her, and the rest of the guests took their seats—in order of their rank. As the Duchess had previously told her, Constance sat in the back row.

"No need," said Susanna, holding her hand, "to bring too much attention to you."

The Duke motioned to a servant who left the room; and a minute afterwards, the play began. The actor playing the Duke of Gloucester and the future Richard the Third limped angrily on stage, his hunchback highly visible and his withered arm hanging useless by his side. He glared around the audience and then raised his good arm and clenched his fist in a gesture of disdain and loathing. Quietly, and then with greater force, he spoke the opening lines that Constance had changed dramatically from Will's original. She listened in suspense to every word.

> Now is the winter of our discontent
> Made glorious summer by this sun of York

The play moved smoothly. The actors performed with power, skill and grace. Will, in her opinion, was superb. The story was intense, compelling and familiar to everyone in the room. The audience listened attentively with none of the catcalls that could emanate from the apprentices and workmen in the pit of The Rose. Excitement rising in her gorge, Constance listened raptly, and anxiously, as the play neared the climactic battle of Bosworth Field. Richard's fate was sealed in the penultimate scene as he uttered the lines that gave her the greatest satisfaction.

> I think there be six Richmonds in the field;
> Five have I slain to-day instead of him.
> A horse! a horse! my kingdom for a horse!

The audience applauded politely, but enthusiastically; and the actors took their bows and retired. The Queen spoke to the Duke who signalled to a servant to come over. He gave instructions to the servant who hurried into the room where the actors were preparing to leave. A mere seconds later, Will appeared, approached the Queen and bowed deeply.

"A handsome work, Master Shakespeare," said Elizabeth. "You did a fine job portraying my grandfather as well as that evil monster, Richard. You are to be commended both for your writing and your acting. The other members of the company did an equally fine job. Please give them our congratulations. You shall be suitably rewarded."

The Queen then dismissed Will with a nod of her head. She again said something to the Duke who gave instructions to a servant. Immediately, a Murano glass filled with hippocras, a spiced and sweetened wine of which Elizabeth was fond, was brought to her along with a pewter plate suitably arrayed with the finest of the Duke's delicacies. After the Queen had been served, the other guests—again by rank—made their way to the table groaning with food.

The company would leave by a rear exit. Constance walked towards the front door, which she knew so well. On her way out, she overheard a young noble saying to a companion: "This is clearly an improvement on his Henry the Sixth plays. The language is much finer. And the story.... well, it's obvious that Master Shakespeare wanted to be in the Queen's good graces. I believe he has exceeded his expectations. His career has just taken a step forward."

Constance stopped at a grocers on the way home and still arrived ahead of Will. She set about preparing supper. A half hour later, she heard Will climbing the stairs. He entered the front room and grinned at her.

"A remarkable performance," she said. "Your acting was excellent."

Will nodded. He drew a leather purse from a doublet pocket and held it up in the air. "A hundred sovereigns for the company: sixty from the Queen and forty from the Duke. One hundred and fifty pounds, not to mention the increase in our reputation and standing." He did a jig and pranced around the room. He took a second, smaller purse from a different pocket. "Ten sovereigns from the Queen—for me alone."

"Oh, Will, that's marvelous."

Constance turned back to the fire.

Will crossed the room, turned Constance around and took hold of both her hands.

"Thank you," he said.

And nothing further.

Constance and Susanna continued their visits through November. Towards the end of the month, the first cases of the plague appeared; and people became frightened. At the beginning of December, Constance decided to restrict her outdoor activities to the market (for shopping and to check for a signal from Susanna) and to walking to Madge's house. She avoided, to the extent possible, close contact with people, not knowing who might be infected and who not. She didn't know for sure that the disease could be passed from person to person; but if not, she reasoned, why were houses with plague cases closed up. She shunned dogs like... well, like the plague... as dogs were reputed to carry the disease. She took such precautions because no one knew if this were just the normal round of cases or the start of an epidemic. Either way, she noticed that people stayed further away than usual from each other on the street; and she was not eager to give Madge a hug. She begged Will to observe the same care and go out as little as possible; but he told her that, as long as the theaters remained open, he would have to go.

Sometime in the second week of December, she began to worry as it had been a good two weeks since she had seen Susanna. For the next few days, she went to the market every day and stayed longer than necessary for her purchases. After several days, which was longer than they had ever been apart, she became consumed with fear and decided on the desperate step of going to the house without having received a signal. As she walked up Poultry and Cheapside, she noticed that a number of houses seemed closed. Bastrow House also had a forlorn, empty look with not a single light shining in the windows, which had always before been gaily lit with candles. Trembling with fear, she approached the front door and rang the bell. No one answered. She rang several times; and still, no one answered. With despair mounting rapidly, she banged on the door, increasing the intensity by the second. Finally, an ancient servant, who appeared likely to die any moment, plague or no plague, slowly opened the massive door and then stepped backwards.

"Is the Duchess at home?"

"You Mistress Shakespeare?"

"I am."

"Wait."

The servant closed the door. In a few minutes, he re-opened the door and stepped out only far enough to hand Constance a leather case before immediately closing the door again. Back on the street, Constance opened the case and found inside a folded piece of paper.

December 2, 1592

My esteemed Miss Shakespeare,

The Duke, myself and all our household except one are leaving for our country manor to escape what may be a serious incidence of plague in the city. I am afraid that, for the present, I cannot continue with your French lessons. Perhaps, we can resume on my return. If you can find your way to our manor, which is in May-field, East Sussex, you and your brother would be most welcome.

With all due regard,

Susanna, Duchess of Bastrow.

Constance walked home, feeling more desolate than ever before in her life.

Christmas was a sad business; and as the plague deaths continued to increase, Will contrived to spend more time at home, reducing the rehearsal time for two court performances that had come about because of the success of the Bastrow House production. In January 1593, a terrible blow shook not only the theatrical world but also the entire city of London. To contain the spread of the plague, the authorities ordered all the theaters to close, reasoning that places where numerous people crowded together represented fertile ground for the generally lethal disease. Will no longer had a source of income nor any meaningful work so he sat home every day and moped. After two weeks of this, Constance told him to find something to do.

"How about writing some more poetry?" she suggested.

"I'll think about it."

Several weeks later, at the end of January, she stopped by Master Thursby's stall. She was in no mood for conversation, which she normally enjoyed with the ebullient butcher, as the long hours at home with little to do except clean, cook and read were fraying her nerves. When he started to talk, she said sharply: "Not today, Master Thursby. If you please, just a leg of mutton."

"Of course, Mistress Shakespeare, but I do have news."

"Concerning?"

"The Duchess of Bastrow."

Fighting to control her emotions, Constance asked: "Oh, has she been to the market?"

"No, Mistress Shakespeare, the news is not good." He paused as if preferring silence but forced himself to continue. "I'm sorry to say that the Duchess was killed in a riding accident. Apparently, her horse slid on a muddy road and threw the Duchess, who hit her head on a large rock and died instantly."

Constance could not contain a gasp.

"I know that you and she were companionable. She was a fine lady: kind and generous. I'm very sorry."

On the verge of tears and hoping it was simply a rumor like so many others, Constance stammered:

"How... how... do you know?"

"I have a supplier who is a tenant on the neighboring manor. He brought the news." As if intuiting Constance's feelings of hope, the butcher added: "I'm afraid the report is reliable."

"I'm... I'm... sure it is. Thank you, Master Thursby."

"The leg of mutton?"

"Not today."

When she arrived home empty-handed, Will studied her curiously. "Something's wrong," he said. "Madge?"

"The Duchess," was all she managed before the tears flowed down her cheeks. Will found a handkerchief which he gave her. She dried her eyes. "I am composed now."

"Go on."

"The Duchess was killed in a riding accident."

"My God," said Will. "How did you find out?"

She told him and then sat at the trestle table and stared into the fire. Will came over and put a hand on her shoulder.

"Did you, perhaps, have a deeper friendship with the Duchess than I am aware of?"

She looked up at him and said: "No... it's just that she was so kind to me... to us."

"I see." He gently squeezed her shoulder. "I am no fool, you know; but have it your way. I understand."

He removed his hand from her shoulder and picked up the shopping basket.

"I'll do the shopping for tonight's supper," he said.

"Thank you." She forced a smile. "Tell Master Thursby to give you the same price he gives me."

Late the next morning, after she had finished the cleaning, she went to Madge's who was alone as her father and husband still had passengers although fewer than before the outbreak. They sat by the fire, in silence, for a few moments. Madge could tell that something important was troubling her friend. She waited patiently, rubbing her huge belly.

"Ouch," she said at one point, "whoever is in there knows how to kick. He—or she—will be a brawler."

After a full five minutes, Constance spoke: "The Duchess is dead—an accident—riding her horse."

"Oh, no," said Madge.

"There's something I need to tell you, but you must swear never to tell another soul."

"I'm not sure I want to hear this."

"Do you swear?"

"Yes."

"You are the only person to whom I could tell this although I think Will has discerned it."

"Now I am truly worried."

"The Duchess and I were lovers."

"Would you repeat that."

"The Duchess and I were lovers."

"Dear God!"

The two women sat quietly for a few more minutes. Finally, Madge said: "I agree. This must be kept a secret between you and me: for your safety and the

Duchess's reputation."

"Truly."

"Do you not like men?"

"No, I do."

"Which do you prefer?"

"The Duchess asked me that. I don't know the answer, much as I have thought on it."

"How did it happen? I mean, she is a duchess."

"And a very lovely person." Constance paused to collect her thoughts. "You could say she seduced me but only the first time. We were together many times after that." Constance sighed. "I came to love her deeply. And she loved me. I will miss her more than I can say. I had to tell someone, and you're the only person I could trust."

Madge took Constance's hand. "I feel honored." She uttered a sharp cry of pain. "Definitely a brawler." She smiled at Constance. "We are wonderfully good friends. I've not had such a one before." She patted her stomach. "I'd like you to be the godmother of my child."

Two nights later, she dreamed of the Duchess. Susanna was in bed, beckoning to Constance. The scene shifted; and Susanna, clothed in a riding habit, cantered down a country lane, away from Constance. She stopped, turned and signalled for Constance to follow. Now walking, Susanna continued along the lane as it passed through fields of barley and corn and then open meadows. In the distance was a wood partly hidden by fog. Susanna reached the wood and turned around again. Now attired in a funeral shroud, she spread her arms wide, then turned away and disappeared into the wood.

Constance woke with her body drenched in sweat and tears flowing like a fountain. The dream, or ones similar to it, recurred for months.

On a cold but bright, windy day in mid-February, it was almost possible to forget the plague. Leaving Will busy at his poetry, as he had been for the past couple of months, Constance went to the market. The wind rustled her skirt as she walked past the stalls in Grace Church Market. Pennants snapped briskly, and curlicues of smoke raced over the rooftops. The air in London seemed fresher and cleaner than it had in ages. She determined to take a walk in Moor Fields after dinner. Little chance of the contagion spreading in the open ground. She would have liked to take Madge; but her friend was staying close to home, venturing out only for food shopping. Mistress Fowler, the midwife, stopped by the house every day in case the birth began early. The last time Constance had visited, she had pressed two crowns into Madge's hand to help pay for the midwife. Madge had resisted; but Constance was adamant, and Madge finally accepted with gratitude.

"I wasn't sure we had enough for the midwife," said Madge, "so thank you, this will help. I am going to watch over this child like a hawk."

Will was writing furiously when she arrived home with her basket full. After dinner, he said that he had to take some air. His brain was becoming addled from being indoors so much. He said he would stroll in Moor Fields and then along the country lanes. The cool, fresh air would clear his brain, and he would meet few people so he had little fear of infection. Constance was tempted to suggest accompanying him but decided he needed to go by himself. She would stay home, read for a while, fix dinner and walk either in the afternoon or on the morrow. Will's papers were strewn over the table. When he left, he made no effort to straighten them up or put them in the box under the table.

She read Chaucer for an hour; but curiosity then got the better of her, and she went over to Will's table. One manuscript, entitled "Venus and Adonis", was stacked neatly and was, apparently, a long narrative poem. She read a few pages and then put it down. Other poems, which she saw were sonnets. were scattered about the table. She read a couple and thought: "Not bad but need work". She liked the idea of one in particular but felt it unusually clumsy. The first lines, especially, needed adjustments.

You an incomparable summer's day
But prettier and master of my fate.
The freezing rain shall have too large a say,
And summer gone before I do thee mate.

She thought long and hard before picking up a

pen; but when she did, the words flowed like a sparkling stream.

> Shall I compare thee to a summer's day?
> Thou art more lovely and more temperate.
> Rough winds do shake the darling buds of May,
> And summer's lease hath all too short a date.

This time she heard his footsteps but decided to remain right where she was. Will flung open the door, exclaiming: "I feel so much..." before seeing her and stopping. "I see you pay little heed to my warnings. You obviously cannot help yourself." Constance said nothing. She simply looked at him. He went slowly to the table. He looked at his poem and then the piece of paper that sat next to it. He picked it up and read her lines first to himself and then out loud. He thought for a couple of minutes.

"All right," he finally said. "From now on, we work together."

# Hard Work: 1593-1594

She doubted it was ever going to be easy collaborating with anyone, much less her strong-minded brother; but she had no idea how hard it would actually prove to be. They began immediately. Will said that he had liked her suggestion of writing poetry while the theaters were closed, had pretty much completed one long poem—at which, Constance admitted to having read a few pages and Will saying: "I should have known"—and had written down some notes for a second one that he tentatively planned on calling: "The Rape of Lucrece". Since he already had a publisher for "Venus and Adonis", he saw no reason for them to work together on it; but when the time came, he would like her to help him with the second one. Constance readily agreed and thought they were off to a good start although she wondered at the title and inquired about Lucrece.

"The wife of a Roman nobleman who is raped by the son of the reigning monarch, the foul deed producing tragic, but also momentous, consequences for the state."

Will then mentioned that he had begun a sequence of sonnets, one of which—and here he laughed although Constance could not be sure if it was a good-humored laugh—she had so graciously amended, thus leading to the current state of affairs.

"I never imagined a helpmeet, much less a woman and even less my own sister; but it is clear that you have a felicity with words. Only time will tell if that ability will translate into working constructively with me, a recognized master, on poems and plays."

"I will do my best, dear brother, and will always look to you for instruction and guidance."

"That goes without saying."

"But I just said it," said Constance and laughed. Will did not laugh. "Sorry, I thought it was a good joke."

"I shall teach you to distinguish between good jokes and country humor."

Handing her a thin sheaf of papers containing the first of the sonnets, Will told her to start their work together by making suggestions for improving the poems but to be sure to maintain the rhyme scheme and the meter. He also told her that it would advance her progress if she read works by other contemporary—if inferior to himself—poets and playwrights. He suggested that, for plays, she read Thomas Kyd's *The Spanish Tragedy* and Christopher Marlowe's *Tamburlaine the Great*, copies of both of which he gave her.

"You are familiar with *Richard the Third* so you can compare my work... our work... to theirs."

Constance could not tell if his smile contained a degree of sarcasm.

For poetry, he recommended Edmund Spenser's fairly recently printed Books I to III of *The Faerie Queene*, of which he would procure a copy, and further stated that nothing could teach her the secrets of poetry better than *The Canterbury Tales*.

"I have read some of that work. It is magnificent and funny."

"How did you procure a copy and why have I not seen you read it?"

"I saved a penny here and a penny there from the coins you gave me and purchased a copy. I planned on telling you once I had finished. I had hoped you would be proud of me."

She deemed it wise not to mention the Duchess since it would only serve to confirm Will's notion about the relationship. This was not a topic she wanted to talk about with anyone except Madge.

"I am."

"I have also read the first two books of *The Faerie Queene*. Father had a copy. I would have read the third except that your letter interrupted my progress."

"You shall have your very own copy so that you can re-read it at your leisure, what little leisure you will have in the future."

HIs smile now seemed not sarcastic but portentous.

She read through the sonnets and was surprised to find them apparently addressed to a young man and containing a suggestion—and on occasion, more than a suggestion—of romantic longing and sexual desire. She wondered if her brother might be as uncertain about his preferences as she was and, if so, whether it coursed through the Shakespeare family veins. She, of course, refrained from raising the topic with Will but decided to seek Madge's opinion at the first opportunity.

She wrote down her ideas for changes and used a numbering scheme to indicate where in his text she meant them to go. He accepted some without demur, even praising several enthusiastically; but others he rejected as preposterous. He got quite angry when she wanted to change the opening lines of one sonnet that, in his version, read:

> A woman's face with Nature's own hand painted
> Hast thou, the master-mistress of my passion;
> A woman's gentle heart, but not acquainted
> With shifting change, as is false women's fashion;

She especially disliked the words: "false women's fashion" and recalled Susanna having said on several occasions how narrow-minded and contrary quite a few men were about women. "They lack respect for our abilities, which lack in nothing compared to theirs." It was at moments like these that she intensely missed her lover. She had simply wanted the lines to read:

> Nature has designed a woman's face

To reflect the varied hues of passion;
Her giving heart and limbs carved with grace
Belie the foolery of courtly fashion.

He said that she had completely missed his meaning and that, furthermore, her last line contained one syllable too many and that if she couldn't do better than this—at which, he slapped the paper on the table—maybe he should think again about their writing together. At which, she stormed out of the room and strode furiously from Fish Lane to Grace Church Street and back before returning to the lodgings. She apologized for leaving and said she would re-work her lines but that his were insulting to women. He replied to let the not-so-sleeping dogs lie for the time being and that there would be time aplenty to take a fresh look at both versions.

"A little temper will only serve to add spice to the work," he said. "Perhaps there is a Shakespeare temper. Father certainly has one."

At which, they both laughed; and Will said he had a play he wanted her to read. It was something of a farce, which he thought would be an excellent first piece when the theaters, as sometime they must, reopened. Its title was *Two Sets of Twins Lost at Sea and Found on Land*, which Constance changed, after one reading, to *The Comedy of Errors*.

He greatly liked her new title and felt the play was ready to be performed either when the theaters re-opened or in a private setting. He then gave her what he characterized as an early draft of a play he was thinking of calling: *The Taming of the Shrew.* Constance became so engrossed in *The Taming of the Shrew* that she completely forgot about the sonnet lines to which she had so vociferously objected and which forever remained as Will had originally written them. Will, meanwhile continued work on "The Rape of Lucrece", which he planned to give her for possible edits once he had a reasonably satisfactory draft.

She had last seen Madge early in February; and she planned on sharing the exciting news on her next visit, which occurred ten days after she and Will had started working together. She especially wanted to ask Madge's advice about *The Taming of the Shrew*, a play she found funny in places but difficult to accept in terms of its characterization of women and descriptions of how they should be treated. When Madge opened the door, Constance gasped. In a mere three weeks' time, Madge's abdomen had swelled to the size of several balloons—the leather balls that men used in a rough game of tossing, batting and kicking.

"I know," said Madge as she waddled to her seat by the fireplace where, when she wasn't doing her work, she now spent all of her time. "I've got a baby giant inside me. I can hardly imagine what it's going to be like when this creature decides to come out and greet the world."

"I'm worried."

"Don't be. Mistress Fowler is excellent and very experienced. She has delivered hundreds of babies. And remember, it's not my first time."

"Make sure someone fetches me when your labor begins. I want to be here to, if nothing else, hold your hand."

"I will."

"I have news."

"You have another female lover?'

Constance laughed. When she told her friend the real news, it looked as if Madge, had she been able to, would have leapt from her chair.

"So he didn't threaten to thrash you this time? Or send you to a nunnery?"

"He was calm. He read my lines to himself and then out loud. Then ... well, I told you what he said."

"When do you start?"

"We already have. I've worked on sonnets and two plays."

"Tell me all about it. Don't leave out a thing. This will be the most exciting thing that's happened to me since the baby last kicked."

"He has written quite a few sonnets and intends on a long cycle. They can be difficult. Some I understand, others, no matter how often I read them, I cannot grasp his meaning. My brother has a complex mind. He uses a lot of what he calls metaphors where, as he explained, one thing stands in the place of another to give more meaning and interest to the line. Do you see what I'm saying?"

"If I understood a word of what you just said, do you think I'd be married to a waterman?"

"A lot of plain, ordinary folk go to his plays and seem to follow them," said Constance. "You and I saw them at *Richard the Third*."

"How difficult is it to understand: 'A horse, a horse! My kingdom for a horse?' I mean you're the king, you're in a fierce battle, you're about to have a sword sever your gullet—or, ha ha, stuck up your ass—if you don't find a horse mighty quick so you can gallop the hell out of there. I understood all that perfectly. Now the sonnets sound like a different matter altogether."

Madge groaned and shifted in her chair. She asked Constance to bring her a glass of ale. Constance found the flagon in the cupboard where Madge kept bread, cheese and fruit. On an upper shelf were pewter tankards and other utensils. She filled a tankard and carried it to Madge, walking carefully so as not to spill any. She went back for a tankard for herself. They raised their glasses and drank deeply.

"Ale is good for the monster inside me," said Madge, "Maybe that's what has caused him, or her, to grow so much. I always gave my children a glass at dinner and supper." A sob escaped her lips, and a few tears formed in her eyes. Constance moved her chair and grasped Madge's hand. "I've thought of them often lately," said Madge. "I hope this one lives to a ripe old age."

"If good food and physic can serve their purpose, by God, this one shall."

"You have forgotten the plague."

"Damn the plague," said Constance. "You and

the baby will stay inside until it passes. I will bring you food and drink. It will be fine. I take stern precautions these days."

"I fear the plague respects not the most earnest of precautions."

Deciding that a change of subject was needed, Constance told Madge about the furious argument she and Will had over the lines in a sonnet. When she finished, Madge burst out laughing and said that Constance had only herself to blame for getting entwined in this spider's web.

"That," said Constance, "would be a metaphor."

She told Madge that the sonnets she had read so far were addressed to a man and, in her view, had romantic and, possibly, sexual undertones.

"You're worried that your brother might be like you?" Madge asked, unable to conceal a touch of sarcasm. "Two sodomites in one family? What a scandal!"

"Stop it."

"I'm only jesting with you—in private."

"I'm concerned for his safety."

"And you weren't for your own?"

"The Duchess and I were very careful."

"So long as brother Will keeps his longings on paper; and they are as difficult to follow as you say, he will be safe."

"And if he doesn't?"

"You may have to start writing plays on your own."

"Bite your tongue," said Constance.

She then told Madge about *The Comedy of Errors*, which she considered a frivolous play, but one that would draw plenty of laughs from the ruder sort when it was finally performed. "And maybe the quality as well," she added.

"Laughter will be welcome," said Madge, "once this plague has departed—if it ever does—without striking dead the whole world."

"God would not let that happen."

"You have," said Madge, "more confidence in the Almighty than I do right now. If He loved us so, why would He send the plague in the first place?"

"If I knew the answer to that question, they'd make me the Archbishop of Canterbury."

When the two women stopped laughing, Constance took up the topic she most wanted to discuss: *The Taming of the Shrew*.

"I freely admit there are some funny moments; but, overall, it gives a harsh view of women and how they should be treated. It is, in places, cruel and demeaning to women. I have some ideas for softening it but am not sure my brother will listen. He seems quite opinionated when it comes to women. I realize that we are not the equals of men, but we still need to be treated with respect. I would very much like your advice on this. I fear spoiling our working together before it has gone very far."

"Maybe someday we will be the equals of men but not in our lifetimes. I don't think you can ask for that. At the same time, I would talk to him about your ideas.

Otherwise, you're not a true partner. Insist on some but not all of them. Choose the most important on which to stand your ground. And remember: Will is a grown man. You don't have to pamper him."

"You are as wise as anyone I've ever met—except maybe Susanna."

When, that evening, she raised with Will her feelings about *Shrew*, he responded, not angrily as she had feared, but in a polite yet rather condescending fashion.

"You have much to learn about the theater and composing plays. I have no doubt, however, that under my guidance, you will in time become quite adept. You have native ability, but it requires channeling and maturing before it will bear fruit."

"Thank you, dear brother; but you did not address my apprehensions regarding *The Taming of the Shrew.*"

Will gave her a look that, he hoped, would suggest she remember who was captain of the ship. Delving deeper into condescension, he said: "The play is a paradox: on the one hand, a farce with broad humor, on the other, a mockery using sharp wit and satire. Much depends, as in any play, on direction and acting. A skilled actor, like myself, can enhance and deepen the meaning of a play with only a gesture or the cadence of a speech or the way a single word is pronounced. A lout, on the other hand, can turn a tragedy into a comedy and a comedy into a tragedy. I am attempting, in this play, to condemn, through humor, the abuse of one's wife while, at the same time, showing that wives need to honor, love and obey their husbands. Katharina, the former shrew, describes, at the end of the play, not only her obligations as a wife but also the duties of a husband, one of which is to protect her even at peril to himself. She does this with dignity and feeling because she has fallen in love with Petruchio. She is happy now but, even while obedient, maintains her own sense of worth and is perhaps not as "tamed" as might be assumed. When, after her speech showing obedience, Petruchio says: "...kiss me, Kate", the actor playing Katharina may demur or simply blow a kiss and then dance away. As I said, the play is a farce but also much, much more. I believe it to be my most intricate work yet. Not easy roles for the principal actors."

Constance gaped at Will, her mouth half open.

"If you have other suggestions regarding the play, I would be happy to consider them.

"I'm not sure that I do."

"It is time that we tried working on one play at the same time."

"That will be interesting... and most instructive."

Will laughed.

"Now you're starting to understand."

Some few days later, on the First of March, late in the morning, someone in the street called in a loud and excited voice for Mistress Shakespeare. Constance and Will had spent the past couple of days discussing a new play that Will had been thinking about for over a year although he had not gotten around to putting quill to paper. It dealt with two young lovers from rival families: the Capulets and Montagues in the Italian city of Verona. The basic story had been treated in English some thirty years earlier, but Will had ideas to far surpass anything previously written on the subject. He also thought it could likely be his best and most popular play to date, surpassing even *Richard III* and *The Taming of the Shrew*, the latter of which had not yet been performed due to the plague outbreak. Constance was equally excited about the new play that they had been calling *Romeo and Juliet*, although they had discussed and were considering other titles such as *Two Young Lovers and Their Untimely Demise*, which Will seemed to favor. They had begun work that very morning and had written the Prologue and a few lines in the first scene when they were interrupted by the cries from the street.

Having a good idea what was afoot, Constance jumped up and ran downstairs. A young boy in tattered clothes and a wool cap stood in the street, looking up at Will's front window. Seeing Constance, he removed his cap and made a slight bow.

"Are you Mistress... Shakespeare?" he asked, unsure of himself.

"I am".

Scratching his head then and searching his memory for what he was instructed to say, he blurted out: "You are summoned... I mean... they want you to come... right away."

"Who wants me to come?"

"My neighbor... the waterman's wife. She's... she's... having...."

"A baby?"

"Yes."

Constance gave the boy a penny and said she'd be along in a few minutes. She rushed upstairs and—gathering her cloak, a loaf of bread and a large hunk of cheese—told Will she'd be back as soon as the baby was born and Madge was all right.

"Can she not manage with the midwife?" asked Will. "We were accomplishing so much."

"Can you not manage with your pen?"

"This was good practice for you."

"Madge is my only friend in London. I'm going."

"Have it your way. I'll rework some passages in *The Two Gentlemen of Verona*. It is largely completed. I must say I prefer working on Romeo. We are working well together."

Constance colored with pride.

"We'll resume soon enough," she said, putting on her cloak and hurrying out of the room. The boy had waited for her possibly, she thought, in gratitude for the penny—something he rarely received. As they hurried along, it began to rain and soon the back lanes were coated with mud. She opened her cloak and pulled the boy inside, but he was already wet and dampened her dress. "What if he's infected?" she thought but continued along, only faster. As they neared Madge's house, she heard screams. The rain eased, and she let the boy out from under her cloak. Madge's husband, Peter, answered the door. His face was white as a linen sheet.

"She's having much more trouble than with the others," he said. "This one must be big as a horse."

Constance moved past Peter, who retired down the hall to a back room. Madge was seated near the fire, in a large wooden chair with cushions and with her feet resting on a small chest. A pillow had been placed behind her neck so that she could partly recline her head. Next to the chair stood a large tub of warm water and a table with a pile of clean linens, several folded towels, a pair of scissors that had been washed (but not sterilized as that process was not yet known), a ball of thread and a candle. Mistress Fowler stood at one side of the chair and held Madge's hand. She was telling Madge that it would soon be over but that she needed to push harder and more constantly.

"I'm trying my best," gasped Madge.

Constance moved in front of the chair and, seeing her, Madge smiled weakly. "Hello, my dear," said Constance, placing her cloak on another chair along with the bread and cheese. "Brought you a small present," she said, nodding at the food.

"I'm bringing the world a huge present. I'm not sure the world—or me—is ready for it."

"I'm quite positive that both are although you might not realize it at this particular moment."

Constance moved to the opposite side of the chair from the midwife and, taking Madge's other hand, said: "Now, do what our friend here tells you to do."

Madge nodded and then felt a major contraction,

causing her to scream loud enough to wake the deceased.

"Scream as loud as you wish," said Mistress Fowler, "so long as you keep pushing. I want this baby, huge as it is, out and at its mother's breast in time for me to be home having a hot supper with my husband and my unmarried sister who has lived with us these many years."

"You cannot leave me," said Madge, a note of panic in her voice.

"Just a joke, my dear. I'll be here all night if need be. A cold ham, carrots, pears and apples from last night's supper will suffice for my husband and sister than whom a worse cook would be hard to find. Not that she doesn't try for which my dear husband, being more gracious than myself, showers compliments on her that the foolish woman takes to heart. Isn't life fun?"

"Perhaps," said Constance, "along with your midwifery, you should begin writing books of enlightenment for the general public."

"I would, Mistress Shakespeare, if only I knew how to write."

Madge screamed again. Mistress Fowler dampened a cloth and wiped Madge's forehead and cheeks.

"It won't be long now," said the midwife. "Didn't you say you had birthed one, or was it two, of your infants with no help whatsoever?"

"Just one and not an experience I care to repeat. Unlike my mother, I am not some tenant farmer's wife dropping children hither and thither in the fields or vegetable garden."

"That you are not," said Constance, giving Madge a little kiss on the cheek.

Contrary to the midwife's optimistic prediction, two hours passed; and while the time between contractions shortened, no baby deigned to appear. In order to pass the time and stay calm, the three women conversed about a multiplicity of things ranging from the best herbs for rubbing into the cavity of a goose prior to roasting to why husbands can be such dolts to how lucky they were to live in the greatest time in history in the greatest city in the greatest country on earth recognizing, however, that they were not familiar with all the possible options. Madge wanted to ask Constance how the work with Will was progressing but felt it might embarrass her with the midwife present. Their conversation was frequently punctuated with groans and screams from Madge and Mistress Fowler's instructions and encouragement. Once, Peter took a few steps into the room, smiled at his wife and said that he had prayed fervently for hers and the baby's health. Then he abruptly left. Suddenly, Madge cried hoarsely: "It's coming."

The midwife quickly moved to a position in front of Madge. She gently lifted Madge's feet off the chest and placed them on the floor. She sat on the chest, lifted Madge's skirt to above her knees and placed her hands at the sides of Madge's vaginal opening.

"Push really hard."

Madge groaned and pushed. Constance

squeezed her hand as if it were a rubber ball. Madge breathed rapidly.

"Out you come, you giant," said Mistress Fowler.

Constance looked down and saw the baby's head and the midwife gently pulling its body out of the birth canal. The midwife cut the umbilical cord and tied it off with a piece of string. Suddenly, Madge cried out: "I feel something else."

"Take the baby," the midwife said sharply to Constance. "Wash it in the tub. Gently."

Constance took the baby and moved to the tub. Mistress Fowler put her hands back alongside Madge's vaginal opening and said in a loud, but calm voice: "Twins" as she delivered a second baby boy. In a loud voice, she called for Peter to come change the water in the tub. When both babies had been washed in clean water and wrapped in linen and wool cloths, they were handed to a weak, but smiling, Madge who cradled one in each arm.

Constance left soon thereafter, telling Madge that she would visit every day and that Madge could count on her to do the cleaning, the wash and the food purchases.

"How can you manage all that?" asked Madge.

"How can you manage any of it with two lusty boys wailing for their mother's teats?"

"What about your own housekeeping and..." Madge hesitated as if searching for the correct word under the circumstances.

"And...?" asked Mistress Fowler, mildly curious.

"...and the new tasks that lazy brother of yours has come up with? Does he do anything but lie around and scribble all day?"

"Not much," said Constance, failing to suppress a laugh. "Do you have a name for even one of these two giants?"

"No but we will next time you visit. And now you're the Godmother of not one, but two children."

"God preserve me."

From March through May, they worked steadfastly on the play Constance insisted would resonate with potential audiences better as almost anything other than *Two Young Lovers and Their Untimely Demise*—the title that Will, but not Constance, had taken to using.

"It doesn't sound right," said Constance. "Awkward... clumsy. I'm unsure how to say it, but it bothers me."

"In that case, how about: *Two Star-Crossed Lovers and Their Dismal Fate*?

"You're borrowing from the Prologue."

"No harm in that."

"It sounds better—more intense, less awkward, but it still gives away too much."

"Then," said Will, with a touch of exasperation in his voice, "what do you want?"

"What we called it at the beginning and what I've been using all along: *Romeo and Juliet*."

"How will that attract an audience?"

"With *Richard the Third*, your reputation is growing and, in and of itself, will be sufficient to attract an audience."

"Would that were true."

"Have confidence," said Constance. "Furthermore, *Romeo and Juliet* is simple, direct and obviously about a couple and that will draw attention. Be sure the handbills show, in a subtle fashion, intimacy, daring and a suggestion of lust. The balcony scene should do nicely."

"Not all your victories will come so easily."

They most often worked together with Will generally, but not always, suggesting lines and Constance nodding in agreement or commenting if she didn't like a particular line or speech. When she thought something was brilliant, she didn't hesitate to tell him. She, likewise, was not loathe to offer alternatives. As she became more familiar with the fluid rhyme scheme and the iambic pentameter metrical structure, he asked her to come up with lines on her own while he concentrated on a different part of the scene. She quickly became adept both at understanding his intentions for characters and thinking up complex lines that moved the story forward and shed light on the character's inner workings as Will had conceived them. The next step was not far behind—where she developed her own interpretations of characters and revealed those in her lines. This caused disagreements—sometimes vociferous—between them. One sharp conflict occurred when Constance, bothered by a nagging thought regarding the first scene, had revisited the scene and raised her concern with Will.

"Romeo bemoans his unrequited love for Rosaline. One of his first lines, which you wrote, is: 'Sad hours seem long.' His cousin, Benvolio responds:

> Benvolio: What sadness lengthens Romeo's hours?
> Romeo: Not having that which, having, makes them short.

And a few lines further on, you have him say:

> Romeo: Out of her favor where I am in love.

All that is fine," continued Constance. "You show the desperation caused by his unrequited love for Rosaline. But that same evening, at the ball, he sees Juliet and forgets Rosaline. I would like to add lines that, in showing how quickly he makes the leap from Rosaline to Juliet, reveal something about his character. For example:

> Did my heart love till now? Forswear it, sight,
> For I ne'er saw true beauty till this night."

Will objected in the strongest terms. "You've made him into an overheated boy. That's not how I described him. Why, he's as fickle as an adolescent girl."

"So only girls are fickle?"

"That's not what..."

"He is fickle," said Constance. "He just flew from one blossom to the next like a honey bee."

"He stays constant to Juliet unto death."

"That means he's capable of change, not that he wasn't fickle the evening of the ball."

"He was overwhelmed..."

"With her youthful beauty. Dear God, how shallow! He hadn't yet said a word to her. For all he knew, she was visiting from France and spoke not a word of Italian."

"That is absurd."

"I imagine it has happened."

Will got up from the writing table where they both were sitting. He paced back and forth. Constance watched him closely, wondering if the joint effort was about to end. That, for her, would be a disaster but not as great a one as giving up her convictions merely on Will's insistence. She would need to be proved wrong through close and logical reasoning. Will paced silently for several more minutes. Then he went to the cupboard and took out the flagon of ale. He filled two glasses and gave her one.

"Drink up," he said, which they both did.

"You have not convinced me that my interpretation is wrong."

"Who is Master here?"

"Neither of us."

Will laughed.

"I wouldn't want to be your husband."

Constance said nothing. The work was too engrossing for her to think of marriage at this time as that would likely put an end to it. Perhaps for the same reason, Will did not further pursue the topic.

"Let's both think about this question and examine it further on the morrow. In the meantime, let's work on what Romeo and Juliet say to each other at this first meeting."

The next day, Will agreed to leave in her lines, seeing merit in having Romeo mature through his love for Juliet. He even further emphasized Romeo's fickle nature when, drunk with love having spent a sleepless night wooing Juliet, he asks Father Laurence to marry them without delay—in fact that very day. Will has the earnest priest express his shock at learning that Romeo now loves Juliet instead of Rosaline by saying:

> So soon forsaken? Young men's love, then, lies
> Not truly in their hearts but in their eyes.

After showing Constance those lines, Will chided her: "So, your victory is complete. Romeo is as fickle as any young girl. But do not let it swell your head. This won't be the last contest before our work with yon swain Romeo and his beloved Juliet is done."

During these three months, Constance kept her promise to Madge and faithfully did all the tasks she had committed to although after a month, Rafe and Ned would often sleep contentedly while the two women did the chores and then sat by the fire, sipping a drink and sharing the latest parish gossip. They tried to avoid talking about the plague, but it was nigh on impossible with carts piled with bodies rumbling through the city's streets on a daily basis. Madge knew people in the parish who had succumbed; and, several times, Will had brought home news from his occasional visits (when he could no longer stand being confined to the Fish Lane lodgings) to the actors' favorite tavern, The Golden Goose, that such and such an actor had either died or had decamped for greener pastures.

"Even with far less plague," said Madge, "the countryside is not necessarily safer. Look what happened to your ... your friend, the Duchess. It was a riding accident, but the result was the same."

A tear sprang to Constance's eye, and she turned her head away. Madge took her hand and said: "I'm sorry. That was not thoughtful. I can only imagine how much you've grieved. I need to be more considerate."

"No, you are sufficiently considerate and have been a true friend through thick and thin."

"Thank you, and I will do better."

"We can all do better."

After a brief moment of thoughtful silence, Constance said: "The streets, while not empty, are noticeably less crowded; and people go to obvious lengths to avoid close contact with each other."

"I'm still not taking any chances," said Madge, nodding at the twins who were peacefully sleeping in a crib near the fire. Neither she nor the twins had yet left the house. "If it weren't for you, I can't tell how I would manage. I worry about you being out so much."

"I'm very careful and have even taken to wearing a handkerchief over my mouth."

At that moment, as if they had identical internal clocks, Rafe and Ned both woke up and immediately started crying. Madge untied her bodice and, with Constance's help, made herself as comfortable as possible with a baby at each nipple. "If they keep suckling like this, there won't be a bed that will fit them."

"When I'm not here, how do you get them both attached at the same time?"

"Magic," she laughed. "No, it's tricky; but I settle one firmly and then, with my free hand, I manoeuver the other into position. So far, I have not dropped either one."

The twins suckled peacefully. Madge gazed into the fire, her cheeks glowing and her expression one of deep satisfaction. "Pretty picture if I were a painter," said Constance and then, glancing at Madge's milk-swollen breasts and not thinking, continued: "Beautiful teats."

"You stay away from my teats," said Madge, at which both women burst into gales of laughter. Rafe stopped sucking and looked briefly at his mother as if wondering what was so funny about his having a good meal and then put his mouth back on her nipple. "He'll be the curious one—maybe a man of science."

"Wouldn't that be a cause for celebration?"

"You have said nothing about your writing. How

goes it?"

"Not badly. Sometimes we write jointly, sometimes apart, although more often together. Will is learning to compromise. It's not easy for him, but he sees the value of my work and ideas—sometimes. We each have victories and losses; but in the end, I believe the plays will benefit from our working together."

"Will your brother ever publicly acknowledge your work?"

"I don't know, but I doubt it. He would say the world is not ready for a woman maker of plays and sonnets, even one who only assists a man."

"I wonder," said Madge, "if you are the first woman writer."

"Probably not. Susanna told me of an ancient Greek poetess named Sappho who is believed by some to have had women lovers. Her work is now known through quotations from other writers although Susanna had heard of a French edition of Greek poets which included fragments of her poems. Susanna had not been able to get a copy."

"Did Susanna know about your writing?"

"No. I had thought about mentioning my changes to *Richard the Third*—the only thing I had done at that time; but she left before I was ready. I don't know why I hesitated. Maybe because I hadn't done that much. She would have been proud of what I'm doing. I am so sorry she is not alive to see it. She used to say that our Divine Monarch, Elizabeth, proves that women can do anything we set our minds to."

"Can a woman be the Captain of a ship or Commander of an army in the field?"

"Of course not. Don't be foolish. She meant that a woman can be a ruler, a painter or a composer."

"Or a writer."

By the beginning of April, they were, in Will's view, almost through a first draft of "the star-crossed lovers" as he fondly called them. Will frequently, in Constance's opinion, displayed a caustic sense of humor that she found out of sorts with the material they were laboring over. Will pressed her to develop her wit.

"Otherwise, your writing, be it comedy or tragedy, will be dry as a dead man's bones and about as interesting."

She tried, not very successfully at first, because to her way of thinking, *Romeo and Juliet* was a serious play composed of reckless actions and heartrending consequences. She came to understand, however, that humor and wit were necessary to relieve the tension of a tragedy and to highlight, by contrast, the doom inherent in the main action of the play. She thus learned to appreciate the ribald jests that Will sprinkled like stardust in various parts of the script. At the same time, she considered the fundamental story to be as sad as anything she could imagine. She wished she could think of a happy ending but agreed with Will's concept of the lovers' end: that it was inevitable and that no happier concept fit his relentless logic.

She, nonetheless, felt that, in at least one particular instance, Will's wit was out of place considering the circumstances. Romeo's friend, Mercutio, has just been stabbed by the Capulet Tybalt, a bitter enemy of the Montagues and thus by extension of Mercutio. Because of his love for Juliet, a Capulet, Romeo had tried to prevent the fight in the first place by standing between Mercutio and Tybalt. This inadvertently causes Mercutio's fatal wound since Tybalt stabs him under Romeo's arm. Dying, the witty Mercutio jests when asked by Romeo how serious is his wound:

'Tis not so deep as a well, nor so wide as a church door, but 'tis enough; 't will serve. Ask for me tomorrow, and you will find me a grave man;

Constance challenged her brother's view of how a dying man would react in this context.

"Why would he not," she insisted, "cry out in anger at his fate?"

"Although you've made a good start, you have much to learn about both life and plays."

"Enlighten me, please, oh omniscient playwright."

"Sarcasm will not serve you in either love or writing."

"What the devil has love to do with this?"

"I mention them together," said Will with a smile whose charm was one of his most endearing qualities, "as love and writing are the two most important aspects of life."

"I am only interested in the latter."

"That was not always the case."

"I have no notion of what you mean."

"As you wish," he said. He looked at her in a curious fashion. "But as I said before when this topic arose, I am no fool. The Duke of Bastrow is not known for giving such fine opportunities to newly-minted playwrights. Your secret, for both our sakes, is quite safe with me." Constance stared at him. He tapped the manuscript with his forefinger. "Shall we proceed?"

"Please but first let me say that neither am I a fool. Your secret is equally safe with me."

Will nodded.

"We understand each other."

"We do," she said. "Now I better understand your feelings about Anne."

"I enjoy seeing her—infrequently."

"Does she have any idea?"

"I certainly hope not." Will smiled. "Work beckons."

"Indeed."

"To begin: neither a play nor a poem are intended to mirror life. They heighten and intensify life and can, thus, take certain liberties. Next, Mercutio does express anger as well as wit. Are you forgetting these lines, which are almost the last he manages to utter?

> A plague o' both your houses!
> They have made worms' meat of me;

"Do you not find anger aplenty there?" asked Will.

"Yes."

"I think it quite likely for a dying man, especially one who has been attached to witticisms his entire life, to mix anger and wit in his final utterances."

"You win."

"And finally," said Will, "I still know more about this business than you do."

"Tell that to Richard the Third."

They worked on the final scenes in a white heat, each contributing lines and even words to match the other's thoughts. Then they began revisions. By the end of May, they had completed two drafts of the play; and Will told Constance that she had contributed much to the work. At which, her cheeks turned red with pride and pleasure.

"It lacks only a final polishing," said Will, "and that can be easily done. When the theaters reopen, soon God willing, it will enhance both my fame and our fortunes."

Choosing prudence in a battle she could not win, Constance simply replied: "That will be excellent."

A few days later, Constance went to Leadenhall and found Master Thursby's stall empty and the table barren of any meat. Fearing the worst, she turned to the neighboring butcher, to whom she had said "Good morning" on occasion, and remarked that Master Thursby was not at his place as was his daily custom except Sundays.

"Have he and his family gone to the country?" she asked, hoping against hope.

"Aye, he's gone somewhere but not the country. Master Thursby bargained hard; but he was a decent man and never cheated a customer, not like some here in the market, so I hope his soul's in heaven rather than anyplace else."

Through her sobs, she asked: "The plague?"

"What else takes a man in a couple of days?"

"His family?"

"Closed up in the house. Myself and the other butchers leave victuals by the front door every morning."

Constance took a gold sovereign from her pocket and handed it to the man.

"From the Shakespeares in their time of need."

"Very kind of you, Miss."

"Now, what are you charging for that loin of pork?"

In early June, it seemed to Constance that the number of carts bearing bodies was increasing, thereby confirming the general knowledge that, for the plague, the summer months were by far the worst. It had not rained for several days; and while the dry, warm weather hardened the mud in the streets, the city stank worse than ever of urine, feces, offal and other forms of refuse. Even with a handkerchief covering her nose and mouth, Constance was reluctant to venture out except to go to market or to Madge's. Once, however, she went to Moor

Fields for fresh air and a country walk. Flowers bloomed along the lanes, and the leaves were thick on the spreading trees. The outing refreshed her spirits, and she returned to Fish Lane eager to resume work on the new play she and Will had begun: *A Midsummer Night's Dream*. It was a light-hearted, comic fantasy which greatly appealed after the darkness that swallowed up "the star-crossed lovers". Were it not for the work, life would now be tedious indeed for she could only spend so much time at Madge's. The work, however, was absorbing; and when not writing, she eagerly read the plays Will had given her in order to increase her understanding of dramatic techniques.

She was, therefore, thunderstruck when, arriving home from the market one day, Will announced that they were going to Stratford for the summer months. He had just learned of the death of another prominent actor, albeit in a different company, the Earl of Waverly's Men.

"I thought we could stay behind when my company left for touring, but I am now even more concerned. Father has already written begging us to come to Stratford for the summer."

"You didn't tell me that."

"I didn't want to upset you."

"Given our work as equals..."

"Hardly equals."

Speaking deliberately, Constance said: "Almost as equals..."

Will laughed.

"...don't you think," she resumed, "...that I should

have a say in this decision."

"No."

"And why the devil not?"

"You are a..."

"...a what?" she interrupted.

"A younger sibling."

It was Constance's turn to laugh.

"Regardless, I cannot go."

"I beg your pardon."

"Beg it all you wish but I'm not going. Madge is my best... no, my only... friend here, and she cannot manage without my help. I promise to stay indoors as much as possible."

Will began pacing, which he often did when he was stuck on a line or a rhyme would not appear as they generally did as if by magic. Constance watched him, knowing that he needed to think. He rubbed his hands over the fire, which burned low at this time of year, despite the room's being almost too warm. He resumed pacing. After a minute or two, he stopped in front of the chair where she was calmly sitting.

"It would not be safe for you to stay in the lodgings without me."

"Because your expert swordsmanship keeps me safe from robbers, murderers and rapists?"

"I said to develop your wit in your writing, not in debating with me."

"I will ask if I can lodge at Madge's. They could use the few shillings we can afford to pay."

Will pointed to the two large boxes on the floor

underneath the writing table.

"Do you want someone to steal these?"

"I will take them with me."

"You are the most stubborn Shakespeare of them all." He paced again and stopped again in front of her chair. "All right, if you can stay at Madge's."

"And what of the work on *A Midsummer Night's Dream*?"

"I will work on it at Stratford."

"And what do I do in the meantime?"

"I am tempted to say, 'nothing'; but you can try your hand at poetry. See what you can make of a sonnet. You can also have a look at 'The Rape of Lucrece', of which I now have a draft that wants only the polishing and trimming at which you are becoming increasingly skilled. Little though I care to admit it, I occasionally—very occasionally—allow my romance with words and the sword-play betwixt them to confound the clarity and discipline of my writing. You could also cast a sharp eye over my latest sonnets, which you will surely misinterpret." Will laughed heartily and remarked that, of course, he was only jesting. She replied that she wished for a shilling for every one of his jests as she could then buy herself a string of pearls. "Nicely parried," he stated before returning to the original topic. "That should keep you busy along with helping with those monsters, Rafe and Ned. It is only for the summer."

Madge was overjoyed and had Peter fix up a corner of the front room with a trundle bed, a chest for Constance's things, and several hooks in the wall. In the middle of the room stood a rectangular table, where they took their meals, and five chairs. Constance could work at this table. Part of this large front room served as the kitchen, and large cupboards—filled with utensils, plates and bowls—stood on either side of the fireplace. The door of one of the cupboards had a painted tableau, of which Madge's father, Hugh, was quite proud; it showed Peter and three other disciples standing before Christ, who was the tallest of them. They were in an orchard surrounded by a wall; fields bordering a river and filled with grazing cows and sheep extended towards distant hills. Villages and solitary farms stood astride a country lane that followed the river in the direction of a body of water on which sailed a number of single-masted ships. A fourth disciple, apparently Judas, stood outside the orchard, his head hanging down and a leather purse hanging from his belt. He was smaller than the other figures.

Two large chests, which had once been in the corner where Peter placed Constance's bed, now were in the opposite corner and parallel to the table. The house was somewhat larger than Will's lodgings; but the chimney didn't work as well, and the air had an acrid, smoky scent, which Constance actually found pleasant except that it sometimes irritated her throat. Madge and Peter along with the twins slept upstairs while Hugh slept in a tiny room in the back of the house.

Constance was ready to move two days later. She packed her things into one of Will's larger chests and the satchel she had brought from Stratford. Will hired a cart to transport her chest, the boxes with the manuscripts and a few of the more valuable household items, also packed in a chest. He had paid the landlord three months' rent; and in turn, the landlord agreed to close up the lodgings and keep a close eye on the place. Will kissed Constance good-bye and said he'd be off within the hour. Leaving Fish Lane, she asked the driver to stop for a moment. She told Davy, who was at his usual spot smoking his usual pipe, where she could be found and to watch out for strangers entering the building. Davy said he knew a couple of rough fellows who could handle any strangers leaving the building with more than they had possessed on entering. She gave him a shilling. He said he would enjoy a better class of tobacco for a while.

"I won't be gone long," she said, "and I'll stop by now and then to see you."

After getting settled, Constance went to the market. Madge nursed the twins and gossiped with her as she prepared supper, which she had ready for the table exactly when Hugh and Peter arrived home, hungry as oxen and thirsty as camels. Learning the previous day that Constance would be staying with them for the summer, both men had expressed their delight at the news. This evening, Peter told Constance that they would all benefit from having an additional participant around the table at dinner time.

"Our conversation can grow dull, and you will certainly enhance it to a great degree."

"Thank you, Peter," said Constance.

"There are only so many stories Hugh and I can tell about the passengers we take across the river."

Hugh was particularly effusive, following Peter's compliment by saying that a woman of Constance's beauty and refinement could only add luster to the household. Constance dropped a short curtsy, which caused general mirth, and said that the refinement was all Hugh's.

"Father," said Madge, with a pleased grin, "you either stopped at a tavern on the way home or you've been reading poetry behind our backs. Which is it?"

"Neither. Cannot a sturdy man, even of my years, compliment a lovely young woman without being accused of being a drunkard or a reader of poetry?"

"Certainly you can," said Constance, "and I much appreciate the compliment. It lifts my spirits, in these harrowing times, to be so warmly welcomed."

"Furthermore, would Peter and I still be thirsty had we indulged ourselves at a tavern?"

"Father, dear, when it comes to ale, your capacity for thirst is unlimited."

"Can we not eat?" interjected Peter, "before we all starve."

This resulted in further laughter and the serving of dinner, which consisted of a cut of roast oxen, turbot poached in ale, cabbage stuffed with diced onions, garlic and seasoned mutton and a fruit tart that Constance had purchased as a special treat at a shop in Cheapside. Both men said the dishes were all beyond compare as they drank enough ale to prove Madge's point. The conversation revolved around the incursion that coaches were making in their trade.

"Why anyone," said Hugh, "would prefer traveling around London's rough streets in a coach to the comforts and convenience of a wherry is beyond me."

"It is the fashion among the quality," said Peter.

"It's hurting our business," said Hugh, "and it will only get worse. Consider the result if they put up more bridges."

"In your opinion, then," said Constance, "not every new-fangled bauble is a good thing."

"You hit the nail on its head. You're as clever as you are comely. A formidable combination." He took a long swig and wiped his lips with the back of his hand.

After supper, Madge cleaned up while the men drank more ale and smoked their pipes by the low fire and Constance dangled on a string in front of first Rafe and then Ned the toy figure that Peter had carved for them. Each twin gurgled with delight and reached for the toy when it was in front of him but whimpered when it was taken away.

"You'll need to carve another one," Constance said to Peter, "so that each will have his own."

"We'll have a lot of that sort of behaviour before they're grown," said Peter with a laugh. "And possibly even afterwards."

Bone tired all of them, they retired early. Hugh was a little unsteady on his feet as he started down the hallway. Peter took his arm to help, but Hugh brushed him aside. "Do ye think I'm a child?" he asked angrily, his speech slurred. He stumbled once but otherwise made it safely to his bed. Madge and Peter glanced at each other but said nothing and, bidding Constance a good night, carried the twins up the stairs.

The fire was out but the room still quite warm so that Constance fell quickly asleep. She had no idea how long she'd been asleep—but later estimated a couple of hours—when she was suddenly awakened by being roughly shaken. Then a calloused, scaly hand covered her mouth; and she heard—so close to her face that his breath, stinking of onions, garlic and ale made her gag—a rasping man's voice whisper: "Don't ye utter a sound or ye'll regret it." With his free hand, Hugh lifted the blanket off the bed and let it fall to the floor. For an instant, Constance was frozen in terror. Taking his other hand from her mouth, Hugh pushed her night dress up to her waist and hurriedly took off his drawers. Whether it was his odor or the sight of his stringy thighs (as a waterman's arms did the work), Constance unfroze. As he started climbing onto her, she snapped: "You filthy drunk" and, with all her strength, slammed her hands into his chest and heaved him off the bed. Hugh's head and back hit the floor with a thud. He whimpered in pain. Constance got out of bed and kicked him in the side.

"Get out of here," she said, accentuating each word.

Hugh staggered to his feet and stared at her. Then he tottered to the hall where he turned and hissed: "I'll be back." Clutching his side, he made his way towards his room.

Constance replaced the blanket on the bed but did not lie down. Fearing that Hugh might carry out his threat, she sat on the bed and watched the hall. If he came back fully sober, she might not be able to fight him off. And then, there was tomorrow and the day after and the day after that and on and on until Will returned. Sooner or later, he would succeed. Fighting her increasingly powerful need for sleep, she forced her mind to concentrate. She had both to think and keep an eye on the hall. What choices did she have? Will had convinced her that she would not be safe alone in the Fish Lane lodgings even with Davy on the lookout. If she went to Stratford, she might never return to London. Her father might well marry her off faster than she could snap her fingers, which she did to show herself. Even Will might not be able to talk him out of it. Just as her work was beginning to show promise, all her hopes could be dashed forever. She felt sick at the prospect. She could bear almost anything but that. And as important as her other considerations, Madge needed her help.

"Madge," she said to herself. "Of course. Madge would think of something."

She would've liked to talk to Madge right away but that would possibly result in waking Peter. She sat on the bed, anxious and impatient and fighting to stay awake. Finally, sleep won the battle and she literally fell over onto the bed. She covered herself with the blanket, and the next thing she knew it was morning. At breakfast, Hugh looked at her in a funny way but said nothing. After he and Peter had left for work, she asked Madge to sit with her for a moment. She worried that Madge might not believe that her father was a monster or if she did, she might be devastated. As it turned out, Madge not only believed Constance but was more angry than devastated.

"Men," she snorted. "Even the old ones. Maybe they're the worst. Thank God for my Peter. Not the smartest, maybe, but gentle as a lamb and as faithful a man as you could find in all London. I'll take care of this, but first I have to tell Peter what I'm about. I'll take him aside before supper. Pretend nothing has happened and be sure you stay up until my damned father has gone to bed. Then come up to my room and climb into bed with Peter."

Constance looked shocked.

"Don't worry," Madge continued, "Peter won't lay a hand on you. I'll get into your bed and give my father a surprise and a talking to that he won't soon forget. He considers himself a religious man; but fortunately for my idea, he is also superstitious and no better versed in formal religion than I am."

"Was the fault mine?" asked Constance in a wretched voice. "Was there something I did to lure him, even unintentionally, to my bed?"

"The old goat is to blame, not you. Be absolutely clear in your mind on that."

After a quiet supper, with Hugh leering occasionally at Constance and drinking less than the night before, and a short spell by the dying fire, Peter said he was ready for bed.

"You men go ahead," said Madge. "I want to talk briefly with Constance."

Hugh kindly offered to carry one of the twins upstairs. Coming back down, he said: "Good night. Sleep well" to the women, glanced again at Constance and walked down the hall. The two women conversed a few minutes in quiet voices and then Madge said: "Time." Constance climbed the stairs, and Madge slipped into the downstairs bed.

Madge had to struggle to stay awake; but fortunately, barely an hour had passed before she heard light steps in the hallway. Her body tensed as the steps drew near. She closed her eyes and fought to keep her breathing steady so as to mimic sleeping. The steps halted, the blanket was pulled away and she groaned as if waking up. At the same moment, her father started climbing on top of her without looking at her face. She opened her eyes and cried out: "Father!"—loud enough to startle and frighten him but not loud enough, she believed, to awaken the rest of the household. Hugh scrambled off the bed and stared at his daughter with a mixture of bewilderment, dismay and anger.

"What the devil are you doing here?" he snapped.

"I could ask you the same question, but I already know the answer."

Hugh raised a hand and leaned towards Madge who, quick as a cat, jumped out of the bed on the side opposite her father. Snarling like an enraged dog attacking a chained bear, Hugh moved towards the end of the bed with the clear intention of catching and beating Madge.

"Before you take another step and certainly before you strike me," said Madge, "consider your soul which is right now in the gravest danger."

Hugh stopped and said: "What shit are you talking?" but his voice was beginning to tremble and doubt creep into his expression.

Madge uttered a brief, but very harsh, laugh. "Shit is it? For what you attempted last night and were hoping to accomplish tonight, you could burn in hellfire for all eternity."

"Hellfire?"

"Yes, Father, eternal hellfire." Her voice was firm and confident, as if she were speaking for the Deity. "You dishonored our house where you should offer comfort and hospitality, not rape. You are most fortunate that Constance was able to throw you out of the bed. Otherwise..."

Hugh interrupted: "But she wanted..."

"Father," said Madge, now in a stern voice. "Do not add lying to your other sins." Hugh said nothing, and she allowed her voice to resume its measured tone. "Yes, you tried to rape my dear friend. Had I not awoken in time, you would have committed incest by raping your daughter—both sins being heinous and deserving of the most fearful retribution. Need I remind you that incest, in God's eyes, is damnably close to bestiality. Which of these horrific sins do you think would earn you, on your death, a passage to Hades, there to burn in liquid fire for the rest of time?"

"Which one?" asked Hugh, his voice now quivering with fear.

"Both of them, Father."

Hugh moaned and seemed to shrink before Madge's very eyes.

"What can I do?" he asked plaintively.

"You must pray to God to forgive you. Whether He, in His ultimate wisdom, will choose to absolve you may take some time to discover. Possibly only on your death so you must promise to never again commit such damnable acts and keep this promise until you depart this world and meet your Maker."

"I will do that. Anything further?" asked Hugh, his voice now quaking and his knees trembling. He was not certain he could remain standing so intense was his fear.

"Yes, you must, on your knees, confess to Constance that you have been exceedingly wicked and that you hope she can find it in her heart to forgive you and that she will consent to continue residing under our roof so long as her brother is away. You will further promise never to molest her in any way and will ensure her safety and comfort should she decide to remain here."

"I will be humiliated."

"Your choice: humiliation or hellfire. I know what I would choose."

"Must I do this in front of you and Peter?"

"No, tomorrow morning, Peter and I will stay upstairs while you speak with Constance."

"Thank you."

"Now let us have some rest."

Hugh walked slowly down the hall. Madge went upstairs, woke up Constance without waking Peter and the twins and the two went downstairs.

"Will you forgive him and will you stay?"

"I will forgive him, but I will never forget," said Constance, "and yes, I will stay. You are my friend for life." Constance was silent for a minute and then sobbed as tears sprang from her eyes. "Curious thing," she said. "Will wanted me here so that I would be safe."

"You will be safe from now on," said Madge. "If he ever does that again, or even looks at you crosswise, I will slit his throat."

Six weeks passed while Constance read admiringly through the sonnets Will had given her, finding little to change except a line or a word here and there. It took a full three of those weeks, however, for her to work up the courage to pick up "The Rape of Lucrece", a narrative poem that she already knew dealt with the horror of rape and its aftermath. When she finally did, she realized, to her dismay, that no matter how elegant and drawn out were the descriptions in the poem, rape—or near rape as in her case—was always brutal and terrifying; and she could not stop her breath from coming faster and tears from rolling down her cheeks. She wondered whether Will fully grasped the dichotomy of putting Lucrece's emotional devastation from the rape on the same plane as a theft of Lucrece's husband's property. Constance had no wish to contest a husband's dominance in his home; but that didn't mean classifying a wife as equivalent to inanimate goods. She was confident that Susanna would agree with her. Perhaps, in all fairness, Will was portraying, in a critical fashion, the position of women in the England of their day and saying that it needed to change. Without revealing why, she intended to broach the subject on his return—at the same time as she gave him her suggested changes, which were not that many as the poem was exceptionally well-written. Lucrece's suicide, which occurred in history as well as the poem, shocked Constance to her core. While unsure that suicide was inevitable for Lucrece, she understood the desperate woman's feelings of guilt and the horror at the shame brought on her husband's house. She wondered how Will, or her Father, would react were they ever to find out about Hugh's attempting to rape her. She vowed to herself that they never would–at least, not from her lips.

Her thoughts drifted to the passionate, willing and eager love making that she had experienced with Susanna and, to a lesser extent given the brevity of their time together, with Edmund. She would have loved to show Will's poem to Susanna, the impossibility of which brought a lump to her throat. She would never again, in this life, see the Duchess. She wondered if the same could be said of Edmund. Will had told her to try her hand at poetry, and these musings led her to start writing "The Duchess." Will had meant sonnets, but so be it.

A longer poem better fit her mood right now. She decided to try the rhyme scheme, complex as it was, that Will had used in Lucrece.

> Fairest of all in England yet conceived,
> Her beauty matched by purity of thought,
> My heart torn asunder and much bereaved
> When like a bounding doe by hunters caught,
> Her soul thus by Death's scythe so cruelly bought.
> Ne'er will be forgotten her milk-white breast
> By a lover whose name shall not be guessed.

By mid-August, she had finished the poem, twenty-six pages in all, using throughout the same rhyme scheme and including details that she knew about Susanna's life and thought but disguising both in name and context and not mentioning Susanna's passion for women. Considering the poem to be a work of fiction, she made up particulars when she exhausted her knowledge of Susanna's life. In truth, she had no idea whether Susanna rode to the hounds; composed dances, marches and fantasies for the virginal and lute; owned an almost completely nude portrait of herself done by a student of Titian (which was kept in a secret room off her bed chamber and viewed only by her husband and lover) and, unbeknownst to the world at large, was a key political advisor to the Duke, who held an important position in the realm. The Duke knew of and accepted that she had a lover since she was more than discreet and since he himself had a mistress of long standing. When, however, she read the poem to Madge, her friend said simply: "Burn it!"

"Burn it?"

"It is really quite good. You have a gift and need to use it; but if the truth ever came to light about this, your Duchess's reputation—in the grave, though she may be—would be destroyed. As for you, I shudder to think on the consequences. Hanging until death would be the best you could hope for."

"But I've left the Duchess unnamed. I could give her a false identity. I do not say whether her lover is a man or a woman. People will suppose a man, wouldn't they? After all, I don't go into details."

"How long would you last in the Tower in the Rack or the Iron Boot or with your thumbs in the Thumbscrew before you told everything?"

"I'll keep it anonymous."

"That's not likely to be possible if you try to have it published, especially since you're a woman."

"I doubt that's possible for a woman."

"What then do you intend doing with it? Hide it? Take it out every year or so and read it to yourself or to me?"

"I hadn't considered it."

"Were my father to come across it, he would be delighted to take it to the authorities. You've surely observed that, while polite, he's not precisely friendly towards you."

"Only to be expected."

"When you return to Will's, what would you do

with it? He's guessed about your connection with the Duchess. Who can tell how he would react if he found it? Better to confine your writing to working with him. If you must write on you own, be sure it's something he'd be happy to claim authorship of."

Constance nodded in agreement but felt a biting sadness well up in her.

"Read it to me once more," said Madge, "before we burn it."

One morning in late September, there was a knock on the door. Madge was nursing so Constance went to the door. She opened it, and there stood Will, a broad smile on his face.

"Will," she cried and flung herself into his arms.

While Constance got her things together, Will tickled Rafe and Ned, causing each of them to giggle and wave their arms. Will thanked Madge for her generous hospitality, chatted about his stay in Stratford and gave her a large ham. Constance said she would resume her regular visits to help out, and she and Will headed home. It took her two days to clean the lodgings of the dust and grime that had accumulated over the past four months.

When, a couple of days later, after she had given him her "Rape of Lucrece" edits, she asked Will whether he intended the poem as a critique of a woman's place in English society, his answer was noncommittal. He acknowledged that some changes were called for in that regard but that women would always be subordinate to men. His real purpose was to show how evil, vicious acts by those in power could lead to upheavals in a country's social and political system. In some cases, as with Rome at that time, the changes could be beneficial; but, in his opinion, they were harmful more often than not. He hoped he had satisfied her curiosity. Constance let the matter drop.

Their first task together was to go over *A Midsummer Night's Dream*, which Will had largely finished in Stratford. Constance thought it a wonderful play and one that, along with *The Taming of the Shrew* and *Romeo and Juliet*, would put Will at the forefront of London playwrights.

"Us at the forefront," said Will, graciously. "Now is not the time but who knows: maybe—just maybe—at some future time, your contribution can be publicly recognized."

"Do you mean when I have turned to dust or some grave robber finds my skull and says: 'This looks to be the remnant of a veritable poetess and playwright?"

"If I could predict the future, I'd stop writing plays and do nothing but buy property."

"You could no more stop writing than a drunk can stop drinking, a knight stop jousting, an accountant stop counting, a banker stop lending, a jester stop prattling, a robber stop thieving, an owl stop hooting, a rooster stop crowing, a lecher stop...."

"Enough," cried Will. "I surrender."

For the balance of the year and through the winter, they worked on a number of plays, including *Love's Labour's Lost* and *King John*. Constance wrote sonnets on her own which Will said were so like his in style and spirit that, with minor changes to fit the sequence, he added them to his own pieces. When not writing, they talked about writing: the theory and nature of drama and poetry. Will did most of the talking while Constance absorbed every word, but she chimed in when she had a point to make. He had her read selections from Holinshed's *Chronicles*, which she found fascinating, to better prepare her for the work on the history plays, which were not only the rage but, with his plays, increasingly close to home. One of his aims, Will told her, was to demonstrate how the Tudors had restored England to peace, prosperity and stable government.

"And perhaps," teased Constance, "to get more invitations to play at court."

"To have multiple goals," said Will, refusing to take the bait, "can only serve to enrich life."

Gradually, deaths from the plague diminished until, by and large, the disease had spent its fury, at least for now. In the spring of 1594, the theaters reopened.

# By A Hair: 1596-1597

Constance had been right: *Taming of the Shrew, Romeo and Juliet* and *A Midsummer Night's Dream* had caused Will's star to rise, which resulted not only in considerable prestige but also in a dizzying increase in their income. In 1594, Will became a shareholder in another company's new incarnation, the Lord Chamberlain's Men, which would achieve fame and fortune as the company of Playwright William Shakespeare and Actor Richard Burbage. The company performed at The Theatre, north of the city walls, and, in 1596, produced work at The Swan on Bankside, south of the Thames. Outside London's boundaries, both theaters were thus unaffected by a prohibition against theaters operating within the city limits.

In November of 1595, Will stunned and thrilled Constance by assigning her a history play to write on her own: *Richard II*.

"You will have to use Holinshed as a main reference, but you should also look through my collection of books and pamphlets for further information. I would be most pleased if you could have a draft ready for me to peruse in, at most, a couple of months. If you run into problems, let me know."

Constance was too excited to speak.

"Cat steal your tongue? Not likely since we haven't got one—a cat, I mean. You most certainly have a tongue."

"I will start right away."

A month later, Will started a play the title of which, he told Constance, would be either *The Jew of Venice* or *The Merchant of Venice*. He was not sure which made made more sense. From the fever with which they were both writing, Will commented, early in the new year, that he wouldn't be surprised if they had drafts to exchange before winter departed and spring warmed their aching bones. Well before spring—at the end of February 1596, in fact—Will's prediction came true; and they exchanged drafts. Constance eagerly began reading *The Merchant of Venice* (Will having decided on the title), but she had not gone far before she began feeling uneasy about the play's tone, especially pertaining to the character of Shylock. She knew almost nothing about Jews—having, as far as she knew, never met or even seen one, a curious fact that puzzled her—but she wondered why anyone would regularly act in such a mean-spirited, greedy, vicious, vengeful and even, yes, violent a manner. When she finished reading, she felt like heaving the manuscript across the room—not caring whether or not it hit Will in the head—or, at the very least, tossing it into the crackling fire. Instead, she sat pensively at her table (Will having purchased one for her to work at over a year ago), keenly aware that Will was, as unobtrusively as possible, observing her. As unspoken tension mounted in the room, Constance felt a desperate need to get away. Taking her cloak off a peg, she told Will she needed fresh air and left. Will said not a word.

Her mind a blur, she walked to Leadenhall and then along Corn Hill towards Poultry and Cheapside. The air was smoky and raw, the cobblestones glistening from a morning drizzle. The dark-windowed houses stared at her like blank faces. Since the abatement of the plague well over a year ago, London's streets had again become crowded with people on foot, on horseback and in carriages, not to mention the carts loaded with goods moving at a snail's pace (not that she had ever seen a snail pace) and the sheep and divers other animals being escorted to their doom. Oblivious to the bustle around her, Constance could only despair at how her beloved and much-admired brother, notwithstanding their literary arguments, could create such a heinous character based solely—or so it seemed—on the fact that he practiced a different religion. She had no idea how to even begin thinking about this when she remembered the proprietor of a book shop where she had occasionally bought penny romances and other books. He was always friendly and seemed knowledgeable. She had to find out something about Jews, and he might be her only hope. His shop was just off Cheapside, not far away. Pulling her cloak tighter against the late winter damp and cold, she quickened her pace.

"I don't know much," said Master Huddleston, the

proprietor of the shop.

"Tell me whatever you know," said Constance.

She was sitting across from him at a narrow table piled with papers in a cramped space set among shelves crammed with books. A crude map of Europe hung on one of the few open walls. The proprietor was elderly, bald except for white tufts of hair stationed, like soldiers on guard duty, around the perimeter of his head. A curlicue of a hair extended from each of his nostrils. He wore a long gown; and a cap, long out of fashion, sat aslant on his head. He was smoking a pipe; and a not unpleasant, smoky odor permeated the shop.

"The Jews were expelled from England," said the proprietor, "over three hundred years ago, in 1290, by order of Edward the First. No Jews have lived in England since that time. Over the centuries, a few converts have resided in what's known as the House of Converts. A few foreign Christians of Jewish descent, such as Roderigo Lopez, have also been allowed to settle here. Occasionally a Jew has been given a special permit to visit England."

"Who is Roderigo Lopez?"

"Who was Roderigo Lopez?" Master Huddleston sighed. "A sad case.... a very sad case."

"Go on," said Constance, a touch impatiently.

"Lopez fled the Portuguese Inquisition—the filthy dogs—and arrived in England somewhere around 1559. Trained in medicine, he took up a practice here and, being well-skilled, rose to become chief physician to our Glorious Queen, may God grant her long life. Rumors circulated that he secretly practiced Judaism which, of course, is against the law. He also made an enemy of the Earl of Essex, not someone you want as your enemy, by, it has been said, revealing that the esteemed Earl had the pox, if you know what I mean."

"I do," said Constance. "It is a disease one catches from too free a life."

"Precisely. Not to make too long a tale of it, the Earl got his revenge: implicating the Doctor in a plot to poison the Queen. I'm told that, while Lopez did have secret contacts with Spanish officials, the evidence of a plot was not only inconclusive but was obtained from Lopez's supposed associates either through torture or the threat thereof. Lopez was hung, drawn and quartered about..." The proprietor thought for a minute. "...about a year and a half ago."

"It appears that you don't believe he was guilty."

"I don't honestly know; but I am no great believer in torture, especially when used to extract, like a rotten touth, a confession. Faced with the rack, men ... and women ... will confess to killing mothers or dear friends, who happen to have just brought them food to the Tower."

"Is it true that Jews are greedy money-lenders and routinely practice usury to the ruination of honest Christians?"

"Who told you that?" angrily hissed Master Huddleston.

"I'd rather not say."

"Is that playwright brother of yours writing

something about Jews?"

"Perhaps you would just answer my question, Master Huddleston."

"I see," said the proprietor, with a knowing smile. "I will answer your question if you'll first answer one of mine."

"I hope I can."

"How is it that you know what your brother is writing?"

"You are perceptive, Master Huddleston."

"That's not an answer to my question."

"Will occasionally—very occasionally—mentions the subject of a new work. I was curious so came to you as the only scholarly gentleman of my acquaintance." Master Huddleston beamed with pride. "Please not a word to anyone. Who can tell when, or if, it will be produced?"

"Silent as the tomb."

Constance cast a quick glance around the shop and thought: "Yes, an appropriate simile."

"And now for my question, Master Huddleston?"

"Yes, the Jews lend money at interest; but when most other means of caring for one's family are denied to a man, he does what he must. Were I to lend a fellow yeoman my team of oxen, I would expect to get paid for it. If I rent you a house, I would expect to get paid for it. Pounds, shillings and pence are the plow and house of the Jew; and he has the right to be paid for its use. Now, surely some Jews over-charge as some landlords do, but I imagine that sometimes Jews suffer losses from ill-advised loans just as some tenants flee the city without paying their last month's rent. And just for the record, although you haven't asked, the stories about ritual murder and the use of the blood of innocent babes to make their unleavened wafers come from the diseased, addled brains of village idiots and, I'm ashamed to say, educated people whom one would like to think knew better."

Constance pushed a shilling across the table; Master Huddleston shook his head and pushed it back. Thanking him profusely, Constance rose and departed, leaving the shilling where it rested. Master Huddleston watched her and smiled. It was rare—exceedingly rare—that a beautiful young woman not only entered his shop but engaged him in conversation for the better part of an hour. And left a shilling to boot. His wife, may she rest in peace, had once been, if not as beautiful as Mistress Shakespeare, surely on the comely side and eager in certain matters. He had missed her terribly these past eight years. His children and grandchildren seemed to have forgotten his existence. He picked up the coin, studied it and smiled again.

On her way home, Constance stopped at the Bell, ordered a cider and asked the barmaid, with whom she was on a friendly basis, for paper, a pen and ink. Sipping her drink, she wrote furiously. She then hurried back to Fish Lane and, bursting into the room, said to Will, who looked up in surprise from whatever he was working on: "You have to change *The Merchant of Venice*."

"Do I now? In what way, pray tell?"

"You've made Shylock into a despicable character."

"That's what most people believe about Jews."

"Are you in the habit of concerning yourself with what most people believe?"

"I am in the habit of writing successful plays."

"I thought we were in the habit of making people think and of looking at life from new perspectives."

"What is so damnably wrong with Shylock? I am rather intrigued by the fellow."

"Dear God, where do I start?"

"Wherever you like but why don't you first sit down. In fact, why don't you also get us each some liquid refreshment and fix up a plate of cheese and bread. It looks like we might be at this for a while."

Constance scowled at Will but did what he asked. She hung up her cloak, poured the drinks and placed a slab of hard cheese and a round loaf of white bread on a platter along with two sharp knives.

"Let's be careful with those knives," laughed Will, "and confine ourselves to slicing bread and cheese, not each other's throats."

Angry as she was, Constance could not help but laugh. Will's humor always disarmed her.

Sitting next to him at his writing table, she began.

"You have Shylock lending money at high rates of interest."

"Which is what Jews do."

"And the Christian merchants in Venice hate him

for it, but nowhere do you mention or indicate that the Christians recognize that it's one of the few ways he's allowed to make a living and support his family. Nor that he must charge high interest to cover loans that the Christians either conveniently forget to or cannot repay. Besides, if a Christian merchant uses Shylock's money to his profit, wouldn't he be taking advantage of Shylock if he didn't pay interest?"

"Did you think of this all by yourself?"

"Are you suggesting that I cannot think?"

"I know all too well that you can. I will consider your point. Go on."

"You have Shylock virtually ignore his wife in his mad pursuit of money."

"I've killed her off. Shylock makes a wonderfully sentimental widow."

"What about his son who, if allowed by the authorities, would like to be a doctor. Shylock scorns his ambition and says sarcastically that if he wants to be a successful doctor, he'll need Christian patients as well as Jewish and for that he'll need to be better than all the Christian doctors in Venice. Shylock cares little, it seems, for the happiness of his family."

"Not a bad point so I'll take the son out as well. Voila, gone with the stroke of a pen. Not a mention of the bugger."

"Do you consider me," she said, barely restraining a laugh, "just another one of your tavern companions?"

"Come, come, my dear sister, you've long since

ceased being an innocent babe in the woods."

Constance guffawed and nodded her agreement.

"Great thing," said Will, "about this business: I... we... have the power of life and death over our characters although they don't always realize it—not in time anyway."

Constance stood up and walked around. She arched her back to get rid of a cramp. She cut herself a large piece of cheese and took a deep draught of ale.

"What I object to most," she said, wiping her lips with the back of her hand, "is all the cruelty and murdering. Shylock makes a loan to a foppish, heavy-drinking Venetian wencher and, knowing the man will not repay the loan on time, takes as security the poor fool's hand. The Venetian authorities who would normally favor the Christian but instead—lacking in funds and fearing the loss of the lucrative taxes they extract from the Jewish community—decide to enforce Shylock's claim. That is beyond cruel."

"Would a pound of flesh please you better?"

"No," she hollered. She gulped down more ale. "Then, Shylock makes a loan to a solid Venetian merchant and takes a share of his estate as security. When the loan comes due, Shylock claims, successfully, his future interest in the man's estate and, soon thereafter, arranges an untimely—or shall I say timely—end to the poor fellow. The authorities barely investigate the murder, particularly as Shylock arranges, in this case free of interest, certain well-placed loans."

"I intended," said Will, chewing on a hunk of

cheese, "that there be a humorous side to these peculiar events."

"Do you also think it humorous that, when his daughter runs off to marry a Christian, he arranges to have both the daughter and her husband murdered? That makes three murders and a mutilation in the course of a few scenes."

"Christopher Marlowe has far more murders and mayhem in *The Jew of Malta*."

"We are not competing with Christopher Marlowe who has been dead for almost three years."

"Oh, but we are."

"Be that as it may," she said angrily. "just because his Jew is worse than yours is no excuse."

"I'm describing the world as I see it, not as I might like it to be."

"So you have nothing against Jews?"

"Not that I can think of."

"You could have fooled me."

"The Christians do not exactly exude the milk of human kindness in their dealings with Shylock. They mock him; they curse him; they bite their thumb at him; they spit on the ground in front of him. They never address him by his name but simply as: 'Jew'. As if all that were not enough, they call him, a highly religious man, a godless worshiper of mammon—not that he doesn't love his gold. So you cannot say I haven't been equally hard on the Christians."

"No, I cannot."

"How would you like me to portray Shylock?"

"Less violent," said Constance. "More loving and tolerant towards his daughter. Tough in his business dealings but not criminal. Angry at his treatment but more moderate in his revenge." She handed him the lines she had written at the Bell. Will read out loud but in a barely audible voice.

> I am a Jew. Hath not a Jew eyes? Hath not a Jew hands, organs, dimensions, senses, affections, passions—fed with the same food, hurt with the same weapons, subject to the same diseases, healed by the same means, warmed and cooled by the same winter and summer as a Christian is? If you prick us do we not bleed? If you tickle us do we not laugh? If you poison us do we not die, and if you wrong us shall we not revenge? If we are like you in the rest, we will resemble you in that. If a Jew wrong a Christian, what is his humility? Revenge! If a Christian wrong a Jew, what should his sufferance be by Christian example? Why, revenge! The villainy you teach me I well execute, and it shall go hard but I will better the instruction.

Will stopped. He stared at the paper and then glanced at Constance. He looked back at the paper. He placed it carefully on his table. Nervous as a filly, Constance watched him closely.

"You keep getting better," said Will. "This is magnificent. And how would you have me handle the Christians?"

"More sides to their characters. Not all so spiteful. More differences among them."

"I will consider your views. I will make some changes... some. I can assure you, however, that having done so, this play will close after two performances and will never be seen again." Will laughed, as heartily as Constance had ever heard him. "What the devil. We can't make money on all of them. And we won't be able to use the lovely placard I had in mind: a disheveled and coarsely-dressed old man holding a knife to a beautiful young woman's throat. Such a shame!" Will laughed again and set Constance to wondering exactly how many changes he intended to make. To satisfy her curiosity, it transpired, she would have to wait for the opening.

"In the meantime," said Will, "I've read your draft of *Richard II*. It is promising but needs work." He handed her a piece of paper, closely written on both sides. "Here are some general remarks. I will go over the play with you in greater detail tomorrow." He got up and stretched out his arms. He scratched his head. "Not lice, I hope," he said casually, laughing as Constance recoiled. He patted his stomach. "I'm weak from hunger," he said. "Hadn't you better get supper started?"

Will's finances, by this time, had so improved that, early in the spring of 1596, he gave up the inadequate lodgings on Fish Lane and moved to the parish of St. Helen's, Bishopsgate which in distance was not so far from Fish Lane but, in the quality of his residence, was worlds away. He rented a brick house, not so terribly large but elegant in its furnishings and with, of all things, two fireplaces: one in the parlor and the second in the kitchen.

The move was easy as neither Will nor Constance had a superfluity of possessions, the most abundant of which were books and clothes. Both brother and sister were omnivorous readers (and Constance's choices had, under Will's tutelage, become more discriminatory), and both loved luxurious and stylish apparel. Will hired two large carts whose drivers loaded all the goods and started the slow-moving oxen down Fish Lane. Constance bid a sad farewell to Davy who said he would sorely miss her cheerful smile and beautiful eyes. A tear formed in one of them, but she forced herself to smile and said she would visit. Both knew that was unlikely. Will shook Davy's hand, and then he and Constance fell in behind the carts as they rumbled out of Fish Lane and headed north towards Grace Church Street and thence to Bishopsgate.

Keeping house would no longer be Constance's responsibility for Will had engaged two servants although Constance periodically planned to do the food shopping (with a servant carrying the baskets) if only to keep the servant honest.

Constance had, over the past couple of years, taken to attending the theater on a regular basis. She was a sufficiently familiar presence that Will no longer was fearful if she went alone; but when Madge could get her neighbor, for two pence each, to watch Rafe and Ned along with her own children, she was delighted to accompany Constance. Though not well-versed in either classical or contemporary literature, Madge nevertheless had a keen mind and, more often than not, understood both the thematic material and the intricate language of the plays. She didn't hesitate to voice her opinion even when she knew that Constance had worked on a play. She found, for example, *A Midsummer Night's Dream*, delightful but, in contrast, *Love's Labour's Lost* much harder to become enthusiastic about although, she admitted, one could hardly tell based on the audience's reactions.

"Maybe," Madge said, "it's because of all the beer the apprentices in the pit have consumed during the performance."

"Thank you ever so much," said Constance, giving Madge a gentle push.

"If you are going to be a power—even if unrecognized—in the English theater, you have to accept criticism."

"No, I don't." Constance laughed and put an arm around her friend's shoulder. "All right, yes I do. And who better than you and my dear brother to offer it up?"

Will often delighted the two women by taking them to supper after a performance.

Constance saw a variety of plays, not simply the ones that she and Will had written. She believed, and Will agreed, that it was a vital part of her training to see plays of all types and caliber: both good ones and not-so-good ones and some incredibly awful ones. She loved the theater. Sometimes she took one of the seats, and other times she stood in the pit. She wanted to hear comments from all levels of playgoers: from the wealthy sophisticates in the seats to the rowdy apprentices in the pit.

On a warm, bright, glorious day in early June, the kind of day that made Constance think not much could be wrong in the world, she stood by herself in the pit as the crowd dispersed after a performance of *The Merchant of Venice*. She was shocked to hear an apprentice with a scraggly beard, wearing a greasy doublet and a filthy cap, saying to another apprentice: "Damned Jew was lucky to lose only half his fortune and not his wretched life."

"Too, too right, my old friend Bark," said Bite, the second apprentice. "That's what we do to Jews in this Christian country."

"But there are no Jews in England or hardly any that I'm aware of," said Bark.

"Well," said Bite, "that's what we would do if there were any."

"You know," said Bark, "what I didn't like about the play was no murders. What's a good play without at least a half dozen murders?"

Constance moved away in disgust. She refused to believe that these two fools represented the general opinion concerning the play and remained content that Will had made a good many, even if not all, of her changes. Deep in thought, she didn't notice a tall man moving through the crowd in her direction. So many people were milling about that she didn't realize that he had stopped in front of her until he spoke in a quizzical tone: "Mistress Constance Shakespeare?"

She looked up into a handsome face and deep blue eyes that seemed to smile down at her.

"Excuse me, Sir," she said, "do I..." Then, she saw the cane and remembered. "The letter from Will."

"Indeed." He touched the brim of his hat. "What did you think of the play?"

"I... I... have very little experience with...."

"...with plays?" he interposed.

"With plays... or Jewish characters."

"Your brother has a great talent."

"He has and I did like the play; but to tell the truth, I wish he had shown that Shylock had no intention of claiming the pound of flesh. Perhaps, I am an innocent, but who could be so cruel?"

"I think, since the Lopez case, it is not so easy to show Jews in a good light in England."

"More's the pity, Mister...?"

"I apologize for my rudeness." He gave a slight bow. "John Maydestone...." He paused. "Barrister."

"I am pleased to make your acquaintance four years later, Master Maydestone. You did me a good turn."

"I could not be more pleased. May I do another and invite you to a modest refreshment? Unless you are waiting for someone."

"My brother will have little trouble finding the way

home on his own."

"Excellent. I know an inn just over the river that has an exceptionally good claret or, if you prefer, a white Burgundy that some of my... some of my friends say is more than worthwhile."

"Do you mean some of your lady friends?"

"I have a passing acquaintance with one or two members of your sex," he said with an abashed expression that made him, in her eyes, even more appealing.

"And you are, apparently, a disciple of red wine."

"I would not put it in quite such a religious context."

"But there are those in our fair city who do," said Constance with a gleam in her eye.

"You have a way with words," said John, "and a sharp wit. Perhaps you get it from your brother."

"Or perhaps he gets it from me."

"I am going to enjoy my claret even more than usual."

"Let me just tell Will," she said, "that I have a protector."

"Let's hope that won't be necessary. I don't wear a sword as, with my cane, it would not be a practical matter."

Constance was gone only a few minutes.

"Will bids us a pleasant walk and glass of wine. He is sorry not to have seen you in quite a while and hopes to rectify the lapse before long."

Constance took John's arm as they strolled through Finsbury Fields. They passed four men practicing archery. "Not nearly as many as there used to be," said John. "If the Spanish invade us, who can tell what will be the result?" Many young couples were out walking. Other folk out for sport rode prancing horses; a number of women used side saddles while a few rode pillion—in a seat behind their male companion. The horses were as elegantly appareled as their riders. As they neared Moor Fields, they approached a small crowd of people standing in a circle. They stopped at the far edge of the circle—curious to see what had attracted the onlookers. In the center of the circle, a sturdy man was leading a sleek bear through a series of tricks at which the crowd laughed and applauded. The bear stood on its hind legs and waved its front limbs. The creature rolled over a couple of times and then, on all fours, growled at the crowd which quickly moved back.

"Have no fear, gentlemen and gentlewomen," called out the keeper, "for Grace is a kind soul and only wishes to be sure you are awake."

At which, general laughter rippled through the crowd as it surged forward, calling for more tricks. The keeper signalled to another man in the circle who took up his sackbut and began playing a popular galliard. The bear danced a few steps, causing great hilarity as the galliard is a complex dance; and poor Grace looked to be a fat, clumsy, elderly woman. Meanwhile, a young lad circulated among the spectators, holding out a pointed hat. John threw in a sixpence, and they moved on.

"How amusing," said Constance, "and such a beautiful day."

As they walked under one of the three rounded arches of Bishopsgate, Constance glanced up at the massive, crenellated structure with its twin towers. Whenever she passed through the imposing gate, she felt keenly the change from idyllic country lanes to packed London streets with so many of the houses cheek by jowl to their neighbors. They wove among the crowd on Bishopsgate Street, still arm in arm, and turned into Threadneedle Street. Some yards further on, an old man with matted hair and a scraggly, full beard lay in tattered clothes on a pallet covered only with straw. Most passers-by gave him a wide berth; a few tossed a coin that landed on the pallet or, occasionally, in the street. Bright-eyed, probably from fever, the old man scooped up the coins with a hand that more resembled a claw and tucked the coins somewhere in his putrid rags.

"It so distresses me," said Constance, "to see such poor, desperate souls lying in the muddy street on little more than straw and a few sticks of wood. I often give them food or a few pence. I will do so now."

She withdrew a purse from her sleeve, took out two groats and handed them to the old man.

"Thank ye and God protect ye," said the old man.

"You are a kind-hearted person," said John.

"If all were kind-hearted, perhaps there wouldn't be poor folk sleeping in the street."

"Let us hope for such a bright future." John gave her arm a slight squeeze. "There are places that will take them in. I sometimes wonder if they prefer their freedom."

"Perhaps you should try it sometime and make an informed decision."

"I shall have to be very careful in talking with you."

"One should always be careful," said Constance, "in what one says... or does."

A little further on, they came across a stout woman sitting at a table, telling fortunes with cards. A white wimple covered her head and fell to her shoulders while rings glittered on her fingers and strands of multi-colored beads hung round her neck and lay on her ample breasts—exposed just enough to encourage the men. A small crowd had gathered in front of the table, watching expectantly as she turned over the cards and spoke in a low voice to the man having his fortune told.

"Would you like to know your future?" John asked Constance.

"No. If it's good, I'll be doubtful. If it's bad, I'll do little else but wait for it to happen. How about you?"

"I have an idea what mine will involve."

They turned off Threadneedle onto Barley Lane, a street unfamiliar to Constance. Shops and small wattle and daub houses lined both sides of the street. Smoke curled up from several chimneys. At the end of the lane, next to a full-leaved holly tree, they came to The Gilded Lady, a stucco and timber inn. They sat in the hall which, on this bright afternoon, was well-lit from numerous windows. Fully half or more of the tables were occupied—some by couples, others by small groups of men who were obviously well-to-do merchants or professionals. At one table sat three fashionably dressed young women, talking and laughing loudly over their glasses of wine. The dark walls were hung with leather panels embossed with intricate patterns and curlicue designs as well as three large tapestries: one showing lords and ladies riding through a wood, another a hunting scene with the dogs bringing down a terrified stag and, at the far end of the hall, a tall tapestry with an elegant lady standing by a fountain. Pearls adorn her V-cut bodice and gold thread gleams on flowers and plants scattered throughout the dress. In one hand, she holds a book. A small dog rests peacefully at her feet. Birds fill the air and, in the near distance, a manor house is surrounded by fields and formal gardens. In the far distance is a walled town; a procession leaves the town by one of several barred gates. A man on a horse rides towards the town from the manor.

"The inn is named for the tapestry of that beautiful lady," explained John, "although I understand there is a double reference."

"Which is?"

"Rooms are available for gentlemen and their...."

"Strumpets?"

"No, their beloveds. No one is for hire. The lovers simply lack other accommodations."

"I see. Such a nice way of phrasing it."

"If you object," said John, "we can go elsewhere."

"I do not object," she said. "I know something of

life."

"Excellent," said John, "as their wines are the best and this hall, in my opinion, quite beautifully embellished although I know little of such matters. The rooms are more often used by out-of-town travelers than for the other purpose."

They both ordered claret, Constance telling John that she did not frequently drink wine and red even less so but she would follow his recommendation. John also ordered two types of French cheese, a loaf of fine, white bread and sliced pears. The Inn's supply of cheeses, he told Constance, was only surpassed by its wines. After tasting the claret, Constance agreed that it was quite good, although it might take some getting used to.

"How well do you know my brother?" Constance asked, glancing at the doorway as a boisterous couple, laughing and hugging, entered the hall.

"People here generally behave in a more seemly fashion," said John. "I imagine the inn keeper will have a word with them. If they are not careful, they will be shown the door and not allowed back."

He put a sliver of cheese on a slice of bread and handed it to Constance. She averred that it was as good a cheese as she had ever tasted, including from some of the well-provisioned Cheapside shops. She cut a ripe pear into quarters and ate one, savoring the pulp and juice as they slid down her throat.

"I don't know your brother that well. I've been, on a few occasions, in the delightful company of Will and some other playwrights, including Christopher Marlowe, and more frequently that poet or playwright... cannot remember which... or maybe both... and cannot for the life of me recall his name. I usually have an excellent memory." John engaged in an inner struggle to force his brain to dredge up the name. "Got it," he exclaimed happily. "Simpcox.... Simpcox.... Montjoy.... Simpcox Montjoy and he was a poet. Said one time that he wanted to try writing a play. Will and Marlowe burst into laughter. I thought they would have fits they laughed so hard. Poor Simpcox was not happy. But that was all some time ago as Marlowe has been gone these...." John paused to think.

"Three years."

"You would keep up with these matters, wouldn't you?"

"If Will didn't know you that well, why did he entrust you with the letter?"

"Several of us were in a tavern, having a tankard; and I mentioned that I had business to attend to in Worcester. Will asked if I would pass through Stratford as he wanted a confidential letter delivered. I said that I certainly could, and the next day he came to my house and gave me the letter."

"How did you find me?"

"We lawyers have our ways."

"I am glad that you do." She ate some more cheese and half a pear. "I'm surprised that you recognized me. It's been... four years."

"Being in a theater made it easier, and you have a face that is hard to forget."

"I only recognized you because of the cane. Are you in the habit of keeping your face half-hidden?"

"Only when delivering confidential letters to beautiful women."

A week later, having sent a note by messenger and received one in return, John came to Will's house to take Constance on a promenade and a boat ride on the Thames. The note had troubled Will—concerned, as always, about the tempo of their work. Constance had insisted that she could promenade with John and still get the amount of writing done that she had planned for that day. Little assuaged, Will, nonetheless, had conceded that Constance deserved not only occasional recreation but also the company of a man besides himself.

Will greeted John cordially and asked how matters stood in the law courts.

"Busy as ever," answered John.

"Idle hands are the devil's tools," said Will.

"I believe," said John, "that the Bible says 'devil's workshop'".

"A writer's license."

"I'm told of writers," said John, "who are quite licensed or, perhaps, licentious would be the term of choice."

"You are licensed before the courts," replied Will with a grin, "which I'm told can be a license for larceny."

"Litany would be more apt given the soporific nature of most trials."

"Do you sleep, then, through such weighty disputations or perhaps you dream while still awake?"

"Words, words and more words," said Constance. "You, Brother Will, and you, Friend John, are both masters of them; but they will avail you naught unless you can put meat on the bones."

"Why, Constance," said John, "you should be a writer."

"I am glad," said Will, hurriedly, "that Constance can enjoy the company of an honest gentleman. She spends too much of her time managing my household and reading literary works." Will turned to Constance and gave her a smile and a nod as if to say: "Aren't I the ingenious teller of tales?" Constance dropped the hint of a curtsy and bowed her head.

"She's mocking us," said Will. "Watch out for that."

"Forewarned is forearmed," said John with a chuckle. "And what are you working on now: a comedy or a tragedy?"

"Neither for the moment. I'm continuing my series of plays dealing with English history: Henry the Fourth this time. I'm showing, as one theme, how lucky we are to live at this moment in time: under the wise and temperate rule of our gracious monarch. The Tudors, particularly Elizabeth, have given England peace and prosperity when compared to the wars that preceded them."

"An interesting thesis," said John. "Do you delve into the question of religion and man's relationship with

God Almighty?"

"Not as much as some might like," said Will, a note of caution entering his voice. "I prefer matters of state."

"Ah yes, matters of state." John clicked his tongue and smiled craftily. "Well, Master Shakespeare," he said, giving Constance his arm, "we should leave you to your praise of the Tudors." He started for the door but stopped and turned around. “Do not mistake me. They certainly deserve whatever encomiums your agile pen devises. Elizabeth has transformed the kingdom."

John and Constance stepped out of the house onto Parson's Lane and turned left. They walked, passing the fortress-like Leathersellers Hall, in the direction of Bishopsgate Street where they turned south towards the Thames.

"Are you interested in history?" Constance asked.

"Shouldn't we all be interested in history?”

“I meant the history of the Tudors."

“So did I."

"Clever answer, but then I already know that you are a very clever man."

"I hope not too clever."

"For your own good?"

"Precisely."

"I very much doubt that," said Constance, moving closer to him and allowing her hip to brush his.

Constance thought how surprised John would be to learn that Will was writing *Henry the Fourth, Part One* and she, *Henry the Fourth, Part Two*. But maybe he wouldn't be so surprised, clever as he was.

As they walked down Grace Church Street, John explained that, after their walk along the river and across London Bridge, they would have a light supper at one of his favorite inns and then, as the light faded, would settle themselves comfortably in the boat he had hired to watch the evening's fireworks.

"The Duke or Prince," said John, "of some minor, German Protestant principality—are not they all minor?—is granting us the favor of a visit. The fireworks are in his honor. The Queen will be on the river."

"I met her once."

"The Queen?"

"Yes, at the home of the Duchess of Bastrow. Will's company was putting on *Richard the Third*."

Constance did not go into further details.

"The poor Duchess. Killed in a riding accident. I understand she was a kind, gracious lady and not overly taken with being a duchess."

Constance turned towards and pretended an interest in a fine, three-story brick house they were passing so that John would not see the expression on her face. Struggling for composure, Constance said in a forced light, gay tone: "I believe my curtsy to the Queen was acceptable for a sprig of a girl from far-off Stratford."

"I'm sure that your curtsy was the envy of all who saw it, including the Queen."

"You are a courteous as well as a clever man."

On the south side of the Bridge, they turned right

and strolled towards the theaters and animal baiting arenas. As they passed the latter, John asked if she had ever seen a bear or bull baiting.

"No," said Constance.

"Would you be interested?"

"I don't know. I imagine it is quite cruel."

"Ah, we English take our cruelty lightly."

The supper was indeed excellent as was the claret that John, after conferring with Constance, ordered. The inn was crowded with noisy young men and a number of women, all of whom were anxiously awaiting the evening's spectacle. Several men stopped by their table, and John introduced them as law colleagues. Constance was keenly aware of the looks they gave her. So was John.

"They are jealous of me, every last one," said John.

"Surely due to your skill as a barrister."

"False modesty is no better than false pride. Look around." She did. "Do you see a more beautiful woman?"

"Or you, a more handsome man?"

"If not a writer, then perhaps a lawyer."

"If someday we women are allowed to be either."

At that moment, their discourse was interrupted as Phillip Henslowe, the highly successful theatrical impresario and businessman—with, people said, a finger in many pies, all juicy but some more respectable than others—greeted Constance with a bow.

"Mistress Shakespeare," he said, "it has been

some time since I've had the pleasure of beholding you."

"The time, Master Henslowe, would be less if you came to more of my brother's plays."

"I do have my own company, the Admiral's Men, whose performances I must attend, and so many other matters to see to."

"Careful," said Constance, "lest you put money ahead of other, more uplifting satisfactions." She turned towards John. "May I present my good friend and admirer of the works of William Shakespeare...." At which, John stood up. "...John Maydestone. John, this is Master Philip Henslowe, a..." Constance paused ever so briefly. "...gentleman of many talents."

"Who has not heard of Philip Henslowe?"

John tilted his head in a slight bow, perhaps to emphasize his superior rank or as a comment on Henslowe's standing in some quarters. Henslowe returned the slight bow as if to say that while not all of his businesses met some people's moral or religious scruples, all of them were profitable.

"The lawyer?" asked Henslowe.

"Yes."

"Also, a gentleman of many talents. I might call upon your services someday."

"I shall attend upon you whenever you choose to visit."

Henslowe nodded again and strolled to another table where three women, heavily made up and all with low-cut bodices, were drinking ale.

"Strumpets," said Constance with a low laugh.

"You do not seem to care for him."

"He once was involved with Will's company; but a few years ago, there was a quarrel over money, and Henslowe left to partner with the Admirals' Men. Will said it was nasty." She lightly touched John's hand. "Nor do you seem much taken by him."

"He is famous, I grant; but he is involved in some businesses that I would prefer not to associate with."

"Such as a brothel?"

"You never cease to amaze me."

"Nor you, me."

The two-oared wherry was sleek and wider than most of the craft in which she had crossed the river. The gunnel was lacquered and the body painted a smoky red. They settled themselves comfortably in the middle of the wherry, and the oarsmen propelled them to mid-stream where a great many boats were milling about as their passengers waited for the fireworks to begin. Suddenly, John, who had glanced down river, said: "Look"; Constance turned round and saw the many-oared royal barge slicing through the water and moving rapidly up-stream. Cheers for the Queen rang out as the other boats made way. The royal barge slowed with the oarsmen, all in brightly colored livery, keeping up enough speed to prevent the barge from slipping backwards in the current. It was not yet completely dark, and Constance could see the Queen sitting on a high dais behind a gilded and brightly painted edifice that separated the throne from the oarsmen. As the barge slid past their wherry, Elizabeth looked at Constance, nodded and said: "Mistress Shakespeare, I believe."

"Your Majesty," said Constance, her voice trembling.

John said nothing but bowed his head ever so slightly, almost as if it pained him to do so.

The barge passed. Trembling, Constance gripped John's hand.

"You must have made quite an impression. One can easily see why."

Soon thereafter, the sky turned black; and the spectacle began. Brilliant lights flashed overhead. Explosions like thunder emanated from cannons stationed on shore and could be heard up and down the river. Smoke drifted past; an acrid smell filled her nostrils. Although it was June, the night air had a chill. She shivered and pressed close to John who put an arm around her shoulders.

"Has there ever been an accident?" she asked.

"Not recently... that I recall."

Just as he spoke, they heard a roar and a fire burst out directly across from them. "I hope it's a bonfire," said John. He told the oarsmen to pull closer to shore. Soon, they could see that it was no bonfire but a building engulfed in flames. Their forms silhouetted by the fire, people ran towards the building with buckets that looked to be slopping out half their water before they could be used.

"I know it's a disaster," said Constance, "but it's a strangely beautiful sight."

"It is, and also fortunate that there are no other

buildings very close to it. Otherwise, much of the city could burn to the ground."

"Dear God, I didn't think of that. Should we go help?"

"Not much we can do without buckets."

"We have two, Sir," said one of the oarsmen.

"Then head to shore," said John. "I'm almost certain it's a merchant's warehouse. They probably stored gunpowder for the cannons, and someone mishandled it. Lit a pipe or some other stupid act."

When they reached shore about fifty yards from the burning building, an oarsman handed a bucket to John who stepped out of the boat onto the muddy bank, the bucket in one hand and his cane in the other. The oarsman was about to follow with the second bucket when Constance said, in a commanding voice: "I'll take that one, if you please."

"This is no work for a woman," said the oarsman.

"It is if you expect a tip this evening." Confused, the oarsman looked at John. "Do you not see," Constance said to John, "women carrying buckets?"

John was about to say that those women were not of her standing, but he thought better of it.

"Give her the bucket," he said, "and wait for us."

They filled the buckets and, trying to spill as little as possible, hurried towards the fire—John's limp hardly slowing him. As they got close, the heat blasted their faces; and the smoke curled around their bodies. Getting as close as possible, they hurled the water towards the flames and hastened back to refill the buckets. They did this over and over until Constance's arms ached beyond what she had ever experienced, her clothes were covered in soot and her face was streaked with grime. By this time, the fire had substantially diminished so John led her back to the boat. Men from other wherries that had also come to shore returned to their boats. One oarsman had a torch, which John borrowed to examine Constance.

"My God," he said, trying to stifle his alarm, "how am I going to explain this to your brother?"

"Leave Will to me."

The oarsmen took them upriver to just past the Bridge. Fortunately, the current was moving slowly upstream so they had no trouble with the arches. John tipped the oarsmen generously, bade them a good night and, taking Constance's arm, led her towards Parson's Lane. When they reached Will's house, Constance told him that he could leave her.

"Not on your life. We'll face this together."

"Then give me a kiss."

Which he did, lightly on her lips.

They went inside. Will was facing the fire. Hearing the door open, he swung around and said: "Where the Devil..." He stopped and then said, in disbelief: "What the Devil?"

"There was a fire by the river," explained Constance. "A merchant's warehouse. Probably gunpowder. We helped put it out."

She smiled as endearingly as she knew how.

"You let my sister fight a fire and then bring her

home in this condition. And here I thought you were a gentleman. Were you mad?"

Constance began to answer; but John, having rehearsed all the way home, said: "Have you ever tried to stop Constance when she had a mind to do something?"

When his gales of laughter subsided, Will said: "Out you scoundrel and next time you take my sister for a promenade, stay away from fires and other natural or man-made disasters."

When the bear was led into the arena and tied to a post, Constance grasped John's arm and whispered: "I'm not sure I'm prepared for this." John had purchased seats in the lowest tier so they could see, hear and smell everything clearly. Constance felt she was practically in the pit with the bear, who stood on his hind legs and growled. Eight dogs were brought into the arena on leashes, two each to a handler. Behind the handlers were two men with long pikes. Seeing the bear, the dogs snarled and yipped and strained furiously at their leashes. The handlers let four loose, and they raced for the bear. One leaped for the bear's throat, biting to get through the heavy fur. The bear swatted the dog with a sharp-clawed paw; and the dog, bleeding heavily from the side, flew through the air and crashed to the ground. The dying animal whimpered and crawled towards its handler. One of the men with pikes stepped forward and stabbed the dog through the throat, killing it instantly.

Meanwhile, the bear had lunged forward, to the end of the restraining rope, and grabbed a dog. The dog snapped at the bear's face but to no avail as the bear slowly crushed the dog to death.

The stands were packed full with men and women of all classes. As soon as the dogs had started for the bear, the crowd shouted and cheered, roaring their encouragement now for the dogs and then for the bear. When the bear snatched another dog off its chest and slammed the yammering beast's head onto the ground, the crowd's noise was frightful.

John leaned over and, because of the overwhelming noise, whispered in Constance's ear: "You needn't fear for the bear. It's too valuable to let the dogs kill it."

Constance looked at him in horror.

"John, take me away from here," she cried over the noise of the crowd.

Not hesitating, John took her hand and, ignoring their vitriolic complaints, led her past a row of spectators, one of whom stuck out a foot and tried to trip him. John started to lift his cane but immediately changed his mind and simply glared at the stout fellow.

"You are lucky today," John growled at him and continued along the row with Constance following closely behind him. They left the baiting grounds and walked towards the Bridge in silence. Finally, when they reached the other side of the river, Constance spoke:

"I care for you, John," she said, "but never, ever take me to such a disgusting spectacle again."

They continued to go on promenades, sometimes along the country lanes beyond Finsbury Fields and sometimes exploring various London parishes. John loved both the city and surrounding countryside and was an excellent companion. They had dinners at London's finest inns and went several times to the theater with supper afterwards. One afternoon in late July, on the fifth day in an unusual string of steaming hot days that had caused tempers to flare throughout the city, they were leaving The Swan in Southwark, having seen a delicious comedy by a new playwright, when they noticed a tightly-packed group of about twenty young men, mostly shabbily dressed, standing about thirty yards from the theater's entrance and all carrying long-handled clubs.

"Apprentices," murmured John, taking Constance's hand and leading her quickly, not allowing his limp to hinder them, along the side of the building.

Shouts rose from the group: "Close the Evil Theaters", "Out with the Whores", "Pray God for Mercy", "Down with Brothels", "A Pox on Sinners", "Drive out Foreign Artisans", "Murder the Irish" and "Hang the Devil Playwrights".

Hearing the shouts, Constance stopped and turned back.

"Come along," said John, urgency in his voice. "I must get you out of harm's way."

"What is going to happen?"

The words were hardly out of her mouth when about ten well-dressed gentlemen, brandishing swords, emerged from the theater's grounds and advanced on the apprentices, many of whom began to holler: "Clubs.... Clubs.... Clubs...." More apprentices ran from the side streets and joined the group facing the swordsmen who were reinforced by other gentlemen leaving the theater. The two groups moved towards each other with the apprentices growling: "Damn Nobles" and the gentlemen responding: "Arrogant Scum." With a roar of "God Bless the Queen," the apprentices charged the aristocrats who met the onslaught with slashing swords and cries of "God Bless Elizabeth." Within seconds, a general melee was in progress with apprentices bashing gentlemen on the arms, shoulders and heads and the gentlemen giving as good as they got with whacks of their swords and even occasional thrusts, which dispatched a couple of apprentices to the hereafter. Blood flowed profusely, staining the ground and spattering men and women attempting to flee the brawl but trapped among the fighters.

Constance stood frozen, staring in horror at the fighting and unaware of John pulling her hand. An apprentice broke free from the crowd and strode towards her, club raised and bellowing: "Whore."

Constance screamed: "No.... no.... not a whore."

John pulled harder, but she couldn't move. The apprentice was within ten yards when John stepped in front of her and raised his cane, which would have done precious little against the long-handled club. Suddenly, the apprentice dropped to his knees, his head partly severed from his neck, and then fell forward to the ground. A handsome young man stood a few feet from John, holding his blood-drenched sword at an angle.

"Thank you," said John.

"Get her out of here," said the young man.

"I'm trying."

Constance stared at the young man and then uttered a single word: "Roberte."

He looked at her, confused, but then a smile spread across his face. "Ah," he said, "the beautiful young woman in the street." He made a slight bow and turned back to the fight.

Having spoken, if only one word, unfroze Constance; and John was able to lead her to the river where all the wherries were taken due to the crowd fleeing the theater. They decided, therefore, to walk and headed towards the Bridge. Fortunately, the riot had not yet spread beyond the theater; but within the hour, as John told Constance the next day when he visited to see how she was, it would engulf much of Southwark leaving a couple of buildings burnt to the ground.

"Does trouble follow you wherever you go?" Will asked John; and this time, he was not laughing.

John tactfully waited a couple of days before asking about Roberte. Constance explained that, several years ago, he had almost ridden her down in the street. John surmised that one would not forget someone who had done that.

"Maybe trouble follows us both," said John, turning to other subjects.

Apart from the riot, however, July furnished them

with numerous pleasures. They went to a party at the home of an acquaintance of John's. Near St. Paul's, the large house was filled with elegantly-dressed men and women of all ages. The main hall was brilliantly lit by two fires—even on a warm evening—and such a plenitude of candles that the gems flashed and sparkled on the outfits of both sexes. White and red wines and beer were available on a long table, and gaily-liveried servants passed through the crowd with platters filled to overflowing with miniature meat pies, oyster pies and fruit tarts; cubes of cheese; slices of roast goose, lamb and turkey and such fruits as strawberries, gooseberries, apples and oranges. The guests ate heartily, wiping their fingers on handkerchiefs extracted for the purpose from pockets or sleeves; and the conversation flowed much like the wine and beer.

John introduced Constance to Roger Gardiner, an elderly gentleman and their host. Constance felt his hot eyes roam over her face and the new outfit that she had purchased for the occasion. After several minutes' conversation, during which he stared continually at her, Roger said that, regretfully, he had to attend to all his guests but that he hoped she would give him the honor of a dance. Constance replied with a modest curtsy.

John explained that Roger was a prominent lawyer and the owner of numerous houses in the city from which he earned substantial rents and that, at heart, he was a decent fellow despite the fact that the hot blood of his youth had cooled far more than Roger cared to acknowledge.

"He stares," said John, "but, as far as I know, that's all he does these days. Not to mention that he would rarely encounter such a beautiful woman to stare at."

"Stop it," said Constance, but with a twinkle in her eye. Then, more thoughtfully, she added: "I didn't find it very pleasing."

At that moment, the players whom Roger had hired struck up a dance tune; and leaving his cane in a corner, John led Constance into the open space where dancing had begun. The first number was a pavane, which was restrained enough so that John, with his limp, and even the most elderly of the guests could participate. But when a courante was played, because of the fast running and jumping steps, John escorted Constance from the dance floor.

"I don't mind," she said. "I haven't danced for years and have forgotten most of what I knew."

Not a minute later, Roger was at her side, requesting that she fulfill her promise of a dance.

"So now a curtsy is a promise. What trouble we women can get into simply being polite."

"It is only a dance. When it's over, you will still be John's adoring and adorable friend."

Constance gave Roger her arm; and he guided her towards the dancing, saying how much he admired a woman with wit enough to hold her own in the verbal jousting so common in London and as dangerous, perhaps, as the bloodier sort. Once dancing, Constance noted with some satisfaction that Roger's running and jumping steps were considerably less vigorous than those of the young men around them. She silently berated herself for such wicked thoughts.

On the way home, in a carriage that John had hired given the distance between the Gardiner house and Parson's Lane, John thanked her for dancing with Roger.

"I doubt it was entertaining, but he is an important barrister and can influence the business that comes a lawyer's way."

As answer, Constance leaned over and gave John a long, full kiss on the lips.

In order to go on these outings, Constance often worked late into the night on the second part of *Henry IV*. Will once took her to task, wondering how she could keep up with both the promenades and her writing and questioning the quality of her work. She showed him the most recent pages, and he said nothing further.

When she told Madge about John, Madge grinned slyly and said: "So you're back with men."

"Is that all you have to say?"

"No." She grinned again. "Is Will planning on speaking to John about marriage?"

"I doubt Will wants to part with such a valuable slave."

"Is that what you are?"

"I labor without remuneration or recognition, except from you and Will. What would you call it?"

"You are doing what few, if any, women have the chance to do."

Constance was quiet and thoughtful for a few seconds and then said: "A hit, a very palpable hit."

"That's a good line. You should remember it."

"I remember lots of lines. You never know when they might prove useful."

Just then, Rafe and Ned, who had been playing quietly with blocks, decided to get into a fight. Madge and Constance separated them, and Madge scolded them: "If you cannot play together without fighting, then you will have to go to separate corners."

"No," wailed the twins with one voice, "we'll be good."

They started again to build a tower.

"I'm not sure," said Constance, "if I ever want to marry."

"Why ever not?"

"I would lose too much of my freedom, such as it is."

"I think," said Madge, "that the Duchess might agree."

"Yes, I think she would."

"Would she also be amazed at what you've accomplished?"

"That I cannot answer, but I'm sure she would approve of the effort."

Once she cooked a meal for John and Will, also inviting Peter and Madge, who said she'd have to bring the twins as Hugh drank too much for her to trust him to watch the rambunctious three-year-olds. Will was pleased as he had a fondness for Madge and, never having met Peter, looked forward to gaining further insights into the ways and character of watermen.

"It will be as if Peter is on trial," Constance reminded Madge, who nodded in assent. "As you may recall, when he meets a new person, Will is worse than any lawyer. They could use him in the tower instead of the rack. An hour's questioning by my brother would break even the strongest man."

"Or woman," shuddered Madge, remembering her own ordeal at Will's hands.

Madge wanted to help with the meal, but Constance declined.

"Jane does almost all the cooking now anyway so she can help me. I'm doing it to show my love and appreciation to the people dearest to me in the whole world."

The dinner was on a Sunday to accommodate work requirements. The main dishes were a roasted swan, a baked capon bathed in cider and well-seasoned before putting in the oven and a poached eel. Everyone praised the meal to the skies, and Will's interrogation of Peter was mild by comparison with his normal standards—perhaps because there was a lawyer present. In any event, the lively conversation revolved around such topics as the prices for commodities, the increase in foreigners settling in London, the building boom in the suburbs and the rise in crime, in particular pick-pocketing, which had become so pervasive that one had to exercise great caution if one left home with more than a few pennies in one's purse.

"It's gratifying," said Peter, "that the authorities are taking these crimes in hand by matching their increase with a suitable increase in bodies swinging from the gallows. If you rob a man of his purse, it's no better than robbing him of any other sort of property, such as his ox or his horse or his wife. In fact, one could say it's worse as the crime may prevent the victim from caring for his family."

"Peter," said Madge sharply, "don't be daft."

"What's the matter?" said Peter in an innocent, quizzical voice.

"Later," said Madge, giving her husband a look that suggested a reckoning would be forthcoming, probably in bed.

Meanwhile, John gave Constance a quick glance as if to say: "We're all friends here. Let's keep it that way." Constance said nothing, and John changed the subject. "How are things on the river these days? Plenty of business?"

"Enough to keep us in beer and cider, " Peter said with a smile at his wife.

As they were leaving, Madge whispered to Constance: "Now I see why you've gone back to men. John is splendid."

A few days later, on the fourth day of August, John asked if she would like to have supper at The Gilded Lady where they had not been since their first promenade.

"Yes," she replied, "but only if you show me one of the upstairs rooms."

To her surprise, the room did not strike her as all that different from the one at the inn that she shared with Edmund some four years ago. This room might be nicer, she thought, but maybe her memory was playing tricks on her. So much had happened in the meantime, and she felt herself to be a very different person from the innocent young woman who had found herself in bed with the eldest son of an Earl. She had also had a Duchess for a lover and now, it seemed, would in short order be making love with a successful, kind-hearted and wonderfully handsome lawyer. She did not reflect as to whether she was moving up or down in the world. Such thoughts, to her way of thinking, would be callous and calculating in the extreme. But in the minute or two since John had unlocked the door, shown her gallantly into the room, limped to a chair against which he rested his cane and lit the two bedside candles, she also realized that one of the truly astounding things that had happened to her in these four years was becoming a writer—even if likely to be forever unknown. And, of course, she had made friends with Madge—a better friend being hard to imagine. She glanced around the room—no unusual furnishings: a large bed with two immense pillows, two chairs, a dresser and a wash stand. Then her eyes fell on a large painting which, in the dim light, she had not immediately noticed. It portrayed a couple making love with the man behind the woman. Interestingly, thought Constance, the lady was obviously a number of years older than the man. Both were only partly undressed.

She looked around to see if there were other paintings but found none.

"Is it all right?" asked John, a little nervously.

As an answer, she crossed the room, put her arms around him and kissed him ardently, letting her tongue slip between his lips. He responded in kind. She broke away from him and stepped towards the bed.

"What's wrong?"

She looked back over her shoulder and smiled. She then began undressing, having worn very simple clothes for the occasion, and letting each garment fall in turn to the floor. When naked, she turned to face him and stood with her arms hanging loosely by her side. He audibly sucked in his breath, gazed rapturously at her full breasts, flat stomach and rounded thighs and said: "My word." Then he undressed.

"I felt pretty certain that this would not be your first time," he said as they afterwards lay in each other's arms.

"I have been in love."

"Do you want to say more?"

"No. And you?"

"I've not been in love but I've made love."

"I think," she said, "that's all we need to know—at least for now. Let us make this a new beginning for both of us."

"You are indeed a remarkable woman. I wager there's not another one like you in London if not in all England."

"Shame that I'm not the wagering sort."

"How did a common lawyer with a limp find himself in bed with a veritable goddess?"

"Stop now. You're being foolish."

"It's pleasant to be foolish at times." He turned thoughtful. "Why have you never asked about my limp?"

"Because it didn't matter; and if I wanted to know, I got my answer today. Your right leg is shorter than your left."

"And has been since birth."

"I don't need to know more; but if you'd like to tell me, I'd be interested in how it's affected your life."

"Not so much. A few boys at school teased me until I beat one soundly. And I have yet to play football."

"So much the better."

She ran a finger down his cheek and then reached between his legs.

As they were dressing, she stopped and studied him. She wondered if now were the right time. "No better," she thought.

"John."

"Yes, my dear."

"We should have no secrets from each other."

"Agreed."

"Are you a secret Catholic?"

John regarded her with shock.

"Whatever gave you that foolish notion?"

"Things you've occasionally said."

"Put it out of your mind. I am a loyal subject of the Queen."

Madge's reaction was: "I knew that wouldn't take long." She hugged Constance and added: "I certainly approve of him if only because it's so obvious that he loves you."

"What would I do without you?"

"Get into all sorts of trouble."

They went to The Gilded Lady again a week later. They had supper after making love, which had left them giddy and hungry. John said he would invite her to his residence except that his neighbors were too close and too inquisitive. And while he had the utmost confidence in the discretion of Rycharde, his long-time servant, the man would think it odd to be given an afternoon off without any logical reason.

"When shall I at least see it?" she asked.

"I shall have you for dinner next week and shall escort you home during the afternoon."

"And who does your cooking?"

"He does. He is unusual in that regard; but he seems to like it, although it's plain fare, nothing sumptuous. When I have guests, I bring in a woman who lives in the parish and is extraordinarily talented in the kitchen."

"Do you often have guests?"

"Occasionally... a few male friends. We talk and talk and talk some more. Often it's idle chatter."

But "next week" had to wait. That very evening, when Constance arrived home, she found Will sitting at his work table, holding a letter and weeping.

"Hamnet.... Hamnet," he kept repeating. Constance gently extracted the letter from his hand. It was from his wife, Anne. Their son, Hamnet, had died and would be buried on August 11th which, Constance realized with a shock, was today.

"I am so sorry, Will," she said, kneeling by his side.

"He was my only son."

"Yes."

"He was only eleven... born in February of 1585. Anne doesn't say, but it was likely the plague. I've heard it's been a difficult summer in the provinces."

"Will you go to Stratford?"

"Yes. Will you come with me?"

"Of course."

They took a coach and were in Stratford two days later. Anne, Will and their two remaining children, Susanna and Judith, were joined by Constance, hers and Will's four living siblings and parents, John and Mary Shakespeare, in visiting Hamnet's grave. Will walked arm-in-arm with Anne, whom he had not seen recently; and each of them had one of their children by the hand. So it was a large group bidding farewell to poor Hamnet, in whom Will had placed such hopes. Constance thought with surprise about the coincidence of her niece and the Duchess having the same first name. She wondered why she had never thought of it before, especially as she was quite fond of Will's oldest, who was only nine when she last saw her four years ago and was now, by the looks of it, growing up quickly.

During their brief stay, John asked Will whether it wouldn't be better if Constance remained in Stratford since Will didn't seem to be doing much about arranging a marriage. Neither of his two children, Richard and Constance, who were born but eleven months apart and were now either twenty-two or close thereto, seemed to be in a hurry to marry, although at twenty-two: "Tempus fugit as you witty scholars would say."

"I may come up with the odd witticism; but as to scholarship, I make no claim. You seem to forget that I missed university altogether and have learned what I've learned from books."

"Your modesty is as hollow as a dead tree trunk."

"Excellent simile, Father."

"Don't start with me."

"Wouldn't dream of it."

"As I was about to say: Your reputation and literary accomplishments are well known even in your provincial birthplace. So please spare me the bullshit."

"Elegant.... very elegant. But I will spare you. As to the question of Constance and marriage, I should point out that during her time in London, she has become quite a different person from the girl who left home four years ago. In case you hadn't noticed."

"I have noticed, but I see no reason why such a change should make a difference when it comes to the subject of marriage."

"To put it another way, she has developed a mind of her own."

"Mind of her own," exclaimed the elder Shakespeare. "Women don't have minds of their own. I'll show her a thing or two. And, furthermore, I still have not forgotten, or really forgiven, the manner of her leaving."

"As you wish, but I suggest refraining from delving too deeply into those topics. You might find the conversation less than satisfactory."

"I'll delve into whatever topic I damn well please. I am master in this house. And you as well should watch your tongue, famous playwright or not."

"Yes, of course." Will thought quickly. "Perhaps, before you become too entangled in this subject, I should advise you that she is being courted by a prominent and wealthy lawyer. I hope that this will bear fruit and that I'll have good news before too long. These things do take time."

Will failed to mention that he wasn't sure who was courting whom in this case or whether he would have any news at all. For the time being, however, it was a suitable diversion and would avoid what he feared would be a fierce and rather malevolent encounter.

"Ah," said John Shakespeare, quickly changing his tone, "that's a tune more agreeable to my ears."

While this conversation was going on, Constance was visiting her old friend, Emma Loveney.

The first thing Emma did after hugging her dear friend was to introduce her two-year-old daughter and then have her taken away by a servant. Emma then mentioned her beloved husband, Harrye "Blockhead" Shawe with whom it turned out—mother of all surprises—she was deeply in love.

"He is the sweetest, kindest man you could imagine and while not as dumb as his old nickname might suggest, the conversation at dinner is limited. But so what! He treats me like a princess; and since he started working with my father, they have sufficiently expanded the mill so that he earns enough for us to have this nice, if modest, home and two servants. As to the other part, with patient instruction he has continued to improve and has turned out to be a more than satisfactory pupil—in fact, quite an outstanding one. But I want to talk about London, not my husband's skill between the sheets."

"That would be unusual for you," laughed Constance.

"We all change—some," said Emma with a wide grin. "Tell me what it's like. I can only imagine how wonderful it must be: the theaters, the taverns, beautiful mansions, elegant inns for dining, fireworks on the Thames, musical concerts and bear-baiting. I've heard all sorts of stories and am so envious. Nothing happens in Stratford—well, not nothing but how can it compare to London. We have touring companies but mostly when the actors are fleeing the plague. There is the making of babies, which is fun, birthing babies, which is not, and burying them, which is the saddest thing imaginable. I've buried one of mine. I still think of the little fellow; and when I do, I can't help crying." Emma paused for breath and a thought. "I'm so sorry about your nephew. He was a nice young lad."

"I'm afraid I don't remember much about him."

"I don't expect you would. He was only seven when you snuck off in the middle of the night without saying farewell to anyone, including me."

"I'm terribly sorry, but my father would've locked me up if he had discovered my plan or gotten the slightest hint of it."

"And you couldn't trust me? I did read the letter and said not a word."

"I know, but once I'd decided, I could think of nothing but leaving. I didn't tell George either for which I'm sure he never forgave me."

"Whether he forgave you or not, I couldn't say; but he forgot sufficiently to be married with two handsome little boys."

"Wish him the best for me and tell him the occasion wasn't right for me to call on him. Next time, perhaps."

"I will do so."

The second servant brought in Emma's nine-month-old son who was crying furiously. Emma undid her bodice, pulled out a breast and proffered it to the child who immediately ceased crying and began to suck contentedly.

"It's all it takes to keep a man happy," said Emma, "from birth to death."

"I shall refrain from comment."

"Which brings me to the most important question."

"Yes, I have," said Constance before Emma could continue. "More than once."

"Well, for God's sake, don't be modest. Tell me about it."

"I think you know all there is to know about it."

Emma laughed.

"Life," she said, "would be much more fun if you had stayed in Stratford."

"But not for me."

When, on the Twentieth of August, she and Will arrived back in London, she sent Rose, their other servant—a young girl who was devoted to Constance and quite trustworthy—with a note to John asking if he might care to have supper on the following day. Rose came back with a note that had one word printed on it. When they got to their accustomed room, Constance flung herself into John's arms and whispered hoarsely: "I've missed you so."

"It's only been just over a week."

"Too long not to be in bed with you."

"Point made, and I have missed you." He kissed her passionately. "And, dare I say it, I love you."

"You may dare indeed because your love is returned in full measure."

With that, she turned and started to undress, knowing it was something he liked to watch.

A few days later, on August 24th, they passed through Aldersgate and strolled out to the Priory of St. John in West Smithfield (northwest of the city walls) to amuse themselves at the world-famous St. Bartholomew's Fair. They arrived at the beginning of the Fair when rabbits were turned loose and, to general hilarity, chased hither and thither by a swarm of young boys.

A dense, noisy crowd had gathered in the Priory's precincts to inspect the wares of numerous cloth merchants spread out on tables and to gawk in wonder at wrestlers, boxers, wire-walkers, acrobats, jugglers, fire-eaters and exotic animals such as a dancing bear, a thieving monkey that snatched mince pies from well-dressed and not-so-well-dressed ladies and a tiger prowling in a cage. Some murmuring approval but many audibly grumbling, the crowd made way when the Lord Mayor, in his scarlet robes and gold chain, entered the grounds preceded, as always, by his Swordbearer.

John had suggested that they invite Madge and the twins to join them. Peter unfortunately was working. Despite using his cane, John alternated carrying Ned and Rafe on his shoulders so they could get a better view. Constance carried the other one in her arms so that Madge had the rare freedom of not watching them like a hawk. She took advantage of the opportunity to stuff herself with a leg of mutton and also treated everyone to a meat pie. The particular twin on John's shoulders kept up a stream of "Look at this" and “Look at that" while the other squirmed in Constance's arms and begged for his turn.

When they came to a fire-eater, they looked on, horrified, as the young man in a parti-colored, red and green outfit lit a wooden rod from a torch held by his assistant, leaned way back and guided the flaming rod down his throat. Ned, on John's shoulders, gazed in fascination; but Rafe buried his head against Constance's chest. The fire-eater pulled out the rod, without apparent harm to himself; and Constance comforted Rafe: "It's all over. No harm done to anyone."

The assistant passed among the crowd with a hat into which John tossed a pair of groats.

"Do you know how he does that?" Constance asked John.

"Not an idea in the world, but he apparently has one."

"If he didn't," laughed Madge, "they'd need a substitute."

Madge decided it was high time the twins walked on their own so, despite vociferous complaints, they were put on the ground. Constance took Ned by the hand and Madge, Rafe, and off they strolled, the complaints quickly dying down.

They came upon three musicians playing a viola da gamba, a sackbut, and a small drum. They stopped to listen. When the players finished the piece, the audience enthusiastically applauded; and several ladies called for a love song. The viola da gamba player nodded, put down his instrument and picked up a lute. He began to play a bitter-sweet tune, and the sacbut player stepped forward and sang:

> Come again! sweet love doth now invite
> Thy graces that refrain
> To do me due delight,
> To see, to hear, to touch, to kiss, to die,
> With thee again in sweetest sympathy.

John took Constance's free hand and gave her a squeeze which she returned in kind.

The twins jumped up and down at the sight of the monkey, having never before encountered one, but were calmer when they came to the bear. On at least one outing with Constance and their mother, they had seen a tame bear in Moor Fields. Seeing the acrobats ignited their innate sense of mimicry; and they were shortly, to the immense delight of the crowd around them, tumbling over each other on the ground. Seeing the twins and keenly aware of the adage about not competing with children, the acrobats stopped and vigorously applauded. Constance and Madge each picked up a finally-exhausted twin and advised John that home was beckoning. Thanking them profusely, John handed a shilling to one of the acrobats; and with now sleeping twins, they left the Fair, vowing to return the following year.

Just over a month later, as they were lying snug against each other's naked bodies in bed in The Gilded Lady, John said that he would like Constance to move in with him, hoping that it would be agreable to her. John, by this time, well understood Constance's independent spirit and mind—qualities which were among those that most endeared her to him.

"I am not entirely surprised that you asked; and yes, I am agreable. Delighted is a better word."

He put his arms around her, kissed her full on the lips and said: "Since your father is in Stratford, I shall ask Will for your hand in marriage."

"I don't want to marry you."

"But you said you would move in."

"I will live with you, but I won't marry you."

"But that is preposterous. What will people say?"

"Whatever they choose to say. What they say now. Surely you don't think our frequenting this inn has gone completely unnoticed?"

John sat up and gazed down at what he knew to be the most beautiful, intelligent and passionate woman he could have ever conceived of loving him.

"I should have known," he said.

"Does that mean you only want me to move in if we marry?"

"I am neither crazy nor a fool."

At that, Constance took him in her arms and kissed him with intense feeling.

"What will your brother say?"

"Leave Will to me."

"What happens if we have children?"

"Then we shall see."

"I assume," he said, tenderly, "that you take this position because you don't want to give up your freedom."

"You are very wise," she replied, "and now may I suggest we build up an appetite for supper."

Saying that, she climbed on top of him and began to move rhythmically until he was ready.

"I have not done my duty," stormed Will as he paced up and down. "I've known what you were up to, but I cast a blind eye because.... because...."

"Because it suited you."

"Why you... how dare you?"

"Do you wish Jane and Rose to learn all of our secrets? If not, please lower your voice."

Will kept pacing, but he spoke more quietly.

"We will be disgraced."

"We will not be disgraced. We are in the theater. No one in the theater has ever been disgraced—except, possibly, Christopher Marlowe."

"Stop being clever," Will snapped. "We're not writing a comedy."

"I'm not so sure. And what's more, you can hardly call your behaviour saintly."

"I'm a man."

"Will," she said in a cautionary tone, "you should know better."

"I don't have to accept this."

"Please stop pacing. It's making me nervous. Shall we sit down? I'll have Rose bring us glasses of ale."

After Rose had left the room and they had sat drinking for a moment, Will repeated: "I don't have to accept this."

"Do you like," she asked, "having me work with you?" She drank some more. "Delicious. None better."

"Are you threatening me?"

"Such an unpleasant word but under the circumstances, an accurate one."

"Will you ever marry him?"

"If we have a child. I will not put my interests

ahead of the child's."

"What shall I tell Father?"

Constance put her two forefingers to her lips and thought. She rose and walked around the room. Will watched her closely. With her back to the cold fireplace, she faced Will. She drank. She admired the elegantly carved tables that Will had acquired since the move in April. She would miss living here, but she would be here often to work and visit. She drank more ale.

"Tell him," she said, "to send a wedding gift."

Will laughed uproariously and then, in a serious tone, asked: "Have you finished the new draft?"

"Almost."

And so, in October of 1596, Constance Shakespeare moved into the home of John Maydestone, a wealthy and prominent lawyer, as John Shakespeare proudly described his daughter's husband. When one of his neighbors asked John when and where they had been married, John smiled and mentioned something about Will Shakespeare's elegant home in Bishopsgate.

Shortly after the move, Madge brought the twins over for a visit. "I am glad," said Madge, "to see you safely married at last." And laughed so uncontrollably that the twins, panic-struck, thought their mother was having a fit.

Owing to problems with the landlord, in 1597, the Lord Chamberlain's Men moved from The Theatre to The Curtain, which was in the vicinity. It was there that

*Henry IV, Parts One and Two* were first performed. Madge accompanied Constance and John to the opening performances of *Parts One and Two*. Constance had written the latter mostly on her own. Will praised her work but decided to add an Epilogue and some other material of his own. Rafe and Ned were left in the care, at John and Constance's house, of Rycharde and Rose, who had agreed to come over for the occasion. John gave her, as well as Rycharde, a handsome tip.

"They will earn every pence," said Madge. "At four, these two have become, shall we say, lively."

The performances were excellent and the audience most appreciative. As they were leaving the theater, Constance said to John: "Among Will's better history plays, don't you think?"

Madge gave her friend's arm what, she thought, was an imperceptible squeeze.

"I would agree about *Part One*," said John, "but not *Part Two*."

Constance looked unhappy.

"Why ever not?"

"It's not a question of the quality of the work. It was superb."

"Then what, my darling, is the problem?"

"The authorship." John grinned like the cat who'd eaten the canary. "Will didn't write it. You did."

Constance fought back a surge of pride.

"Whatever makes you say such a foolish thing."

"I know you. I know your brother's style. And, while she thought she was being ever so clever, I saw

Madge squeeze your arm so she knows and, I imagine, has for some time."

"You cannot tell a soul," said Constance, a hint of anxiety in her voice.

"Your secret is quite safe with me." John paused. "And yes, both parts are among the best Shakespeare history plays."

"Now I don't always have to work at Will's."

"Just be careful of Rycharde who, for all his other good qualities, likes to snoop."

They turned into Shoreditch, which led into Bishopsgate Street. It was a pleasant, if somewhat windy, afternoon in early spring. It was a substantial distance—across most of the city—to the area just east of St. Paul's where John and Constance lived on Mutton Lane (off Wood Street); but they all thought the walk would refresh them after sitting in the theater for so long. John said that he would send Madge and the twins home in a carriage. On Mutton Lane, they walked past comfortable looking homes although not as elegant as those on Cheapside or the stately mansions along the Thames.

"What I would like to know," said John, as they neared his house, "is whether this is the first play you've written. I doubt it given how polished it is."

"It is the second that I have written by myself. I have also worked together with Will on a number of others and helped with sonnets and "The Rape of Lucrece."

"Remarkable. Who could imagine that a man with one leg shorter than the other would be living with not only the most beautiful woman in all England but also one of the country's finest writers?"

"I'm glad you realize that," said Madge, "but I would've left out the 'one of.'"

About a month later, in May of 1597, as they were having supper, John asked Constance if she had ever seen a tennis match.

"No."

"Would you care to?"

"Why, yes."

"I've been invited to play this Sunday in the afternoon at a court where I've never before played. I understand it's a well-planned court in a beautiful garden both of which we should enjoy seeing."

The court was indoors set along one wall of the Earl of Redding's opulent mansion on the river. John explained that some courts were squeezed into spaces between buildings and that poorer folk played in the fields. The Earl's court, on the other hand, was reputedly the best in London.

"I don't play as often as I should. It's great fun and good exercise. Good for the body and the soul."

"But how do you manage...."

"With my limp? I'm not as fast as the other players, but I make up for it by hitting the ball harder. They ignore my limp and give me no quarter. I would have it no other way."

The other players were already there when they arrived. The court had a low wood ceiling, wooden walls on three sides with a viewing gallery on the fourth. John introduced Constance to his good friend (and source of the invitation), Dr. Humphrey Claybrook who, in turn, introduced them to the Earl's second son, Thomas Ufford, and then to Thomas's cousin, Anthony Ufford.

"Dr. Claybrook," said Thomas, "is a brilliant physician who has helped my poor father tremendously with his gout."

"He is also physician," added Anthony, "to half the gentlemen in London and one of our best tennis players. He said you would be an excellent fourth."

"You embarrass me with such undeserved compliments."

Two women stood in the spectator's gallery, which ran the length of the court. Dr. Claybrook took Constance to meet Frances Ufford, Thomas's sister, and her friend, Sara Hargreve, and to get her settled to watch the game.

"Lady Frances," said Dr. Claybrook, "may I present..." The good doctor hesitated. Frances leaned forward slightly as if to say: "Yes?" The doctor continued: "Mistress Constance Shakespeare." Constance made a proper curtsy.

"Welcome, Constance," said Frances. "We do not stand on formality during a tennis match. Please call me Frances." She turned to the second woman. "This is my good friend Sara Hargreve."

Constance did another curtsy.

"Delighted," said Sara. "As with Frances, please call me by my given name."

Dr. Claybrook returned to the men, and the game

began. Before playing an actual match, on which, John had told her, money was wagered, the players warmed up by hitting hair-stuffed balls back and forth over a somewhat sagging net.

"Are you related to the playwright, William Shakespeare?" Frances asked Constance.

"He is my brother."

"How wonderful!" exclaimed Sara. "I was in tears over *Romeo and Juliet*. Such a sad story."

"I saw *Merchant of Venice*," said Frances. "I never in my life met a Jew nor do I hope to. What a frightening monster that Shylock was."

Constance wanted to say: "You should've seen him before I jumped in," but kept quiet.

"Imagine," continued Frances, "cutting off a piece of a gentleman's flesh simply because he fails to pay you a few silver coins. The nasty fellow never deserved to be paid—not a single pence."

In light of Frances's comments as well as the ones at the theater, Constance reflected that Will might've had a point about how the English viewed outsiders, which would include foreign merchants and artisans as well as Jews.

The match began, and conversation ceased. Constance watched in fascination as the ball flew back and forth across the net at what she considered outlandish speed. John and the Doctor were paired against Thomas and Anthony. Early on, it became clear that, because of their youth and superior skill, the two noblemen had the advantage. Thomas served the first game, and

Constance thought John and Humphrey were lucky to return the ball at all. But they did, and she was delighted to see that John was quite good—surprisingly so as she had no idea that he even knew how to play. She had to admit that he looked funny chasing down a ball with his limp, but he got to most of them. The limp, she realized, forced him to anticipate where the ball was going so that he started more quickly than the others.

"It is remarkable," said Frances, "how well your future husband moves around the court with his limp."

"Isn't it?"

Thomas and Anthony won the first game.

"Sixty to thirty," said Frances who went on to explain the strange scoring system of sixty points divided by four. "For example," said Sara who, like Frances, had obviously seen a great number of matches, "You can win the game by sixty to thirty as Thomas and Anthony just did. Or by sixty to fifteen or...."

"Sixty to forty-five," said Constance.

"Indeed."

The match continued with many points going on for quite some time and the players breathing hard as they ran up and down the court. John was the last to serve, and his powerful arm muscles not only drove the ball extremely hard but made her think of how he held her in bed. Moving too fast for a powerful shot to the corner of the court, John stumbled and fell. Constance let out a gasp; but he quickly got up, waved to her and called for the game to resume. The match consisted of three sets of six games each with Thomas and Anthony winning two of the sets and, therefore, the match. Coins quietly changed hands, and the men strolled over to the gallery. They were all dripping with sweat and still panting from the exertion.

"Good sport," said Thomas. "Wasn't it, ladies?"

"You were wonderful," sighed Sara, and Constance realized there might be more to tennis than met the eye.

"It was terribly amusing," said Frances. "You were remarkable," she nodded at John.

"I should like to try," said Constance cheerily.

The men stared at her, and John looked horrified.

"I'm afraid..." said Thomas.

"Why not, brother?" interrupted Frances. "Father is not here. No one will know if we swear secrecy. Women ride and hunt. Why not tennis?"

"All right," said Thomas, "but no one, absolutely no one, must know."

They took turns with a man and a woman on each side. Constance completely missed the first three balls hit at her, hit the next two into the gallery and, finally on her sixth try, hit one over the net. The women could not move quickly in their long skirts but compensated with enthusiastic swings and incessant laughter.

"What fun," said Frances to Constance when play ended, "you and John must join us again someday."

"You should not have done that," said John angrily as they walked up Bread Street towards

Cheapside.

"Why ever not," retorted Constance. "After all, Frances invited us to play again."

"That was merely aristocratic courtesy. We shall never be invited back."

Neither John nor Constance could know how right he was.

"That would be a shame since everyone had such fun."

"Shame or not, it was not your place to make such a.... a...."

Constance's cheeks reddened in anger. "Renowned lawyer lost his tongue. Hope that never happens in court." She quickened her pace so that he would have to struggle to keep up.

"Such an unusual request," he said as he caught up.

They walked in silent anger until they reached the corner of Bread Street and Cheapside, which was within sight of the towering steeple of the ancient church of St. Mary-le-Bow. From here, they could take either Milk Street or Wood Street to the warren of lanes that comprised the well-to-do neighborhood where they lived. Constance stopped abruptly and faced him, her hands resting squarely on her hips.

"Do you like, John, what we do in bed?"

She spoke quietly but strongly emphasized the words, "John" and "bed." He looked around, embarrassed; but none of the passers-by swirling around them seemed to be paying them the slightest attention beyond an occasional curious glance. Still feeling awkward, he asked: "Should we perhaps discuss this at home?"

"I want an answer now."

Keeping his voice low, he said: "Yes, of course, I do. It's wonderful. Nothing could be better." His expression became worried. "You're not thinking of stopping, are you?"

"No, but I need you to consider whether our pleasure would be as intense were I unwilling to rid myself of ridiculous social customs?"

"You could've been a lawyer as easily as a playwright. Forgive me."

She enfolded him in her arms and, in the middle of Cheapside, gave him a lingering kiss.

Every day, or at most every other day, Constance gave Rycharde, who did most of the food shopping, a verbal list (as Rycharde was only semi-literate but possessed of a prodigious memory) of what was needed. John trusted him with money, and the trust was never misplaced. Constance, furthermore, knew what everything cost. She sometimes went with Rycharde and, occasionally, told him that she would like to do the shopping herself.

One afternoon, having that morning forgotten the gooseberries for a pie, Constance decided on a quick trip to the market without Rycharde. She was walking on a quiet street when she saw John in deep conversation with a fierce-eyed, sunken-cheek man dressed in simple attire. Constance approached them. The man, noticing her, hurried away.

"Who was that?"

"No one in particular."

"John, please. Everyone you know is someone in particular."

"An old acquaintance whom I haven't seen in some time."

"Did he not want to meet me?"

"He does not know how to behave around women."

"Then he's a silly fellow and not worthy of your acquaintance."

Constance laughed and continued towards the market. She wondered who the odd stranger might be but decided that John, in his professional capacity, probably had dealings with all sorts of people. He could, for example, be representing the fellow in a lawsuit. Or other business dealings might be involved.

She shrugged and turned her thoughts to where the freshest gooseberries could be found.

When they went together, Rycharde was invariably polite and outwardly respectful; but, no matter how much Constance sought to draw him out about his past, his likes, his dislikes, their conversations were stilted and mostly one-sided. Constance concluded that, for whatever reason, he did not care for her.

"Maybe he's in love with John," she once said to

Madge, "and is envious of me."

"Love is not behind every emotion."

"Pretty much," said Constance.

"You, of all persons, should know better."

"I meant love in all its guises: love of another person, love of love making, love of power, love of money. Should I go on?"

Having become an observant writer, Constance had correctly assessed Rycharde's feelings towards her but had not discovered the cause, which would have become apparent had she been privy to a certain conversation between John and Rycharde. Furthermore, whether to spare his beloved's feelings—or some other reason—John did not tell Constance of this conversation. Having served John for a number of years and also due to John's open and trusting nature, Rycharde felt free to express himself on whatever subject he so chose. The conversation in question took place on a hot August morning in 1597. Constance had eaten a hurried breakfast and then left to go to Will's.

"I have no doubt," Rycharde said as he served John a glass of ale before John left for court, "that Mistress Constance is a good and loving companion but I cannot help wondering why she spends so much time away from the home."

"Her time away from here is generally spent at her brother's although she occasionally visits her friend, Mistress Whitton, of whom I am also quite fond."

"But why should her brother require so much of her time?"

"As one of London's foremost playwrights, Master Shakespeare hardly has the time to oversee the servants and otherwise manage his household."

"Excuse my saying this, but how can you be certain she goes to her brother's home, or Mistress Whitton's, just because she says so?"

"Caution would be well advised at this juncture."

Whether, unusual for such an astute person, he misconstrued John's meaning or, more likely, chose to ignore the warning, Rycharde plunged on.

"The other day, Mistress Constance said she would do the food shopping; but she returned home with scarcely half a basket's worth of provisions."

"That, Rycharde, is none of your business."

"I am sorry to say this, Sir, but I feel I must. I wonder if the Mistress is entirely trustworthy."

John slammed his fist on the table. Rycharde, who had been standing close to John's chair, jumped backwards.

"Sirrah, you have overshot your mark. Simply because you have been privy to certain meetings does not accord you the liberty you have just taken. I beseech you watch your tongue. Were it not for your years of service and the confidences I have entrusted you with, I would dismiss you on the spot. I shall overlook your impertinence this one time. See that it does not happen again or you will have seen the last of this house."

"I am truly sorry, Sir. I will guard my tongue in future."

"See that you do."

Bowing, Rycharde turned and started for the hall that led to the kitchen. John picked up a paper that he wanted to re-read before he left so he failed to see Rycharde stop briefly at the entrance to the hall and glance backwards at John with an expression of disdain, hot anger and murderous intent. Rycharde made a brief, obscene gesture and hurried from the room.

Two days later, in the middle of the afternoon, Constance told Rycharde that she had some shopping to do but that he needn't accompany her as there were other tasks, such as sweeping and mending some of John's clothes, that required his immediate attention. He could then start roasting the pork for supper. She would bring home greens for a salad to go with the meat and fruit for the second course. Having eaten a substantial dinner, she added, they only desired a light supper. She would also purchase the provisions for tomorrow and, possibly, the following day.

"But Mistress, will you not require assistance carrying all those items?"

"I can manage perfectly well."

"As you wish, Mistress." Rycharde thought a second. "Would you also be going to Master Shakespeare's?"

"Not today but likely tomorrow."

Rycharde tried but could not conceal a look of arrogant satisfaction.

She left Mutton Lane, turned right on Wood Street and walked in the direction of Cheapside. She carried a basket on her arm and, in the basket, her purse with her shopping money. A brutally hot, damp August afternoon, she was soon perspiring and stopped to wipe her brow, cheeks and neck with a handkerchief. She began to wonder if this had been such a good idea. She looked forward to finishing her shopping and returning home where it would be cooler. As she walked, her thoughts turned to Rycharde. She had caught his smirk and was considering whether she should ask John what might be the source of the fellow's hostility.

At Cheapside, she turned left and moved slowly east towards Poultry. She planned to make a few purchases at shops along Cheapside and Poultry and at one stall in the Stocks Market after which she would go home. She had not gone far on Cheapside when she saw a man on the side of the street dancing up and down, shaking his head and jiggling his arms as if he were having a fit. She stopped briefly to look. The other pedestrians ignored him. Not long ago, John had mentioned an increase on the streets of madmen, diseased people and poor folk without homes. It might be a good idea, he had said, to contribute funds to organizations that helped such unfortunates or even to start one of his own. Suddenly, Constance felt a jolt as she was bumped by a passer-by. Before she could say or do anything, the man had snatched her basket off her arm and was running down Cheapside. The man having the sham fit ran in the opposite direction.

"Thief," cried out Constance. "Stop that thief."

The thief was about to turn off Cheapside into a side street where it would be difficult, if not impossible, to find him when a man stepped in front of him. The thief raised a fist to strike the man but stopped when he saw the man quickly slide a sword from its scabbard. Keeping the sword point firmly against the thief's chest, the man backed the thief up Cheapside followed by a group of onlookers that included several young boys who danced around making fun of the thief. The other people walking on Cheapside stepped back to let what had become a small crowd pass. When the crowd reached Constance, who was hurrying towards them, the swordsman stopped. Constance looked gratefully at him and then said, not concealing her surprise: "Roberte."

"Give the lady her basket," Roberte said to the thief, who readily complied. Constance checked to be sure the purse was there. The adults in the crowd cheered, and the boys continued frolicking all the time hollering: "Thief.... Thief...." Roberte continued: "You can count your lucky stars that I'm not in the mood to slit your throat which is only because I don't care to take the time and, furthermore, I wish to speak with this lady. If I ever see you playing such tricks again, I will separate your head from your body."

With a final cheer, the adults in the crowd dispersed; but the boys, jumping up and down, hollered: "Slit his throat.... Cut his head off.... Gouge out his eyes...."

"Be gone," commanded Roberte, giving the thief a whack on the behind with the flat of his sword. The thief ran off in the direction his cohort had gone, and Roberte chuckled: "I will likely have to make good on that promise."

The boys ran off, except one who said to Roberte: "You could've at least cut off one of his hands."

"I'll cut off one of yours if you're not gone by the time I count to five." Roberte started counting at which the lad took to his heels, causing Roberte to smile broadly. Then, bowing to Constance, he said: "If, my beauty, I'm to keep saving you from disaster, the least you can do is to allow me to buy you supper."

"I humbly thank you for the offer, my lord, but that would not be possible."

"Because of the man I saw you with at the riot? That would be about a year ago."

"Yes, my lord."

"Please call me Roberte." He looked at her hand. "But I see no ring. Are you not married?"

Constance looked down demurely and thought it was high time she got a modest ring to wear when needed. It would help her avoid awkward situations.

"I do not always wear it out of concern for what just happened. We live in troubled times. I should be devastated to lose it."

"At least, let me accompany you while you shop and see you safely home," he said, offering his arm.

"My name is Constance," she said as they walked.

"And the surname?"

"Maydestone." Constance thought that, having started the lie with the ring, there was little point in stopping. Despite the coincidence of their three accidental meetings, her falsehood was unlikely to be discovered. Should they meet a fourth time, she would deal with it then. "And yours?"

"Underhill."

"You carry a sword and know how to use it so I presume...."

"Correctly.... Sir Roberte Underhill at your service."

"More than once," she laughed.

"But I am not a peer so no Lord This or Lord That. I was knighted for some services I performed for the Crown. Nothing extraordinary, and my family has but modest connections."

"And the lady with you the first time we met which, had you run me over with your horse, would've been the last time?"

"My wife."

"So you're married."

"Widowed."

"I'm terribly sorry. May I ask the cause?"

"Puerperal fever that she caught within days of giving birth to our first child—a daughter named Marie. She is three now and the apple of my eye. Do you have children?"

"Sadly, not yet."

He waited patiently while she made her purchases and then walked her as far as Wood Street where she asked him to leave her. "It is but a short distance from here," she said, "and I will be cautious." He bent over her hand and kissed it and said that he hoped they would meet again only under happier circumstances.

"Whether we do or not, I shall always be grateful for the services you have rendered me. I wish you and your daughter much happiness and good health."

Sir Roberte bowed and strode off. Constance hurried home eager to tell John about the amazing coincidence of Roberte saving her yet again from calamity. When she opened the door, she heard male voices coming from the small library off the front parlor. Not thinking whether she might be intruding, she went to the library door and looked in. John, Dr. Claybrook, Rycharde and three men she did not know were seated around the table in the center of the library. Tankards stood on the table. Evening had started to fall, and the room was dimly lit by only a few candles in sconces. John was speaking:

"The time for action has come. We must...." He paused when Rycharde, having spotted Constance, audibly cleared his throat. All the men looked at Constance who said, apologetically: "I am sorry. I wanted a word with John."

"Can it wait, darling?" John asked. "We are almost finished here."

"Of course. I will be upstairs."

She left the basket in the kitchen.

When John entered their bedroom, Constance was sitting in a wooden armchair elaborately carved with swirls, flowers. leaves and geometric forms. A cushion supported her back while she read the latest draft of a play Will had sent over yesterday for her comments. It was a comedy, *Much Ado About Nothing*; and she found it quite funny. She made only a few marginal notes. She got up and embraced John. When she told John about her adventure, he was also astounded at the coincidence but worried about her shopping alone.

"Nonsense, I will just be more careful. I'm not going to lock myself in the house. Madge does all the shopping at her house and even takes the twins along."

When asked about the group in the library, John explained that they were potential contributors to the charitable organization he had mentioned to her recently. Dr. Claybrook was hoping to include in their plan a small hospital to serve the indigent.

"How wonderful that you are actually moving forward, but why was the man who doesn't like women there?"

"Despite his appearance, he is quite wealthy."

"I see, and Rycharde?"

He had finished his work and asked if he could listen. We had a disagreement a few days ago, and I thought this might set matters straight. You know that I've never treated him like a typical servant."

"I know all too well."

"Speaking of Rycharde, I have given him the night off so he could visit his mother, whom he says is not well. Do you mind preparing supper?"

"Not in the least so long as we prepare something else first."

A couple of days later, on the fourth of September, 1597, at two in the afternoon, a date and time Constance would never forget, they were having dinner when there was a loud, repeated knocking at their door.

"Rycharde, please see who is there," called John.

No answer came from the rear of the house so John wiped his mouth with a napkin, rose and went to the door. A gentleman in somber dress and wearing a flat hat stood at the door, his hand resting on the hilt of a sword. Two Queen's Body Guards of the Yeomen of the Guard flanked him, each armed with a halberd and dressed in scarlet and gold uniforms. Behind them stood a carriage with a coat of arms on the door.

"John Maydestone, Barrister?" demanded the gentleman.

"I am he."

Constance came into the front parlor and approached the door.

"What is it, John?" she asked.

Before John could answer, the gentleman spoke in a calm but disdainful voice: "Are you Constance Maydestone?"

"We are not married," said John.

"Please answer the question, my good woman."

"I am Constance but what is this about?"

"You, John Maydestone, and you, Constance Maydestone,"

"But she is not...."

"...are charged with high treason against the person of Her Majesty Queen Elizabeth and by order of Her Majesty's Privy Council are to be taken into custody forthwith by myself, Sir Oliver Stoughton, Representative of said Privy Council, and removed to the Tower of London there to await trial and sentencing."

Constance screamed and John again tried desperately to say that Constance was not his wife but was again interrupted by Sir Oliver.

"You will come with us now. Later, you may be permitted to send for a few personal items."

Having regained his composure, John asked: "May I speak briefly with my servant?"

Sir Oliver stepped into the parlor and told John to call the servant but not to attempt leaving the room. To emphasize his point, Sir Oliver pulled his sword a couple of inches from the scabbard and then replaced it. John called several times for Rycharde, each time louder; but no response was forthcoming.

"He must be occupied elsewhere," said Sir Oliver. "We must leave now. I have others on whom to call."

At a brisk trot, the four horses pulled the carriage through London's streets. The curtains were drawn so they could not look out; but from the feel and sound of the wheels on cobblestones, Constance was certain they were on main thoroughfares. Sir Oliver and one of the Guards sat in the carriage while the second Guard, with both halberds, sat on top with the driver.

"John," said Constance, struggling to contain her anger, "you have...."

"Silence," barked Sir Oliver.

No one said a further word. Constance looked stonily at John. The carriage passed through two gates and stopped in the Tower forecourt where two other Guards were waiting. A jailer carrying a ring of keys stood between them. In contrast to the Yeomen Guards, the jailer wore ordinary clothes. The Guard in the carriage got out first while Sir Oliver told John and Constance to wait. The second Guard handed down the halberds and then climbed down from the top of the carriage. These two Guards arrayed themselves at either side of the carriage door while the two from the Tower stood a few steps away. Sir Oliver then indicated for John and Constance to step down from the carriage. Constance looked around at the place she had last been with Madge, all those years ago, on their first outing. This was a far different occasion, she thought fearfully, and realized that she was trembling.

The jailer stepped forward and spoke: "Welcome to the Tower. We who work here have no reason to harm you. So long as you behave properly, we shall endeavor to make you as comfortable as circumstances permit." He glanced at Constance and smiled. Then, he made a sign, and each of the Tower guards took one of the prisoners by the arm. With the jailer leading, they walked to the left around the main building. They passed through a heavy oak door, climbed two flights of worn stone steps and entered a hallway. Here John and Constance were separated, and each led in a different direction.

"John," said Constance in anguish. He looked

back but said not a word.
She was led past two doors, and then the jailer stopped in front of a third door. He searched among his keys, found the right one and opened the door. The Guard left. The jailer pushed her, not roughly but firmly, into the room. He took a step into the room. She noticed an unidentifiable, but distinctly unpleasant, odor. She turned back to the jailer.

"I want to speak to... to John."

"Not possible."

He then advised her that, as a woman, she was entitled to straw for the stone platform that would serve as her bed and blankets—if he could find any—to help with the night cold, which could be bitter even at this time of year. He looked her up and down and smirked.

"Delicate women such as yourself don't do well in the cold. I've seen one or two that could barely walk to their executions." Constance's lips moved, but no sound came out. "You're also entitled to one or two meals a day—unless I forget. In any case, they won't be like what you are used to." He laughed, left the room and closed the door. The key turning in the lock made a grating sound that caused her to shake uncontrollably.

She looked around and screamed. Two rats crouched on the platform staring at her as if annoyed that their games had been interrupted. Flailing her arms and hollering, she rushed at them; and they fled, scrambling into a corner where there was a hole through which they disappeared. Sobbing she sat on the one piece of furniture in the room: a wooden chest. The chamber was divided by stone arches into three sections. The middle one contained the platform above which was a stone shelf on which sat a large candle in a brass holder. A tinderbox was next to the candle. To the right was a narrow space separated by a crumbling wall from the platform. A stone basin was built into the wall, and a pitcher stood next to the basin. Drying her eyes with a handkerchief that she found in the sleeve of her outer garment, she got up and walked to the basin, a matter of a dozen steps. It was caked with a greenish growth that turned her stomach. She fought not to get sick. The pitcher was full of what appeared to be clean water; she wet her handkerchief and cleaned, as much as possible, the basin. She doubted she would succeed, but she determined to ask the jailer for soap, no matter the quality. She needed to keep herself and her surroundings clean. A chamber pot stood by the basin.

The third section was as large as the other two combined and was empty. But there was a window, albeit unglazed and barred. It would let in the cold and provided no means of escape, which she knew was anyway out of the question; but through it, she could see the courtyard, the very end of Thames Street and a sliver of the river on which she saw a wherry. Scant comfort but at least she didn't feel quite so isolated. Yet how could she prove that she was completely innocent of any charge of treason and that she knew nothing of the matter.

A horrifying thought struck her. Was Rycharde's disappearance today significant? Did he really have a sick mother—or any sort of mother—in London? Had he informed on John, the man who had treated him for years with such extraordinary kindness? Tears flowed again, but these were of anger.

John had lied to her. Was he protecting her? She snorted. His protection could end in her death. She would stay with the story of a group of men planning a charitable organization. Who would believe that she had lived with a man who plotted treason in his own home without her knowing, or at least suspecting, the truth?

She sat again on the chest. Although the jailer's attitude boded no good outcome, she must at least try to ask—beg, if necessary—for a book, any book; otherwise, she would tell him, she would certainly go mad—and whom would that help? A welcome idea occurred to her. She could work on a play in her mind and later, if she survived, write down from memory as much as possible of the script. Maybe it should be about treason. She got up and paced, working out a list of characters. She worked out the first few scenes in the story and even composed a number of lines, some rhymed, some not. She liked what she had accomplished but, as of yet, had no ideas for a title. That could wait. She had no idea how much time had passed when she suddenly thought there might be something useful in the chest. She opened it and found a disorderly pile of clothes. She took out a few pieces. Clearly feminine, they were of good cloth and reasonably well cut. A former prisoner, no doubt. She wondered what had happened to the woman and shuddered. She tried on a cloak. On the big side, it still fit tolerably well and would help keep her warm should the promised blankets be thin and moth-eaten. She heard the key turning in the lock, and the door opened. The jailer entered with one folded blanket and a plate on which were a small wedge of cheese and a slice of bread. He looked at her curiously.

"Where did you get that cloak? You hadn't it on when you arrived."

Constance nodded at the chest.

"Give it to me."

Slowly, she took off the cloak and handed it to him. He gave her, in return, the blanket and plate. It was, as she feared, very thin and old. He noticed the other clothes on the floor. He scooped them up. Constance thought there could be no harm in trying to change his attitude. Maybe it was due to the treason charge.

"John and I are innocent," she said in as humble a voice as she could muster, "of treason. We are loyal subjects of Her Majesty, whom we revere. John is a barrister and respects the law."

"That is not for me to decide."

"But do you believe me."

"I've never had a prisoner say they were guilty. It would have gone easier on them had they done so."

"This blanket will hardly keep me warm and this food barely alive."

The jailer shrugged.

"May I have another blanket?"

The jailer shrugged.

"May I ask," she said, "what your name is?"

"Josias."

"No surname?"

"No surname."

"I'm Constance."

"I know."

He was shorter than Constance by an inch and looked to be about thirty or so. His beard was neatly trimmed; and he wore simple clothes—in contrast to the elegant uniforms of the Yeomen.

"Have you always worked in the Tower?"

"A number of years. It's not hard work."

"Do you have a wife?"

"I had one, and two children. They all died in the plague four years ago."

"I am very sorry. Your pain must be unbearable."

The jailer shrugged.

"I need to contact my brother."

"In due course."

"May I at least have a book?"

The jailer didn't reply. Taking the clothes with him, he left the room and locked the door. Although she had protested John's innocence, she had her doubts but could not understand what his motives for treason might be. He had everything. But his reaction at the time of the arrest—and Rycharde's disappearance—suggested that it's exactly what he had done. She resumed her pacing and did the only thing left to her: work on the play that was taking shape in her head.

When it grew dark, she lit the candle. Having put

it off as long as possible, she ate the bread and cheese. After another hour of pacing, she became tired and, wrapping the blanket around her, lay down on the bench. She shivered throughout the night and slept only in fits and starts. She had never been so cold in her life—not even the night she left Stratford. In the morning, she got up, haggard and exhausted. As the sun rose in the sky, she warmed a little. The jailer unlocked and opened the door. With him was a young lad carrying a chamber pot and pitcher of water; he exchanged the pots and pitchers and left. The jailer had a plate again with a slice of bread and cheese. He also carried a flagon.

"Ale," he said, handing her the flagon and plate.

"I almost froze last night. May I please have more blankets?"

"Not unless you have money."

"More food?" she asked in desperation.

"Money."

"If I could contact my brother, he would bring money."

"As I said yesterday, he will be notified in due course. I have nothing to do with it."

"Do you want me to die?"

The jailer shrugged and left.

She spent the day working on the play. As the room was somewhat warm, she was able to sleep for a couple of hours. Late that afternoon, the jailer and the lad appeared again. The lad changed the chamber pots and pitchers and left. The jailer handed her a flagon and a plate, this time with a small apple in addition to the bread and cheese.

"I must have another blanket or I could die tonight."

"That is of little concern to me."

"Could I at least have a bar of soap.'

"Money."

That night was the same as the first although colder and her shivering worse so that her teeth chattered. She was barely able to get up when she heard the key in the lock. When the lad had changed the pots and gone, the jailer stared at her. Her shoulders were hunched over, and she had the blanket wrapped around her.

"You do look cold."

"I.... I.... couldn't stop shivering."

"There is a way."

"What?"

"You are a beautiful young woman, and my wife died four years ago."

Constance straightened up.

"Never."

"As you wish." He stopped at the door and turned around. "it would mean blankets and hot food and soap. You would be comfortable until ... well, until."

"No."

She heard him laughing as the key turned.

Two days later, she succumbed. After the lad had left, she walked unsteadily up to him, smiled as best she could and ran a finger down his cheek.

The jailer was as good as his word. Later in the morning, he brought three thick blankets, the cloak and a pillow. He also gave her two books, a bar of crude soap and several cloths. In the early afternoon, he brought hot porridge with fatty pieces of meat and diced vegetables floating in the broth.

This went on for three more days. She had hot food three times a day and a new book when she finished the other two. All were romances. She stayed warm with the blankets and the cloak. She was relatively clean and spent those days reading, working on the play in her head and gazing out the small, barred window. Josias took her once a day. She sat on the platform afterwards, filled with self-loathing but knowing she had no choice.

Despite begging Josias for news of John, he invariably shook his head whenever she asked.

The morning of the fifth day, when the door opened, it was not Josias but two men in ordinary clothes. Without a word, they grasped her by the arms and half-dragged her out of the room, down the hallway to a circular stone staircase and then down three flights to the basement.

"Do not say a word," they cautioned her as they descended into the bowels of the Tower. The hallway in the basement was barely lit so she would have stumbled had not the two men held her firmly. They passed several doors; at one, she heard a man screaming in pain. She tried to hurry, but the men did not change their pace. If anything, they slowed so that she would hear the screaming longer. Her body shook with fear. They opened a door at the end of the hallway and pushed her into a room that was bare and devoid of any furnishings except a wooden box with low sides and rollers at each end. A stick and two coils of rope were fastened to each roller. Two men in jerkins, short trousers and stockings stood on the near side of the rack. Their biceps bulged. Two men in flowing robes and wearing hats stood on the far side. The two men who had brought her left. Without a word to her, one of the men in a robe said to the men in trousers: "Prepare her."

One of these men went up to her, roughly undid her bodice and jerked it free. He took it off and dropped it on the tiled floor. He pulled her outer dress over her head, dropping it on top of her bodice. He grabbed her arm and pulled her towards the rack. She felt her legs go weak. She resisted, but it was no use. He forced her onto the rack and tied a rope to each limb. One of the robed men looked down at her.

"We will start slowly with just a little pressure. As it increases, the pain will begin. It won't be long before it is excruciating, but we are not here to cause you pain. Whenever you are ready to confess to your participation in your husband's treason plot, we will stop." He addressed the men in trousers who now each held a stick. "Begin," he commanded.

The rollers started turning, and she felt the pressure in her limbs and torso. The men kept turning. Little by little the pain began. She groaned.

"Are you ready?" asked the man.

"I know nothing of any plot. I don't believe there was one. They were talking about starting a charitable institution to help the poor and also building a hospital for the indigent. How is that treason? Rycharde made it all up as he despises me."

"We don't want to hear lies."

"I'm not lying. I swear."

"Faster."

The men turned faster, and the pain grew worse. She cried out. The pain became acute. She screamed. The rollers turned, and she screamed louder. She thought her body was being torn asunder. The pain was unbearable. She would tell them anything. She started to speak when she heard the door open and a somewhat familiar voice bark: "What in hell is going on? Stop immediately if you value your lives. Now slowly and carefully roll back."

Her pain eased slightly.

"But Lord Pennyford," said one of the men in robes, "she is the wife of the traitor Maydestone."

"She is nothing of the sort. She is a common whore whom Maydestone hired from time to time."

"But Rycharde told us..."

"Rycharde was mistaken on that point—or lied. Perhaps he wanted Maydestone for himself. Who knows? Get her up. Let her dress."

"But Lord Pennyford, she was about to confess. Surely the Privy Council will be interested...."

"She knows nothing about which to confess. She was not part of the plot. We have all the confessions we need. I have spoken to both Lord Burghley, who will advise the Council, and the Queen, neither of whom want the blood of an innocent person, especially a woman, even if she is a common whore, on their hands. She is to be released now. I have it in writing signed by Her Majesty."

"How do you know she is not his wife?" asked the robed man, unwilling to easily release his prey.

"Do you doubt an Earl? Do you doubt Lord Burghley? Do you doubt the Queen?" Edmund laughed as if this were the best joke he had ever heard. "Have you all grown tired of living?"

They knew when they were defeated. Constance was untied, helped to her feet and given her clothes. She dressed quickly, not caring that five men were observing her, of whom only one counted.

"Edmund," she said, her voice quaking, "I.... I...."

Before she could say another word, Edmund had crossed to her and slapped her hard across the face.

"Lord Pennyford, whore," he spat out.

"Is that how you know she's a whore?" asked the younger of the two men in robes.

In barely a second, Edmund's sword was out of its scabbard; and he had turned to face the speaker. Slowly and deliberately, he approached the man, sword extended, until its tip was under the man's chin. The man's mouth moved, but no words came out.

"It is fortunate that I don't, today, want to explain to Lord Burghley how one of the service's better investigators fell on a sword."

"I'm... I'm... sorry."

"That will do—for today."

Edmund took Constance by the arm and left the room. He led her quickly down the hall, up the stairs and into the courtyard. From there, they passed through the gates and circled the walls of the Tower until they reached Thames Street where he stopped. Until then, he had not said a word.

"Lord Edmund," Constance said. "Or Lord Pennyford? I am not thinking very well."

"Who could blame you? It is Lord Pennyford as my father is no longer with us; but as we are now alone, you may call me Edmund."

She fell sobbing into his arms while people gawked but did not stop - not advisable when a man with a sword is holding a woman. He untangled her and, taking her arm, started up Thames.

"I will explain," he said, "but let's find a tavern. We could both benefit from a glass of wine."

They walked in silence up Thames until, just past the Fishmongers Hall, they spotted a tavern on a side street. Constance thought that the name on the sign—The Swan—that swayed in the gentle breeze off the river was sadly appropriate. She doubted that Edmund would be able, or even willing, to save John: but she was determined to try. She looked briefly at the painting of the lovely, white bird with its long curving neck, and then they went inside. They sat at a corner table in the front hall. Edmund ordered a claret and Constance a glass of white, not caring nor specifying whether it was French or Spanish or malmsey from Crete or piss from wherever. She just wanted to drink and find out what she could.

"I am sorry about your father. When did it happen?"

"A year ago, and I'm not sure why you should be sorry given the circumstances of your only experience with the late Earl. On the other hand, what he called you at that time probably influenced my plan for freeing you."

"I hold no ill will. We were in a compromising situation that could easily have been interpreted as he did. I would offer congratulations on your becoming the Earl; but the death of one's father, particularly at what I take was a somewhat young age, should not be the subject of congratulations."

"My dear Constance, you have greatly matured from the beautiful young woman that I...."

"Deflowered?"

"Yes, very much matured. And your way of speaking has changed: so refined and ... literary is the word that comes to mind."

"One doesn't live with Will Shakespeare without acquiring some literary phrases."

"I suppose not."

The serving girl brought their wine and, as Edmund had requested, a plate of cheeses and tiny mince pies.

"You must be starving. Did you get anything decent to eat in the Tower?"

"Eating was not my first concern."

They drank briefly in silence.

"Before we go further," said Constance, "I must thank you for saving me."

"John asked to speak to me privately. He convinced me of your innocence—which I already suspected was the case—or much as it would have pained me, I would not have done it."

"Why did you need to say I was a common whore?"

"It made for a more credible story, and I knew that Lord Burghley would need convincing. Less so the Queen. She is, and rightly so, less skeptical than Lord Burghley. I told John of my plan so that he would, if necessary, corroborate my story."

As it was early afternoon, and past the dinner hour, the tavern was not crowded; and Constance felt she could speak freely. Two tables in the dark wood-panelled hall were occupied by what appeared to be merchants and professional men. Three women, fashionably dressed so daughters of prosperous merchants or, less likely but possibly, women of the street sat at a table across the hall while nearby she heard four well-dressed men—one in a sable lined coat—speaking a foreign language. Dutch, she guessed, or German. She felt that now was the time to address the question even if there was little, or no, hope. Keeping her voice as steady as possible, she asked:

"Edmund, can you save John?"

Edmund looked at her, almost sadly, shook his head and then spoke in a low voice so as not to be overheard.

"He is guilty of treason. All have confessed, three with torture, two—John and Dr. Claybrook—without. Nothing can be done to stay their executions."

Constance's hand shook as she reached for her wine.

"Nothing at all?"

"Nothing."

Edmund took her hand and held it briefly.

"Why then was I tortured?"

"Because you had insisted to the jailer on your innocence, and the investigators were convinced of your guilt. They thought torture was the way to find the truth. Such men, while good at unearthing true traitors, are not good at accepting those who are innocent. They had convinced Lord Burghley of the necessity of torturing you. My task would've been not impossible but more complicated if Lord Burghley had thought of you as John's wife."

"I am not."

"I know."

"You seem to know many things."

"I do. So I had to change Lord Burghley's mind. Telling him that not only were you not John's wife but also were nothing more than a common whore rather than an intimate lover made the story that much more convincing. I told him that men such as John do not entrust secrets to common whores—or strumpets—as Father once called you. He listens to me as does Her Majesty. And so here you are."

"But why?"

"Why what?"

"Treason? Why did they commit treason? And what did they hope to accomplish?"

"They are Catholics. One of them is a Jesuit priest in disguise."

"I once asked John if he were a secret Catholic; he denied it. Said he was loyal to the Queen."

"Did he say which one?"

Constance did not try to conceal her anger.

"He did not."

"There you have it."

"John lied to me, but I..."

"But you still love him."

"In a way, yes, and it is agony to think of what awaits him."

Constance put her face in her hands and sobbed.

"Careful," said Edmund softly.

Constance quieted. She touched Edmund's hand.

"I understand."

"This is a tricky business in dangerous times. Some say your brother has Catholic leanings, but I don't believe it and will ensure that he is safe."

"Dear God," she said. "This is too much to bear."

"I know, and I am sorry to tell you all this; but if I didn't, you would never understand. I am not personally, as I think you know, against Catholics unless they represent a danger to our beloved Monarch and the tranquility of our country. In this case, they intended, through the services of the Doctor, to find a way to poison the Queen. They then hoped Spain would invade and return the country to the Catholic faith. I am not a particularly religious man, but such a deed would have wreaked havoc and destroyed the hard-won peace and prosperity—not to mention the greatest religious tolerance and freedom of any society in the modern age—that the glorious Tudor, and especially Elizabethan, age has bestowed upon us. As a woman, and without heirs, Elizabeth is in a vulnerable position and always has been. It's due to her political skills, and our constant vigilance, that she has not been assassinated. Not that there haven't been numerous attempts."

"I am astonished, to say the least."

"I thought you would be."

"Are you one of her spies?"

"Not a question that I intend to answer."

"You just did."

"I hope you will go to your grave with that information. Walsingham's role was no secret. My methods are different. Who can say which is better? Just to be clear, after Lord Burghley, I am the most powerful man in the government which means in the country. I say that with all modesty. My position has nothing to do with my rank. I earned it. For me, what's truly important is that our Queen is alive and in good health."

"I will go to my grave as you requested."

"Yes, very much more mature. It pleases me greatly to see it."

She took a large drink of wine, draining the glass, and asked for another, which Edmund readily ordered and the serving girl promptly brought. "So,' she continued, "John is doomed."

"I cannot speak for his soul but, as for the rest, yes."

Constance forced back tears. She would not again cry in public.

"He has, however, done a very brave thing, of which I must inform you as it deeply affects your future."

"What do you mean?"

"John will remain silent at his trial, pleading neither 'guilty' nor 'not guilty.' This is called *'peine forte et dure*' and means that the Crown cannot take his property nor deprive his heirs of their rights. I understand that, as he had no other living family, you are his sole heir. You will inherit the house where you are living as well as a substantial income."

"And the penalty involved in this *'peine forte et dure*' which, remembering my meager French, means something like 'hard and forceful punishment'?"

"Your French is correct."

Constance shuddered.

"What is the penalty?"

"I would rather not say."

"Please, Edmund. It will be worse not knowing."

Edmund took her hand.

"He will be placed under heavy stones and, although given a little water and bread, will starve to death—or crushed depending on the weight of the stones. The latter would be preferable as faster."

Constance raised a fist to her mouth and bit on it.

Fearing that she might even scream, Edmund squeezed her hand tightly and continued in a voice, not loud, but one that that could be heard at the nearby tables: "These mince pies are excellent, don't you think, my dear?" He released her hand and gave her one that she forced herself to eat. Finishing, she said: "I have myself under control. Thank you. I know the effect an outburst would've caused." She drank some wine.

"Another glass?" asked Edmund.

"Not yet.... I must see him."

"That would not be wise."

"Edmund, I must."

"He expressly asked that you remember him from happier times. He is a traitor, for which I roundly condemn him; but I will honor his final wishes. I will not permit you to see him."

"And I presume that is within your power."

"It is." Edmund lowered his voice so that she had to lean forward to hear him. "There is another reason for you not to see him. Were Lord Burghley to discover that you had seen John at this time, he might wonder why a common whore would do that. Who knows where such speculation might lead? He might have someone besides me investigate and discover that the inheritor of John's property was the supposedly common whore. Better for the authorities to forget you." Edmund drank some wine. "It really is quite a good claret," he said, approvingly and loud enough to be heard.

"I cannot accept the property if it means adding to John's suffering."

"John thought you might say that and asked me to convince you otherwise."

"You cannot. I am a stubborn woman."

"John also said that but implores you to accept the only token of his love that he can now give you."

"What is that token worth if it means causing him greater torment?"

"What is a love worth that denies a man his last wish? It is also his last chance to perform a meaningful act. He will die more at peace knowing you are provided for."

"I could go back to Will's. He is now well-to-do and has a large home."

"John also thought of that and remarked on how you cherish your independence."

"He was an excellent lawyer and very perceptive."

"Do him this favor. Allow him what little peace is possible in his final days. He knows that he foolishly endangered your life and wishes to atone."

"You were always very persuasive."

"You cannot prevent John from experiencing pain, and worse alternatives exist."

"May I leave you for a moment?"

"Of course."

Constance went outside and walked up and down in front of the tavern. When she reentered fifteen minutes later, she told Edmund that she would accept the property if he promised to tell John that she loved and forgave him.

"Agreed."

"I will cry later and mourn in private. But now I have a practical matter to discuss."

"Go ahead."

"What of our neighbors who may have assumed that I was John's wife? We never said one way or the other. Won't they be suspicious of my being released?"

"Make it known that you were not his wife and knew nothing of his treasonous activities. Say that the authorities became convinced of your innocence. Say nothing further. Do not discuss the inheritance. If there is gossip, I will put a stop to it."

"Thank you, my dear friend. It is an excellent solution."

"That's why I'm good at what I do."

"What do I tell Will?"

"The truth except the part about the common whore. Tell no one about that."

"And my father who thought I had married John?"

"The same."

"He will be angry and ashamed if he has to tell his acquaintances that I never married John."

"When he learns of your inheritance, he will forget his anger. You will be wealthier than he is. And you can convince him that not marrying John saved you from the gallows. At the same time, tell both Will and your father that the less said about this whole business the better, including the subject of your marital status. They should at all times avoid discussing any aspect of John's treason. If pressed, they can say it's simply too painful."

She took one of his hands in both of hers. "I cannot thank you enough. I won't even try." She released his hand. "I have one favor to ask."

"This will not be a surprise."

"I know from what was said in the torture chamber that Rycharde reported us. I will not blame Rycharde for betraying John. He may have seen it as his duty although John told me they recently had a disagreement. I have no idea what it was about so perhaps Rycharde wanted some kind of malignant revenge. I will let that pass, but I cannot forget that he incriminated me for no valid cause. I'm sure he disliked me, but that is hardly a reason for sending someone to be tortured and executed. Did I hear correctly in the torture chamber?"

"You did; and as you know, I seriously doubted that part of his story, which is why I agreed to speak privately to John when he asked to see me alone."

"I almost wish it were in my nature to ask you to torture Rycharde. God may take care of that, but I cannot be the cause of inflicting such pain on any human being no matter how evil."

"I only approve of torture when we absolutely must have the truth in order to protect Elizabeth or to solve a particularly odious crime. But even though you don't want Rycharde tortured, I imagine you'd like him to disappear."

"I want..."

"Don't answer. He attempted to destroy someone I care deeply about. Whatever you were about to say, he will not see twenty-four hours after the trial, where we do need his testimony."

Constance bowed her head as if in prayer.

"My dear: one thing I must ask," said Edmund.

"Whatever you wish, I grant."

"This whole conversation never took place."

"Just two close friends having a glass or two of wine. And speaking of which, if you don't mind, I will now have another."

After their glasses had been refilled, Edmund said: "Do you recall the two nieces of Mistress Sedley?"

"In the carriage—yes."

"It seems that Ester, the younger of the two, whom I encountered recently by chance, does not find my company wholly disagreeable."

"Who would?"

Edmund laughed, and then his tone turned somber.

"I will," he said, "send you word when John is gone."

"Thank you. I would very much appreciate that."

"And now let me escort you home. I have a carriage waiting down the street."

# The Prison Play: 1597-1600

Constance could never recall whether the year after John's execution went by quickly or crept at a snail's pace. She knew that, for several months, she did little but sit by the fire. She thought continually of John, mostly with great sadness but occasionally angry that he could have allowed his political beliefs to cause them both so much pain. She missed him terribly. She also thought that, so far in her young life, she had been in love with two persons, both of whom had met violent, untimely ends. She wondered if there was something wrong with her and, also, if she would ever experience such love again. Of course, she loved Will and Madge; but that was different.

True to his word, Edmund had advised her, in person, of John's demise. He had also obtained for her the services of a good lawyer, and the inheritance process went smoothly. No one, the lawyer told her, had questioned why John Maydestone had left his entire property to Constance Shakespeare—a person who had lived with him for not even a year.

Will had wanted her to write a play about Henry V—following up on her *Henry IV, Part Two*—but she declined, saying she wasn't up to it. Maybe he could give her something in a few months. She did tell him she would be happy to read through his first draft and make comments. Will reluctantly agreed but told her that work would be the best antidote against the poison of the mind that, he argued, was consuming her.

"Please," she said, "give me time."

"As you wish." He got up to leave. "Is the income from John's estate sufficient for you to maintain the house and live comfortably?"

"I am well provided for."

"I should, nevertheless, like to give you money as I used to, only now I can afford to more amply reward your work."

He gave her ten sovereigns, said he would do so periodically and left.

She did think occasionally about the play she had started in the Tower—the one in her head—which she thought of as the prison play.

Edmund visited periodically. He liked, he said, to sit comfortably by her fire and talk with her. She was not only the most beautiful woman in London but also one of the most, if not the most, intelligent. Their conversations ranged widely from politics to religion to literature. He admired her collection of books, some but not all of which, had been John's.

"Do you," he once asked suspiciously, "help Will

with his work?"

"Good heavens, how could I do that?"

"Easily, given how well read you are."

"Put that idea out of your head."

He never attempted intimacy, for which she was grateful. In fact, he once brought Ester who was delighted to see Constance and reminded her of the time, many years ago, that they had met by chance in the street.

"Oh yes, I was... shopping."

In November, she told Edmund that she would like to hire a servant and asked if he had any ideas.

"I know just the person if you don't mind someone whose father is African and whose mother is English."

"Not at all. How do you come to know her?"

"Her father works as a carriage driver for a friend of mine. My friend mentioned just a few days ago that, now that she is eighteen, the father would like to find her a place. He is afraid that not everyone would want such a girl and, also, that she might be ill-used. My friend does not need another servant but says that, having done some chores for him, she is hard-working, well-spoken and pleasant."

Helena turned out to be a treasure. She and Constance got along from the start. Which was fortunate since, only a month earlier, Constance had discovered that she was pregnant. She was thrilled and only hoped the baby was John's and not the jailer's. She realized, to her distress, that it might take considerable time after the baby's birth before she would be sure—if she ever would. She turned over and over in her mind whether she was wrong to give herself to Josias in return for the blankets, hot food, soap and books. But she had no idea, she reminded herself, how long she would be kept in the barren room and or whether she would have survived without Josias.

Helena was as cheerful and out-going as she was industrious and efficient. She took on all the work involved in maintaining the household: cleaning, washing clothes, food shopping (although Constance liked doing part of the shopping—old habits being hard to break) and cooking. To no small degree, she reminded Constance of how she had managed Will's home during her earliest years in London. Helena also—without knowing anything about Constance's relationship with John nor any of the specifics of his death nor of how Constance came to be in possession of the house—instinctively understood that Constance needed quiet time.

After Helena had been with her a few days, Constance, who had been staring gloomily into the fire, noticed that the rasping sound of Helena's broom had ceased. Constance turned around and saw Helena standing in the door to the hall—where she had just been sweeping—that led to the kitchen and back rooms.

"Should I sweep the parlor and change the rush mats now, Mistress Shakespeare, or do it later?"

"Why don't you fetch us each a glass of cider and come sit by the fire for a few moments."

"But I couldn't."

"Yes, you could."

Their conversation began with the basics. Constance asked Helena if she liked her work, and Helena replied that she did. They talked about the cold and damp of an English winter and how it made one's bones ache. They talked about the tasty foods available in the nearby Cheapside shops and in the market at the intersection of Poultry and Threadneedle Streets. Then, without giving it any real thought, Constance asked her how her father had come to England.

"I don't know all the details, Mistress; but he came from Africa on a merchant ship. He was a young man, hungry for adventure but may have been tricked into boarding the ship. I don't know as he has never said and goes quiet when I ask about certain aspects of his life. His father was a chief, a fierce warrior, back in Africa. When he arrived in London, he went into the service of Lord Markeley, I don't know how, and has remained there ever since."

"Does he ever feel, as a black man, looked down upon here in England?"

"Most people, especially in Lord Markeley's household and among the Lord and Lady's circle of friends, treat Father with respect and perhaps awe. He is very black and tall and imposing. On the streets, sometimes, people stare and, occasionally, make comments; but I think they are careful. He can look quite fierce although he is a gentle man. He is proud of his black blood and his family."

"Yes, a chief's son. Quite a distinction."

"I've also heard comments about myself and, once or twice, jokes. Some people must think we don't speak English."

"I am truly sorry. I was neither kind nor thoughtful in my questioning."

"No, Mistress, you have been exceptionally kind in all things. I am happy to be part of this household."

"Your English, moreover, is far superior to the gibberish that many in this city pride themselves on as proper English."

Thus commenced a routine that both women enjoyed. The few minutes, which over time grew longer, of conversation two or three times a day did much to improve Constance's spirits and slowly lift her out of the doldrums.

"She is remarkable," Constance said to Madge when the latter came for a visit with the twins.

Constance once asked whether Helena's father missed Africa.

"Mother said that, before my brother and I were born, he occasionally considered going home for a visit but decided that it would be too arduous and dangerous a journey. He also recognized the possibility that he might get captured and sold as a slave. I've never heard him mention the subject. His life and immediate family are here in England. He thinks of himself as English."

"Tell me about your mother."

"She is a kind, if stern, woman, Mistress. She had a stall in Leadenhall Market, selling fruits, which is how they met. You cannot imagine a more unlikely couple. Father, as I've said, is tall and imposing while Mother is short and a little on the plump side. On the other hand, I would rather get in a fight with Father than Mother. She now works in Lord Markeley's kitchen and is quite content."

"Sounds like a perfect match."

"And your family, Mistress, apart from the famous playwright?"

Constance talked about Stratford and her parents. She said that once the baby was old enough to travel, she would go home for a visit. She was a little distressed to have gone back only once since she'd come to London.

"But then my life here is so complete." She thought for a moment and then said: "Except when we might have guests, other than Madge, please call me Constance."

"But Mistress...."

"Constance."

The baby came in June of 1598 with Madge, Helena and Mistress Fowler in attendance. Will strode back and forth in front of the house, holding Ned and Rafe each by the hand. Constance named the baby, a healthy girl, Audrey. One look at Audrey and Constance knew that John was the father. Nor did she ever have occasion to think differently.

"Mothers," she said to herself, "do not make mistakes in such matters. I was wrong to ever be concerned on that score."

As Constance sat by the fire, nursing Audrey, Helena did chores and kept an eye on Constance's glass to see if it needed replenishing with cider or ale. Plenty of either, they felt, would be good for Constance's milk and, thus, the baby.

In August, after three days of declining ability to function on the wherry and two days unable to rise from his bed, Hugh, at forty-nine, died of old age. Madge was sad but had never been particularly close to her father, a situation which only worsened after he had tried to rape Constance. When, however, her husband, Peter, died of typhus three months later, Madge was devastated. At Constance's urging (and payment of the fees), Madge had taken a vial filled with Peter's urine to a physician recommended by Edmund. Fearing infection nor much liking the neighborhood where Peter and Madge lived, the physician had insisted that Madge bring the vial to him rather than his coming to them. He advised her to be careful not to spill any as so many of the paid messengers did (and subsequently substituted their own). After discussing Peter's diet with Madge and describing the urine as "thin," the physician recommended bleeding, which a surgeon performed, and an herbal concoction, which was obtained from an apothecary. Neither worked and, in late November, Peter succumbed after an illness of three weeks.

Constance comforted her friend as best she could. Perhaps the greatest comfort was insisting that Madge move in with her. It took a few days of persuasion; but Madge ultimately agreed, came to an understanding with her landlord and moved in December. She and the twins shared a large room on the second floor down a short corridor from Constance's bedroom. The spare room had been used for years for storage, and the three women worked vigorously for two days to dispose of or relocate items and to thoroughly clean the room. Madge brought a little furniture, such as two beds and a few chests. She and Constance went on a shopping expedition and acquired other items, including a wash basin, two chairs, a table and even an inexpensive painting of a farmhouse, barn and farm animals to hang on a wall. By the end of the year, Madge and the twins were comfortably settled.

Constance had gone through Will's *Henry V*, making marginal comments and changing dialogue—especially some of Henry's martial speeches. Just before the end of the year, she started written work on the prison play and was pleased to discover how much she remembered from the work she had done in The Tower. She told no one about it, not even Will or Madge, and worked quietly at a table in her room.

So, 1598, which had begun as a lost year, ended for Constance with a renewal of hope, energy and work. And little Audrey put into perspective the notion of an apple of one's eye. Constance never tired of holding her, tickling her (which made her giggle), talking to her and breastfeeding her. The hours melted away. The time with Audrey was as completely absorbing as her work. Will, a little to her surprise, turned out to be a proud and attentive uncle. He visited often, bringing wooden toys. Audrey was fascinated by a spinning top and tried, without much success, to spin it herself.

In 1599, the Globe Theatre, in which Will was a shareholder, opened; and the Lord Chamberlain's Men (where he was also a shareholder) moved back to the south side of the river. Large enough to hold up to three thousand spectators, the Globe was a twenty-sided polygon with a main stage that extended into the pit (where folk stood for a penny). There were also three tiers of seating for well-to-do patrons and changing and storage rooms behind the stage. Will was delighted with the new theater.

Remembering their extreme difficulties with Giles Allen, the owner of the land on which The Theatre stood, Constance laughed uproariously when Will told her that the company had found a clause in the ground lease that gave them the right to dismantle The Theatre. Unbeknownst to Allen, therefore, the actors tore down the building and transported the timber and other materials across London and stored them in a waterfront warehouse. These same materials were subsequently used to build the Globe. Allen, according to Will, was enraged.

"Fortune smiles in odd ways," said Will drily. "If that scoundrel had not raised the price of the lease at The Theatre to such an absurdly high level, forcing us to move to The Curtain a year ago, he might have profited by a goodly sum. We might still be at The Theatre, and The Globe would not have been built."

"Such, indeed, are the mysteries of fate," said Constance with a bright, teasing laugh. "If you hadn't sent for me to manage your household—rather, to be your servant—I might be married now to a Stratford merchant, bored to tears and certainly not the foremost unknown playwright in all of London."

"Such are the mysteries of fate," agreed Will. "Speaking of writing, can we talk for a minute about work?"

"Certainly."

"It's been far longer than the few months you originally suggested."

"I know, and I'm sorry."

"I need your help. With acting and working on several plays at the same time, I feel overworked. I would like to give one over to you."

"I'm ready."

"It's set in the Roman era and deals principally with the assassination of Julius Caesar and its aftermath. Are you familiar with the life and ambitions of Julius Caesar?"

"Yes, but I would have to go back to Plutarch to do a play about him."

"Myself as well. I've done some background reading but haven't written anything yet."

"I should also tell you that I'm working on a play that I thought of on my own. While I was in the Tower."

"Well now, that's interesting. What is the subject matter? Is it tragedy or comedy or, perhaps, history—at which you are quite good—or tragic comedy, or comic tragedy?"

"Are you, by any chance, making fun of me? Because if you are, I will set Audrey on you."

"Not in the least or maybe just a little."

"Are you annoyed that I've thought of my own idea rather than employing one of yours?"

"Such a thought never crossed my mind."

"Will..."

"You must admit that you caught me by surprise."

"Which is a bad thing?"

"Do you wish to get this work performed under your name?"

"Too much to hope for."

"In that case, when might I expect to see a draft?"

"Within a few months. I do have a baby to care for."

"You didn't tell me the subject matter or what type of play it is."

"I would prefer to leave that for now. I will say that revenge plays a significant role."

"I always like a good revenge play."

"There is more to it."

"I expect so. I look forward to reading it."

The work progressed more slowly than Constance had expected. It was harder than anything she had yet written. The problem was not so much in the dialogue as in the characters: their shifting motivations, their complex feelings, the subtleties of thought she was trying to express. She felt in unfamiliar territory but pushed forward as best she could.

Her work on the prison play was not made easier by her simultaneous labor on *Julius Caesar*. She would have liked to defer the work on Caesar, but she didn't want to disappoint Will, especially as she had made almost no contribution to their partnership (other than reading and commenting on a draft of *Henry V*) in the sixteen months since John's execution. True, she had Audrey to care for; but it was time to get back to work in earnest. If that meant working on two plays simultaneously, so be it. She was not prepared to postpone the prison play, finding it a constant source of stimulation and challenge. Not that *Julius Caesar* wasn't also demanding; but the story was simpler, and she had Plutarch's *Life of Caesar* as a helpful foundation on which to build.

She established a routine for the household that facilitated her dual responsibilities. She rose early, nursed Audrey and ate the simple breakfast of porridge, fruit, bread and cheese that Helena had prepared. While Helena played with Audrey, Constance was joined at the table by Madge who had already taken Ned and Rafe to their petty school in the neighboring parish. Run by a competent, well-regarded schoolmaster, the twins had studied reading and writing and the basics of figuring for the past two years. Next year, they would move to a grammar school where they would be expected to become proficient in Latin—using it as the everyday language in school—and also acquire the rudiments of Greek. The school also offered composition, rhetoric, geography, history and mathematics as part of the curriculum. As with their petty school, Constance would pay the grammar school fees. She had done so even before the inheritance, which only made it that much easier.

After breakfast, Madge took over responsibility for Audrey while Helena did her chores and Constance retired to her room to work. With breaks to nurse and play with Audrey for a half hour, she worked on *Caesar* until late morning when Madge and Helena went out for the daily shopping and Constance again took charge of Audrey. After the shopping, Helena fixed dinner, the main meal of the day, while Madge fetched the twins who were allowed home for the meal. After dinner, they returned to school. Constance then worked on the prison play with Audrey napping in her room—where the baby also spent her nights. When she woke from her nap, Madge would play with her while Constance continued to work, again taking nursing and play breaks. In the late afternoon, Madge retrieved the twins and Constance, Madge and the children gathered by the fire to play and sing. Constance often read to them from one of the many books in her library. Helena occasionally joined them if supper were bubbling on the fire and no longer needed her immediate attention.

In this fashion, Constance was able to move both plays forward at a steady pace. The stories and characters were so different that she generally did not confuse the two although once or twice she caught herself inserting a name from *Julius Caesar* into the prison play. She merely laughed and made the correction. As she progressed with the latter work, she became more at home with the intricacies of character, plot and thematic material. She believed she had mastered the complexities and was writing a good play. She wouldn't, of course, be sure until Will had read it. She was fond of the *Caesar* play, especially the Mark Antony oration that she began with: "Friends, Romans, countrymen, lend me your ears." She thought the bit about the ears a particularly felicitous, double-meaning phrase and one that would resonate with an audience for whom the slicing off of a criminal's ear was not an uncommon event.

But the prison play was her passion. Every day, she regretted stopping work. She wrote slowly but steadily, adept now at the poetic structure, but choosing her words carefully to best convey the powerful sentiments being expressed. She also relished the subtle humor that was an important aspect of an otherwise dark, foreboding play—one that sprang from depths in her own character of whose existence she had been unaware. This process of personal discovery not only excited her but drove her forward with ever greater intensity.

"You look tired," Madge said to her one evening as they sat by the fire after everyone else was in bed.

"It is tiring work."

"But you also look happy."

"I have much to thank God for, not the least of which is your friendship."

"My thoughts as well."

In June of 1599, she gave Will a draft of *The*

*Tragedy of Julius Caesar*, telling him that she had worked quickly and that he might want changes. A few days later, he sent her a note, saying that the play was quite good and only needed work in a small number of places. He would make those changes himself and send her a draft to review. He was most favorably impressed with how her language and dramatic skills had progressed.

"Soon, I fear," the note ended, "you may surpass me; and I'm the best playwright in London."

"In the whole, civilized world," she wrote on the bottom of the note and returned it to him the next day.

Two weeks later, he brought over the manuscript as he was not willing to entrust manuscripts to messengers. It was late morning so Constance invited him to stay for dinner. He readily agreed and settled down to play with Audrey who, at almost one year, was able to crawl, walk more than a few steps, say a few words and had become as curious as a monkey. It also took very little to start her giggling and clapping her hands. Will sat her in front of him, took off his broad-brimmed hat and hid his face behind it.

"Where's Uncle Will?" he chortled.

Laughing as if this trick were from one of his more farcical comedies, Audrey pulled aside the hat. Will did the trick again and got the same reaction. He played the game for five minutes and then, tired of it, put his hat back on. Audrey burst into tears.

"Careful what you start," said Constance, who was sitting close by. She picked Audrey up and rubbed her back, which caused the crying to stop.

Will took the baby back and again sat her on the floor. "I've brought you something," he said and took a small, wooden cart from his pocket. Audrey gurgled with pleasure and clapped her hands. A string was attached to the front of the cart, and Will pulled the cart around in a circle. He gave the string to Audrey who put it in her mouth. "No," Will said, "pull it." He demonstrated again. This time, Audrey pulled the cart a few inches and then picked it up. She turned it over and examined it from every side. She turned one of the wheels, turned another and lost interest. She crawled over to Constance and said: "Muh."

"That would be me," said Constance, picking her up and, with a mother's sure insight, giving Audrey her breast. The baby nursed contentedly.

At dinner, whose main dish was a well-seasoned beef and vegetable stew—one of Helena's specialties—and which tempted Will to have two large portions, Madge asked Will what Shakespearean works would be opening soon.

"A comedy titled *As You Like It* and a play about the Roman, Julius Caesar, that...."

"...Constance," interrupted Madge, "worked on ceaselessly."

"Yes, I know," said Will, thus acknowledging openly what Constance and Madge had long assumed: that he was aware that Madge knew who was working on what. "She does excellent work."

"And should be recognized for it."

"Ah," said Will, "a turn of events greatly to be desired but which may have to wait for a civilization more open-minded than our present one."

Constance listened closely but said nothing.

"The work tires her," said Madge, thinking to attack from a different angle.

"It tires us all. The London theater is not for the faint of heart. One slip in a production or a delay in getting a work performed and the crocodiles of the stage will eagerly devour you. Given half a chance, even friends will gleefully quaff your blood. It's a dog eat dog world. Young Ben Jonson, for example, off to a good start last year with *Every Man in His Humour*, will soon be snapping at my heels, anxious to knock me off my shaky pedestal."

"Surely, no one can displace William Shakespeare," said Madge.

"Kind of you to say but a great exaggeration."

"Don't you think that a small bit of recognition would seem her due."

"You are a true friend and deserve much credit for that."

"Which is as far as I will get."

"I am afraid so."

Having complimented Helena on her extraordinary culinary skill, Will left shortly after dinner; and Constance went upstairs with the *Caesar* manuscript. Will's small number of changes turned out to be on every second or third page; but in general, Constance agreed with them. They dealt primarily with wording rather than the plot or the characterizations. She made further changes and crossed out two of Will's. She finished in two days and asked Helena to take it to Will.

Constance expected it would take Helena an hour and a half so when she hadn't returned in two, Constance feared something had gone wrong. At that moment, Helena came through the door. Her hair was awry, and her bodice and skirt were badly stained. Her eyes were puffy from crying.

"Dear God," cried out Constance, in a voice quivering with alarm and dread. "What happened?"

"I was walking on Church Lane when a boy tripped me and ran off, shouting 'blackamoor.' I fell into the mud. It got all over my face and clothes and the manuscript."

Constance enfolded Helena into her arms.

"You poor thing. Are you all right? Not injured?"

Helena replied that she was fine but that the last few pages of the manuscript had been spoiled. She had continued to Will's house, and he had been most kind. He supplied her with water, cloths and a towel; she cleaned off as much as possible. Will admonished her not to worry about the manuscript: he would rewrite the spoilt pages from memory.

"He can do that. HIs memory is prodigious. Now you change into clean clothes and have a glass of hot cider by the fire."

Two days later, Will sent word that he now considered *Julius Caesar* finished and expected an opening within a month. The incident with Helena caused Constance to think she needed another servant—a man who could take care of things that maybe a woman shouldn't be asked to do. Since she wouldn't need him all the time, she discussed the matter with her neighbor, Master Throckmorton, an accountant, who had purchased the next-door house four months ago and with whom she was on friendly terms. She had, twice, invited the gentleman and his chatty wife to dinner; and they had reciprocated. He told Constance that he could easily use a part-time servant to ease the burden on his current two employees. A man servant would be suitable so they decided to jointly employ whomever they could mutually agree upon. Within a week, Master Throckmorton had found Anthony, a sturdy young fellow with an agreable manner. Recently in from the country, he had been working as a porter and was delighted with the change. He would sleep at the neighbor's house. Constance liked him immediately and had no trouble figuring out with Master Throckmorton how to divide Anthony's time and wages. His duties for Constance included accompanying Madge or Helena, or both of them, when they shopped and acting as messenger to and from Will's house. Anthony carried a stout stick wherever he went. No further manuscripts ended up in the mud.

A couple of weeks after the completion of *Julius Caesar,* on a hot evening towards the end of August, Constance and Madge were sitting in the front parlor reading. The twins and Audrey were sound asleep. Helena had gone to visit her parents and would not return until morning. Anthony had left for the day. The house was quiet. Over the years, Constance had encouraged Madge to read. Semi-literate when their friendship began, Madge was now fully literate and read a good book as eagerly as Constance although she preferred a colorful romance to history—even if the historical work were mostly concerned with intrigue, dynastic struggles and heroic battles.

At one point, Constance realized that her friend was looking at her somewhat quizzically.

"What is it?" Constance asked.

"Nothing."

"That's not true. We've been friends too long to deceive each other."

"I've been wondering."

"About what?"

"What it's like to make love to another woman."

"Are you simply wondering or do you really want to know?"

"I'm not sure."

Constance got up, walked slowly to Madge, leaned down and kissed her on the lips. Madge started to pull back but then, swept up as if by a tidal wave, kissed her friend back, opening her mouth to receive Constance's tongue. Constance took hold of both Madge's hands and gently pulled her from the chair, Madge's book falling to the floor. Constance put her arms around Madge and kissed her again, this time both with open mouths.

"Shall we?" asked Constance.

Madge stepped back. An expression of confusion

flitted across her face.

"I don't know."

"Be sure of yourself. It's fine if we don't."

Madge walked around the room. Constance stood quietly, watching her. Madge looked into the cold fireplace and then paced some more.

"Did you learn to pace from my brother?"

Madge laughed but said nothing. She stopped in front of Constance. She looked into Constance's eyes.

"I've decided," said Madge, reaching for Constance's hand. "Why not?"

They climbed the stairs and went into Madge's room, the twins now having a room of their own. They undressed each other. Madge stared in amazement at Constance's slim, but full-breasted, figure. She had never before seen a naked woman except in a mirror. Her heart beat faster as she ran a hand over Constance's breasts and down her stomach, stopping before she reached the triangle of thick hair. Constance whispered: "Keep going" and Madge did, although feeling awkward. Constance did the same, and Madge shuddered.

"You're beautiful."

"Not as beautiful as you," said Madge, "and I need to lose a few pounds."

"Not that I can see."

Constance led Madge to the bed, and they climbed between the sheets. They began kissing in earnest and stroking each other. Madge felt she was floating on a cloud. It was not long before both women climaxed and fell asleep in each other's arms.

"Do you want to do this again?" Constance asked when they woke up an hour later.

"Now?"

"We could, but we could also wait."

"I hadn't planned on this."

"I know."

"May I think about it?"

"Take all the time you need."

"I'm pretty sure that I will."

"No one can know," said Constance.

"I recall telling you that some years ago."

"Ah, the Duchess."

"Do you miss her?"

"I miss her and John."

*Julius Caesar* opened in early September to great acclaim, and Will decided to give a party in celebration. The function was held in Will's new home in Southwark where he had moved earlier that year. Not far from the Globe, it was convenient for him and larger and nicer even than the house in Bishopsgate. Constance helped him select a few new pieces of furniture and was delighted that Will was so happy. She only wished that his family would join him in London as he saw them so rarely. She accepted, however, that Will had no interest in Anne as either companion or lover. "Must be hard on her and the children," she thought. She also wondered from time to time if he were still enamored with the man or woman, or both, to whom the sonnets were addressed—one hundred and twenty-six to the man, twenty-eight to the woman. Neither she nor Will inquired about each other's intimate lives. Which, Constance mused, was at present a good thing.

Will hired three musicians and asked if Helena and Anthony could help Jane and Rose prepare and serve the refreshments. They brought the three children who, under the servants' watchful eyes, played happily in the kitchen.

The house had been thoroughly cleaned, the floors covered with fresh rush mats (sprinkled with sweet-smelling herbs) and vases filled with flowers placed on every table. The house was cheerfully lit with candles everywhere. A fire blazed in the front parlor. The musicians struck up lively tunes in the panelled dining room, which boasted pilasters carved with human figures—some of which were quite sensual including a nude satyr and a woman with exposed breasts. The center table had been moved to one wall to leave space for dancing, which began soon enough.

Constance and Madge stood talking by the fire. They could easily hear the music across the hall. The musicians had moved on from popular tunes to a stately pavane and then, to cries of "Faster!" from the younger men and women, to a galliard and the even faster lavolta—or *la volte* as it is known in French. The faster music was accompanied by shouts and clapping. Will, whom they had barely said "hello" to since arriving, approached them.

"This is an excellent party, brother," said Constance. "The house looks magnificent."

"Thank you." Will turned to Madge and bent low

to kiss her hand. "And how are you, my dear? In good spirits?"

"Excellent spirits."

A young actor, named Emanuel Carew, came over, bowed to Madge and asked if she would care to dance. She glanced at Constance who smiled and nodded.

"I should very much like to," Madge said to the handsome actor whose brown eyes sparkled, whose beard was neatly trimmed and whose cheeks were flushed from copious draughts of the strong ale Will was serving, "but I must warn you that I've had little experience."

"Do not be concerned, most beautiful lady. I shall instruct you. You will find me an easy partner as I've danced on stage in a goodly number of foolish comedies."

"None by Master Shakespeare, I should hope," said Madge, with an ill-suppressed laugh.

Embarrassed, Emanuel glanced at Will, who said: "Well, Emanuel Carew, you had best answer the lady whose name, by the way, is Mistress Madge Whitton and who is a very good friend of my sister's."

"None at all, Mistress Whitton. Your brother... I mean, your friend... I mean, your sister's brother... I mean..."

"It would seem, young Emanuel," said Madge, "that ale has removed whatever meaning was left in your head, but I sincerely pray that it has not done the same for your dancing."

"Not at all. I can dance a lavolta with the best of them so long as I don't trip over my own feet. And what I meant was that William Shakespeare is a genius and that *Julius Caesar*.... Have you seen it?"

Madge nodded.

"...is a masterpiece."

"Do you truly think so?" asked Constance.

"Oh, yes, indeed. I had three small parts: a cobbler, one of the Senators who stabs Caesar and a soldier in Cassius's army. It is a veritable masterpiece."

"Come, friend Carew," said Madge, "if we delay further our dancing, the musicians will have all gone home."

So saying, Madge took Emanuel by the arm and led him into the dining room.

"He has some promise as an actor," said Will.

"But not as a drinker of ale," laughed Constance.

Richard Burbage, the leading actor in the Lord Chamberlain's Company, strode up to Will and Constance, bowed gracefully and, saying: "Good evening, Constance", took her hand to place thereon a light kiss.

"May I join you? Or would I be intruding on a private conversation?"

"No one as handsome as you could ever intrude," said Constance to the man whose high forehead, thick wavy hair and slight beard was known far and wide in London.

"How kind of you, if completely untrue." Burbage glanced around. "Will, the house is most cheerful. And this blazing fire, most welcome. It is rather a damp and chilly evening for this time of year, don't you think?"

"I do," said Will, "but we mortals are no more privileged to choose our weather than the time we meet our Maker."

"Now, Will," said Burbage, "don't be composing lines in the midst of a party. And if you must, pray choose a more joyous subject." Burbage turned to Constance. "How did you like *Julius Caesar*?"

"Very much."

"I've often wondered, my dear Constance, given your keen intelligence...."

"For a woman?"

"For anyone. As I was saying: ...and sharp wit and apt way with words, whether you ever help Will here with his writing? A little revising here and there, perhaps, or critical commentary? Brilliant as he indisputably is, your brother does go on at times. If you are helping him, please remember that cutting back makes our lives easier."

"I hardly know what to say, Richard. The thought of helping Will never occurred to me."

"I wonder," said Burbage.

Will stepped close to Burbage and whispered something in his ear.

"My God," said Burbage. "How extraordinary." He lowered his voice even though no one else was standing near them. "I congratulate you, Constance. The work is superb, but this must remain a closely-guarded secret. Many people would not credit it—that a woman could write so brilliantly. But even worse could happen were it to be credited. The authorities would certainly take a dim view of this and possibly use it as a reason to close us down. You are, I am sure, well aware that many ignorant, narrow-minded people consider the theater to be a fount of evil. Think what they would say were it known that a woman was involved in a production—in any fashion, much less writing a work. Although I hope you will continue to write, mum's the word, I'm afraid."

"I understand even though I don't like it. At the same time, recognition from the foremost actor of his day lessens the sting."

Burbage turned to Will.

"Thank you for telling me. It will change the way I think about women if nothing else."

"It has certainly changed how I think about my sister."

Madge and Emanuel returned from dancing. Madge was breathing hard. "I should do more exercise," she gasped.

"We'll have to see to that," said Constance.

Emanuel bowed unsteadily and wandered off down the hall to the kitchen. Helena was slicing fruit at a table. Hearing Emanuel's irregular, deep breathing, she glanced around, smiled at him and returned to her work. At the sight of a beautiful, black woman, Emanuel's eyes opened wide. He stepped to the table, put his arms around Helena and pushed his pelvis against her butt. He rocked back and forth.

"Stop that this instant," said Helena sharply.

Emanuel continued.

Helena struggled to free herself; but ale or no ale, Emanuel was too strong for her.

"Stop it," she said in a louder voice.

Suddenly, Emanuel was pulled away from her. She turned around. Anthony had the drunk actor in a bear hug and was squeezing him hard. The actor's eyes bulged, and he made a gurgling sound.

"Don't hurt him," said Helena.

"Why not?"

"Please, Anthony. You'll get in trouble."

"Over a drunk actor attacking an innocent woman, I doubt it."

The gurgling continued.

"Then for my sake."

"In that case."

Anthony let Emanuel go. Gagging, Emanuel dropped to his knees. In a minute or two, he recovered. Anthony helped him to his feet.

"If you come back to the kitchen," said Anthony, "I'll kill you."

Terror spread across the actor's face. He hurried from the kitchen, made his excuses to Will, telling him how much he had enjoyed the festivities, and left.

"Curious," said Will. "Did you not sufficiently compliment him on his dancing?" he asked Madge with a laugh.

At that moment, Helena, followed by Anthony, each with a platter piled high with fruit, entered the parlor and set the platters on a table across the room from the fireplace. They bowed to the guests and left the parlor. Constance noticed Helena taking Anthony's arm as they walked down the hall.

Constance and Madge continued their intimacy although not as frequently as either of them would have liked. They had to be sure the children were asleep and that Helena was either visiting her father or likely—having retired sometime earlier—to be asleep. Audrey, having nursed prodigiously by the fire, generally fell asleep in her mother's arms and would be dead to the world for some hours, if not the whole night. Constance expected to breastfeed the baby for another year or more. She loved the feelings of comfort and satisfaction that she, and apparently Audrey, derived from the practice as well as her belief, which a doctor had affirmed, that a mother's milk was the healthiest food for babies and even toddlers. Little Audrey, as she was affectionately called in the household, now walked on her own.

Rafe and Ned were altogether a different story. They resisted bedtime like tigers; and the two women—feverish with desire—used all the wiles at their disposal to drain the twins' manic energy. They played hide and seek throughout the house and, if it was light out after supper, judged foot races in Mutton Lane—always under Anthony's watchful eye. Neighboring children joined the fun which soon became a ritual. After a half dozen or more races, Anthony went home. Helena excused herself to go to her room behind the kitchen, and either Constance or Madge would read stories to the twins. After a few pages, they were more often than not ready to be taken upstairs.

Constance and Madge returned to the fire and took up their books, although neither could concentrate on reading. After one of them deemed that enough time had passed, she got up, crossed to the other and began kissing her neck.

One night, having made exquisite love, they were talking quietly in bed. Constance reminded Madge of her once asking whether she, Constance, preferred men or women.

"Let me now ask you the same question."

"I cannot answer any better than you could. I loved Peter deeply and would never have thought of betraying him. I miss him terribly; but he's gone, and I love you: first as a friend and now as a lover. As I don't expect, nor am I trying, to meet a suitable man, I don't see the need to answer the question. If I meet Peter in the hereafter, I think he'll understand. He was always very fond of you and might prefer this to my being with another man."

"You were always cleverer than me."

"Clever comes in many guises. I doubt there are many as clever as you, Mistress Shakespeare, with the written word."

At that, Constance kissed Madge good-night and felt her way silently the few steps down the darkened hall to her room.

A few days later, while the twins were at school, Audrey was napping and Madge was shopping, Constance, feeling quite thirsty, got up from her work to go to the kitchen for a drink. Descending to the parlor, she was surprised that Helena was not there cleaning. Neither was Anthony in evidence, and she assumed he was working at Master Throckmorton's. Constance walked down the corridor and entered the kitchen to find Helena and Anthony in a passionate embrace. Helena's bodice was unlaced and her blouse pulled down on one shoulder, exposing a bare breast, which Anthony was caressing. Their attention fixed on each other, neither were aware of Constance standing in the doorway.

"What the devil," said Constance sharply, and both reacted with the terror of a deer set upon by hounds. Helena turned away from Constance, adjusted her blouse and did up her bodice.

"Anthony," snapped Constance, "go immediately to Master Throckmorton's and stay there until called for." Anthony hurriedly left, and Constance turned her ire on Helena. "You're lucky I don't dismiss you."

"Why would you do such a thing? Am I not an excellent servant?"

"Yes, but I won't have that sort of behavior in my house."

"You mean the sort of behavior you and Mistress Whitton engage in?" Constance stared at Helena, speechless. "You are not as quiet as you imagine. Or the walls as thick. I have, on occasion, returned to sit by the fire when everyone else had gone to bed."

"You've spied on me."

"Not intentionally." Helena took Constance's

hand. "I don't need to spy. I only need to observe how you look at each other. It's how Anthony and I look at each other."

Constance tried to pull her hand from Helena's grasp, but Helena held fast with great strength.

"What do you intend?" asked Constance.

"I will not reveal your secret, if that's what you're asking. I care for you too much to even think of doing that."

Helena released Constance's hand.

"Thank you," said Constance, inwardly breathing a sigh of relief.

"I only ask that you respect Anthony's and my feelings for each other and allow us to express them."

"There's a difference. We are... are... shall we say, more advanced in years."

"He loves me and wants to marry me."

"Then he should ask your father for your hand before he starts unlacing your bodice."

"I undid it." Constance could not help a soft laugh, and Helena joined in. She quickly, however, turned somber. "I am not sure Father will give his permission. He wants me to advance in the world which, he believes, is much harder for people of our color. He may not find Anthony suitable."

"Anthony is a fine young man. I will ask Edmund—Lord Pennyford—to have a word with your father—with Lord Markeley's permission of course—and also to think what can be done to advance Anthony. Perhaps Lord Pennyford has a position open although I would hate to lose Anthony—or you, for that matter. In the meantime, until you are married, you and Anthony will confine yourselves to the occasional kiss in the kitchen; and your bodice will remain laced up."

Helena threw her arms around Constance and hugged her tightly. Constance disentangled herself.

"That will do," she said.

"Aren't you being just a little hypocritical?" asked Madge when they were alone. "After all, I've not noticed you waiting for marriage before entangling yourself."

"Oh hush and kiss me. I'm a writer. What would we writers do without a little hypocrisy?"

Anxious to show Will a polished draft, Constance intensified her work on the prison play. She wrote draft after draft, in each one refining the characterizations and the poetry. She knew that Will did not write many drafts, counting on his great skill as well as the rehearsal process to produce elegant stage productions. Nor had she ever before written as many drafts; but she felt strongly that this play was far superior to her previous work, and she wanted it to be as perfect as she could make it. On numerous occasions, she toiled far into the night, which brought complaints from Madge who said that the play could wait a little while.

"Just let me work a little longer," Constance said one night. "You go to bed, and I'll be there soon."

The candles were burning low when, two hours later, she stopped working, put on her night clothes and slipped quietly down the hall to Madge's room to find her sound asleep. Constance kissed her on the lips and stroked her cheek, but Madge simply murmured something unintelligible and turned away. Constance was tempted to pull back the sheet and blankets and get into the bed, hoping that a few well-placed touches would wake up her lover; but the hour was late, she was tired and there was always tomorrow. Sighing, she returned to her room, blew out her candle and climbed into bed. She was instantly asleep.

But the next night proved no different nor did the following three until, with everyone else in bed, Madge crept up behind Constance—head bent over the manuscript and lost to the world—and whispered: "I cannot go another night without holding your naked body in my arms." Madge then left as stealthily as she had entered, and Constance put down her pen.

In early spring, 1600, Constance was finally satisfied with the play. She read it aloud to Madge who said that, while she didn't understand it all, she felt it was overpowering and magnificent. Constance sent Will a note saying that the "revenge play" was ready for him to read and asking when she could come over. Anthony returned with Will's reply: tomorrow morning. He had a performance in the afternoon.

"I want to stay while you read it," said Constance after Will had asked after Audrey and had Jane bring each of them a glass of cider.

"That's unusual."

"You may have questions."

"You mean you're nervous about my reaction."

"No, curious."

Will started on the manuscript, periodically reciting a few lines out loud.

> Oh, that this too, too sullied flesh would melt,
> Thaw, and resolve itself into a dew,
> Or that the Everlasting had not fixed
> His canon 'gainst self-slaughter.

"Good, very good."

"Thank you.

"It is reading well, and the story looks to be compelling. I've always liked ghosts taking a hand in the affairs of us poor mortals."

Will returned to his reading, pausing after a couple more pages.

> Neither a borrower nor a lender be,
> For loan oft loses both itself and friend,
> And borrowing dulleth th' edge of husbandry.
> This above all: to thine own self be true,
> And it must follow as the night the day
> Thou canst not then be false to any man.

"Ah, this is subtle. Words of wisdom but from a man whom, if I suspicion correctly, is all too readily mocked. Am I wrong?"

"Read on and you shall see."

Will read for some time, silent except for the occasional murmur of approval or nod of his head. At one point, he seemed to stop and re-read a number of lines. He looked at Constance and uttered a single word: "Astounding." Constance felt her heart racing. Will read aloud:

> To be or not to be: that is the question.
> Whether 'tis nobler in the mind to suffer
> The slings and arrows of outrageous fortune
> Or to take arms against a sea of troubles
> And by opposing end them. To die, to sleep,
> No more, and by a sleep to say we end
> The heartache and the thousand natural shocks
> That flesh is heir to—'tis a consummation
> Devoutly to be wished.

Will put down the manuscript. "The writing is brilliant," he said. Constance smiled and said nothing. Will returned to the manuscript. He had been reading for a good three hours when he came to the final scene: the duel. Constance had mostly sat by the fire, a book in her hands that she glanced at occasionally. A few pages from the end, he said aloud:

> A hit, a very palpable hit.

"I like that line: pithy and sums up these final moments. You have a gift, but then we've both known that for some time."

"I've had the line in my mind for a while."

He finished the manuscript and laid it carefully on the table. He rose from his chair at his writing table, went to Constance, pulled her up and enfolded her in a hug. "It is magnificent. If it were in my nature, I would be speechless. I do not know if I could've done this. It's likely the best play ever written."

Constance turned away from him to hide the tears in her eyes. Her emotions were beyond description. All she could muster was: "Thank you. I am speechless. I thought it was good, but not that good. Thank you."

"Is that what speechless is like?"

They both laughed.

"This will be on the stage within a month or not much more."

He returned to his table and picked up the manuscript. "I notice that you have not given it a title."

"Do you have any ideas?"

"Something simple yet appealing: *The Tragedy of Hamlet, Prince of Denmark*."

Some six weeks later, on a fine afternoon in early May of 1600, Edmund, Earl of Pennyford, arrived in a carriage at Constance's front door. He stepped down from the carriage and knocked decorously using the brass lion's head. Dressed in their finest, Constance and Madge came out of the house. Edmund handed each one into the carriage and then called to the driver: "The Globe, Toby, and quickly."

Toby drove swiftly down Bread Street, scattering pedestrians right and left; he slowed only when he approached Thames Street where he turned left and picked up speed again until he turned onto London Bridge. From the bridge, it was a short ride to the theater.

"Are you familiar with the play?" Edmund asked Constance as they clattered over the cobblestoned streets.

"Somewhat."

"And you, my dear Madge?"

"Not quite as much."

"Well then, in brief, what is the story?"

"Hard to say in a few words," said Constance.

"Betrayal.... murder.... revenge.... doubt.... plots foiled," said Madge.

"Sounds like one of my typical days," laughed Edmund. "Is there, hopefully, some comic relief?"

"Hopefully you will find some humor therein," said Constance.

"Most enigmatic answers."

"Perhaps, my lord, you should wait to see for yourself," said Madge.

"It is an honor to go to the theater with two of the cleverest, and certainly the most beautiful, women in London. I shall wait with anticipation to see what your brother has planned for us. I confess that only a few of my friends attend the theater, but I quite enjoy a good play and greatly admired *Julius Caesar,* especially the fact that the assassins were quickly dealt with."

Edmund had insisted on paying for seats in the uppermost galleries—the most expensive—although

Constance had said that she and Madge could attend without paying.

"We must contribute to Will's income. After all, he has that elegant house to maintain."

They were transfixed by the play, especially Richard Burbage's riveting performance as Hamlet. During the intermission, they strolled in the grounds outside the theater; and at one of the numerous stalls, Edmund bought a pastry for each of them. When the play ended, with bodies askew on the stage, Edmund said: "Outstanding. We must congratulate Will."

Will bowed his head slightly when Edmund and the two women approached, and he blushed at Edmund's praise of his elegant writing.

"Undeserving of such praise," said Will, glancing sideways at Constance.

"Not in the least," said Edmund. "I know there are those who insist the theater lowers public morals, but a play like your *Hamlet* can only serve to enhance the intelligence and character of the populace." Edmund rubbed his chin thoughtfully and then continued: "At the same time, I would've liked to see Claudius dispatched more directly than as the side effect of the duel. Regicide, even—or especially—on the stage, must be punished with great cruelty. Perhaps you could arrange to have him beheaded although off stage. We should hate to lose Master Burbage's services."

Edmund laughed softly in appreciation of his own joke, and the others dutifully joined in. He then nodded to Will, hooked one arm in each of the ladies' arms and guided them to the waiting carriage. Will stared after them in some astonishment. When they arrived at Constance's house, Edmund asked Madge if he might have a word in private with Constance.

"Of course, my lord."

Edmund escorted Madge to the front door and then returned to the carriage. Settling himself comfortably next to Constance, he took one of her hands and pressed his lips to it.

"Sitting next to you in a carriage brings back fond memories," he said.

The horses stomped impatiently, eager to be off.

"That was..." Constance thought briefly. "...eight years ago, and I remember it quite distinctly."

"You are as beautiful and alluring now as then."

"Hush now. We can't have the head of Her Majesty's spy service caught in a lie."

"In the course of my work, I dissemble frequently—as you should well remember. I am not doing so now."

"Then, thank you."

Edmund ran a finger along the back of Constance's neck.

"Would you consider," he asked, "paying a visit to Pennyford House? I guarantee you that the servants will be suitably polite this time."

"I thought that you enjoyed Ester's company."

"Not for some months."

"I am sorry to hear that." Constance paused briefly. "It is a flattering offer, Edmund; but I would fear someday losing your friendship, which is far more meaningful to me than a dalliance, no matter how gratifying that might prove."

"As well as beautiful, you might also be the only honest woman in London."

"No, Madge is as well."

"I too value your friendship so we shall say no more on that subject."

"Edmund, will you keep a secret if I tell you one?"

"Secrets are the coin of my profession."

"I wrote *Hamlet*."

Edmund stared at her, wordless for a moment, and then laughed.

"So my suspicions were correct. You've not been as honest with me as all that, but I forgive you." He smiled. "You are even more amazing than I imagined. Just think: that girl of eighteen in the carriage growing up to write a masterpiece. Extraordinary. Perhaps you will consider my suggestion to Will of having Claudius beheaded. More fitting for the killer of his monarch than as part of a duel when he's not even dueling."

"It might change the meaning of the play as the point is for Hamlet himself to finally revenge his murdered father."

"I suppose so and, in the end, the fellow is killed."

"So you're satisfied."

"Yes. Have you written other of Will's plays?"

"*Richard II, Henry IV, Part Two* and *Julius*

*Caesar.* We worked together on others."

"You are right to keep this a secret. Who can tell what the consequences of this becoming known would be? Have you told others?"

"Richard Burbage knows as does Madge. Both will keep the secret. John figured it out, and I'm sure died with his lips sealed."

"I am honored that you told me." He kissed her hand. "Yes, friendship is about as valuable a commodity as one is likely to find."

"He wanted you to sleep with him, didn't he?" asked Madge when Constance entered the house. They were alone in the parlor. Rafe and Ned were in their room. Audrey was seated at a table in the kitchen playing with blocks while Helena prepared supper.

"He did."

"What did you say to him?"

"I told him 'no,' that I valued his friendship too much to risk losing it."

Madge felt her face grow hot and suffused with anger.

"Meaning that, if you didn't fear losing his friendship and the advantages that come with it, you would sleep with him?"

"Madge, my beloved, of course not but what would you have me say: 'Sorry, Edmund, but I'm sleeping with Madge?'"

Madge took both of Constance's hands,

squeezed them and then kissed Constance fervently on the lips.

"I'm the one who should be sorry. How could I have doubted you even for a second? We were friends years before we were lovers, and we have been honest with each other for all that time."

"No matter the circumstances, I would've turned him down. Our intimacy is in the past; our friendship is in the present. I value it both because I like him very much and because it never hurts to have a powerful friend. If not for Edmund, I would not be alive today."

"For which, I am supremely grateful." She kissed Constance again. "Tonight, I will make up for my foolish remarks."

"I am on fire with anticipation, but enough kissing where curious eyes might see us."

For the next two weeks, Constance did little but play with Audrey, help the twins with their lessons and try her hand in the kitchen to see if she remembered how to season a mutton stew and roast a stuffed capon. Helena expressed some surprise at how tasty were the results.

"Don't be so shocked," she chided Helena in jest and picked up Audrey, who had divided her time among building a house with her blocks, knocking the house down, and watching her mother doing what Helena normally did. "I cooked all my brother's meals for a good number of years: four to be exact."

"I had no idea. I assumed you were always a fine lady."

"Now you know the truth. But mark this well: one can be a fine lady and spend one's life in a kitchen."

At that moment, Anthony's younger brother, Miles, entered the kitchen with two baskets heavily laden with groceries. Madge generally took him with her when she went shopping. She liked the company of the strapping young man and knew that no thief would try to steal from her with Miles carrying the baskets. Miles had taken his brother's place when, not long before Anthony and Helena had taken their marriage vows, Edmund had given Anthony a position on his staff as a junior butler, a position in which he was expected to learn about wines, food and the other details of managing a household. Edmund told Constance that Anthony had certain other responsibilities, but he refused to elaborate. Constance suspected they had to do with the spy service.

Anthony and Helena slept in the back room while Miles slept at Master Throckmorton's house since the arrangement between Constance and the good accountant had remained in place. Master Throckmorton advised Constance that, in his opinion, Miles was every bit as good a worker as Anthony. Constance agreed wholeheartedly.

After unloading the provisions, Miles went to the Throckmortons' to take care of some chores.

"Mistress Shakespeare...." said Helena.

"This must be serious. You're not leaving me, are you?"

"Not for the world, but I must unburden myself."

"Go ahead."

"Anthony and I have been married for several months...."

"And you are not yet with child?"

"It is true what they say: you are very clever."

"And it is true that you should not worry. It can take time."

"But it will happen?" asked Helena, a hint of anxiety in her voice.

"One can never be sure but chances are better than good."

"Thank you, Mistress...."

"Constance."

"Constance."

"I wonder," thought Constance, "who considers me clever."

Shortly thereafter, Constance invited Will, Edmund and Richard Burbage to dinner. Richard brought his wife; Edmund did not—and would not have even if she were not at their country manor. Winifred Burbage was a lively, intelligent woman who would ultimately bear Richard eight children. Constance knew that it was unusual for an earl to socialize with theatrical people, but Edmund was no ordinary earl. As she glanced at the table laden with elegant dishes prepared by herself, Helena and Madge, Constance realized that everyone there, with the possible exception of Winifred, knew of her writing accomplishments.

Although well into May, the evening was chilly so a fire blazed in the dining room fireplace. Opposite the fireplace hung a painting of the gate to Lincoln's Inn, one of the four Inns of Court and the Inn where John had been a member. The painting showed the arch and the two flanking square brick towers as well as lawyers and law students passing through the gate.

After Miles had served everyone, according to their taste, either claret or a white burgundy and the guests had, using their own knives, cut portions of roasted meats: goose, lamb, peacock and mallard as well as slices of fine, white bread, Richard began the conversation by addressing Edmund:

"I understand, Lord Pennyford, that you attended the opening of *Hamlet*. May I ask what you thought of the play?"

"Before answering, I would request that, in this intimate setting where several of us are close friends, we dispense with formal titles. Please, therefore, call me Edmund."

"I will have to get accustomed to the idea," said Richard, "but as you wish."

"Come now, Richard," said Constance, "It's not that difficult. I've known Edmund for years; and in public, it's Lord Pennyford, but when he pays Madge and myself a call, we all use first names."

"Lord Pennyford, I mean Edmund, calls on you?" asked Winifred, failing to conceal her surprise.

"I do, indeed. I greatly enjoy the witty conversation of both Constance and Madge. And I especially enjoy playing with little Audrey. I see so little of my own children as they are in the country, and my work keeps me in London."

"Yes.... yes," said Winifred, "of course." She turned hastily to Constance. "Your late husband...."

"I have no late husband. Audrey is the daughter of a dear friend who lost her husband to a fever and then, a month later, on her own deathbed, asked me to care for Audrey who was then only a few months old."

"Returning to your question, Richard," said Edmund, "I thought the play was superb. You did an excellent job portraying Hamlet, and the writing is peerless. Wouldn't you say so, Constance?"

"All of my brother's plays are magnificently written."

"Thank you, dear sister. I would be tempted to agree with you, but that would be less than modest."

"One can hardly expect," said Winifred, "the foremost playwright of our times to be modest."

"Well spoken, dear wife, or are you jesting?"

"Would I dare jest in such refined company?"

"Such company might lead you further into jesting," laughed Richard.

At this point, Miles cleared the silver platters (which along with the silver plates and wine goblets had belonged to John) in the center of the table and brought in a large bowl of salad—dressed with olive oil, vinegar and sugar—and platters of sliced fruits and cheeses. The company cleaned their plates with bread and helped themselves to the next course.

"I have an idea for a game," said Madge.

"I hope it doesn't involve making fools of earls," said Edmund, "as from some that I know, it would be all too easy to accomplish."

"Present company excepted," said Constance.

"Thank you, my dear."

"Oh, no," said Madge. "The game involves discovering who among us is the least modest and requiring that person to drink two glasses of wine in quick succession."

"What an excellent idea," said Richard. "Whether I win or lose, I win."

"I shall have to refrain from playing," said Constance, "as I am by nature and by society's customs modest in the extreme."

"A hit," said Madge, "a very palpable hit."

"I'll play," said Will, quickly.

"And I," said Richard.

"*Pourquoi non?*" said Edmund. "Why the devil not?"

Winifred and Madge agreed to play, and Constance said she would be the judge and choose the winner. "You go first," she said to Will.

"I am, as has been already asserted this evening, the foremost playwright of our times and, most likely, of all times."

"Would that include Rome and Athens?" asked Constance.

"Most assuredly."

"Well, your plays would not be worth cow dung were I—the greatest actor of all time—not around to make sense of your complicated lines and rhymes," said Richard.

"And your acting, dear husband, would be stale indeed did I not make your meals, darn your trousers, raise your children, sweep your house, clean your plates and lie in your bed."

"You do far more in bed, darling wife, than lie."

At which, the company burst into laughter which grew only more raucous when Will said: "I hope you do not lie about the lying."

Miles entered again, this time with a bottle of claret in one hand and a bottle of white Burgundy in the other. He liberally refreshed everyone's glasses and quietly left the room.

"Is he a good worker?" asked Edmund.

"Excellent," replied Constance. "Every bit as good as his brother."

"I guess it's my turn," said Madge. "I suspect I'm the most, not the least, modest person in this company. But if I'm immodest about anything, it would be my two fine sons, Rafe and Ned, who are currently doing their lessons upstairs."

"That," said Edmund, "is something truly deserving of immodesty. I am also immodest about my sons. England has need of fine sons—and daughters..." And here, he glanced at Constance. "...if we are to preserve the freedom of our great island and its people."

"God save and bless our glorious Queen," intoned Richard. "And death to any who would betray her."

Constance looked at the fire and then turned back to her guests.

"Hear, hear," said Will.

"Would your work, whatever that is, cause you to be the least modest among us?" asked Winifred of Edmund.

"Let us not bring up my work. Such a tedious subject."

"I have decided on a winner," said Constance.

"Who is it?" asked Madge. "Surely not Edmund nor myself."

"The winner..." Constance paused for effect. "...is none other than Winifred, a perfect example of the truth that, without a woman, a man would accomplish little, if anything, in this world. I will ask Miles to bring Winifred her choice of wine; and to ensure our continued conviviality, I must insist that the entire company join Winifred in raising a glass or two."

Constance rose from her chair and went down the hall to the kitchen where she instructed Miles to bring as much wine as necessary to fulfill what she considered her judicious decision. Before returning to her guests, she went upstairs to check on the twins, who were bent over their books, and Audrey, who was fast asleep and didn't move when Constance bent down to kiss her brow. The guests remained another two hours with the conversation ranging from the serious, including the fighting in Ireland, to the frivolous. Edmund then rose and, saying that sadly he still had work to finish that afternoon, offered to take Will and the Burbages to their respective homes. He had a carriage waiting.

That night, lying together in bed, Constance said to Madge: "Everyone there tonight with the possible exception of Winifred—and Richard has very likely told her—knows of my work, yet do you think one of them would mention it or give me credit for it? No, not even in the privacy of my own home, where the secret would be safe."

"I think you need to stop concerning yourself with this issue. Things are unlikely to change, and you are tormenting yourself to no avail. Take your gratification where you can and stop thinking about matters over which you have no control."

"It would seem that you are eager to move on to other activities."

"Over which we have a great deal of control."

Madge then ran a hand over Constance's bare stomach.

In June, Will brought over an early draft of a new play. "Do you recall," he asked, "when you first arrived in London that I was acting in a miserable play called: *The Moor's Wife, A Tragedy*?"

"I do."

"Do you also recall that you suggested at the time that I might want to consider improving on that piece of dung by writing my own version?"

"That too although it was eight years ago."

"Nothing wrong with your memory."

"May I assume that this manuscript represents your version of that awful play?"

"You may. I've called it: *The Tragedy of Othello,*

*the Moor of Venice*, and I would like your views. I've also been wondering if you'd started any new work of your own. It's been some time since *Hamlet*."

"I was hoping to start soon and was planning on asking you for suggestions, but I've not been feeling well lately so I've held off. I will, however, start on your manuscript right away."

"Take good care of yourself."

"I shall."

Constance read the play but not feeling well enough to go to Will's house wrote him a letter with her comments.

My dearest Will:

I have read *Othello* and was greatly taken by it. Your usual eloquence and facility with language is on powerful display and will, I am sure, captivate the audience. The work moves with unrelenting logic to the tragic conclusion and the inevitable, but undeserved, doom of Othello and his innocent bride, Desdemona, as well as the deserved doom of that foul, conniving devil, Iago. One wishes the two lovers' fates could be avoided but, as with Romeo and Juliet, the powers that prescribe man's destiny have determined otherwise.

The characters from the highest to the least important are drawn convincingly and in sharp detail. One longs for Desdemona, admires and then pities Othello, despises Iago and Roderigo, all the while sensing the very human—and thus flawed—aspects of all their natures. As the story moves forward, I was consumed with dread and anxiety as I waited, trembling, for events I knew to be just over the horizon.

So far so good but now I must comment on aspects of the play that I did not find so agreable, of which three stood out as most memorable. Women are uniformly treated badly—from Othello's mad, and ultimately murderous, jealousy towards his pure and innocent wife to Iago's cruelty towards his own wife, Emilia, in the end killing her in parallel to Othello's murder of Desdemona.

I know that many of our countrymen hold blacks in disdain and, secretly or not so secretly, despise them for the harmless color of their skin, which they no more choose than we do ours. Blacks are too often looked upon as superstitious, idolatrous, dominated by lust and violent when their passions, such as jealousy, are aroused. I knew nothing back in Stratford about this race; but having spent much pleasurable time conversing with and keeping company with Helena, I can assure you that these disreputable sentiments about the black race are, in the particular—and in the general case—completely false. I also know from Edmund that Helena's father is a kind, gentle, diligent and highly intelligent person who speaks his adopted tongue of English as well as myself and, I daresay, yourself. My sample, you may say, is small but, I believe, indicative.

You may respond that you are simply reflecting common feelings among our misguided fellow Englishmen; but I say, as I did in *The Merchant of Venice*, that such reasoning is unacceptable in a man of your superior mental capacities. I understand that you consider the ease with which Iago leads Othello into believing that Desdemona has slept with Cassio to be caused by the characteristics of his race, but I urge you to change not only your view of the black race but also the basis—wholly or at least in part—on which rests Iago's evil success in duping the noble Moor.

And finally, I found the business with the missing handkerchief a bit too obvious. Perhaps, you could make those circumstances more convincing.

If you agree with me, these are matters easily resolved. If you don't agree with me, it is your play.

I am feeling increasingly unwell. I am feverish, have dire headaches and frequent spells of harsh coughing. I will go to bed and may even ask Edmund if he can send his doctor.

Your adoring sister,

Constance

Constance sent Miles with the letter and then, after dinner, took to her bed. Over the next day and a half, her fever grew worse as did her coughing. She experienced stomach and back pain and excruciating headaches. Madge sat with her hour after hour, talking with her and holding wet cloths to her forehead to bring down the fever. Audrey looked in, said: "Mama, come play" and started towards her but Helena quickly lifted her up and said: "Let's go see what Rafe and Ned are doing."

Audrey chortled and said: "Play trick on them."

Both Madge and Helena feared that, if Audrey went near her mother, she might catch the fever which would be even more severe for a child than an adult. On the second day, Helena having explained to Audrey that Mama needed to rest, the child stood in the doorway staring miserably at Constance who stared back, equally miserably, in return.

"Mama better soon?" asked Audrey.

"Soon. Then I will read you good stories."

Early in the morning on the third day, Madge sent Miles with a note to Edmund, describing the situation. Miles returned with a glass jar and a note from Edmund's doctor requesting a urine sample. Madge took charge of obtaining the sample, and Miles delivered it an hour later. Late in the afternoon, Doctor Snelling himself came to the house in Edmund's carriage. He was a plump man with only wisps of gray hair on his head and a high-domed forehead. He had a large, wrinkled nose and puffy cheeks. He was obviously a man who relished his roast meats, his apple pies with cheese and his wine; but he exuded an air of assurance and competence, which gave comfort to Constance and Madge, who was sitting by her side.

Doctor Snelling asked Constance about her symptoms and then felt her forehead and cheeks and studied the rash on her shoulders and neck that she said had spread from her abdomen. He then announced that, based on his examination and study of her urine, he was confident that bleeding Constance was the remedy most likely to be of benefit. He then politely, but firmly, asked Madge to bring him a bowl and clean cloths and then to leave the room.

"I normally," he said to Constance, "defer to surgeons or barbers to bleed my patients, but Lord Pennyford has asked me to personally handle all aspects of your care."

"Thank you, Doctor Snelling. May I ask a question?"

"You may ask as many as you like."

"Am I going to live?"

"I cannot tell for sure. Despite your high fever and other symptoms generally associated with typhus, I think it more likely, given the spotless condition of your home, that it's one of those fevers about which, sadly, we know little. The bleeding will help. I will also have an apothecary send over an herbal mixture that is reputed to be effective in cases such as yours."

"All these fevers are serious, are they not?"

"Yes, but rest assured that you are getting the best care available in all of England. Lord Pennyford does not casually pick a physician, and he told me that you are a friend of long standing. Any further questions?"

Constance shook her head. The doctor opened his thin leather case, took out his instruments and began the bleeding. When he finished, he told Constance to stay in bed and that he would return the following day. He had not been gone more than a minute or two before she fell into a deep sleep. When she awoke, she thought the fever had somewhat diminished; but she had a severe headache, and pain had spread through much of her body. She was not hungry but forced down a little mutton and vegetable pottage for supper. By the next morning, the fever was as bad as ever; and the rash had spread further. She asked Madge, whose eyes clearly showed the effects of crying, to send for Will.

"And stop crying. God giveth and God taketh away. I've had a wonderful life."

"I love you," said Madge.

"And I love you. I shall only hate to lose my friends and to miss seeing Audrey grow up."

"It's not over yet."

"It's moving in that direction."

About an hour later, as Madge was holding a cold cloth to her forehead, Constance heard a horse neigh as a carriage pulled up to her front door. She heard footsteps on the staircase, and Edmund came into the room. He looked at her carefully as he came to the bedside and took her hand. Madge discreetly rose and stepped back a few feet. Accustomed to dissembling, Edmund concealed his shock at seeing Constance's gaunt face and the rash that had sprouted like a weed. He could not credit the change that had taken place in a few short weeks. No longer the most beautiful woman he had ever seen, she had aged almost overnight. Lying was all he could think of doing.

"The doctor," said Edmund, "tells me there is hope and that he is doing everything in his power for a recovery. Did you get the herbs?"

"Yes," Constance said, her voice strained. "Helena put them in a soup. I think they helped."

"Doctor Snelling is the best physician in London. You must do exactly as he says."

"I shall."

"I could not bear to lose you nor could Will nor Madge so you must get better."

Constance looked at Madge who did not try to hide the tears that had sprung to her eyes. She managed, however, a weak smile.

"Madge, could you please leave Edmund and me alone for a few minutes. There is a matter that I wish to discuss with him."

"Of course."

Madge left the room, too overcome to remember to curtsy to Edmund.

"What is it, my dear?" asked Edmund still holding her hand.

"You were my first lover," Constance said, choosing to ignore her juvenile kissing and touching with George Clopton, "and you've been a dear friend for a long time. You saved my life three years ago; and we have enjoyed each other's company long after our, perhaps unfortunately brief, romance." She struggled to speak clearly and to keep her brain functioning. "I have one further service to ask of you."

"Name it and if it is in my power to accomplish, it shall be done."

"It is kind, if deceptive, of you to speak of recovery. We both know that is most unlikely. I am getting worse, not better. Doctor Snelling is doing his best, but I doubt it will be good enough. Nor could anyone, I suspect, do better."

"If you insist, I will not dissemble; but please... please, dear friend, do not give up the struggle."

"I will do my best."

"Thank you. What is the service?"

"I wish to make a will. Would you please ask the lawyer who handled John's estate—or some other competent lawyer—to come over?"

"That poor fellow has gone to his Maker; but I know of an excellent one, whom I will contact directly."

"Thank you. I wish to leave this house and my income to Madge and, after her demise, to Audrey. Would you ensure that this is done?"

"Nobody will interfere with Madge's or Audrey's inheritance. I can promise you that."

"And finally, I plan to ask Madge to care for and raise Audrey. Can you help her if any difficulties arise?"

"There will be none, and I shall help her whenever needed."

"I cannot thank you enough. If it comes to that, I

can now face death at peace. In a very real, if symbolic, way, you helped me into the world; and now you are helping me out of it. I owe you an enormous debt of gratitude."

"No, I owe you. Very few are privileged to have known as lover and friend one of the greatest playwrights of all time."

"Quite a compliment from an earl."

"There are more useless earls than fine playwrights. Many of my fellow peers would not agree with me, but then they haven't seen *Hamlet*."

They sat in silence for a few minutes, and then Constance asked Edmund if he would bring Madge back. The three sat quietly until Edmund rose and said he had to leave. Madge accompanied him to the front door and then returned.

"Madge, I have to ask something of you."

"Yes."

"Will you take care of Audrey?"

"Yes, of course, I will."

"Please make sure she remembers her mother and how much I loved her."

"Have no fear on that score."

"I am making certain arrangements. Edmund will explain them to you when the time comes."

"I don't want to...."

"Not now but later, you will."

Constance fell into an uneasy sleep for an hour. Doctor Snelling arrived later in the afternoon but, after looking at her, decided that further bleeding would be futile. The lawyer arrived soon after and, in privacy, noted Constance's wishes. Realizing the urgency of the situation, he retired to the parlor and drew up the will, which Constance signed with Madge and the lawyer as witnesses.

Will came later in the evening, and Madge left them alone.

"Just think: eight years ago, you came to London, an unschooled girl, to take charge of my untidy household. Now you have a household of your own, a beautiful, clever daughter and have written the finest play to yet appear on the London stage, not to forget your other superb works. Such a transformation occurs but infrequently. You are, in a very real sense, a woman of the world."

"Thank you, brother. You are too kind."

Constance's voice had become exceedingly weak. She now had chills as well as the fever. She felt confused and not able to focus her thoughts as clearly as was her custom. The headache was almost constant; she was nauseous and had no desire to eat. Before Will's arrival, she had thrown up the little bit of pottage that she had managed to get down. Helena and Madge had cleaned her and changed the bed linen while Miles, whom Master Throckmorton had kindly told to stay at Mistress Shakespeare's house as long as necessary, played with Audrey and kept an eye on Rafe and Ned as they did their lessons.

Audrey occasionally looked wistfully at Miles and said: "Mama?"

"It has been a great pleasure," continued Will, "to have worked with you on so many fascinating and difficult projects. To say your contribution has been invaluable would be the most extreme understatement."

"I did my best."

"If all writers did their best as you have done yours, who can tell what great works of literature might have been produced."

"One request, brother."

"Yes."

"Consider, please, the changes I have suggested for *Othello*. It has great potential."

"I am already doing so."

At that, Constance fell back into a fitful sleep.

As Will left, he put a hand on Madge's shoulder and said: "Life will be a great deal more difficult going forward."

"Without doubt."

Madge sat by Constance well into the night and, when she could no longer stay awake, reluctantly went to her room for a few hours' sleep. Constance had, during Madge's vigil, woken once to mumble something about a new play and how she had walked through half the night to get to London.

"It was cold... so cold... field... there was a field... lay down with the sheep... still cold... horses... straw... stable... warm... finally a little warm... coach... Edmund's han ... oh, my... so many cows... my kingdom... my kingdom... my kingdom for a cow... no, a horse... a stable... a horse, yes... oh my... again?... *peine forte et dure*... oh, my... another... make love... another... what is it like... another... make love... woman... a horse... yes, that's... that's... that's it... A horse, a horse! My kingdom for a horse!"

Next morning, the fifth day since Constance had taken to her bed, the fever had worsened; and she was unconscious except for occasional mumbling. Madge sent Miles to tell Will and Edmund to come right away and to ask Edmund to bring the doctor. Meanwhile, she sat by the bed, holding Constance's hand. She had kept the twins home from school, and they read while Helena played with Audrey.

The three men arrived in an hour. The physician took one look at Constance and said there was nothing further he could do.

"Stay, anyway, please," said Edmund.

"Of course, my lord."

Helena appeared in the doorway and asked if she could come in. Madge nodded yes, and Helena went to the bed and took the hand Madge was not holding. She pressed her lips to the hand, said: "Good-bye, Constance. I shall never forget your kindness" and left. Madge would always swear that Constance smiled.

Will, Madge, Edmund and Doctor Snelling gathered around the bed, hoping for a miracle they knew would not happen.

Constance could no longer speak, but she could hear: the sounds of people walking and talking in the street outside her house, the rumble of an occasional cart passing by, the barking of a dog, the shouts of small children playing, the heavy breathing in the room, the voice of Madge saying something she couldn't understand and, then, as the end approached like a wave, she distinctly heard Audrey cry out: "Mama".

In her mind, she reached out to Audrey and all the others she had loved; but she could not move. It was love, she understood, that counted. And the sea closed in.

# Epilogue: 1606

Queen Elizabeth died on March 24th in 1603, having reigned for forty-four years, four months and a week. James VI of Scotland, her cousin, became James I of England and began the Stuart dynasty. That same year, the Lord Chamberlain's Men were renamed the King's Men and came under the patronage of King James.

In the six years since Constance's death in June 1600, Will had written several comedies, including *Twelfth Night* and *As You Like It*, and the powerful tragedy, *King Lear*. He had also made some changes, if not all the ones Constance would have liked, to *Othello*. He was, without a shadow of a doubt, London's foremost playwright and wealthy beyond what he could have imagined that spring day in 1592 when Constance arrived at his doorstep.

The work had gone exceedingly well, but oh, how much better had Constance been there to prod, to challenge, to argue and to write. He missed her more than he would have ever dreamed possible. He had once asked Madge if she missed Constance, and her reply was: "Every day."

He had recently written a play set in Scotland; and he wanted to talk to her about a matter concerning the play. Will had moved again, this time from Southwark across the river to an area north of St. Paul's and was, therefore, quite close to Madge. He frequently stopped at her house after a performance for supper and a talk by the fire over tankards of ale or cider. The talk turned regularly to Constance although less often as the years passed. Will suspected that Madge's friendship with Constance had been intimate, but he never raised the subject.

Interestingly, Edmund also dropped by Madge's with some regularity. Madge had to pinch herself whenever she dwelt on the fact that she, the daughter of a poor farmer and waterman and wife of a waterman, had an earl for a friend, and not just any earl but one who had been head of Elizabeth's spy service and was now a close advisor to James. And a Pennyford as well. He had told her about the spy service because Constance had known and because he wanted someone else that he trusted to know. She promised to keep his secret.

When she once asked him why he visited so often, he replied that she was one of the most, if not the most, interesting persons—man or woman—in London and that, furthermore, she stirred fond memories of Constance. Madge—astute as ever—turned the conversation to the book she was reading. Although she worried about it, Edmund never attempted to transform their friendship into intimacy.

For Madge, those days were over; she would never again welcome anyone—man or woman—into her bed.

It was a brisk fall day, and Will whistled as he walked the short distance to Madge's house. He hoped she would be in as he was excited about what he had to show her and wished he had—the evening before—sent a servant with a note saying that he would be calling in the morning. Constance would have loved a day like this and most certainly would have approved of what he was about to show Madge.

Helena, who now had two children, opened the heavy oak front door and greeted him warmly, saying that yes Madge was at home and would be glad to see him. He stepped inside and, just at that moment, heard a young girl shouting: "Uncle Will.... Uncle Will" as eight-year-old Audrey ran across the room and leaped into his arms. Holding her firmly, Will twirled her in a circle while she squealed with delight. He put her down, and the lithe girl danced around him shouting: "Play hide and seek. Let's play hide and seek."

"Not right now."

"Oh please, Uncle Will."

"All right, just once."

Madge had entered the parlor during this exchange.

"She does understand the word, 'no,'" said Madge.

"Not that you use it very often," laughed Will.

"Nor do Rafe and Ned. She orders them around shamelessly."

Will found her, after several false tries accompanied by groans and shouts of: "Where oh where can Audrey be?", in her favorite hiding place: under Madge's bed. She begged Will to play again; but he shook his head and, protesting only briefly and for form's sake, Audrey made a polite curtsy and went off with Helena.

Settled by the fire with glasses of cider brought by Miles, who now worked exclusively for Madge—poor Master Throckmorton having gone to his Maker the year before—Will and Madge engaged in a few pleasantries about the invigorating fall weather and a new shop on Cheapside before Will turned serious and said: "I have written a play set in Scotland and want to show you the manuscript. I hope you will attend the opening."

"You know that I will."

Will handed her the manuscript. She opened it, glanced at the title page and gasped.

The Tragedy of Macbeth
by
William Shakespeare
Dedicated to
Constance Shakespeare,
Beloved Sister,
Companion,
Fellow Writer
and

True Author
of,
Among Other Works,
The Tragedy of Hamlet, Prince of Denmark.

It is well past time that women should get their due when it is, indeed, their due.

"Oh, Will," Madge exclaimed. "This is so brave of you. Constance would be so pleased. You have struck a blow that will resound through the ages. Now not only are you the foremost playwright of our times, you will turn out to be the foremost man of our times and of many more to come."

Audrey and Helena entered the room. Audrey ran to Will and stood by his knee. He laid a hand on her shoulder.

"Audrey, say thank you to your Uncle Will."

"Is he giving me a present?"

"You could say so; but most importantly right now, he is giving one to your mother."

The End

CPSIA information can be obtained
at www.ICGtesting.com
Printed in the USA
FSHW010534051219
64754FS